Do Not Forget

Ollie Trotter

Contents

Chapter 1

I n a posh neighbourhood about 30 minutes south of San Francisco, Heller High School stood out proudly. Across a busy street from the neighbourhood was a strikingly modern structure that served as a useful buffer between it and the locals. There were some grassy fields next to the street, but they were too marshy for most people to use them other than a few dog walkers early in the morning. The athletic track was located on a platform covered in ivy; the groundskeepers had long since given up trying to keep the area around it, as well as many of the facilities on the far corners of the campus, free of that green threat. A rough-paved path similar to a bike trail wound between one of these fields and the track. The campus was built on a modest slope, just enough to allow discouraged students to gaze out windows and dream of freedom in the metropolis below. The path twisted and curved slightly as it rose in height. The end destination, a series of concrete steps leading to one of the numerous entrances inside the school proper, became more obvious as the trail passed the chain-link fence and gate that too many PE students were familiar with well.

A basketball court that was infrequently used and a shed that only a select few could properly comprehend were situated in a flat, grey area to the right. If one walked the side stairway up a level and then obtained a copy of the key, they could reach what amounted to the theater's garden. The dancing team would occasionally practise here as the coach yelled instructions from above. A few students chained their bikes to the fence in this location, but the more daring ones forwent taking any safety measures in favour of believing that nothing bad would ever happen to them. These gullible pupils were rarely disciplined because of the ubiquitous surveillance cameras, which were strategically placed to give students the impression of freedom.

This was once again the sole domain of PE students, many of whom were familiar with the uncomfortable sensation of having one of those wooden shards stuck in their shoe while trying to run laps. The path forked into two here, taking a lazy arc to gain some further elevation that most ignored by walking across the wood chips. The tranquilly, semi-forested surroundings (much of the vegetation is ivy), and complete inutility of this walk would all become apparent if one continued on it. Who needed to get to the teacher's parking lot, anyway? With those two exceptions, the majority entered through the hefty glass door that sometimes sat ajar onto the central courtyard after ascending the thin steps, a new addition hailed by many as a sign that the school was starting to appreciate convenience and modernity.

Although the central courtyard was hardly a creative design miracle that would make Frank Lloyd Wright blush, it was unquestionably efficient. Another lawn, this one less marshy and perfect for students to enjoy the sun while eating, located in the centre of the enclosed space. A concrete pathway that encircled it and surrounded the school's swimming pools. Of course, nothing ever happened during lunch hours, but when the pools weren't covered by blue tarps (presumably chosen as a hint to the viewers that there was in fact water present), they could enjoy the water's stillness and block out the smell of chlorine and memories of pain and suffering. Students who chose to eat lunch outside could walk down and easily observe whatever festivities were taking place down there.

This central area was surrounded by various flowerbeds and picnic tables that were sufficiently apart to allow each student clique to quietly ignore the others. A few semi-lucky instructors who liked the sunlight but didn't like the rambunctious students had their classroom doors open into this communal area as well. The classrooms of the remaining teachers were distributed across the school buildings' grid of passageways. One path dipped down, then up, to allow students to access the lower levels of the school, and one path remained straight so they could take in the beauty of the lunchtime hubbub. This dual walkway was located on the side of the central courtyard opposite the administrative offices, which were housed in their own building and were therefore infrequently visited casually. These had an overhang to protect them from the sun, and when viewed from the pedestrian side, they featured an odd mesh covering a network of pipes. Sometimes, until someone took the effort to use a broom to chase them away, pigeons would peck holes in the mesh and nest among them.

Lockers were free-standing and lined the walls, and at any time of day, someone may be seen urgently opening one to remove a textbook or a piece of overdue homework. One nest of these lockers was situated adjacent to another door, this one identical in construction and utilised for a similar purpose. It could be accessed from the hefty door by making a sharp right and stepping across the bridge. It led to a different outdoor promenade that received more sunlight and was lined with the classroom doors of STEM professors. It was just as cold as anywhere else on the chilly mornings that preceded every school day, but it was frequently the first place to warm. There were no flowers in this area, but a few stalks of bamboo peeked up from the lower level, which was otherwise same but greener and darker. The upper path came to an end at a fork where a narrower path led straight ahead to the remaining science classrooms, whose doors were concealed by an awning, and one lone, dilapidated picnic table that appeared to be there solely because no one knew where else to put it. Another route that encircled the school buildings could be reached by turning left directly, and there would be another picnic table outside the ceramics teacher's classroom. A broad stairway that went to the student parking lot was also to the left, but it was further forward as well.

It was a little misleading to refer to this area as the student parking lot because any teacher who thought this was a more practical location was welcome to do so as well. They regretted the times when too many kids used this public space, shoving them out and forcing them to park on the street or, even worse, in the teacher parking lot, which is more peaceful and shaded. Throughout the day, cars would frequently circle the parking lot and drop off visitors who had taken an Uber, students, and parcels before they surveyed the massive structures in front of them and confidently decided where to walk. The busiest times were in the mornings and afternoons, especially on holidays and important days like the opening day of school. The cars would form a multicoloured snake during these times, and despite the staff's best efforts, the train would still move slowly.

"Go on, move along! "Go ahead, go ahead!" One teacher beckoned, directing a parent who was trying their best to ignore the directions and go at their usual pace by firmly guiding them with her hands. A kid was hastily shoved out of the car as it reached its peak, their backpack in hand, with a kiss and a farewell. They then blinked and walked past upperclassmen and professors cheering them on as they made their way to the theatre. A second automobile turned around, releasing two students: a freshman who followed the first through the thunderous thrum and a junior who avoided the entire hubbub by going up the stairs.

The new students entered a place that was familiar to some but the stuff of dreams for many, moving through it one by one like loose drops of water from a showerhead. They were only a few months older than their previous selves, who had graduated from eighth grade with far too much pomp and fanfare, but many had made a promise to become more resilient in that interim period. Others just read books and played video games. They were amazed by the multitude of clothes, colours, shapes, and expressions in the crowd at that point, at least for some of them. The most precocious of them had already acquired flippant attitudes appropriate for their status as teenagers. These students disregarded the vice principal's instructions to put their phones away and smile while sneaking glances at their phones and messaging friends who were already at the theatre and those who were still on the way.

"O brave new world that contains such individuals!" John was amazed and relieved that no one else had heard his impromptu remark; the last thing he wanted was for someone to hear his Shakespeare and find it odd. Although John hadn't actually read The Tempest, the remark stuck in his mind because it was from a play his parents and he had once seen in a park. The only significant variation in mood between this entry and middle school was the size of the buildings and the number of pupils. His watch said he was still early, but he could already see a queue building in front of the theatre, so he obediently took his position and waited. He tiptoed down the steps as quickly as he could and touched his pockets to make sure his belongings were still there. He was disappointed that he could not join the kids in front of him in their enthusiastic conversation since they were speaking Spanish, not that he would want to, anyhow. He chose to take in the size of everything around him, including the softball field, the elementary school across the street, the "HELLER HIGH SCHOOL" written in enormous metallic letters on one of the buildings, etc.

The theatre teacher's car was parked to John's right by yet another gate that led onto what was unquestionably the theater's land and had a higher fence. A few students had the audacity to check inside the automobile, but were disappointed to see only a Starbucks cup left behind; they quickly forgot what they had seen. The green room door was locked, and if anyone peered inside, they would see nothing but darkness and a jacket that had been abandoned last year that the janitors had decided to leave there in the off chance that someone would remember to retrieve it after three months. If the school day had started and drama class was in session, some students would be in this fenced-off area practising scenes. The larger woodworking area was accessible through the second door down. The walls were heaped with abandoned props from numerous prior shows, and the floors were covered with a thin layer of sawdust. This room was connected to the theatre teacher's office, a modest area with a little sofa, a few special posters and props. It had two windows—one to let in light and the other to keep an eye on the building site.

The theatre instructor showed there on time since it was the first day of class; ordinarily, he would arrive late, just in time to prepare for his first lesson. The vice principal had sent him an email asking if he would be available to oversee the use of the theatre for that morning's assembly. He had started his early morning by responding to emails, only to find that there were remarkably few to do so. Some of the emails were administrative drudgery, but the most interesting one was from the vice principal. This wasn't quite correct, though; he was meant to wait patiently in his office and vanish during school functions in the theatre. The drama instructor was required to stay in the rear since he was too indulgent of students' desires, but other teachers were compelled to stroll the seats and oversee while occasionally allowing pupils to choose their own seat placements. The acting teacher opened a game of Minesweeper because he was bored and tried to channel his inner Zen. He spent countless hours playing the game during downtime (including some staff meetings) and thought he was fairly adept at iden-tifying precisely which squares presented the most danger of failure. The majority of motions just required a brief moment of thought, however some especially difficult ones necessitated a massage of the chin or the temple.

It's "Mr. Cathcart!" The vice principal who had done her best to smile for all the new faces knocked on the drama teacher's door, and she then let herself in. She politely declined to comment on his current meditation as she stood over him. He continued to click until he heard the minefield detonate, at which point he swivelled in his chair and walked towards the vice principal, his face in dire need of a cup of coffee.

What, Ms. Wolfe, do I owe the pleasure? He seemed friendly and professional, as if they were old friends, but he was grumpy because he knew he was about to be handed work.

As you are aware, this year's freshman class is exceptionally large, so it would be very helpful if you could help keep an eye on them. I guarantee that they will still behave properly. We just would adore the additional assistance. Mr. Cathcart gave it some thought, hoping for the inspiration of an excuse. Ms. Wolfe could see him playing Minesweeper right then, so he couldn't really say he was engrossed in his work. He could say he was waiting for a call; it was always a good excuse because he did get calls at odd times anyway, so he wasn't exactly lying. After all, it was certain that he would get a call at some time during the gathering, even if it was from a stranger with a strange accent requesting nicely to know his Social Security number. He was also exempt if there was no call because he had made his statements without making any assurances of their accuracy.

"I was anticipating a call from one of our cork-board suppliers to confirm that we'll be ready to start building sets in a few weeks. I can still come, but I might eventually have to leave.

"Oh no, don't be concerned, then! I'll send for another person. Since calling in another teacher didn't cost her anything and if the supply of cork boards was delayed, well, she didn't know what would happen, but it was probably a bigger inconvenience, Ms. Wolfe didn't want to be rude. Mr. Cathcart checked the clock and started another round of Minesweeper as she hurriedly exited the office.

Ms. Wolfe navigated the theater's intricate labyrinth with amazing assurance. In her perspective, there were only two ways out: one led to the lobby, and the other led to the audience. She entered the lobby through the door in front of her after leaving the exclusive, employee-only area. Before going into the public facilities, she stopped to have a drink at the water fountain. A few pupils focused their bored eyes to look through the glass for any movement. Several of their coworkers were waiting for the signal to open the doors as they relaxedly strolled back and forth or sat on the benches. They had to adhere to the schedule that had been previously discussed at a staff meeting: the doors would open at 9:00, the assembly would last for 60 minutes, and the new students would have 30 minutes to mingle and panic before their classes started. Every teacher in the school was aware of this schedule, and several of them had set their phones to alert them when the final countdown was about to start. After a few minutes had passed, someone got up to fix the velvet rope obstructing the staircase to the second floor. Due to a lack of monitoring, it was normally forbidden for students to go upstairs. Some people were concerned that it would be too simple for a curious person to break the spotlights or, worse, slide down the smooth wood and injure themselves on the main seats. That would be terrible.

9:00. The moment was now. In response to Ms Wolfe's order, the teachers all stood up at once and dramatically opened the doors to the main lobby. They did so at the same time as the teachers who had been waiting in the foyer and those who had spent the previous half-hour inside the building playing I Spy because they had nothing better to do. Students were hurried inside to fill the chairs as they entered in pairs, fumbling with their wallets to find the shiny ID cards they were so eager to receive.

"Which seat should I occupy? Is it a given? Alan questioned, his focus completely on abiding by all social conventions, and his feet instinctively following those in front of him.

The mathematics teacher gave a rote, "Don't worry, just keep moving," reply. A small percentage of pupils were always concerned that they were already acting improperly during the first thirty seconds of class. Did it matter that a few kids broke the pattern and sat in "the wrong seats," as opposed to everyone else? No, not at all—all the chairs would still be occupied by the end of the day, and nobody would remember how things were supposed to be. He believed that it was a common misperception that students who arrived on time were more likely to be well-behaved; in reality, it always took a few days for students to settle and reveal their actual selves once their mental fortifications broke down and they were unable to maintain the façade of success and casual calm.

Students continued to enter the theatre in a steady stream while still holding onto their stuff in the lobby. Many people disliked being corralled like the primary school pupils across the street since they were used to a certain level of independence during their summer break. Some believed that their intelligence and maturity were insulted by the fact that they could not be relied upon to behave appropriately; nevertheless, the most mature students showed little concern and simply followed instructions. The physics teacher guessed that after a few minutes, the ground floor of the home would be awfully crowded, and someone would certainly radio in to confirm the earlier drawn inference that, yes, this was in fact a sizable class of freshmen.

He addressed a small group that had split off to use the restroom and get water, "Any of you want to go to the second floor?" This wasn't meant to happen, and the teacher sitting next to him shot him a scathing glance, but he didn't care. The pupils joyfully nodded, and Mr. Ivanov allowed them to rapidly climb the stairs without being observed by the other students by squeezing past the rope.

The other teacher glared at him and said, "You'll have to oversee them, you know.

"Sure, that. In any case, I like to sit upstairs.

The students who were wise enough to sit with their pals sighed in relief when the lower level of seating swiftly filled up as expected.

"Assemblies. My preferred. Beth snoozed. The stage was still covered when the event began, and soon she was getting bored. She thought about pulling out her phone, but she figured there would be no reception.

It's high school time! Why don't you seem happy? Regina spoke fast and a little giddily in her reply. She knew that the next four years would be the pinnacle of her life up to that point, and she was in for a wild trip no matter how those four years began. She shifted slightly in her seat as she relaxed into the cushion's softness.

Naturally, I'm content. But not for this section.

Juliet exclaimed, "I never knew the theatre was this big," as she stared in astonishment at the ceiling's gradual fading into obscurity. She hadn't seen many theatres before, at least not the kind where films were shown, but this was still spectacular in her thoughts because she was still in awe of the actual cityscape she was in. The three of them were seated on the home's right wing, close to the entrance that all of the pupils used to enter.

Frank and Jason followed them while speaking animatedly as they moved along the straight aisle. Normally, they would arrive earlier, but because they were taking calculus, they had to sign some paperwork in the office. They had anticipated some trouble when they sat in the counselor's stark white nothingness, but she grinned and remarked that since they were better at maths than she was, they were more likely to have sound judgement. They were exhorted to return right away to the theatre in order to secure good seats while she dramatically signed some paperwork.

Calculate the best theatre seat as soon as possible. Jason scoffed at Frank's joke as he looked at him. Jason almost got at school late and was already considering how he could get some extra sleep. Frank was a morning person and had plenty of jocular humour.

I simply want to take a seat in the back. They sat down next to an instructor whose eyes were already glazed over with boredom after Jason murmured grimly.

In the foyer, Ms. Wolfe tapped her feet anxiously. Only a few minutes had passed, yet it already felt like they were running late. She returned through the same door she had used to enter the common room, made her way through the shadows to a location behind a curtain, and signalled to one of the student volunteers to open the curtains and turn on the spotlights. Some students gasped as the lights went out in the theatre. She emerged from behind the curtains with a bright smile towards the crowd and proceeded to the podium, where a laptop had already been set up. When she cleared her throat and started speaking, "Uptown Funk" stopped playing through the speakers, a deliberate attempt to get the crowd energised.

She said, "Good morning, Tigers!" and several of the teachers applauded properly. The moment the students realised what was going on, they began to applaud. Your first day of high school is starting today. This day is significant. We look on you for maturity." Ms. Wolfe continued droning on while maintaining an enthusiasm that was completely out of character with the specifics of high school life being detailed.

They could have hired cheerleaders or anything, right? Jason was already asleep when Frank made a gentle comment to him. In an apparent attempt to convey that he was even less interested in being there, the teacher who was standing behind them grinned at him and nodded. Jason lucked out. Alan and John were seated down, somewhere in the crowd, and they both sat silently with their hands in front of them. When something that looked essential came up, John would periodically jot it down on his notepad. He paid particular attention to references to fundamental Heller ideals like bravery and honesty. John saw these instructions as suggesting that, absent intentional effort, he and his contemporaries would inevitably veer towards cowardice and deceit.

One of the several counsellors took the microphone after Ms. Wolfe finished speaking and did so in order to remind the children of the bell timetable. People in the crowd who hadn't already committed their schedules to memory pulled out their paper and listened closely. Some of the audience members, at least the more artistically inclined, drew diagrams on the back of their schedules as mnemonic devices; the counsellor even went so far as to present a map of the school to lead them through the broad layout. Instead, Beth decided to place happy smiles next to the classes she was most looking forward to. Following the counselor's remarks, a few members of the student body spoke, making additional guarantees of high school excitement and overdone empathy: yes, they too were freshman once, and yes, they too were lost once, but everything would be OK!

Tom muttered, "This is stupid," and Ted grunted in annoyance, "Yeah." They turned and rolled their eyes as a teacher scowled at them to quiet them. Naturally, everything would run smoothly. College is where high school graduates go after graduating, not the crazy institution. They had heard it again and time again that high school kids had carefree lives. They were adults; no one needed to instruct them on proper behaviour. They were unable to see many more faces in the pitch-black room besides those that were illuminated on stage and covered in orange and black face paint, but they were certain that this was all for nothing.

All of this appeared to be a tremendous success to Ms. Wolfe, who could still view the audience while avoiding the heat of the spotlight. She hoped that the chairs up top were simply extra space because the ones down below were mostly occupied, and she could just about make out Mr. Ivanov's physique up there, so she assumed everything was good.

It wasn't difficult at all, even though this was only the second time she had personally led one of these orientation meetings. It was the obligation of returning students to mould new students swiftly before their exteriors hardened. She stepped out of sight to avoid setting a bad example while checking the time on her phone. On schedule yet.

The upbeat beats of "Uptown Funk" resurfaced as the assembly came to a close, and some of the less restrained youngsters mouthed the lyrics and danced as they walked. The teacher behind them, who introduced himself as Mr. T, advised they follow Jason and use the side exit to leave the theatre more quickly. Jason soon roused himself. Mr. T waved them off as they left before the pathways became congested and he stayed behind to enable a few more shrewd kids do the same thing. They moved quickly enough to leave before the routes became clogged. Under the watchful eye of the teacher, John hurried out of the room after the rest of the group while Alan was left behind—possibly trampled—and unaccounted for. John, who hadn't really done it before, used the chance to look around for people he knew and waved hesitantly at those who appeared to recognise him. John struggled to remember names, so he identified people by looking at their clothing and faces. There was that kid with the growing moustache, that kid with the much less growing moustache, the kid John remembered as his student council president last year (whatever that meant), and that trio of females he dimly remembered from middle school. He thought Regina was the taller one and Juliet was the shorter one because they both appeared to be acquainted. maybe in the opposite direction. In any case, he had never spoken to them before. The third one was less well-known, and John felt she was somewhat adorable.

The other kids in the residence were advised to leave as soon as possible by any exit, provided they did so fast. They had never before had a half-hour of free time, and it was quite unlikely that they would get two in a single day. Even the pupils who were moving slowly because they were chatting happily with their new acquaintances were advised to move quickly because a healthy mind required fresh air. Teachers searched the aisles for misplaced items while placing food wrappers, empty water bottles, and loose schedules in file folders. Inquisitive about what had transpired while he was away, Mr. Cathcart emerged from his hiding place and urged the teachers who were still there to clean carefully. Because she had dared to try to give him more work earlier, he planned to assign Ms. Wolfe in particular with garbage duty as payback. However, she had already left. He left disappointed and went back to his office. The lights were switched off and the tiled flooring turned a dismal grey in the shaky morning light a few minutes after the motion detectors lost track of the last teacher gently closing the double doors leading into the lobby. The stairway was still blocked off with what seemed to be a brown velvet rope.

Chapter 2

A ll 1,000 of the other students had left the school by the time the incoming freshmen ascended the steps and entered the main courtyard. They travelled in small groups, visiting with old acquaintances and eagerly exchanging tales of their summer vacations. There was a long line of people waiting to contest their class schedules in front of the administrative offices. A few freshman tried to cut through the line by pushing their way to the front before being relegated to the back. All of the seasoned students moved fast, pushing those who weren't yet accustomed to the flesh's currents to duck and weave or be forced to sidle along the walls. The metal seats were still too chilly to sit on because the sun hadn't yet poked its way through the clouds above.

Frank was a quick walker, but the unrelenting river of students nearly carried him away before he dodged to the side and into a hallway. The entire corridor was lit by fluorescent lights, and because of how their light reflected off the tiles, it initially appeared sterile. The school made a special impact by welcoming its new pupils with calm in the hopes that they would be inspired to maintain this status quo, even though there would typically be crumbs near the margins, driven there by natural foot activity. Since most students were enjoying the cool air outside, he could hear every teacher's and student's step and count how many others were around. Normally, this would not be visible. The posters were diverse, ranging from a couple of food safety reminders to pleas to uphold Heller ideals. One banner honouring the junior class at the time caught his eye. It was covered in a jumble of green scribbles that appeared to be autographs. Nobody eating their hastily prepared breakfast in silence acknowledged him.

Chinese was his first lesson, and it was outside. As Frank turned left at a crossroads, he nearly collided with another student who was examining his class schedule and carefully drawn map and appeared bewildered by the directions directing him to leave the building.

Frank said nervously, "Are you looking for Mrs. Huang's class? It's outside and to the left." Did they bite? This was the first interaction he had with a new student. He most likely wouldn't.

Yes, I am. Thank you, Ernest replied, his eyes fixed on his itinerary and then the intimidating glass door in front of them that led to an unfamiliar area of the school. "When does she get her period?"

I did. I reasoned that I might as well make sure I was in the proper location.

Frank sternly nodded in reply to "Chinese III."

What did you think of the assembly, by the way? The students sitting next to me were extremely disrespectful, always whispering to each other.

With less vigour, Frank nodded once more. Ernest laughed, sighed again, then continued to complain about the morning's assembly, "I was sitting in the back next to one of my friends, Jason if you know him, so it was quiet. He even took a nap."

John had just finished his own rambling tour of the school on the opposite side. Following the mob for a while, he eventually found himself back where he had started. He pulled a granola bar out of his pocket and started munching on it because he didn't see any special reward for his efforts beyond a few more recognisable faces in the crowd. He cautiously tried one of the benches but decided it was too cold, so he settled for a seat on the concrete rim of a planter with a view of the still-wet central grass. He went through the fundamental algebraic formulas from last year before his next maths class out of concern that he could forget them. He was enrolled in the accelerated geometry programme, which was equally made up of freshmen whose parents envied the kids who were closer to calculus and sophomores who, like their friends, had pledged to no longer fall behind.

John finally dropped his granola bar wrapper in the closest garbage can and entered the closest hallway to find his math lesson when it became evident that he would be unable to identify any hidden insight in the weaving masses. Heller High School's main floor plan was roughly symmetrical; on the two sides of the central courtyard that weren't occupied by the administrative offices and gymnasiums, two or three looming doors with white-painted letters on them led to a regular grid of classrooms that were numbered according to the hallway they were in. With the exception of the newcomers, many of whom found it difficult to process the system while already experiencing sensory overload, both students and teachers thought it was an excellent system. Numerous classrooms had illogical numbers, generating a long list of exceptions that everyone with experience was familiar with.

With the rare artwork attached to the wall, these halls were more gaudily adorned than the ones Frank had previously seen. The majority of the paintings featured tigers, either tigers baring their fangs in the forest or tigers jumping through rings of fire at the circus. Some great artworks were replicated, some more skillfully than others. Edvard Munch's The Scream took on new meaning when the subject's face had stripes and was standing with the school theatre in the background, looming over a landscape that looked like an oil slick. The poor student who had been commissioned to paint these clearly was told to ensure some connection to Heller as a whole, and tiger motifs were present in every painting.

When John noticed that the autographs listed years far in the past of his own, he quietly stood before them as though he were at a museum. He wondered what the school was like during the time period depicted by the rusty trophy cases and plaques. Obviously more original.

In actuality, Alan had avoided being crushed and had survived to leave the theatre. He followed the crowd, picking one guy at random who was taller than the others, and followed his journey through strange hallways and to the science wing, when he realised he had returned to his starting point and was still unsure of his whereabouts. He took another look at his schedule. The doors around him had numbers 2 and 3, and his first classroom's number began with a 1. In the hope that the numbers on the paper might somehow move, twist, and distort into ones that made more sense, Alan turned his schedule 90 degrees, then again. He was aware that there were several locations on the campus where huge university maps were posted, but he needed to know where he was in order to find one of those. He had no idea whether choosing the wrong door would lead to a parallel universe or reveal yet another area of the school that he would need to memorise.

Alan clinched his hands in fear as a voice from behind him questioned, "Do you need help?" When he turned around, he was expected to see an instructor, but all he saw was a student carrying a map and his own schedule. With a smile, the student said, "I'm new here too," noticing Alan's apprehension.

After taking a deep breath, Alan hesitantly asked if he could describe how the numbering system functioned. The science wing went into the 300s, the maze of hallways next to them would be in the 200s, and the location Alan wanted to go to would be all the way on the other side of the school, according to Behrooz, who pulled out his map and leaned towards Alan. He also explained that each quadrant roughly corresponded to an interval of 50. Behrooz urged Alan to travel with him because he was concerned that after he crossed the campus, Alan would encounter yet another confusing situation. Alan grinned again and uttered an artificial "Thank you." Behrooz brought Alan to where he would need to be in a few minutes, and then strolled off to his own class. Alan found it simpler to move around in Behrooz's wake and stopped feeling the need to say "Sorry" and "Excuse me" all the time.

Being a highly flexible individual, Behrooz had already decided that nothing was really that horrible before the first day of class. He shook hands with those he knew and told himself to relax. Some of the handshakes were personalised, while others were firm and formal. At the morning meeting, the counsellors had assured them that while the opening weeks would be difficult, they would emerge from them reborn and completely at ease with their new position. Even if none of the inspirational quotes on the walls had yet engraved themselves in Behrooz's mind, he nevertheless saw everything with a wise understanding. He was a rapid learner; in a few days, it would seem as though he had spent his entire life at the school.

The school bell rang just as some of the newcomers were becoming unhappy with their new surroundings and feeling as though they had once more regressed to elementary school recess. Some were attending for the first time, and in an instant, the environment surrounding them turned hostile. They waited motionless, while everyone else seemed to know where to go, until social pressure finally compelled them to dash towards where they believed their first class was. Frank and Ernest waited outside Mrs. Huang's door, watching for activity within. There was no teacher, despite the fact that everything appeared to be in order—groups of four desks, tri-folds at the rear on various cultural issues, and word posters they well understood. The majority of the class, which was made up of sophomores and juniors, grumbled when they realised there were too many freshmen in their class as more students gathered, many of whom knew each other from elementary or middle school. They believed that by this time in their senior year of high school, dealing with annoying kids was a thing of the past.

Mrs. Huang hurried around the corner just as the second bell rang to signal the start of class, saying aloud, "Sorry, I'm late," to no one in particular. As the kids let themselves in, she swiftly opened the door and took a position behind them. Frank used his foot to open the door from behind him, giving Mrs. Huang the extra second she needed to enter without seeming awkward or unpolished. She was rather taken aback as she turned to face him and saw a freshman who didn't appear to be Asian.

Frank asked in Chinese: "Chinese III. First period, correct?" Mrs. Huang's frown abruptly warmed into a smile: "Sorry, my mistake. Are you Chinese? How are you in this class?" Frank responded in Chinese, looking confused. "This is the Chinese III class. Chinese I is next period," she stated severely.

Frank paused, unsure of why he needed to explain why he was in her class. After all, Mrs. Huang had given the placement test over the summer and had welcomed him with a warm greeting after being impressed by his absolutely excellent linguistic abilities. He shook his head so as not to anger Mrs. Huang or cast doubt on her recall. She continued:

The other students rolled their eyes as they said, "You aren't Chinese? You speak so well, you must be very smart! What other classes are you taking?" He had undoubtedly set the record if there were one for the quickest time to become the teacher's favourite. Frank, however, made a promise to speak with her later because he felt too modest to demand all of her attention. He sat next to Ernest, and Mrs. Huang began her lesson beautifully. She spoke in a mix of Chinese and English, which caught many of the freshmen off guard, but by the end of the class, they were effortlessly imitating their peers' gestures.

John was delighted to discover that geometry was as simple to understand as he had anticipated. Polynomials could not be created from scratch using a piece of paper and a compass, nor could they be held and rotated. After carefully and distractedly examining the calculus posters on the wall and concluding that they were clearly not geometry, John did not allow himself to be intimidated by them. Hard plastic that was occasionally strengthened with wide girders served as a sort of window on one of the classroom's walls. Ms. Bracknell made a joke about everyone running into the hills in case of an emergency as she pointed outside to the student parking lot and the driveway that curled around behind it and into the forest. Few people laughed. John sat with a group of unknown acquaintances, all of whom, happily, appeared to be at his level of comprehension. He observed that Juliet and the other cute girl were seated at a table nearer to the window, where they and the mottled carpet were bathed in light. Perhaps "the other cute girl" would be a better designation, as John did not want to put her on some pedestal over any other cute girls, of which there were undoubtedly plenty. John concentrated on Ms. Bracknell while occasionally sneaking looks elsewhere because she rarely moved and tended to stand on the opposite side of the classroom.

When their first class was over, John departed at a leisurely pace, see-ing Beth (Elizabeth sounded strange—John could only recall one name) following suit. He continued to move forward in the hope that he could follow other people to Mrs. Huang's classroom. As Frank passed him by, he was giddy about calculus. He would perhaps be able to blend in a little better. With any chance, Jason wouldn't reveal his genuine identity despite having a different period and knowing from the counsellor that they were the only two students enrolled in BC. Frank's tablemates were amused enough by having a young and innocent freshman that they helped him determine his email address and password, and after a few wisecracks everything was kosher. Unfortunately, the first activity of the class period required logging into the school computers, something that as a new student, he had not previously had to do. The young man seated next to him was a sophomore who was glad to see another student of his age. Frank and Pranav quickly bonded over a love of video games and grew close friends.

When John walked outside and was met by a gust of chilly air, he trembled. Only a few of the classrooms had doors that opened outward, and after searching through each one, he discovered Mrs. Huang's space. There, she sat and gave each pupil a number as they entered; the number corresponded to a rather haphazard arrangement of labels on the desks. He sat down and retrieved his notebook and pen while facing forward. About a minute later, Beth entered and by some amazing coincidence was given the seat opposite from him; as a result of Mrs. Huang's confusing seating arrangements, Beth had to twist in order to view the board, and John had to lean to the side in order to see past her head. They exchanged a timid wave in passing acknowledgment of one another but kept their mouths shut. Beth saw that John—she did, after all, remember his name—was unusually quiet; on occasion, his expression twisted, as if he were torn between wanting to talk and not wanting to. At the second bell, Mrs. Huang began her lecture and spoke passionately about the advantages of studying Chinese. John was disappointed but encouraged to learn that half the class, including Beth, had some prior exposure to Chinese when she quickly called for a show of hands. John had learned that while they were learning Mandarin, or literally "ordinary speech" in translation, many other varieties of the language existed. He reasoned that this was his chance to shine. When Mrs. Huang confidently introduced him as James at the end of class, his spirits took a little dip as he briefly questioned his own identity.

Soon after their passing period started, Frank and John arrived at Mr. T's classroom at around the same time and found the door open. At his desk in the rear of the room, Mr. T greeted them with a friendly smile. A variety of patterns were used to decorate Mr. T's classroom; a skeleton with a limp dangling jaw was hidden in a corner near to posters for Casablanca and the trigonometric functions. Back in the spacious classroom, behind

Mr. T's diminutive desk, were cabinets. He turned around, unlocked a cabinet, and brought out a banana for each of the two early corners after deciding to reward their punctuality. John politely rejected, but Frank accepted his, examined it, shrugged, and then began to eat.

Mr. T spoke briefly about himself before making fun of the fact that they were fortunate to have him instead of the other instructor since he attempted to make class interesting—a difficult effort considering that he taught health education—but if the skeleton was any indication, his class had some personality. After his lecture, which lasted around fifteen minutes, he urged everyone to start working on their other classes' homework. Mr. T permitted the sporadic chats as long as they were ostensibly intellectual. As he began working on his math worksheet, Frank hoped no one would notice that he was acting strangely. Mr. T, however, did.

Mr. T softly said: "Don't forget the negative sign there; the integral of sine is negative cosine." He drew a circle with his pen to indicate where Frank had erred. After Mr. T departed, his fellow diners turned to him inquisitively to find out what he was working on, and he nodded in appreciation.

Frank addressed one of them, who appeared particularly interested, "I'm doing my math homework. What are you working on?"

I'm interested, too. Is that geometry?" he retorted, his interest still piqued.

Thankfully, Frank only got a long "Damn..." in response to his statement that "No, this is calculus." He then quickly got back to work. Surprisingly, towards the end of the lesson, Mr. T knew everyone's names and wished them good luck. He hastily arranged the desks after they left and waited for his senior English students to show up.

Jason was grateful that their first few PE days would be spent in the gym and the locker rooms getting accustomed to their surroundings rather than engaging in any physical activity. Jason was startled by the

PE teacher's whistle and managed to veer to the right just in time to avoid running into Louis, who scowled at him. Even after the bell rang, Ms. Stevens continued to separate the pupils by gender as they walked in. She spoke loudly and made large, sweeping gestures. She was shocked that so many people had trouble locating the gymnasium they were in, but she was sympathetic.

We're in the digital age, so I'll post your assignments online and go over them in class. If you don't finish a week's worth of work during class, you can make it up by working out more on the weekend, so make sure to keep a strict journal of what you do. If you go running, I want to see a map of your route.

Unexpectedly, Ted was paying listening, so Tom questioned him, "Does she really think anyone will do this?" His thoughts were already racing with schemes to trick the system and obtain free credits. On the weekends, he worked out, and if Ms. Stevens saw him going above and above, she would be impressed. Ted did not realise that Ms. Stevens did not care exactly when her students exercised as long as they were maintaining a healthy lifestyle since he was too preoccupied with the thought of obtaining something for nothing. Ted mouthed the word "yes" in answer because he didn't want to cause any trouble on the first day.

Ms. Stevens pointed at them and yelled, "You two! Quiet!" All of their classmates' heads turned to look in that direction.

Ted said, "Sorry, Ms. Stevens," and Tom said nothing.

The pupils rushed out of their classes after lunch with a fresh perspective on the new life that awaited them. Even though they would eventually drift away over the next weeks, many people stayed with old pals they knew from earlier grades because they found the familiarity comforting. Their social activities and the locations of their meals were governed by the individual schedules of the students. The less brave youngsters tried to attract attention by walking close to the popular kids, but all social circles were in flux. Freshmen were shunned by upperclassmen like the plague, and if a bunch of them happened to occupy a popular dining location before previous territorial claims could be made, so be it: it was theirs. Whether they knew it or not, other students filled the gap left by the graduating class of the previous year. Beth, Juliet, and Regina chose a pleasant area by the grass to talk and exchange ideas. They were thrilled to learn that they would be taking the same English class the following session, and their conversation instantly turned to the experiences they did not have in common.

After everyone had completed their lunches and felt like gossiping, Juliet said, "You won't believe this, guys. There's someone in my health class taking calculus."

Regina said, dismissively, "Jason? He's kind of creepy. I don't like him," and then she pulled out her phone.

No, it's not Jason; I'm sorry, I can't remember his name.

Regina asked, unsure if this was news worth sharing: "Is that unusual?" She didn't know this individual, but if Jason was creepy, there was a considerable chance that this youngster would also be disgusting.

They resumed idle conversation until the bell rang, at which point they joined their colleagues waiting outside Ms. Baldwin's doorway. "I think it is. We're both in the accelerated geometry class, you're in the regular one, and we're ahead of schedule. They must both be geniuses," Beth said.

At first glance, there was love. Regina was instantly smitten with John the moment she first laid eyes on him. He had a roving eye, a razor-sharp haircut, and an even razor-sharper chin. His jumper, a carpet of blue and grey diamonds on a brown backdrop, suggested not only pragmatism but also a keen sense of colour and fashion, which promised, at least to her, a fast pathway to success through his imagined charisma. It didn't matter that his attire wasn't the usual high school student's first pick because those sleeves undoubtedly covered some muscle. a straightforward theory to confirm.

Regina turned abruptly and said, letting her hair flutter. "Are you cold?" She stood around John's height and looked into his eyes, hoping for a response.

John said hesitantly, "Uh, I don't think so," and took a tiny turn away. The question "Who are you?"

She extended her hand for a handshake and said, "I'm Regina, and I'm looking out for my fellow students, you know." He had chilly hands. Strong grasp, she observed, extremely admirable. Beth and Juliet looked perplexed, but John did not appear to be brushing off Regina's questions. Although this did not involve a beer keg, he felt it odd that Beth and Juliet were observing him as they were talking to him. It reminded him of one of those fraternity hazing ceremonies. Soon later, Ms. Baldwin showed up and opened the door for them.

Ms. Baldwin firmly believed that seating charts had the ability to shape the minds of impressionable freshman. As a result, she always created the seating chart at random and didn't realise how regrettable her initial choice was until after the fact. She could already see that some old acquaintances were discouraged by being separated by a few desks, while others affectionately hugged as if they had just finished a conversation. John was fortunate to be seated with three well-known individuals: Regina, who was convinced that she was his new best friend; Juliet, who believed that Regina's unusually boisterous behaviour was proof that she had finally lost her mind; and Ted, who listened warily and abruptly fell silent when Ms. Baldwin started speaking so as to avoid receiving verbal abuse a second time.

John loved English; even if he had never read the poetry before, he thought there was no frigate like a book to transport him over the globe. John frequently read books several times, especially when they were new. A happy narrative would dependably impart a warm feeling that would linger for one or two days at most, while a sad story would do the reverse. This basic formula helped them uncover his emotions. Beyond this dichotomy, there were numerous shades of nuance and emotion that John experienced but often struggled to describe. As a result, John delighted in new stories and read them carefully to determine what morally upright qualities they gave. He predicted that he would experience horrifying nightmares because their first book was Frankenstein.

John attended biology, his final lesson of the day, where he ran into Alan, who he was happy to learn had survived the day without suffering any obvious emotional scars, and his new friend Behrooz. Though hardly helped by the sunlight streaming in through the windows, at least John was accustomed to it. In a cunning move he hoped no one would notice, Alan put a pencil beneath his chin to keep from dozing off.

Lab work was what Behrooz most looked forward to. Even though he wasn't a die-hard scientific enthusiast, he admired the quiet discipline needed to combine and pour in the precise amounts necessary to change the world. When Behrooz was younger, his mother, an executive in the pharmaceutical industry, tried to pique his interest in a similar field. A periodic table was still hanging in his room even now, even though he had not given it any attention in years. It was located in a spot where he did not usually look at it. Like most of his friends, he was inclined to doze off until the lab safety quiz was administered. This interactive exercise was skillfully created to help pupils feel at ease with the possibility of having to clean up acid and shattered glass. In order to demonstrate to the other students why it was so crucial to refrain from using the safety shower, Mr. Reinhardt persuaded one brave student to attempt utilising the unsightly maze of pipes that might pass for plumbing in Sparta. When a powerful burst of cold water was sprayed in Behrooz's face after he volunteered, he gasped.

Mr. Reinhardt said dryly, his German accent barely audible, "Not so pleasant, is it?" The students walked about the classroom in search of all the other crucial information as they formed their new lab groups, to which they were to be devoted with unwavering determination.

Some of them had never seen Erlenmeyer flasks or microscopes before, which all stayed in cabinets with a strict instruction to not tamper with them unless absolutely essential. This final point was often emphasised whenever a student inquired whether they may touch some expensive lab apparatus. After class, John asked Mr. Reinhardt about the deflated balloon he had seen curled up in the rafters around another steel beam that was both structurally and aesthetically pleasing. Mr. Reinhardt said he had been waiting for the janitors to take care of it for years and that he would be eternally grateful to whoever found a way to safely dispose of it.

Is it safe to use old balloons?

Mr. Reinhardt kindly replied, as if John hadn't just asked an obvious question, "No, John, I don't want some fool falling off a ladder and cracking their skull." He interpreted John's question as a sign he was volunteering to repair the situation, an approach he looked upon favourably, and clarified: "That was a bit morbid. I apologise. One could try taping a few yardsticks together." The last bell rang before he could make a stronger suggestion that the yardsticks were in the cupboard behind lab table 4, and that if John didn't remedy the issue, he would have to repair it himself. John was tempted to ask Mr. Reinhardt why such a simple solution required such a terrifying discussion about ladders, but he did not want to distract away from those who had more pressing questions.

The students' movement towards the parking lot and bus stop was accompanied by a crescendo of excitement that had been building in the previous several minutes. John looked for familiar individuals who were using public transport since he was eager to do so for the first time in a while. He spotted Beth behind a tree examining her phone; she seemed to be everywhere. John was startled to see Frank continue to follow the street and vanish as he sped past him. Alan didn't know where to go after his final class; his parents had told him to meet them in the parking lot, but which one? He was lucky that the closest and safest option was the parking lot from which he had started his trek. He double-checked his itinerary to make sure everything had gone off without a hitch that day. Alan held onto his now-wrinkled and sweat-stained schecule as he walked out of the school. His parents were thrilled to hear that he had a good time since they had picked him up in tandem on the first day of high school. In a sea of hundreds of other cars, Jason stood by himself across the street from the school and searched carefully for his mother's vehicle. He paced back and forth for a bit before being alerted by a trumpet, at which point he hurried inside and shut the door.

Chapter 3

The music department at Heller was tucked away next to the locker rooms and down yet another level of steps. In the morning especially, arpeggios echoed through the halls before suddenly stopping, as if the students practicing knew others were listening. The more experienced students mentored the younger ones in the idiosyncrasies of the discipline, warning them of silly superstitions that by now they had internalized as fact. One must never walk through the door, they said, that led outside directly from the practice rooms; if they did so, their next concert was destined to be a failure. This custom only reinforced the geographic isolation of the area; as students practiced, they could forget they were at high school. Even the music teachers believed this, and they marked the door with caution tape.

Alan held his violin case hesitantly as he crept through the path of bamboo, past the locker rooms where some seniors in shorts eyed him warily, and down into the dungeon. He had played for a fairly long time, but he was rapidly beginning to believe he was underqualified compared to the rest of his ensemble. Alan felt shame when the teacher walked over to adjust his hand position, even though the teacher made adjustments to everyone's playing, no matter how good, and was too professional to display any signs of animus or exasperation. In fact, the more experienced students bristled most, believing they were worthy by now to play with the upperclassmen. There was a peculiar hierarchy within the music department with no special significance to anyone outside of it: the elders got to sit on the couch and ride shotgun on field trips.

Behrooz arrived at school precisely five minutes before classes began. When he had first came to Heller, he needed extra buffer time to find all his friends and greet them appropriately, but he began to realize that conversations were best enjoyed without the threat of their abrupt end. After slightly less than two weeks, Behrooz had finally learned all his classmates' names. He knew which ones to smile at, which ones were satisfied with a quick flash of a handwave, and which wanted him to ignore them.

"Hey, Tim!"

Tom grimaced, and was tempted to correct Behrooz, but it was early in the morning—perhaps he was sleep-deprived, and thus forgot basic phonics? Tom considered himself a nice guy with no need for petty conflicts.

"Hey, Behrooz, what's up?"

"Just hanging in there, just hanging in there." Behrooz moved speedily toward his first class and the other people he needed to greet, and Tom walked with carefully cultivated leisure around the corner to where Juliet was writing in her journal. Juliet used her journal as a diary and planner combined, using a wide variety of bullet points and arrows to organize her thoughts. If she did not use a variety of colors and possess neat handwriting, her intent would be completely illegible, not as if she let others look inside.

"I love the color scheme," Tom remarked from a safe distance at such an angle that he had no way of looking inside. Nevertheless, it was an educated guess, and by Juliet's warm smile Tom concluded he had started the conversation off on the right foot.

"I appreciate that. It's nothing much, really—I find it helps me keep track of life."

"What do you write inside?" Tom asked, moving closer to Juliet as she moved closer to him.

"My schedule, my diary, dreams, anything that catches my eye." Tom smiled and nodded as if he had an intimate familiarity with everything she mentioned, and Juliet took this as a sign to continue: "Do you keep a journal?"

Tom didn't keep a journal, but he wasn't sure if that was the right answer. After all, Juliet seemed to look favorably upon journals and those who wrote them, if she had any level of self-esteem; a harmless white lie could not possibly do any harm. Maybe it would soften his exterior a little in a way she would like. Perhaps an approach halfway would be best, allowing him the option of a tactical exit should he prove to be in over his head with journal-related jargon.

"Sometimes," Tom offered, rapidly clarifying when he thought Juliet was confused by this answer that he really needed to get back into it.

"Journaling is fun, I promise. I can help you if you want. We should totally spend a lunch period getting a new journal set up for high school, and you can get in touch with your inner self. Wouldn't that be great?"

Tom forced himself to smile and nod, and he was thankful the bell rang before he would have to continue the deception. That went well, he thought. Juliet was always warm and friendly, but this time she seemed exceptionally so, and most importantly, this attention was di-rected toward him alone. In his mind, Juliet's habit of being friendly to everyone she met, even going as far as to frequently utilize the casual hug maneuver, made her quite attractive. Cheerleader, intelligent, nice, not unattractive—Tom was happy his first attempt at making a move went so well. She clearly found him charming, handsome, or otherwise awesome too, otherwise she would not have entertained his inquiry so appropriately.

Juliet walked away thinking only of what color scheme she thought would suit Tom best. This was something that he really should decide himself, but as Tom was only an amateur at journaling, it was her duty to help the less-fortunate by offering recommendations. The purple of the balloons scattered through the hallway outside Ms. Bracknell's classroom seemed appropriate; she had heard somewhere that purple was a regal color that conferred great status on its users. Her last thoughts before she had to switch her focus entirely to geometry were that Tom was not only a friend, but also a cool guy.

"Hey, Frank."

"Yes?" he responded crisply while carefully measuring water into a graduated cylinder.

"Could you help me with this geometry packet? I'm not really under-standing how you solve for the angles." Frank looked over and saw that while he was hard at work jumping into their first lab, one of his lab partners was trying and failing to multitask on both math and biology. Frank wasn't extraordinarily enthused by their first exercise, measuring the quantities of different materials in their household soil (he did not see himself changing his life nor gaining a better appreciation for the universe through the resolution of this activity), but it was good practice and he was being graded on how well he did it.

"If you need help with that geometry worksheet, let's get those soil samples measured out quickly then."

Mr. Reinhardt smiled and nodded when he passed by their lab table during their conversation. Frank had answered correctly—in his class-room, biology came first. He made a mental note of their competence.

The four of them proceeded to finish quickly, and as soon as they returned to their seats, Frank began a miniature lecture on the nuances of geometry fundamentals, everyone nearby listening carefully. When he couldn't immediately think of the term "transversal lines," Mr. Reinhardt, who somehow was listening from his desk despite appearing occupied in grading tests, filled in the blank. Frank spoke slowly and carefully, insistent that all listening understood each concept in sequence and could independently draw their own conclusions. He did not consider himself a natural teacher, but he accepted the title with dignity when Mr. Reinhardt complimented him after class. It seemed like the others took note, and Frank felt punished; he worried that in the future, he would have to divide his attention between too many and thus not give each the assistance they truly needed. On the positive side, he earned respect even from those who did not identify as academics, many of whom were glad to be able to ask questions without shame.

Alan found John in the hallway between periods seemingly lost in an interesting daydream (Alan, who had watched a YouTube video on how to read lips once, thought he was mouthing something about a shrine) and asked him, without waiting sufficiently for him to come back to reality, if he wanted to tour clubs during lunch that day. The club fair was a semi-annual tradition intended to proudly display all that Heller had to offer beyond the classroom. Students set up booths at tables and handed out free food and flyers, telling other students who were only there for the free food what fun they were missing out on. The newer students and those with some inkling of moral character pondered every club extensively, particularly if they had not found their appropriate social circle yet. Clubs were an expedient way to find new friends quickly; some did not even choose clubs based on their subject matter, but by if the people looked cool.

This was one of those days when the full force of the student body was apparent as they perambulated, and Alan and John once again found themselves apologizing for their mere presence as they wandered through the crowd. All the students manning the booths were upper-classmen, and after Alan overheard one of them joke condescendingly about the cute little freshmen, he resolved to show them who was boss someday. He was a high school student, and by now he had earned some privilege. It was time they respected it. The sun beat down on all of them relentlessly, and he resisted the urge to sweat.

Despite Alan's urging to hurry up and get free bubble tea before it ran out, John engaged with most clubs he visited, curious to know exactly what they did and how they did it. John had always found the idea of joining a club of like-minded people enthralling, even if he struggled to find one. Community service seemed appealing, and any club with humanitarian goals—bring menstrual products to all high school restrooms, ensure no child ever goes hungry again—stood out in his mind. He found it easy to sympathize with all their goals. Bright kitsch of sequins and colors repelled him equally, and John interpreted these superficial appearances as important as their professed missions. Some clubs unashamedly lied about how active their meetings were or how much fun they actually had, the savviest gauging based on their conversations which lies would be most effective and the others presenting a marketing spiel that was clearly memorized. John was an easy mark, and he walked away with a few colors of fliers and a wake of promises. He could not find Alan immediately, and quickly forgot that they had been walking together at all.

Just a few minutes after the lunch bell rang, the veterans had staked their claims on prime real estate, the wood chips under the massive oak tree and the one shaded table by the library, leaving Alan to fight for second place with the others who had not yet figured out the rules of territory. He perched on the end of one of the occupied tables, a safe few feet away from a group of juniors who seemed surprised to see him, but did not really care. He avoided talking for a few minutes until they had finished eating and one of them initiated what was ostensibly a welcoming conversation, but came off to Alan as a needless grilling about his classes, his favorite teacher, and whether he needed any advice. Had Alan known, as he would come to realize over the next few months, that these students were relatively delinquent, perhaps he would have avoided their open mirth, but for that lunch period he felt he had no choice but to play Go Fish with them and politely decline their offered junk food. Alan sipped his sugary bubble tea without a hint of hypocrisy (the club handing it out had used their AP Psychology knowledge to connect this excessive sweetness with happy hormones and thus easy retention of new members).

Regina came to English class exactly on time and immediately began telling John about her latest problem.

"Hey, John, you're smart. What do I do if I spilled bubble tea inside my bag?" Regina asked, pushing the bag in his direction so he could see her binders, luckily insulated by the plastic from much direct damage, and her phone and notebook, which were less fortunate. John stared intently at the conundrum, a touch of saliva forming due to the sugary fumes.

"Try using rice," Juliet suggested. Regina immediately turned to John and asked him to verify this solution, and he thought for another moment. Juliet smiled at John too to see if he would pass Regina's test. This was an entirely accidental spill, of course, and Beth and Juliet both doubted Regina's decision to use this as an opportunity for experiment.

"That sounds like it would work, yes," John responded, avoiding eye contact and focusing on his work. Ms. Baldwin was tempted to roll her eyes, but as this spectacle was playing out quietly, she continued as if they weren't there.

"Thank you John. You're so helpful." He was about to appropriately direct credit to Juliet when she shook her head, anticipating what he was going to say. John and Regina were certainly becoming good friends, Juliet thought. Regina shared her woes with John, and he responded with appropriate sympathy. Sometimes, he would respond with his own opinions, and Regina would give them careful consideration with an easy-going geniality. In fact, both she and Regina suspected that John would make the first move and save Regina some exertion. When that happened, it would be a glorious day.

John, of course, had little awareness of their stratagems that were carefully honed over texts throughout the day. Regina had instructed Beth and Juliet to take notes on how John acted during class; when did he show signs of emotional vulnerability that she could exploit? One time, she had tried the classic "bend and snap" maneuver from *Legally Blonde*, dropping her biology binder with a coquettish "Oops" and picking it up slowly while John watched for a moment and then walked right by her. The second time she tried this, John did not anticipate her sudden stop and walked directly into her, a fumble which he copiously apologized for and Regina endeavored to engineer again. When Beth did the same during Chinese class as a control, John bent down to pick up her binder with a gracious smile, which she accepted with a muttered thanks.

Ernest watched their table with barely concealed disdain, remarking to Tom how childish it all seemed.

"Yeah, I know. They're behaving just like kids," Tom responded, emboldened by Ted rolling his eyes and Ernest shaking his head in agreement to do the same. Maybe Tom had the wrong idea in being subtle with his machinations. He had already forgotten what he told Juliet he would do, but it seemed too early to do anything more drastic. Tom wanted to see the latest Avengers movie, but Juliet couldn't possibly be into anything that intense. And Tom was certain he did not want to see any chick flick, no matter who was sitting next to him and eating popcorn from the same giant bucket. Tom turned back to his group and tried to think of something suitably intelligent to say about the paragraph they had just read. At the end of class, John took a minute to fumble with the Chromebook cart and transform the spider web of cables into a neat array, prompting an immediate thank you from Ms. Baldwin and later gossip in the faculty room; John was unique in that he stopped to tidy up even when he was not the last to leave.

After school, Ernest took a pair of safety goggles from the plastic bin and entered the massive supply closet that served as the robotics base of operations. For lack of any better space, the robotics team did most of their engineering work in the same wood shop the engineering class used, an arrangement the teacher only tolerated because they kept their space clean and came with a peace offering of a set of power tools when they began. Ernest had joined the robotics team because his parents insisted he do some sort of activity. He ruled out performing in the musical, as an actor and not part of the orchestra, with a sharp intake of breath and an exasperated sigh of defeat, suggesting robotics instead, which his parents accepted. They weren't picky—as long as he enjoyed whatever he was doing and it built good character, they could not complain.

Pranav directed Ernest to help move some boxes of scrap parts out to a parent volunteer's car, which would take the parts to a storage unit they had rented a few miles away. Due to their perpetual worry that the budget would be cut, the robotics team was hesitant to dispose of anything that theoretically could be salvaged and worked into something new. It was cheaper to rent storage space than to purchase new parts, and this meant that one team member, namely Pranav, had the dubious honor of being in charge of cataloging all supplies the team possessed. He was never seen without his clipboard when he was on duty, where he logged everything that passed his eyes with utmost detail. He had developed a talent for being able to estimate the size of something to the millimeter, although he carried a tape measure for when those estimates were insufficient.

Frank walked past them just as they walked out of the building clearly overburdened by what they were carrying. "Let me help you with those," he insisted, and Frank took a surprisingly heavy box and let out a mild groan.

"How many more of these do you have?" Frank asked after following them back to the room; Pranav did not verbally answer, but instead gestured to a pile that had formed in the span of the first weeks of school.

Frank shook his head and picked up another one, and they walked back and forth until their arms were sore and the room was cleaned up.

"You didn't have to help, you know," Ernest replied, somewhat out of breath. Frank, seemingly not any worse for wear, shook his head.

"I have time, don't worry. I always have time."

"Speaking of that, could you take a look at my Chinese presentation tomorrow?"

"If you trust me to help, as long as you look at mine too, sure." Frank looked behind him and saw the student parking lot largely empty, and knew that it must be late. He waved goodbye and kept walking home.

Meanwhile, John watched the street signs as he rode the bus. All of them were named after presidents, and he spotted familiar names—Washington and Lincoln—and those that if he did not identify the pattern, he would not recognize at all—who were Buchanan and Harding? Some on the bus did their homework as it crested peaks and went down hills, but John found his already not-great handwriting to deteriorate into cryptic cursive when he wrote while moving, so instead he closed his eyes and tried to meditate. John always sat near the front of the bus. He had read once that it was the safest place to be, and he never doubted this fact's veracity. He thus imagined the bus tipping over, and him heroically turning the bus upright with sheer force of will or a sudden surge of adrenaline. If this did not happen, though, would the windows break and shower him with broken glass? Would the engine explode, hurtling him out of the bus and onto the then-cracked pavement? Would he be smothered under someone else's body, their folds of skin and fat choking his breath? He felt no concern at any of these macabre thoughts, as they passed the time.

Beth sat in the back of the bus, happy to have an unoccupied seat next to her, and thought of happier things. Once, she had heard John tell someone sitting next to him, whose face quickly turned to horror, what he thought about to pass the time during bus rides; now she couldn't help but think occasionally if John's prognostications would ever hold true, and if they revealed a troubled mind. Logically, she believed the safest seat ought to be in the middle, safe from a collision in the front or in the back. If the bus were in a collision, would she be launched forward until her head met the metal bar in front of her? Or would she merely be shaken up and mildly perturbed, that is until she realized how narrowly she escaped with her life? She chose instead to browse her Instagram feed, which fortunately was free from anything resembling vehicular manslaughter.

John disembarked the bus at the stop before Beth's, being sure to thank the bus driver appropriately before he strolled carefree back home. He wondered how far Beth rode the bus, as she always was there when he got on and always there when he left. If he were not intently focused on getting home safely, he would have noticed she got off at the stop immediately after his.

Chapter 4

Every morning, when only a few early birds were on campus, the morning fog rolled down from the hills and enveloped Heller, a chill that condensed on lampposts, dampened leaves of grass, and made those wearing light clothing shiver. On particularly frigid days, when the winds were just right, the temperature dropped below freezing, and those who took morning showers had their hair decorated with shards of ice. Sometimes a student walking too quickly without offering the weather the proper respect would slip and fall, and then a good Samaritan passing by would help them hobble to the nurse's office, where the employee on duty would warn them sternly about playing when slippery. Those being tended to were apologetic, regardless if they considered themselves at fault for merely walking as an ordinary person would.

This layer of cloud that rendered the school ethereal tended to burn away in the sun by the first bell if an especially warm day, and if not, it would linger and fester and make the PE students outside cry. Today was a hot day, one when autumn got bored and chose to masquerade as summer. The first students to emerge from the locker room signaled to those still leaving: "It's hot!" They loitered in the shade until they mustered the energy to move downhill toward the track. Some took long sips from the water fountain as a precaution. Ms. Stevens came down exactly five minutes after the bell rang in a visor and black-and-white checkered outfit, showing no signs of discomfort. She enjoyed the warm weather; besides, she didn't have to run. Every lap was a battle against the heat, a lush carpet that smothered all but Frank, who seemed content to jog at a reasonable, if not particularly fast, pace and power-walk slightly slower, all with the intent of running out the clock. The sweat lubricated their shoulders, rigid arms swinging like scythes. Everyone, regardless if they were cross-country all-stars or flabby tragedies, curved on their last lap up the concrete steps and toward the water fountain, which gurgled and spat out an arced stream of frigid water with the press of the button.

Tom and Ted moved immediately to chat with their friends in the shade; they ran quickly and thus had time to relax. Steam rose from Ted's arms, a novel occurrence that Tom immediately commented on. Before they could fully catch their breath, Ms. Stevens's voice rang out:

"Tom! Ted!" They turned in unison.

"You two were late! Run another lap!" They groaned and hopped over the railing, back to the track, and they started running again. The track was scenic: as they ran, students passed by some scattered track-and-field equipment, an athletic shed dedicated to an old coach no students at the school still remembered, and one locked gate in the chain-link that many fantasized about escaping through. There was still no respite from the heat. Ted finished quite quickly, and Ms. Stevens was impressed.

"You should consider doing cross-country. Good stamina."

"I want to join the Navy someday, and for that I try to remain in shape. There is no greater privilege than serving one's country," Ted said with a smile, looking back at Tom out of breath behind him and people like Jason, who appeared on the verge of fainting even after a few minutes' rest.

"Great energy and good work. I respect that. This counts as extra credit for both of you. Now go change," Ms. Stevens concluded with a smile, pointing at the other students who were leaving the field.

Alan still had a few beads of sweat dotting his brow and a mild odor when he left his fifth-period class for lunch, a fact which his peers politely ignored. He walked with no particular destination in mind, but endeavored to project a single-minded determination, tracing the hallways for someone to attach himself to. Behrooz, who held a packet of papers while staring at one of the many posters proclaiming Heller values, proved appropriate.

"What are you looking at?" Alan asked, standing next to him and adopting his same puzzled expression.

"I'm trying to fill out my application to join the leadership program. It's asking me to think of ways I embody true Tiger values," Behrooz responded calmly, as if he was trying to teach Alan.

"What are those?" Alan had never paid much attention to what teachers tried to tell him and others about school spirit. It seemed extraneous. He attended a football game once, where he understood little; Frank was there and also understood little, but Frank explained to him something about being a good citizen that Alan did not understand—it made no sense why he walked back to school, in the dark, to drink hot chocolate and marinate in undefinable energy. If this school spirit did not improve his test scores, he wasn't interested.

"Well, it's the eye of the tiger, it's the thrill of the fight," Behrooz said with a smile, and when Alan did not understand, he explained it was an old song. "You should apply too. It's fun, I promise." Alan obediently went to get an application for himself and pulled a pen from his backpack. Name, date, grade, student ID number—so far so good: this was easy! Describe your favorite experience at Heller so far—Alan's pen stopped. He looked at Behrooz for inspiration, who seemingly had come out of his writer's block and was continuing to write, holding his packet against the wall. Alan had greatly enjoyed acing his first math test. His teacher had written "Great work!" in crisp handwriting along the top, next to a "100%" underlined in red. Alan had looked through his test multiple times, impressed that he had done everything right. It appeared he was close at one point to losing a point because he used an unusual method, but thank God the teacher excused that! His parents and sister seemed so happy when he had showed them later that day; he talked with his mouth full to re-emphasize that this was a hard test where he struggled a lot.

"No, I'm not sure if that's what they're looking for," Behrooz commented when Alan pitched that story to him. "That's not unique enough, it doesn't speak to who you are as an individual. Any ordinary person can do well on a test if they study."

"But this was an especially hard test. I studied many hours for it, sure, but that's considered fighting through adversity. I think my classmates are ordinary, and they did not do as well." Behrooz was loath to admit it, but maybe Alan wasn't quite as wrong as Behrooz wanted him to be. Surely it was some testament to their unique virtue that they were striving to challenge themselves. Ms. Foster had promised everyone during the weekly video announcements that it was easy to become a leader. A journey of a thousand miles begins with a single step; it did not matter what prior experience they had, passion would reign supreme. Still, Behrooz was not swayed by Alan's logic:

"Is there any experience outside the classroom you enjoyed?"

"Well, I'm not sure if this is something I could write about, but..." The bell rang and shattered Alan's train of thought, and Behrooz turned in his application with a grin and wished Alan good luck. He put his own in one of his binders to work on as homework.

Frank was enjoying drama class. He had a natural flair for improv, generally playing the straight man but also perfectly capable of stealing the spotlight when his group members proved lacking. One particular scene proved his magnum opus so far: his character was hosting his own birthday party, but none of the guests he had invited came. It was a silent scene, and through pantomime Frank mimicked setting up tables, preparing a birthday cake, and anxious waiting, culminating in a tragic rendition of "Happy Birthday (To Me)" that received uproarious laughter. Beyond that, many amusing anecdotes populated the first few months of class: near the beginning of the year, Louis's acrophobia was exploited for the class's amusement, his resulting embarrassment driving him to quit the class before word spread of his failure; a week later, a junior had a seizure and collapsed due to a flickering spotlight, which was the talk of the school for a day before students collectively decided it was poor conduct to make light of another student's illness. He was having a blast, and he was about to have even more of one: Mr. Cathcart had put out the call for ushers to apply to assist with the musical starting the following week, and Frank was interested.

"Why didn't you audition at the beginning of the year?" Mr. Cathcart asked, still sitting in his favorite swivel chair.

"The time commitment was the main factor, and I'm not much of a singer."

"I'm sure you could figure it out. But anyway, I'm glad to have you on the team." Mr. Cathcart pulled out a T-shirt matching the theatrical poster, depicting a stylized Don Quixote with a rotund Sancho Panza, and gave it to Frank along with a reminder for him to pitch seeing *Man of La Mancha* to his friends.

"Have you read *Don Quixote*?" Frank asked Mr. Cathcart, who responded with a sheepish grin.

"Once in college, I think. But that was a long time ago. You're smart, you probably read it in kindergarten."

"Over the summer, which at this point may as well be kindergarten," Frank smiled, and they laughed in unison. "I'm also mildly traumatized from the mandatory plays in middle school."

"Oh yeah, that's right, you went to Pemberley. You're one of those kids. I was a student teacher there before I came to Heller. Interesting place."

"Indeed it is. I'll be glad to be on the right side of the stage this time," Frank concluded, and he went to one of the many restrooms in the theater to try on his new shirt. The theater's restrooms were perpetually spotless, and they even had air freshener; every drama student knew to hold their bodily needs until they could swing by the theater and relieve themselves in peace. It fit well, and wasn't out of character for Frank, who generally only wore T-shirts when they were advertising something. He dressed similarly to John otherwise, who also could pass for an university professor if not only due to his wardrobe, due to his temperament too. John had a leg up on Frank in that front because he wore reading glasses, which he kept in a fancy case that seemed to always appear out of thin air.

"What's the musical about?" John asked Frank after noticing his sudden wardrobe change.

"I'm not that familiar with the plot of the musical, but it's based on an old Spanish novel called *Don Quixote*, which is considered by some to be the first modern novel. Don Quixote, an old nobleman living in a ruined estate, wakes up one day suddenly believing himself to be a knight; together with his squire, Sancho Panza, they roam the countryside adventuring. I'm really not doing the story justice, but if you want to know more, you'll have to come to the show next week."

"How much do the tickets cost?"

"Uh, not much?" Frank wasn't sure if he was already failing at his duty as usher.

"I'm intrigued. I'll be there." John reached out to shake Frank's hand; Frank smiled curiously, and responded with similar formality. The timing of this discussion proved fortuitous, as during English class that day, Regina was especially in the mood for conversation.

"What do you do in your free time, John, like let's say this weekend as an example? What do you have planned?" Regina looked John straight in the eye, hoping this would make him respond more quickly. Juliet blushed.

"This weekend, not much. The usual, you know. Maybe some Minecraft. I'm going to see the musical next week, though."

"Oh, really? I knew you were artistically inclined." Regina considered herself extremely artistic, almost excessively so. Her parents enrolled her in piano and ballet from a young age, two extracurriculars she pursued with admirable devotion up until the present day. They controlled her free time to a remarkable degree, and she was fortunate that she never grew tired of performing. Regina could not imagine a life without performance, without an exceptionalism that was so uniquely her; her friends and family were constantly supportive of her efforts, and while they had always offered her the option of doing something else, she never chose to take it. Besides the pride she felt when executing a perfect arabesque or playing a sonata, another primary motivation was the focus on technique and constant improvement. Her ballet teacher frequently explained how there was always something new to discover in even the simplest of steps; any good performance of any sort was the confluence of hundreds of variables, all tweaked to perfection, and Regina resolved to master all of them. Regina did not consider herself entitled, but when success was not hers, there would be hell to pay.

"No, no, I'm really not. I'm a spectator. My drawings are terrible," John meekly responded, turning to his paper to do a quick sketch of Regina with an honest effort; when she figured out what John was doing, she posed appropriately. John did not lie: he was a poor artist. Regina came out with a bulbous nose, asymmetrical cheekbones, hair that appeared to be in the process of ripping itself from her scalp, and a puzzled look that was either a freeze-frame from an electrocution or the result of too much Botox. Regina tried to force herself to say something pleasant about the drawing, but could only comment that John would improve someday. When Regina stood up to grab a tissue and blow her nose, Ted asked John if he could keep the drawing, and John was happy to get it off his hands. Ted would later set it as the background picture on his phone.

The following Thursday was one of the few short days scattered throughout the school year, and just in time for lunch hundreds of students were given premature freedom that they did not know how to use appropriately. The foolish ones had their parents come pick them up, the collective impact of these decisions being yet another long, snaking line of cars that stretched from every parking lot into the street. The smarter ones walked downtown, passing alongside pristine gardens of jeweled flowers and landscapers to gorge themselves on the fruits of society. Beth, Regina, and Juliet had decided to dine alfresco, and Beth and Juliet marveled equally at just how nice that day was. The school schedule was not based on the weather forecast, but if it were, the administration could not have picked a better day to let students leave school early. Regina was not walking with them because she had to make up a math test at school, but promised to hurry over to join them as soon as she could. They had decided on sushi that day, but until Regina arrived, Beth and Juliet could not be impolite and dine without her; they sat in the shade and bantered, distracting themselves from the impending meal that their stomachs growled in chorus for.

Regina wore sunglasses and had a spring in her step as she strode toward Beth and Juliet. As much as she considered them more appropriate for the spring and summer, with such unseasonably warm weather, the prospect of being seen in public, and John once remarking on them in a positive way, her sunglasses seemed suitable. Beth and Juliet complimented her on her outfit, revoking any doubts she had. The Japanese supermarket was air-conditioned, and the girls made an immediate left to the shelves of boxed sushi, displayed next to a few Japanese drinks that Regina used her developing linguistic skills to haltingly read. They then immediately crossed the street and walked another block to reach the park, where many other students were enjoying their own meals.

Regina stopped when she saw a bench looking over the grassy field, where lanky men in T-shirts played volleyball, and brushed off the dried leaves before sitting down. The others followed suit. They had sat somewhere near here before many times, they were sure, when they were a year or two younger and a bit shorter. They had talked then of carefree things, pop idols and movies, and they still talked of the same. But first, they ate. Beth precisely scraped a piece of salmon nigiri through the wasabi, leaving a green dusting on the rice: the perfect morsel. Just a trace of fat rippling between the fish's muscle, which had undoubtedly lived a healthy life in a Hokkaido stream or somewhere up in Alaska until it was reeled in, dissected, and shipped on ice across the ocean to eventually wind up delicately clutched in her palm (Beth and Juliet had reached for their chopsticks before Regina enthusiastically informed them the proper Japanese way was to use one's hand). Thin slices of pickled ginger served as a palate cleanser, and Juliet winced when Beth ate hers without accompaniment.

"I have a great idea: why don't we all see the musical tonight?" Regina suggested suddenly, endeavoring to disguise any semblance of forethought. She had discreetly tricked John into confirming that tonight was the night when he, alone, would go watch the show; its quality and name (which Regina forgot) were irrelevant. When asked, John did not know if the show was best enjoyed alone or with friends, or even one special friend; he encouraged Regina to ask Frank, who inferred from her having been directed by John that her asking was no coincidence.

"I don't know. It's all according to your personal preference, and that's something only you know. Some attend shows for what happens on stage. Some attend for the social experience. Maybe, just maybe, you may find yourself sitting with like-minded people. If you want specific seats,

I suggest you arrive early," Frank said with a grin, and Regina effusively thanked him, despite not having been promised anything specific.

Beth and Juliet immediately saw what Regina was suggesting.

"By any chance is there a special someone there?" Beth insinuated with a smile, and they all laughed.

"I think it's romantic—theaters are always romantic. We don't have cheer practice; we can come." Beth grimaced slightly at being spoken for, but voiced her assent. It was official: they were all to arrive at the theater as early as they could, buy four seats, instruct the volunteer manning the box office to give John the ticket (students were required to show ID when attending all events, ensuring this transfer would happen successfully), avoid being seen by John before the show, arrive at their seats, and then smile as if this was all a coincidence. Their plan was foolproof, Regina declared, straight out of a movie! Juliet giggled with delight.

After they finished their lunch and the volleyball players left, they returned downtown in search of sweet refreshment, which they found remarkably quickly. Only a few minutes standing in line at the raunchily named, although still kid-appropriate, "Snacks and the Ci-Tea" (the pun on "Sex and the City" never failed to amuse Beth, not that she'd ever seen it) and they left with cold drinks in tow. Heat and cold exist in a primal balance befitting their status as natural forces: when it was cold, students crowded Starbucks and coffeehouses even more boutique; when it was hot, students crowded bubble tea shops and ice cream parlors. Beyond merely ensuring the youth remained in caffeinated bliss, these businesses also provided easy employment for older students. It was considered an easy job to dispense drinks—not as profitable as private tutoring, but students could work without thinking secret thoughts of extorting their employers.

Juliet took a moment to stir her bubble tea, waiting for the black pearls to settle again before slowly taking a sip. Regina chose instead to take a boisterous slurp immediately upon exiting the store to express her resounding approval of her refreshment. While they all had homework, none of them felt like they were in any particular rush. They wanted to look their best for the theater, and Beth reminded them yet again that there was no dress code and that they all looked perfectly fine as is. Juliet relayed a text from her mother inviting the other two to study together, relax more, and enjoy life at her house; the other two received the all-clear from their parents, and together they waited in the parking lot of a grocery store for her mother's black BMW.

Behrooz wished he could have left early, but instead he was nervously waiting outside the leadership director's office for his interview. It was a casual affair, really—Ms. Foster and two seniors simply wanted to have a friendly chat about his life at school, more angled toward general mentorship and wellness than anything regarding leadership, and to identify any red flags. Some applicants clearly would not work well with others; they boasted of their own prowess while implying that school was a competition that must be won by them at any cost. Alan fell into that category, and while he left his interview the previous day confident that he aced it, Ms. Foster took the rare step of putting his application through the paper shredder so the two students with her could have no doubts about her opinion. Other applicants defied attempts at categorization, writing at unusual length about strange hobbies or their peculiar fascination with the school's architecture. This weirdness was not a red flag in Ms. Foster's mind, although she prepared for interviews with these applicants with a trace of caution; these sorts of people tended to be subversive, and the last thing the school needed was saboteurs reigning supreme. Behrooz was fortunate to come into his interview without facing any preconception, and he was greeted warmly with a glass of ice water. A bowl of fresh heirloom tomatoes, already washed, lay in the middle of the table; Ms. Foster spoke proudly about her garden, and would often bring in gourmet treats for her students.

They admired her generosity, and she was absolved of some sin knowing that they were being tricked into eating healthily. Behrooz thought this a strange gesture, but he popped one red globe into his mouth, chewed, and smiled. Sweet, but tangy, with a vague herbal note that indicated this was truly the finest of vegetables (once, a smart-ass had told Ms. Foster that well actually, tomatoes were fruits, and received a stern warning not to be subversive ever again).

"So, Bay-Ruse—am I pronouncing that correctly? I want to make sure I'm saying it authentically," Ms. Foster began. Behrooz nodded and assured Ms. Foster she was entirely correct. The students flanking her sides assiduously began taking notes. "What made you apply for this position?"

"Well, where do I begin? At the first assembly, I was inspired by how proud all of the students on stage were to be Tigers, how spirited they were. And I knew then, at that exact moment, I wanted to bring the same joy to others," Behrooz responded.

"Good answer, good answer. I will admit I'm not in charge of how exactly our freshmen are taken care of to begin the year, but I'm glad they are doing satisfactorily, and that our students are doing a good job," she responded, placing a particular emphasis on the "they" while turning her head toward the administrative offices. "Do you have any prior leadership experience?"

"No, but I'm willing to learn."

"Good answer, great initiative there. That's the sort of attitude we need around here. Leaders, not followers. Do you consider yourself a leader, Behrooz?"

"I really don't know how to answer that."

"You will become one."

"I guess that answers that."

"What's a proposal you have for helping the Heller community?" This was an important question—the seniors held their pens in a ready position, as if about to stab their papers. Behrooz looked around the room for inspiration, which seemed to have the highest density of motivational posters on campus.

"Peer-to-peer mentorship. We could have a big buddy system, where upperclassmen like you two," he said gesturing to the seniors, who beamed with delight at their being recognized, "mentor students who simply need a bit of help adjusting to their new surroundings. Academically, socially, emotionally, whatever—you'd know better than I would."

"Great idea! Michael, work on that." Michael made a note on his paper. They engaged in their back and forth for a while longer, Ms. Foster constantly impressed at Behrooz's diplomatic skills. Even when she urged him politely that if any of his classmates needed special attention to absorb true Heller values, he could simply say their names and already be providing the student leadership he desired, Behrooz refused. Not out of any moral principle, he just couldn't think of any. Ms. Foster frowned, but regained her composure. She congratulated him heartily on surviving his first few months of high school, and urged him to go out and enjoy the sunshine.

John arrived at the theater roughly fifteen minutes before the show began, early enough to not be late, but late enough that many already were loitering in the lobby and eating snacks. It was dinner time—was he hungry? He didn't know. He showed his ID and was about to hand over some money when the lady there gave him a ticket with a smile. Before he could ask why, she called out "Next!," so he shrugged and entered the lobby. He saw Frank talking with a parent who was selling flowers, and made a note to ask him before the show.

Frank had already seen the show once, and was rather neutral about seeing it again that night, to be followed by three more performances. The previous night was technically opening night: it was a chance for the show to perform for some teachers who didn't want to risk seeing their students' parents on other nights, relatives of the cast who saw this as their only chance to sit in the front row, and the ushers. There were a few others besides Frank, who kept to themselves and talked in cryptic anime references avoiding all responsibility; they were only there for extra credit. Frank could handle people. He knew people. People liked him. This would be easy.

"You must know Adrian!" One of the parents told him somewhat rhetorically while Frank was making sure the doors worked properly. Frank said that he did not not know Adrian, hoping his vagueness would end the conversation quickly. Mr. Liebkind explained that Adrian was still a freshman, but he was fast-tracked for theatrical talent (despite only being in the ensemble this time—beginner's luck), and that surely if Frank were to stick around, he would meet him. Liebkind was a funny name, Frank thought; it implied literally that Adrian was a bastard child, or that the line of bastard children extended patrilineally for some time. And while Frank did not know it, Adrian did live up to that title in the other sense of the word. It also reminded Frank of something, which he asked Mr. Cathcart about when he emerged from some dark recess of the theater in a suit.

"Mr. Cathcart, has Heller ever done *The Producers*? I loved the movie, and meeting Adrian's father put the thought in my head for a reason you probably understand." Mr. Cathcart checked to make sure Mr. Liebkind was out of earshot, and then laughed. "We're doing *Young Franken-stein* next year, and probably a tragedy after that, but that's the first good suggestion I've heard for what to do next. I'll know for sure by next year, but great idea."

That was awfully abrupt of a decision, Frank thought, but he saw no reason to question it. John came up to him with his ticket, curiously marked with a smiley face in addition to the seat number, and explained what happened to him outside.

Frank could barely conceal his grin, and he looked up to see the three girls standing on the far end of the theater talking among themselves and dressed just formally enough to stand out (despite Beth's pleas, the three of them spent a solid half-hour searching through Juliet's wardrobe for last-minute outfits that screamed Broadway and class). If he did not know them, he'd have assumed they were distant cousins of somebody in the cast. How John hadn't already seen them was beyond him.

"Today's your lucky day," he commented wryly, and handed the ticket back to John without caring to give any more details. Mr. Cathcart gave the signal to start seating, and the doors to the house opened in sequence. Frank was fortunate he knew exactly how the theater's seating plan worked, otherwise he would be lost in the deluge of arrivals. When waiting for someone new to help, he spun his pocket-sized flashlight around in circles. In the short span of five minutes, Frank transformed himself into a hardened professional, walking backward while leading parents, teachers, and students alike to their seats just as he had been led before at other theaters. Familiar faces were addressed by name, the rest sir and ma'am, a somewhat unnecessary touch of formality that was nonetheless appreciated. John was greeted by name, and the three girls that entered a minute or two after him also received personal treatment, including a compliment on the effort they had put into their outfits. Regina realized at this point that they had over-dressed slightly, at least compared to their age group, but it was obviously too late by then to change.

John looked up from his program to see Beth, then Juliet, shimmy past him apologizing for the inconvenience; he had already moved his legs inward out of reflex. Regina sat to his right, then turned toward him and feigned surprise:

"John! You made it!" He looked at his ticket again, searching for a mistake; he could not find one, but apologized anyway to the three of them, certain he was sitting in the wrong seat. They presented theirs in return, assuring him that for tonight, their three now included a fourth. John did not appear terribly enthused, but seemed happy enough. John was too closed-minded to view this as a scheme or clever application of artifice. His first instinct was to assume someone in the box office made an error, and he expected someone fitting the others' demographic profile more closely to come replace him. This must be what it felt like to be popular. And given no other choice, he turned to chat. Regina pondered and savored John's casual questions, trying her best to convey that such refined banter came naturally to her. John did not notice this Herculean effort, but he too tried his best to carry the conversation and touch upon the standards of theater conversation. Beth and Juliet purposely minimized their roles, only jumping in when they saw it appropriate; they laughed modestly at John's Chinese pronunciation because he still struggled to identify tones. Regina tried to teach him a tongue-twister to capitalize on this weakness, which he failed at miserably. Frank, who happened to be walking by, overheard and said it perfectly on his first try, as if it effortlessly rolled off his tongue. Juliet was especially impressed, Beth didn't want to make John feel too bad by applauding Frank's skill, Regina was far more interested in John, and John did not realize at all Frank did more than mimic flawlessly. "Frank's the kid who's taking calculus," Juliet added, but Regina did not seem to care. Probably still a creep, she thought, although at least he didn't pat them on the head for their good effort.

The overture started and the lights dimmed, and Regina went silent out of force of habit; the others followed her lead. John had never seen anything in a theater like this before, and he was too scared to make any comments, even about Juliet and Regina's legs slowly infiltrating his personal space. He stared transfixed at the stage, imagining his mind slowly leaving his body and floating effortlessly over the seats in front of him; inside that musty Spanish prison with rusty chains and the odor of blood; inside Cervantes's mind as he stared at shifty felons in the darkness; inside Don Quixote's mind as he woke up in a village of La Mancha, the name of which he had no desire to call to mind; inside a hardy, gaunt, sporting figure who rose early at the cock's crow; and on and on through such a chain of logic that he absorbed everything with the greatest possible appreciation. John would have made a natural theater critic then, as he remembered every tremulous note the singers hit and every step on stage. The melodies wormed their way into his body and coursed through his veins. He roused himself with the lights heralding intermission, and Regina insisted he come with to purchase snacks. Juliet mouthed a "thank you" to Frank as she left, along with a wave, and he returned the latter gesture. The same general pattern repeated itself at the end of intermission: John reassured the three of them that he could switch seats if needed, Regina responded that everything was perfect as is, and the show resumed.

John's mind was addled and his body was stoic. Juliet worried for a moment, when her arm brushed against his, that he seemed icy. He blinked at regular intervals, so he was probably fine. It helped that John was drowsy, as he often was; he watched the musical in a state of half-dream, half-lucidity, not quite sure if he was watching the show with his companions in a Californian suburb or the Spanish countryside. Regina found that she was enjoying herself, and decided that even if John were absent, this was a perfectly fine way to spend an evening. As the curtain closed, John could not tell if he had spent hours or days sitting still, and along with the others he gave a standing ovation.

Chapter 5

John pounded the water with even strokes, leaving a bow-shaped wake that combined with everyone else in the pool to create choppy interference. Breathe in, breathe out. When he forgot this mantra, the electrifying shock of chlorine in his nose would jolt him back to reality, and he would take a few moments to find his rhythm again. Careful breathing made John perceive Ms. Stevens's voice as an old, grizzled monk at a Buddhist monastery; Jason had told him once about how in middle school, someone matching that exact description whacked him with a bamboo pole during guided meditation. John thought that sounded painful. The sun reflected in the ephemeral patterns, granting everyone a sun-dappled sheen when they emerged for breath. Beth grabbed the concrete lip of the pool, pulled her torso up, and turned back to look at John and the others who were still finishing their laps.

Today was technically the second day of the swim unit, as the first was yesterday during the short day, a scenic tour of the facilities punctuated with frequent reminders not to act like idiots. If they misbehaved, Ms. Stevens and one of the water polo coaches would have to get in the water to supervise them. The students laughed among themselves, blissfully unaware of their impending new routine. The following morning, like many others, was cold. The boys came out of the locker room in small clusters, some in oddly sized flip-flops and some barefoot, most clutching striped towels or plastic bags of clothing and shoes. They paced back and forth to ward off the cold, damp floor, which felt to them like it drained their life force with every second. The girls on the other end seemed more loquacious, but they too were burdened by the cold; some stood on their towels in an attempt to ward it off, but this only delayed the numbness, as eventually the moisture would seep through to every fuzzy filament and they would have to move. By John's period, the day had warmed considerably, but nobody was comfortable. They didn't know how good they had it, Ms. Stevens warned.

Jason barely tolerated running, and he also barely tolerated swimming. At least he was buoyant, unlike Frank, who astonished Ms. Stevens by his ability to sink like a rock despite his light figure; after the first swimming session, Frank innocently inquired to Ms. Stevens about alternative activities, and they came to the consensus that his time would be more efficiently used on the track. She suggested he try scuba diving (Ms. Stevens never had had a student scuba dive for PE credit, although she never explicitly forbade it; if anyone ever did, she would have a cool story to share at the next staff meeting). Coincidentally enough, Pranav's sophomore PE class was on the track during that time, and Frank would blend in perfectly. Jason finished every lap with his head and heart pounding. It wasn't that he was out of shape—Jason could lift weights and do push-ups all day—Jason simply lacked endurance, and PE was nothing but a competition of endurance. He considered asking Ms. Stevens for a similar exemption, but as soon as he walked by her to enter the locker room, she gave him a glare that indicated clearly he had not earned the right to favoritism. Jason could feel the chlorinated water eating at his skin, wicking away moisture and turning it into a crumbly patchwork. He tried blasting away any trace of the chlorine in the shower, scrubbing with a bar of soap, but he left every day feeling raw.

Ernest was frequently bothered, and today was no exception. Mrs. Huang took a portion of class that morning to lecture on Chinese culture, a topic he believed he needed no further education on. The Chinese had invented gunpowder; they had invented kites; they had invented the printing press; they had invented the compass; they had invented poetry—Ernest believed this claim to be a bit dubious, and Mrs. Huang then asked the class if they knew any Chinese poetry. Frank offered up one of the poems that every other student in the class knew by heart from a young age, and Mrs. Huang applauded and told everyone to learn more. If Frank could do it, they could too. Her vaguely racial rhetoric bothered Ernest; a few weeks prior, she had explained to the class how people from the south of China were more attractive due to the clean air and water, while those from the north, like herself, were ugly—but not to worry, they were from the heartland of Chinese culture, and for this they should be proud! These statements ensured most in the class felt insulted in some way; Mrs. Huang looked at Frank as she explained these truths that apparently were common fact. The juniors, who had already heard this same talk their previous two years, made sport of watching the freshmen's jaws drop.

Ernest was also bothered by English class. He had been doing exceedingly well, at least compared to the rest of his period, and in his mind, receiving the highest score on the English essay was a form of personal attack. Did Ms. Baldwin have an ulterior motive by making him feel good? Was she trying to build up his confidence only to pull out the carpet from underneath? Madeline, who received the second-highest score, was far more deserving. She was also too humble and modest—in Ernest's mind, modesty was his right alone. Because she talked little, and she did not have any clear feather in her cap that put her head and shoulders above the rest, she slipped incognito under everyone but the rest of the academic elite and her teachers. That was also because many found her boring, but to Ernest, boredom was the product of a lazy mind.

Jason, another member of that pantheon, had his own eccentricities. Jason fancied himself a bit of a historian, and could talk excessively about World War II on cue. This trait was accepted by few: the other history nerds in his classes, his history teacher, and Mr. T, who casually matched him on every historical intrigue and offered even more as appropriate. This went as far as to turn into an impromptu proctored debate when Mr. Simon happened to encounter the two of them discussing Stalingrad after school, when they enjoyed tea and cookies from Mr. T's cabinets and argued late into the afternoon. Jason found it easier to talk with teachers and older students, as a rule. Ms. Bracknell's TA, who spent the majority of the period in the back browsing Tinder, taught him tips and tricks on succeeding in all his classes while complimenting him on his taciturn wit. There were some exceptions, of course: he still enjoyed talking with Frank, despite his penchant for verbal irony and talking like a character from an Oscar Wilde play. At least he wasn't banal—too many of Jason's peers talked of stupidities, laughing at jokes that weren't funny and refusing to act civilized. They didn't like Jason, and Jason didn't like them.

Frank shared Jason's preference for maturity, but he was a man of the people too. Wisecracks and witticisms were his bread and butter, along with an unabashed demeanor and willingness to speak the truths that needed to be told. These contributed to an eccentricity that was entirely his own, one that many others considered as taking the best parts from all his peers. Life was good.

The previous week, after seeing Ms. Bracknell nearly fall asleep during office hours, Frank asked if she needed any help grading the pile of paperwork in front of her. She said yes without question, and gave Frank the answer key, no questions asked. Frank had nowhere else to sit, but Ms. Bracknell did not want him sitting with the riff-raff in case they peered over his shoulder at the gradebook, so Frank sat in his very own swivel chair a few feet from her. The classroom appeared quite similar from his new vantage point: it was well-lit as usual, and some students played with Rubik's Cubes in the back corner while others tried to study. Ms. Bracknell affectionately dubbed the cube-toting clique the eggheads, and spoke of them fondly to other teachers. As soon as Mr. T heard about this at a staff meeting, he pulled out a cube from one of his cabinets and solved it in under ten seconds, smiled, and told none of the other teachers to ever mention it to their students. The eggheads scared John, and he sat as far away from them as possible.

That day, John was equally occupied by finishing his English essay on a Chromebook as stealing furtive glances at Beth, who did not notice. People-watching was a favorite hobby of John's, and he assigned backstories to many he met without any particular rhyme or reason. He extrapolated from minor details and overheard conversations, and sometimes he would share these musings with others, forgetting that they were entirely figments of his imagination. He looked at Frank, who was so absorbed in his grading that he didn't even take advantage of his swivel chair, and decided he was an agent of MI6, sent as a spy to avert a nuclear apocalypse. Apparently, as part of his deep cover, he had to attend the musical, in case some important foreign dignitary with a funny accent and pocket-watch were sitting in the mezzanine and some stagehand secretly carried a pistol underneath their black shirt.

Frank was indeed conducting espionage, but of a different sort: inside Ms. Bracknell's voluminous gradebook, which had loose worksheets folded inside, he could see the grades of many he recognized. Unsurprisingly, Jason had a near-perfect grade. Frank and Pranav still had As, but their performance was not clearly exemplary. He did not find the calculus grades interesting; any who made it to that level had gotten their act together long ago, and took the even more challenging material as an excuse to study even harder. John, a solid A—not bad. Juliet, A+—out of all people, her? Beth, B+—tsk tsk. Frank found it hard to feel sympathy for his peers when they were numbers on a paper. They were all passing anyway, so they had no cause for complaint.

John found a healthier outlet for his speculations during English class. They were close to being done with *Pride and Prejudice*, which some considered a cause for celebration. It is a truth universally acknowledged that rambunctious teenagers love nothing more than drawing rooms, tea and crumpets, and epistolary flirting. Some affected British accents as they finished their lunches, thinking this made them posh. Mr. T and Ms. Baldwin conspired one day, along with the culinary arts teacher, to give them a traditional British tea service as they watched scenes from one of the many movie adaptations, which the students found a welcome surprise and the teachers thought a great way to spend a period relaxing while still "teaching." Mr. T spoke proudly of how they had baked everything themselves to create an authentic environment; that was a few days prior, and today was more mundane. John was rather ambivalent regarding romance: he struggled to identify it outside books and movies, and thus only knew it as a vehicle for character development. If he were a romantic, and he did not consider himself one, he wanted his romances to be brooding and mysterious, so much that nobody involved knew they were involved.

Regina turned her desk toward John as he explained the evil of Wickham, releasing a faint smile as he leafed through his book and read a passage in a seemingly sexy monotone. She could imagine him riding a horse through a grassy glen, or perhaps through the misty rain, or whatever the scene was in the movie Ms. Baldwin showed where Darcy triumphantly rescued Lizzy. Now was the time. Fate had brought them together in the theater, and it had brought them together in their current seating arrangement—how could he possibly say no? If she admitted so herself, she certainly was a catch.

'My chin?' John asked, searching his classmates' faces for some innu-endo he was missing, but they looked back at him blankly, almost as if they were judging him.

"Yes, I think you have a very attractive chin," Regina continued, not fazed by John's lack of reaction. "From the moment I first saw you, I felt attracted to you. And the more we talked, the more I became certain my initial impression was correct. I have patiently waited for months to confess the feelings I am sure you have for me as well, but I can wait no longer. In vain I have struggled. It will not do. My feelings will not be repressed. You must allow me to tell you how ardently I admire and love you."

John was confused. This was the first time anything of the sort had ever happened to him. How was he supposed to respond? He thought Regina was nice, certainly, but "ardent love" was pushing it a little. She continued clumsily, and everyone nearby said "Aww..." in unison, even Ted, who could immediately detect John's discomfort but wished to see what would happen. The others at the table smiled at first at the pure passion of the moment, but as it became clear that John and Regina were not a match made in heaven, they buckled down and waited. After Regina finished, the silence was palpable.

"Well?" Juliet prompted with a smile.

"I'll think about it," John responded dismissively, and nobody knew what to say. The bell rang to save them from any more awkwardness, and as John left, Ms. Baldwin suggested he keep his options open. Few students were given such opportunities, and those who refused them rarely got a second chance.

Regina was too optimistic to think her chances were ruined, but she also had another class to get to, and so any thoughts of John would have to wait until later. Her parents would ask how her day was, she would tell them of her failure, and they would console her and offer tips for next time. Maybe her mother would tell her the same story again about how her father showed up at her dorm room door at university with a bouquet of her favorite flowers. Regina did not know which flowers John liked. She had made the safe assumption that John, befitting his literary inclinations, would have appreciated her tasteful homage. What had she done wrong?

"You did great, Regina," Beth reassured her after school. Beth wanted to say "I told you so"—the scheme at the theater was ambitious even by Regina's standards, and John also seemed shy, so launching into a dramatic speech in front of the entire class was perhaps not the best idea. If it were Beth's decision and Beth's initiative, she would have eased John into the idea of being more than casual friends, first finding him in the hallway between classes and working from there to the anguished declaration of love.

"I didn't. I messed everything up."

"Well, maybe, but John seems like a forgiving guy. Start with an apology for embarrassing him, and work from there to something healthier. Trust me."

"You ride the bus with him, Beth. Ask him what he likes."

Beth nodded, told Regina that as she was so kind to mention it, she really did need to get to the bus, and bid her farewell. She walked through the shade back to the bus stop and decided she would do John a favor and not mention anything. It would be awkward for her, and she did not want to be tainted by whatever had happened in English that period. John waved to her, which was rare, and she returned the gesture. He still sat in the front, she still sat in the back, and quiet peace returned.

John suffered from insomnia that night, as he did on many when particularly weighty thoughts occupied his mind. It was blindingly obvious, in retrospect, that Regina always had designs on him. It was clear from day one that he was in her crosshairs, and the fact that it took her three months to fire her Cupid's bow meant he had three months of missed signals to compensate for. John was so intrigued by Beth that he was blind to all else. He had promised Regina that he'd think about it, and he set about thinking of pros and cons.

There was one big pro in John's mind regarding Regina: she had made the first move. He disliked her method, but she had tried, so there was that. She was also kind-hearted if a bit blunt, not unintelligent, not unattractive, and not so many other things that he struggled to find room for criticism there. There was also one glaring con: she had made the first move. John was forced to act spontaneously, without thought, in class that day: every moment he thought, every moment the others blinked and Regina stared at him with pouting eyes. John did not mind tests in class that had time pressure, as it was only him and the paper locked in that dance of death. But testing was not a spectator sport—no other people had personal stakes in the outcome of any assessment, only John and John alone. He tried to assume best intent: Regina had no way of knowing how he would prefer to be approached. He wracked his mind for alternatives, feeling his heartbeat's steady rhythm, but could not think of an answer. It had never occurred to him that there was an alternative to being a bachelor. He knew some people with boyfriends and girlfriends—not anyone he knew intimately, but classmates he saw on occasion. They were happy; they stole away to make out in the restrooms and behind the gymnasium. As John tried to imagine the exact path he and any special someone would take from class down the steps and through the paths of fallen leaves to a secret place, now that this case was no longer a hypothetical but a tangible possibility, he fell asleep.

John decided in the spur of the moment that the backstroke was his favorite: it allowed him to stare at the cloudy skies up above, which each lap seemed to shift ever so slightly, and clear his mind. The backstroke was precise, and John counted exactly sixteen circuits of each arm needed to swim the whole length of the pool. That number never changed, although swimming, as with all things, became easier over time. John was so engrossed in his movements that he took a few seconds to process the voice calling his name from the balcony. He turned and looked up, and Regina stood leaning over the railing.

"Hi," she murmured, and John gave a friendly wave. Ms. Stevens blew the whistle loudly to discourage any more fraternization, and Regina walked off before he could process it any further. John had started keeping a notebook of "incidents," as he dubbed them. 1:49 PM: Regina flipped her hair in the hallway near Mr. T's classroom (John had done some online research and learned this was a sign of affection). 7:58 AM: Regina complimented John's sweater. 6:02 PM: John saw someone outside the library with long hair that, from a distance, looked like her. Regina's confession had been a spark in John's mind, and there was ample tinder to stoke the flames. John saw it as clear as day that his classmates held secrets.

John may have considered his swimming meditative, but Ted loathed every minute. It was his mistake telling Ms. Stevens he planned on playing water polo in the spring, as he was chosen to act as her TA, adjusting his classmates' arms and modeling proper form. Most of all, Ted loathed his mandated affability: he really wanted to act like a drill sergeant and chastise those who, after weeks of lessons, still couldn't kick in that rat-a-tat-tat rhythm any swimmer needed to know. But he needed to smile, gently remind them yet again not to kick him in the face, and give Ms. Stevens all the juicy details every period. He could no longer even gossip with his friends, as Ms. Stevens would frequently lean over and join in—to put it mildly, he found it humiliating. Ms. Stevens was perfectly aware of this, but she had discovered through years of experience the last thing her students wanted was for her to try being cool and hip. Generally, one private, informal mention of "yeeting" something was enough to keep her students on task. One minute, Ted was a mentor; one blast of the whistle later, he was ordinary. Ted weaved between the two worlds with little exertion, joking with his friends while treading water yet turning silent when needed. From day one he vowed to "be water," as Bruce Lee advised, and he had moved through the first few months of his high school career without making waves. Nothing fazed him, not the timed miles or the pop quizzes, and he succeeded in strong performance without ever being the best. Some, he thought, viewed this behavior as him "not applying himself"; he interpreted his own behavior more generously as a rationing system: if he were to tire himself, he had already lost the game. Incidents around him were but comic material, interesting ideas to be contemplated and then filed away somewhere in the recesses of his mind. The spectacle of Regina's confession or Jason's exquisite hand-drawn picture of Stalin were not even sticks in the water that bent the stream around them; rather, they were pebbles that made a splash and then sank into the mud.

"You need to work on your attitude, Ted," Ms. Wolfe told him menacingly after he had earned garbage duty yet again for throwing a carrot stick at one of his friends.

"I stick my head out for nobody."

"All I'm saying is that if you want to enjoy your time at high school, you might just want to turn that perpetual frown of yours upside-down." She contorted her face into a grin, as if his disobedience stemmed only from a lack of education. Ted gave her a thumbs up and left quickly.

Final exam week offered an unusual reprieve for Frank due to how the schedule was structured. On each day, there were two exams, following each student's regular schedule. When Frank realized this meant one day only had PE and drama, he saw an opportunity. The sophomore PE teacher, impressed by Frank's good spirits and power-walking, handed out extra credit to him and any other similarly-motivated students like candy (Pranav was annoyed he didn't think of this loophole until Frank came along), and Frank calculated that he could skip his final exam and still end with an A+. He expected Ms. Stevens to object, but she instead congratulated him for his hard work and wished him an excellent break.

In drama class, a similar policy was in place: Mr. Cathcart gave extra credit for seeing the show, but Frank discovered there was no limit to how many times one could see the show and receive a bonus. He and the other ushers decided to group together on the final project, and after the first day of work decided they did not feel like giving it any effort. They presented him with a well-argued case that no matter what they turned in, they would have at least 115% in the class, and that their time could best be spent elsewhere.

"Well, you guys need to do something for the next few weeks. I'm nice, but I'm not that nice."

Frank thought for a moment, then offered something genius: "I remember you mentioning you were struggling to decide which shows to put on in the next few years. How about we watch a variety of shows online, read through the scripts, and prepare some proposals that you can take to the drama council? We can critically review if the subject matter would mesh with a high school audience, and brainstorm how effectively Heller could perform them."

Mr. Cathcart was amazed at their audacity; clearly they had thought this through. "This sounds like more work than my project, but at least it's educational. I'll permit it." Frank and his newfound friends, who he found to be surprisingly likable when they weren't talking about anime, colonized the green room, snacking abundantly as they took notes. They presented their bulging portfolio to Mr. Cathcart the day before final exams started, who thanked them wholeheartedly and also wished them well. "You still have to come to school on finals day, but you just need to be on campus somewhere."

Frank spent many of his four hours in the library reading, and at Mrs. Huang's urging he spent a good chunk of time helping her move boxes and make copies. Mrs. Huang gave him a pushcart stacked high with textbooks and other miscellany, and instructed him to keep going back and forth between the library and her classroom, each trip transferring a new load, until everything was tidy. The sun was out accompanied by a light breeze, which in California passed for winter. The hallways were quiet, and teachers ignored Frank as he walked. When he passed over the walkway by the pool that he had so cleverly avoided the entire semester, he heard Juliet call out, who was on break and lazily held onto the rim. Light broke through the window of the main office at such the right angle to give everyone in the area but Frank a celestial glow.

"What are you doing?" Juliet asked the figure above. Frank turned and looked down; Ms. Stevens was occupied elsewhere and did not blow her whistle.

"I'm doing Mrs. Huang a little favor. Shouldn't you be swimming or something?"

"I finished already. The water's warm. You missed out."

"Life is sink or swim, and unfortunately, I have no choice but to sink." Juliet laughed, even though Frank did not think he was that funny. If the other PE teacher were there, he would have made some crack about things going swimmingly, or Frank's remark being a stroke of genius. Frank preferred dry humor. Before Juliet could think of an appropriate response, Frank kept walking, used to the cart's weight at this point. He walked back along the same route to avoid the sun, and Juliet waved again, he waved back, and the pattern continued until Mrs. Huang ran out of things to give him. Mrs. Huang was so happy about his efforts that she gave Ms. Wolfe a call, who granted permission for "her special assistant" to leave school early. Frank arrived at his house, opened his front gate, stopped to think, closed it, and kept walking onward downtown. He had earned a treat. Sushi sounded good.

Chapter 6

The new semester brought some changes in class schedules, and students thus had to cope with change. Freshmen spent half the year learning history and the other half learning about their bodies in far too much detail, and so the new freshmen sat down in their new classes and lived again the feeling of being new, only this time they weren't as star-struck. It did not take long for the more observant freshmen to discover that there was something funky about Mr. T, whom some lucky ones met for the first time in their health class. They compared notes with each other, and together they tried to explain incongruities. When Ernest asked Frank to clarify what exactly was wrong with him after the first day of class, Frank responded simply with a grin: "Oh, he's just like any other man, only more so." Ernest didn't think that clarified much.

Mr. T spoke Chinese, having substituted for Mrs. Huang one period, and spoke with a strong Beijing accent and a semblance of sanity many thought she lacked. He also taught some of the advanced English courses, and apparently last year picked up a period of AP Gov, and beyond that upperclassmen told them that he had substituted for practically every class, and could easily teach any full-time. The students then worked at identifying gaps in his knowledge; perhaps Mr. T was best defined at what he was not, rather than what he was. This proved to be a hard question because Mr. T was so obliging with their interrogations, sometimes letting students ask him questions at the end of class: yes, he spoke Spanish, yes, he could play piano, yes, he worked in New York, yes, he wasn't always a teacher. He rarely answered no beyond verifying that he was not a CIA agent, although of course, if he were a CIA agent they doubted he would tell them. And so, after a few weeks, most gave up and simply accepted that Mr. T was Mr. T, a mighty fine teacher and a bringer of surprises.

Alan met all these new stimuli with a constantly flickering facial expression that fell between wonder and horror. Alan believed he had a good sense of what constituted polite conversation. There were some topics, like the weather, that were appropriate for every situation. Everyone, regardless if they cared to discuss the weather, had some thoughts on it—some, like Alan, always believed it was too hot or too cold. Sports were acceptable too, even if many did not share Alan's enthusiasm for the Pittsburgh Steelers. Food was starting to veer on the risky side. Everyone had their own preferences, and Alan could not think to imagine what would happen if he said he liked a food that his conversational partner abhorred. But all of these paled in comparison to the big four that he was supposed to avoid: religion, abortion, politics, and economics—Alan personally chose to use those as an acronym to remember a fifth topic to avoid, which made Beth's jaw drop when he shared his mnemonic with a casual, clever grin. Religion was easy to avoid, as Alan did not practice; when reading texts out loud in English, he never read "God," "Jesus," "Allah," "Zeus," "Osiris," or anything that could potentially offend. Alan was unfamiliar with the exact mechanics of abortions until Mr. T explained in class the panoply of birth control options available; it would be easy to avoid those in polite conversation. Alan was able to maintain his commitment to avoiding politics all of last semester until his history teacher, quite directly, asked him to please comment on that day's activity. Economics was rather simple, and he did not see why it was even controversial at all: if they only printed more money, everyone would be wealthier!

Tom disagreed with Alan's approach on almost every count, considering it insipid, boring, and cowardly. His father had always told him oratory was a tradition invented by the Greeks that had been passed down through the ages, and it was every man's duty to maintain it. Tom had asked once when he was younger and knew little how people functioned then.

"I don't know, Tom, maybe they threw rocks at each other? Or maybe they just beat their chests and howled loudly. Why does it matter? We have civilization now," Mr. Langley responded with a sigh. "I'm busy. Go do your homework."

Tom believed every conversation was a transaction: you were always trying to get something out of the other person, who was always trying to do the same. Naturally, one could never admit they were aware of this core philosophy. That wasn't what civilized people did. Any venue could, in the blink of an eye, become an auditorium. There, Tom and his opponent would walk up to their podiums in suits and ties, and wave politely to the cheering audience. The referee would call foul as appropriate, and at the end of the day, the winner would get a trophy in the form of eternal love, respect, and devotion. Tom had not watched many debates, but nevertheless, he considered himself an expert. One of his favorite venues for casual conversation was English class. This was mainly because Ted was there, who had the gumption to not let Tom sit on the throne and revel in his glory forever. Ted would never admit it, but he thought Tom was a wee bit too big for his britches, and his time as the biggest rooster in the henhouse needed to end eventually.

Ted and Tom's sporting rivalry manifested itself in many ways. During PE, each vied to be the fastest; Ted generally won these contests. In math class, each vied to finish not only most quickly, but most precisely; this was generally tolerated by their teacher, as it turned out that finishing quickly and precisely required quiet focus. This did not extend to English class, where any activities with the semblance of discussion involved increasingly grandiloquent speeches juxtaposed with attempts at increasingly thrifty epigrams. Tom once read that brevity was the soul of wit, and as he desired to be witty, brevity proved essential; however, this ran at odds with his natural tendency to pack on layers of interlocking points and a preacher's delivery, resulting in something altogether verbose. Ted attempted to match this with a relatively sensible pattern of speech, always aiming to speak immediately after Tom and dismantle his points, an almost Socratic style of interlocution. This then demanded more refutation from Tom, delivered in an even more garrulous manner as he sought to win over the affections of the rest of the class, which at this point was either taking meticulous notes or staring into the gray void of the whiteboard. Ms. Baldwin generally stepped in once the arguments were clearly becoming too intricate and opened up the floor to other insights. She was torn: the quality of discourse was admirable, but two people were running the show instead of thirty. Granted, other strong voices in the class stepped in on occasion, and the two stars took these moments to recoup and prepare their next verbal landmines, but the net result was still cacophonous. Private conversations did little to dissuade this behavior, as she had to phrase her words carefully so as not to silence the two entirely, so all she could do was wait and hope they would exhaust their seemingly endless reserves of rhetoric.

John was tired and not in the best condition for watching that day's verbal ping-pong match. John's droopy eyes, which did not wander nearly as much as they used to, caught Regina's attention, as they frequently did.

"You need coffee. I'll bring you some tomorrow." John shook his head to indicate it wasn't needed, but Regina was unfazed, asking if he wanted cream or sugar. It was the first time John had ever had to think about that. His parents drank their coffee black, and when John took a sip out of curiosity, he spat it out into the sink. That was many years ago, and now he knew he could handle it plain. The next day, John hoped Regina would have forgotten her promise, but today she carried four cups instead of three. John tried again to drink, this time thinking it pleasant.

"You know, John, it's very mature of you to drink black coffee. It's far too bitter for me," Juliet suggested as she sipped her green tea iced latte, pushing it toward him in case he wanted to try some. She searched his face for any hidden expressions of displeasure, but could find nothing. John occasionally looked down at his coffee cup as if he had forgotten what he was drinking. There was something so strange about seeing Regina's name on the side in black Sharpie. Technically no drinks besides water were permitted in class without teacher permission; Ms. Baldwin did not care to break up the happy moment, which she hoped would be to John what the madeleine was to Proust, and so she allowed it. Later, John thought of the coffee again, thinking it filled some void in his personality, and on a whim asked Frank what he thought.

"I drink tea," Frank curtly responded.

"But when you do drink coffee, how do you drink it?" Frank felt like this was a test of his intellectual stature or something that he wasn't quite comprehending.

"I'm not picky. There's this great café downtown that has brilliant Vietnamese coffee. My parents and I get banh mis and coffee there all the time."

John paused a few seconds to determine if he had received a sufficiently clarifying answer, but was still confused. He had no idea what either of those foods were; he could ask Regina, but then she would think he was inviting her, and that would do nothing to help his position. Over winter break, John turned Regina's confession into an anguished appeal for friendship. She was alone, he thought. She felt lost, just like he did. It was his obligation as an ethical person, a good person, to ask her how she felt, to smile and show interest in what she said, and to return her warmth with something better than a chill wind. John's happy place, entirely imagined, was a cabin in the snow. The door opened inside and led down the hallway to a fireplace that was always going, always warm, always reliably itself. Sometimes he had nightmares that he left the door open, and one gust of wind would blow and echo all the way down until it extinguished the fire and left his house cold, lifeless, and spooky. Strange things moved in the dark—John knew that as a fact. In some other nightmares with the same setting, John woke up in what for the moment was his bed, even if the room was decorated differently, unable to move. Something was in the house, something that made the floors creak and the shadows wander. His heart pounded without reprieve, and just when his door opened and that beast was about to enter, he woke up, safe and happy.

One time, John had asked his parents if everyone had those sorts of nightmares. They looked at him with great sadness and said that they never worried, at least not anymore: they had their friends and family, who were beacons of light in the darkness that could repel any monster. Empathy, that peculiar warmth and care John had always struggled with, was the solution! He vowed to immediately set about acquiring some. He practiced on his classmates, always being sure to say thank you when they did him mild favors, and on his teachers, who appreciated the help. All of this circled around to his current pet project, Regina. All she needed was a kind and caring shoulder when needed. Not in the literal sense, though—he had made that mistake once, and felt like he needed to wash off her aroma in the shower that night.

This extended to others, too; how was Beth? She always seemed nice, and had a mental alacrity that to be frank, Regina did not always maintain. John did not know who she was, at least compared to Regina; but did he know Regina? After Mrs. Huang had shuffled the seating arrangements yet again, still with John and Beth sitting in inconvenient seats, Beth was forced out of some necessity to talk with John. Spontaneous conversation was a part of any language-learning curriculum, although as they were still in the elementary class, it wasn't r veting.

"*Who is this person?*" John asked Beth, drawing out the syllables needlessly.

"*This is my older sister, this is my mother, and this is my father,*" Beth responded with more natural intonation. For class that day, they had to bring in family photos, which weren't terribly exciting.

"*Your father is taller than your mother,*" John remarked sagely.

"*Your shirt is blue,*" she replied offhandedly, then looked at her paper and realized she had a problem. "How do you write 'blue' again?"

So that's what that word meant, John thought. He looked at his own note sheet and sketched out □□, and Beth tried her hardest to copy all the strokes correctly. They made an excellent pair: John had an excellent memory for Chinese characters, imagining many as deformed stick figures engaging in activities, and Beth spoke with excellent pronunciation and vocabulary, using whatever she remembered from her mother's phone conversations. What they had in common was that neither of them enjoyed their mandated chats. Both were listeners: they all understood Mrs. Huang's classroom commands, even if they did not respond in turn. The speakers in the class disguised their sketchy grasp of the fundamentals by speaking with confidence, and in their minds, these students were charlatans. This was why Mrs. Huang put James and Beth, as she knew them, in nearby seats all the time. As far as she could tell, James and Beth were independent learners who knew how to solve their problems without her assistance, behavior she had no qualms with encouraging. This wasn't entirely true: after spending about half an hour working through a weekly homework set that seemed to keep going on and on, Beth found Frank reading his newspaper outside and asked him for help.

"Why ask me? I barely know anything, only the fundamentals."

"You said that tongue-twister perfectly on the first try, I've seen you talking to Mrs. Huang before school, and that newspaper's not in English." Frank looked down and admitted Beth was right, he did know a little more than "barely anything." Today was a poor day to feign ignorance. Frank did not think he lied, however; he was by no means fluent, even if he could get by passably with little embarrassment. He tried his best to take opportunities whenever he could to improve, and when he learned that he could get newspapers in Chinese downtown, he resolved to read one a week. This did mean that by the time he finished reading, his current events knowledge was dated.

"You got me. What do you need help with?" He put his newspaper away, and they spent the remainder of the lunch period working through the homework. Initially, Beth was surprised at Frank's generosity, but it was not out of character for him to help her or any others. Frank often spent his lunch periods sitting down at a lunch table with struggling students, some his friends but more often random classmates, and together they worked through algebra problems or discussed essays. He was never one to say no, seeing this altruism as an easy way to make friends, and he discovered he had a name recognition among his class at large that belied his "nerdy" reputation. In contrast, Jason bristled at inquiries for help, lacking the seemingly endless reserve of patience and discipline Frank possessed; to him, there was such a thing as a stupid question, and his classmates provided them in abundance. Despite this, Frank always knew that Jason was the person to ask for the questions he struggled with, and at least from his perspective Jason was always forthcoming. The school's reticence to accept Jason as the true academic master baffled him, and when he told his charges that if they ever needed more help, Jason would be the best, they laughed and politely refused. One possible reason for this was a lack of intelligence, but no, that couldn't possibly be it: if they were too unintelligent to seek qualified help, then they would not talk to him. Temperament was a second option, but one limited by Frank's narrow perspective. Frank certainly did not see himself as a man of the people, as beyond the occasional bouts of witty banter and quick tutoring sessions, which generally took the form of spot checks rather than intensive lessons, he really did not interact with those he helped. It was a true work-life balance. A third possibility was that Frank was simply wrong, that in reality he was the smartest in the class, but people like Ernest, Jason, and Madeline certainly performed better on average academically, and as for brightness? Brightness was necessary, Frank thought, to learn; and if the three academic titans were truly titans, then they must be bright. The hours people like Madeline spent reviewing their notes were also then indications of "brightness," which was rapidly proving to be a convenient handwave of any difficult questions. Being unable to come to a conclusion, and certainly not wanting to ask Jason to spill his secrets, Frank kept calm and carried on.

Beth and Behrooz sat at the same table in health class, and rapidly bonded over a shared wariness of Alan and a growing appreciation of what they had assumed would be the worst part of their day. As befitting his original promise, Mr. T made health class interesting by telling stories. He told them about one of the Christmas parties at his previous place of employment, where one vice president got so drunk off champagne that he pulled down his pants and urinated on a dare. He told of one night in Hong Kong, when he and a few others were negotiating some sort of deal, and how he woke up to the smell of marijuana drifting down the hall and the sound of unfamiliar morning laughter. He told of how one of his best friends at work discovered some quaint little white crystals that gave him so much energy, so much that he ran with excitement out of work one day and was hit by a car. Mr. T paused to think a moment, as if in remembrance, and his face had the accumulated pain of telling that story too many times. He quoted once how life was but a walking shadow, that those whom he considered his friends turned into ghosts of their past selves. Mr. T did not say as much, but many assumed he decided one day he needed to get out, and thus whoever he was before became their intrepid teacher.

There was comedy too along with the tragedy: for the condom demonstrations, Mr. T took out a bunch of bananas and a box of cucumbers from one of his cabinets and offered the brave student volunteers a choice; at the end of the period, he cut up the cucumbers along with some tomatoes, feta, and olives, mixed some vinaigrette from olive oil and balsamic vinegar that for some reason he had handy, and offered everyone Greek salad. Mr. T had the class watch *9 to 5* to teach them about sexual harassment and spark a discussion on changing gender roles, warning them that every comic moment was rooted in reality.

Ernest accepted his bowl of salad with some confusion. If Frank were not so cryptic, Ernest would think he had deceived him. This was not how class was supposed to be, a fact he lamented to Frank during Chinese class one day:

"Where are the Snowdens of yesteryear?" Ernest asked Frank, eyes wide with intensity.

"On a plane, bloody, dead, and cold."

"What do you mean?" Even by Frank's standards, this seemed a non sequitur, but by now Ernest was used to it.

"What do you mean if not that? You didn't read *Catch-22* last year?"

"I forgot you didn't go to the same school we did. Mr. Snowden was an English teacher we had in eighth grade, who was kind, intelligent, and most of all, sane."

"What makes our teachers insane?"

"Yesterday, I ate Greek salad made from cucumbers that touched condoms. Mrs. Huang thinks her microwave is spying on her. Mr. Galantine spent half of the class talking in a British accent. You have to agree with me here: there's something clearly wrong with this school."

"Well, nobody forced you to eat the salad. But consider this: if you think everyone is insane besides yourself, maybe you're the insane one and we're all sane. How do you like them apples?"

Ernest groaned. "I know I'm not insane. There is nothing you can do to make me think I'm insane. You're being illogical, and I really expected more from you. Why do you think this is normal? You spend all day playing into their antics. We're better than that."

Frank looked disappointed. "I will admit that when Mrs. Huang asked for examples of inspirational leaders, I shouldn't have said Mao Zedong."

"You shouldn't have, and Mrs. Huang shouldn't have agreed with you! Finally, you're getting what I'm trying to say. If you consider yourself an ethical person, you shouldn't be indulging others' sick fantasies."

"That's exactly right. I should be indulging my own instead—who gives a damn about them?"

"I do. With great power comes great responsibility. Let me pose a little dilemma to you: you're walking along the street, and you hear cries for help from an alleyway. Being the good person you are, you rush to help. You see some hooded scoundrel brandishing a knife. What do you do? Do you stay and fight, or do you flee?"

"I take out my gun and shoot him. Everyone knows you never bring a knife to a gunfight."

"Seriously, Frank."

"You aren't seeing my point here. What matters at the end of the day is that the criminal is dead and justice is served. That's the brighter world you say we are supposed to fight for. I agree—this world is a nice place. So we have two choices: the fast solution and the slow solution. Now, if our goal is truly making the world a better place, why should we twiddle our thumbs and sabotage ourselves? Why torture ourselves by living in a gray world of misery, one where people walk with their head down and talk in bitter invective? It is the ethical person's responsibility to hasten the inexorable tide of progress. I'm no coward: I'm not going to flee."

"That's a very clever solution, Frank, but I don't see how you can say with a serious face that your visionary outlook is applicable in practice."

"Is that a challenge?"

"I give up, Frank. You win. Happy now?" Ernest sighed. Frank ignored his temptation to get the last word in and turned back to his work.

Chapter 7

Ted crossed his arms and tried his hardest to look contrite while Ms. Stevens yelled at him and Tom. He didn't see what they had done wrong—they were just a bit chattier than normal that day as they ran laps. The only people they were distracting were each other. She must have woken up on the wrong side of the bed. Tom chose instead to appear aloof, especially as Ms. Stevens was directing most of her attention toward Ted. He stepped away for a moment to grab a drink of water, which Ted noticed and immediately thought disrespectful, but Ms. Stevens did not seem to notice.

"Ted, detention during lunch! Tom, 20 pushups!" she concluded, then turned away to inspect someone else. This wasn't fair.

"Tough break," Tom said, and shrugged as he dropped down to start doing pushups, slackening his arms whenever Ms. Stevens turned away.

"What did he do wrong that I didn't?" Ted asked Ms. Stevens, who refused to make eye contact with him.

"Life's not fair. Today isn't your lucky day," she responded with a sigh, as if to indicate that she knew she was saying something stupid but didn't want Ted to call her out on it. Tom finished his pushups and brushed off his hands, before ambling to another group of his friends. Ted didn't think he was crazy here for thinking that irrational. He went to ask Jason for his opinion, who said something similar:

"You win some, you lose some. It's a hot day anyway. You'll be cooler inside."

Jason clearly had never gotten detention before in his life. Ted assumed it was inevitable: Jason had many habits Ted suspected would lead to his ultimate downfall. Jason was defiant, extremely willing to say no to unreasonable requests. When Ted did this, he was being snarky and talking back to his superiors; when Jason did this, he was being innovative and demonstrating leadership. Jason patted others on the head as a form of greeting, particularly girls Ted thought, although he reconsidered his initial hypothesis when Jason did the same to him. Nobody considered this behavior normal, and eventually, someone would topple the first domino in the chain that would lead to consequences for Jason and maybe something positive for himself. Ted had no choice but to finish class that day without taking any sort of decisive action. In the locker room, nobody commented on what had happened; Ted believed this was because he was being ostracized, but in reality, nobody else had noticed.

A second hypothesis came to Ted as he sat inside, watching the clock tick away and the future juvenile delinquents around him carve their initials into the desks: Tom had bribed Ms. Stevens. Tom's father was a lawyer, and apparently a litigious one too; he was nicknamed "Bulldog" by his peers, which Ted found quite evocative. Tom certainly had the wealth to slip Ms. Stevens a check at some point to keep her on his good side, which was a step too far even for Ted. Ted was not opposed to unethical behavior, but he did not view his teachers as investments. Jason was right, at least: the classroom where detention was being held that day was air-conditioned. Ted looked at his sandwich, which suddenly did not seem that appealing—he needed better food. Ted also did not like being a spectacle; other students walked by the door and stared inside, just like he had done in the past, undoubtedly thinking what scoundrels were imprisoned in there. Ted considered himself better than a scoundrel, and he did not deserve to be embarrassed like this!

While Ted stewed in his own misery, John wandered the hallways searching for somewhere to sit. Occasionally, some spot in the school would draw John's attention, as if there were a neon sign above telling him to come and relax a little. Beth walked by to see John sitting facing a wall; even for him, this was unusual.

"Are you OK, John?" she asked, and John turned around, appearing like he had just woken up.

"I'm fine, yes. How are you?"

"I'm enjoying life. Louis isn't here today, so I was looking for something to do. Mind if I join you?"

"Go ahead, I never mind the company."

"Should I be facing the wall, too? Is there something here I'm not seeing?" John chuckled, and Beth sat down next to him. She turned to look at the wall one last time, just to be safe, and then took out her lunch.

This was the first John had heard of Beth and Louis being together. After some casual inquiries, which Beth responded to eagerly, he discovered that at a friend's birthday party, Beth ran into Louis and chatted a while. The next day at school, they talked more, and this initial warmness escalated into friendship and then romance. They shared few interests and had dissimilar temperaments, but Louis was nice to her, and she was the same to him. Freshman year was early, John assumed, for a relationship; Beth was clearly extremely precocious.

"What do you do at parties?" John asked quizzically; his idea of a birthday party involved party hats, cake, and candles, nothing more.

"Fair is foul and foul is fair. We fly around on witch's brooms, dance naked in the woods, and mix magic potions in cauldrons. If we're feeling especially frisky, we lick toads," Beth joked, and when she saw John was staring at her with horror, she clarified: "Of course we don't do that, except on Halloween. We chat, eat food, nothing terribly exciting. You aren't missing out on much."

"Is love a tender thing?"

"I don't see why it isn't," Beth responded declaratively. That was a good enough answer for John. Simply by not flirting with him at every opportunity, Beth seemed like a kinder, smarter, and cooler person. She could act as an insulator, John thought, against the malign influences of Regina, who began to seem a diametric opposite. If Regina was what was wrong with high school, Beth must be what is good. Especially after the Regina incident, as John noticed, Beth seemed a bit more friendly on the bus, returning his waves and occasionally going as far as to say hello. Just as she did not recoil from his presence, she also did not immediately turn toward him and inch toward his seat, as Regina did when she took the bus one day and along with Beth, decided to sit with their mutual friend John. What else could he ask for? John also realized this was awfully poor timing for any sort of revelation, seeing as Beth was now with someone else.

John had been urged along to consider more of these thoughts yesterday during English class, when Ms. Baldwin triumphantly announced the culmination of their study of *Romeo and Juliet*: the class was split up into small groups, and together they would each perform their own scenes and cumulatively the entire play. Ms. Baldwin had a wicked sense of humor and some unusual theories about how to turn her unwilling students into actors, and had paired John and Regina together as Romeo and Juliet in multiple scenes. This was not entirely driven by a desire to play matchmaker: John and Regina excelled at reading scenes in class, both understanding not only the arcane language, but how to act dramatically. John was not nearly as enthused as everyone else at his table when the pairings were announced; in fact, he felt uncomfortable. While Regina was trying to sell him on the idea of a stage kiss as being extremely pivotal to their scenes, he was juggling words in his mind on how exactly to frame his complaint. He couldn't call Regina a sociopath, as much as he thought that an appropriate epithet. Then again, was it really a big deal? It was only a scene, in a play, one played out on the tiled floor of a brightly lit classroom and not on a stage in London. And with Beth now out of the question, it was too late for second options. It was ironic, indeed: John's only love was sprung from his only hate.

They practiced outside that day in the central courtyard, Regina and John sitting under a large tree in bloom and Beth and Ted, who were performing another scene, sitting a few feet away. Regina and Beth took every opportunity they could to chat with each other, and Regina felt no shame in drawing John in as well:

"Eugh, some pollen or whatever fell into my bra. Hey, John, have you seen a bra before?" John nodded and said yes, when shopping with his parents, he had passed through the lingerie aisle. Regina appeared amazed, and Beth laughed.

"Shouldn't we be practicing our lines?" John responded with a hint of exasperation—this pattern had repeated itself *ad nauseam* for some time, Regina testing John on some sort of trivia and him responding in turn that they needed to get back to work.

"Don't be silly, we have plenty of time for that. We perform on Monday, remember?"

"But if we use up all our class time now, when would we rehearse?"

"You can always come to my place after school, or I can come to yours; I've seen you on the bus before, I kind of know where you live." John did not think this was a particularly professional response, and he indicated as such. Regina laughed again and begrudgingly read some of her lines. To John, school was school and fun was fun: never the twain shall meet. Even when riding the bus with his classmates, he felt uncomfortable because eventually he would slip up and do something untoward. Now, if Beth and Regina were swapped in their pairings, and she had proposed they rehearse after school, he would have been more willing to say yes. She was in a relationship, the ultimate sign of discretion: it would be impossible then for her and John to read any lines with subliminal intent.

John tolerated this amusement for the rest of the period, then left class in a desultory mood. Frank spotted him as John began his daily trek toward the bus stop.

"What sadness lengthens John's hours?" Frank asked with a smile that then turned caring; Frank could only speculate what was wrong, but seeing as it was after English class, Regina was surely to blame.

"Not having that which having makes them short," John responded, still with a minor frown. "Rehearsal was a disaster. Regina was distracted the entire time. How are your scenes going?"

"Our teacher put it up to a class vote after she saw only a small minority wanted to perform romantic scenes, so now we're in groups performing our choice of something classic. My group's doing Willy Wonka."

"Is that really classic though?"

"Our teacher thought so," Frank commented, and started humming "Come with me, and you'll be in a world of pure imagination..."

"You can sing?"

"Oh God no, I'm not singing, Adrian is. I'm Augustus Gloop. But something is clearly bothering you besides just *Romeo and Juliet*. Do you want to talk about it?"

"What do you do when you like someone, but that person's in a relationship already?"

"I can't say what I would do, but for what you should do, you can simply be friends for a while. And maybe, if things go just right, you will have an opportunity to strike. By then, they'll have warmed up to your presence where it will feel natural to say yes. And even if they don't say yes, you will be happy enough already that you won't mind."

"Thank you, Frank. It's nice of you to be so helpful. Wisdom is a virtue."

"It certainly is," Frank concluded, trailing off as soon as he saw John's eyes turn toward Beth, who had beat them to the bus stop. Oh what a tangled web we weave, Frank thought to himself as he walked onward.

In that moment, John's meditations began anew. John thought back to a few weeks before the revelation, desperately searching his memory for indications of "why him?". He remembered one of the swim days, when Regina spotted his bare chest and cold body in the huddle and said hello. He stepped back off his towel (at this point the boys had copied the girls' technique) and turned toward the balcony, where Regina stood smiling; clearly she had not had PE yet, or else she would have discovered the pool wasn't heated that day. He felt as if he was under a spotlight just then, but he had thought it random chance that Regina called out to him and not someone else. Clearly it wasn't. Beth waved at John with what by now was a standard friendly routine, they sat apart, and John returned home still in his dreamy reverie.

The following day, Frank sat at Ms. Bracknell's desk as had become accepted custom during office hours. By now, the cast of characters had solidified: the eggheads kept doing whatever they were doing, which today was putting together some sort of robot with tools that made loud beeps, Beth and Louis looked in each other's eyes affectionately while they pretended to work, and John looked back at them occasionally while he actually did work. It was more than a bit disrespectful to publicly court in class, as Ernest had told him when relaying the latest hot gossip about John and Regina; apparently, there was a betting pool going on in their class trying to predict the outcome. Frank had assumed Ernest would be above such trivialities, but Ernest said he had put in $10. Frank let out a sharp exhale of breath and decided he wasn't above a bit of gambling himself, and put in $20 against them becoming an item. Life is too short not to take risks, he told Ernest, who by now was conditioned to bristle at any attempts at a philosophical discussion. Ms. Bracknell agreed with Frank:

"Sure, it's disrespectful, but if I draw attention to it by shouting 'get your hands away from each other!,' then I look like the creep. As long as their grades don't suffer, I can only do so much to interfere in their private lives and emotional development."

"Hold that thought," Frank said when Juliet walked in. Something about Juliet disturbed Frank, and he thought Ms. Bracknell noticed the same. They had never talked in any great depth before, sharing words before class on occasion, when he would make some remark about the weather, she would kindly agree, and they would proceed as if they were strangers on the street until class began. Indeed, they were effectively strangers, their conversations arising out of happenstance and not desire. Frank did not think it surprising that Juliet had asked him for help, almost running after him at the end of class to ask, and he appreciated her punctuality when she arrived at Ms. Bracknell's classroom. Yet, despite this unfamiliarity, she walked to meet him at their private desks in the corner of the classroom as if they were old friends.

"How are you so smart?" Juliet asked after he walked her through a complex trigonometry derivation, her hands reaching toward his paper and pencil to follow along.

"I'm really not. Discipline is all it is. You can learn anything with enough discipline."

"Fine, fine. How are you so disciplined?" Juliet drew out that last word with a trace of sarcasm, and Frank was mildly offended.

"Discipline, of course."

"But seriously, I want to know how I can be like you."

"If you have a question, you can ask it. I can't guarantee I'll answer though, but you can ask."

"What's your favorite bubble tea flavor?"

"I don't have enough of a sweet tooth for that."

"What if you get it unsweetened?" Juliet was enjoying this battle of wits. It was rare she had a chance to learn so much from such simple subject matter.

"I'm not sure. What's yours?"

"Jasmine."

"Jasmine sounds good to me too."

"What do you do in your free time? Do you have free time?"

"I read, I study, whatever amuses me. I try not to bind myself to needless habits."

"You read books? No wonder why you're so smart."

"Don't we all read books?" Frank asked, seeing Juliet's copy of *Romeo and Juliet* in her backpack still in pristine condition.

"For fun, I mean. I do have my journal. You should try keeping a diary. It's fun, I promise."

"One should always have something sensational to read on the train. What do you write in a journal? I'm afraid I have few thoughts that would ever be interesting enough to remember."

"I would love to know what thoughts you have. Write them in a blog or something and I can remember them for you. You should share with the world what makes you you. I would follow it intently."

"So you're saying that if I were to write a list of quick tips on how anyone, with enough dedication and perseverance, could become just like me, you and many others would be interested?" Frank's mind was running at full gear at this point; Juliet had no idea what a great mistake she was making. Ernest would be so mad.

"I would love to hear your wisdom of any sort, at any time. Everyone would want to become a good person, just like you."

"Hmm... 'How To Be A Good Person.' I like that."

Juliet smiled again, and looked at Frank with such an expression of innocent glee that he was sure she was a fool. Ms. Bracknell shot them a look when they seemed to be having too much quiet fun in their corner;

if they weren't being so productive, she would have considered Frank a hypocrite. The bell rang, and Frank assured Juliet that if she had any more questions about academics (he punctuated that point with some emphasis), she could send him an email or find him in the hallway.

"Email? That's so old-fashioned. Send me a text instead," she responded, and she wrote down her number on a scrap of paper and handed it to him, leaning over to make sure he saved it in his phone correctly.

"I am at your service. Typically I wouldn't do this, but here's my number, so call me maybe." Frank had been saving that line for a long time.

"You're hilarious," Juliet said, giving Frank a brief hug, and Ms. Bracknell saw Frank's face contort into an expression of befuddlement. "I feel like some of your smartness just rubbed off on me."

"You're welcome? Take as much as you wish, but now I do have places to be and people to see," Frank said with his usual geniality, and he walked off with haste, checking behind him to make sure Juliet was not following with more inquiries. After he left, Beth and Louis walked up to her, and Beth gave Juliet a knowing glare.

"Be careful, Juliet. There's daggers in men's smiles." It had not occurred to Juliet, or to Frank for that matter, that her behavior could have been perceived as flirtatious; Frank simply thought it unusual. Juliet was used to a certain element of friendliness and gratitude that she perceived as being neglected in modern society. People who looked for subtext in everything were weird, and she knew Frank was too altruistic to ever be duplicitous in that way.

Frank had largely shelved any thoughts of that interesting experience until after school, when he ran into Juliet and Regina.

"Have a great weekend! I can't wait to see what you write! If I have any ideas, I'll text you," Juliet said to him, and both he and Regina were astonished.

"What are you writing, Frank?" Regina asked, curious to know what had suddenly drawn Juliet's attention.

"He's going to share his wisdom with the world. I'm very excited," Juliet explained to Regina while Frank took the opportunity to slip out unseen.

"He has wisdom?"

"Too much for any of us to understand."

"But more importantly, he gave you his number? I'm impressed."

"I gave him mine first, but yes. He's so nice. I think we will become great friends. You know, you may have better luck with John if you're a bit nicer too. Frank can teach you."

"If I be waspish, best beware my sting," Regina responded as she climbed into her mother's car. Juliet shrugged and kept walking.

As soon as Frank got home, he opened a Google Doc on his computer, wrote "How To Be A Good Person" at the top, and stared at it for a few minutes. What reasons did he have to be treated as a source of wisdom? Sure, he was kind and, he hoped, accurate, but people trusted him without any particular reason. People wanted to be his friend. They wanted to learn how to be a good person from him, all his thoughts on bubble tea, literature, and society at large. He would give them what they wanted and have a little fun with it too. He saw some room for improvement in the school, and if this improvement meant being the beloved protector of all, Frank truly had nothing to lose but everything to gain. Someone more conniving in his position would start a cult; it was too early for Frank to do the same. He could come up with something if given time, and what did every cult need? A sacred text. Through the weekend, he added new thoughts whenever the mood struck him. He would wake up to a text from Juliet every day that, using far too many emoji, would suggest some new topic that she clearly considered indispensable to being a good person; clearly giving her his number was a huge mistake. Writing his manifesto came easily to him: he had by then quite a few months of stories to lampoon, mannerisms to critique, and kernels of genuine advice to season what was otherwise turning out to be a fairly tongue-in-cheek essay. Juliet came to him Monday morning before school, eager to see what he had come up with.

"I have a draft, but I want to spend one more day editing it. Patience, young grasshopper."

"Fine," she huffed, and she walked away disappointedly. He hadn't lied: he did want one more day, but this was so Pranav could review it.

"This is hysterical, Frank. And they're really going to fall for this?" Pranav asked between bouts of laughter.

"We shall see. Any feedback before I release my creation into the world tomorrow?"

"It's perfect, this is perfect as is."

That phrase did not describe John's state of mind during lunch that day while he frantically read through his lines one last time. While John did not need to memorize his lines, he wanted his delivery to be as fluid as possible. The last thing he wanted was to awkwardly stumble and stutter through his scene with Regina; that would only draw out his misery. Thank God he convinced her that the stage kiss would not be needed—and no, he told her, it didn't need to be a real one for "historical accuracy." He hoped Regina would not embarrass him.

Act II, scene ii. Ms. Baldwin's classroom. Enter John, standing on the opposite side of a balcony constructed from cardboard boxes and chairs. He jests at scars that never felt a wound. Enter Regina, ascending the balcony, her head almost touching the ceiling. She stares out toward the class, looking as if she were in heaven. John begins his monologue, Juliet smiling thinly whenever her name is mentioned, and Regina sighs, "Ay me!". He continues, Regina wishing he would call her a "bright angel" outside of class, and she begins her declarations of love, the class marveling at what they view as natural chemistry. They continue their interchange for some time, a few immature people laughing whenever John says the word "breast," ending when Ms. Baldwin turns off the lights with a dramatic flourish at John's last lines. Exeunt.

Chapter 8

1. First, computer fonts. Times New Roman or Helvetica are preferred. Documents should always be double-spaced, especially professional and academic documents.

2. Always attempt to use proper grammar. This includes such arcane topics as pronoun-antecedent agreement and proper use of punctuation; violations of the above indicate you are not properly educated.

3. Spelling should always be perfect unless you are attempting to mock someone else, and even then proper spelling should be encouraged. You will appear to be an ignorant simpleton if you do not conform to proper spelling, with the possible exception of abbreviations such as "LOL" and "LMAO." Even if you are using such media as Snapchat or Instagram, which should be avoided anyway, proper spelling demonstrates to your friends how refined and sophisticated you are.

4. Furthermore, do not hesitate to correct your friends' spelling or grammar; if they are good friends, they will appreciate your helpful feedback. Otherwise, it would be wise to find some new friends.

5. Relating to the topic of social media, all forms of social media should be avoided, with no exception. Social media is the vanguard of the sinister movement to destroy proper, moral society as we know it,

and thus you should not use it. Assume that anyone who uses social media is not as smart as you are, and thus should be avoided.

6. One cause of excessive social media usage, particularly among teenagers, is the proliferation of mobile phones. A mobile phone or cell phone, whichever is your preferred term, should only be used for calling people for the sake of convenience; it is not to be used to mindlessly browse Snapchat or Reddit, or play games which contribute to the moral degradation of our society. I do concede that such games can be a good form of leisurely activity, but this behavior should not be taken to excess. If you find yourself desperately needing to contact your friends, there is no reason not to talk to them in person, as most people would do.

7. Clothing, especially in a school setting, should be relatively conservative and nice. Although there is no reason to wear dresses or suits to school unless you want to flaunt your fashionable status, there is nothing wrong with polo shirts, button-down shirts, or similar items. Avoid logos on shirts, and wear normal sweaters instead of hoodies. As for pants, jeans or slacks are generally a good choice; shorts and skirts should be reserved for hot weather, and regardless of gender should not be too short. Never wear ripped clothing; it implies you are naturally unkempt and do not care about your appearance.

8. Footwear, especially at school, should be chosen based on comfort and convenience, not appearance. However, this is a topic where people often have their own preferences, but remember to conform to the aforementioned rule of being relatively conservative and nice. There is nothing wrong with sneakers, but slippers imply you were too lazy to change into actual shoes.

9. A person's vocabulary reflects their education and intelligence; do not hesitate to use more complex vocabulary to appear more erudite. However, do not use words unless you know what they mean; it can already be perceived as embarrassing to use sophisticated vocabulary,

but it is unfathomable to accidentally confuse words such as repository and suppository, or immigrate and emigrate.

10. In an academic setting, the primary focus should always be on learning; do not engage in behaviors which would prevent this. Take notes if necessary in a class, and always do homework, even if it is challenging. Never cheat or use tools such as Sparknotes, which are practically the equivalent; if you are having trouble understanding material, talk to the teacher or your classmates for assistance.

11. Read frequently to improve your mind. For fiction books, focus on classics, while for non-fiction, read books which interest you. Avoid "pop science" books unless they are extremely well written; you will not achieve true depth of knowledge by blindly reading lists of over-sensationalized facts. Do not be afraid of long, boring books; if you don't understand them, it is not due to them being too sophisticated, you are simply not thinking hard enough.

12. In subjects such as math or world languages where progress is segregated and there are multiple levels, it is extremely uncouth to lie about how capable you are in a subject; if you aren't smart enough to actually be at that level, then study hard enough until you attain that level.

13. Speaking of math, math is good. Everyone should do math.

14. It is a widely known stereotype that teenagers incessantly pepper their speech with such fillers as "like," "um," and "yeah." While this may be an unavoidable verbal tic, do attempt to minimize your usage of these words, for your speech will sound far more refined.

15. Always avoid profanity at all costs. Profanity is yet another one of the factors which is contributing to the moral decay of our society. Instead of using expletives, attempt to replace them with such colorful, but safe words as "butterfly," "cellulose," "senator," and "Bosnia-Herzegovina"; this simple substitution will mask your anger in heated conversations and project an aura of cool, calculated awesomeness.

16. Nutrition is a topic which most teenagers desperately avoid; after all, in the era of Starbucks, Tpumps, and McDonald's, how can one maintain a healthy diet? First, avoid sweetened drinks, with the possible exception of fruit juice, and even then do not drink them in excess; if you are going to have sugary drinks, you may as well ingest a healthy amount of vitamins as well. Eat whole fruit such as apples and bananas instead of their processed forms; this ensures you consume a satisfactory amount of fiber, and whole fruits have more nutrients than processed fruits anyway. Bubble tea is the scourge of the civilized world, and should be avoided at all costs. If it is unsweetened, then it may be considered as a wonderful way to enjoy tea on hot days. Refrain from consuming Frappuccinos and similar beverages, and avoid fast food unless desperate for sustenance.

17. Dessert should be avoided; if you are hungry enough for dessert, you should have had more dinner. This also applies for snacking on desserts such as ice cream; ice cream and related desserts are not substitutes for proper food. If you feel the urge to snack, eat fresh fruits and vegetables.

18. All people should aspire to get at least 8.5 hours of sleep per day, ideally closer to nine hours. It does not necessarily matter when you go to bed, but try to go to bed before 10:00, and wake up before 8:00. There is enough time in the day to do everything you need to do, even if you have numerous extracurricular commitments; if you are unable to manage your time properly, then that is your fault.

19. There are two conflicting viewpoints on having romantic relationships as a teenager; some feeble-minded people say they help develop emotional maturity, while more sensible people say that teenagers are too immature to have successful relationships and they lead directly to moral armageddon. Personally, I am of the belief that people should not date others until they are at least in junior or senior year of high school, but ideally when they are in college; this of course depends on

how mature both people are. It is best to avoid all non-school related thoughts about your classmates altogether.

20. It is important to have a strong sense of moral beliefs, religious or otherwise. This means that you should not commit crimes, and always have a strong sense of justice. Do not feel afraid to right wrongs in society, for how else are we going to make society great again? Do not feel afraid to work hard and persevere, for how else are you going to improve? Do not feel afraid to be shunned by your immoral friends, for how else are you going to find success in life? The only path to success is hard work, and it is important to acknowledge this.

21. Paranoia is a sign of intelligence. Never completely trust your friends, or anyone who appears to be helpful; unsolicited gratitude is an indicator of nefarious motives. If you think someone is being too kind, there is no harm in asking why; in the best case scenario you demonstrate your intelligence, and in the worst case you now know who you cannot trust in the future.

22. Honesty is always the best policy. Even if you border on being blunt, your friends will appreciate your directness, and your interactions with others will be simplified significantly. In fact, others will admire your honesty, and want to become friends with you. Lying always reflects poorly on yourself, and should be avoided. Success in life is caused by being a paragon of virtue. Furthermore, being honest avoids deception and awkward conversations; if you want to tell somebody something which would be humiliating, honesty mitigates this factor because you will be a model human being.

23. Think of life as a video game, where you are competing against a lot of other players in pursuit of victory. Do not hesitate to take actions which improve your relative standing compared to others if it would not be detrimental to your overall success. Take advantage of opportunities where you have the opportunity to give fraudulent advice; giving fraudulent advice to others is a particularly insidious, but effective

way to take advantage of others. If you feel a moral compunction against betraying your compatriots, remember that if given the opportunity, they would do the same to you.

24. A person's taste in music reflects their soul. An educated, sophisticated person spurns pop and rock music, and instead prefers to listen to jazz or classical music. A truly refined person will also enjoy opera; although some people view opera to be boring and soulless, a true aficionado will realize that opera is music of the heart, not random singers screeching high notes. It is poor form to impose your music tastes on others, however, no matter how crude theirs may be.

25. Pride is the downfall of all smart people. No matter how smart you think you are, it is a critical fallacy to assume you are smarter than others; people often belie their intelligence to mislead others. Always downplay your own accomplishments, and remember that even if you feel as if you will become famous, you probably won't. As Shakespeare said, some are born great, some achieve greatness, and some have greatness thrust upon them. You probably are smarter than average, considering how you are reading this, but that is because greatness has been thrust upon you.

26. The concept of filial piety, or respecting one's elders, is one which used to be entrenched in our culture, but now is rejected in favor of social media, the demented spawn of a twisted, neurotic society which favors senseless tactile stimulation over sophisticated thought. In fact, the concept can be extended to a blind obedience of authority figures, ensuring a harmonious society. Teenagers are often rightfully punished for their defiance, which at the core is caused by vicious, modern culture attacking the core of our society. There is a reason why people often reminisce about the "good old days": society was more moral back then; even if there were some abominations in history, there was a refined culture which ensured everyone was happy.

27. Discipline in schools and in home is a contentious topic, although this is mainly because wimpy teenagers refuse to acknowledge that

discipline breeds success, and hard work breeds happiness. The term "tiger mom" is used disparagingly, as a term of mockery for parental views which are viewed to be too strict, but this ethos of the modern day is ultimately detrimental to our society, where harsher methods of parenting are reviled and "special snowflakes" are nurtured. We live in a society where pragmatic attitudes are viewed as pessimistic and edgy, whereas sunny, unrealistic optimism is lauded as inspiring and beautiful. Discipline should forcefully mold students into model members of society, and if this means bruising a few egos, then so be it.

28. To further expand on my thesis of life being analogous to a video game, it is important to note that life is not a zero-sum game: any calamity which befalls a group will affect everyone somehow, and one person's jubilation does not necessarily equate to one person's despair. If planning for long-term victory overall, as you should, it is important to look past shallow victories and focus on long-term goals, since everyone else is also planning. If you owe someone a favor, do not think of it as a detriment; at some point they, too, will be obligated to owe you something, and at that point you prosper. Plan your actions such that they require more effort from others than from yourself; by doing this you will gain tangible benefits. However, benefits of certain courses of action may not necessarily be apparent at first glance; every cloud has a silver lining, and it is important to account for every possibility. It may seem like a pointless endeavor to help your teacher make copies, for you help your teacher while you spend your own time; however, not all actions should be undertaken to selfishly benefit yourself.

29. Despite superficially appearing to be at odds with my confrontational, analytical approach to life, altruism is necessary for a society to flourish, and unless you are a sociopath, the benefits to being nice are obvious. Not every action has to be done with a goal in mind, but if a goal can be developed from a seemingly erratic action, then it is an even greater benefit. By correcting your friends' grammar, you

are helping them, but is there benefit to you? Of course there is a benefit: having smarter friends means you grow more, and through study and camaraderie bonds of friendship form. Helping others study is a selfless act, and no spirit of kindness should be observed in it except for benefiting the school community. No special favor should be assumed from giving others book recommendations, nor should tutoring be seen as a punishment instead of a boon. Altruism in a school community is positive overall.

30. It is often necessary to hold grudges against your friends or classmates, even for faults which they might perceive as slight. No matter how trivial the offense, it is important to know how your classmates' actions affect you, and it is likewise important to know how your actions affect your classmates. Too often do people underestimate how one single remark, a quick, off-hand response to a question, could influence future events. If only a few cab drivers were informed about a change to Archduke Franz Ferdinand's schedule, World War I would not have started. What a smart person must understand is that grudges and unnecessary appreciation are only consequences of the thick web of actions which define our lives. What one person perceives as a compliment may be an insult to the receiver, and a single act of generosity may cast lasting doubts which sour a relationship. Think before you speak, and if you make a mistake it is imperative that you can connect it to your overarching agenda. The largest schemes and conspiracies started as practical jokes.

31. Yet another factor in the complicated game that is life is information imbalance, which sounds complicated but is fairly simple intuitively: you are planning a surprise party for your friend, but they do not know about it. You can't hang out with them at your house because it would ruin the surprise. To your friend, you seem unusually standoffish on their birthday, which could ruin a friendship. To you, your friend is a victim of a deception, where hidden information plays a pivotal role in

your interactions that day. To effectively utilize this concept in your life, you need to think about what benefits you can gain from withholding information: for instance, pretending you do not speak a language allows you the benefit of eavesdropping on others, while having the ability to grade a teacher's papers allows you to make better judgments about your classmates' academic strength, which can then be applied to other things later. By utilizing this effectively, you also have the advantage of appearing far smarter than you actually are; if you strategically share observations you have made about others at the right times, you magnify their impact and appear to be a modern-day Sherlock Holmes.

32. Deduction is not necessarily that important of a skill, but nonetheless it has numerous applications. What is often more important is the ability to make observations about your surroundings, and apply them: a logo on a backpack, somebody's friend group, somebody's shoes. There are numerous online resources on the art of deduction, but by carefully tabulating facts about a person, you build a profile which then can be applied for personal benefit later. If you are able to spot somebody's lie, or notice how somebody's posture changes around another person, then you gain an advantage in information, further highlighting the information dynamic mentioned in the preceding tip. Successful people are successful because they know enough about others to structure their own behavior to gain maximum benefit; to outsiders, their behavior seems erratic at best and maniacal at worst, but in reality they use information gained about others to make their own behavior effective.

33. Even though a lot of these tips so far have related to creating effective plans, none of them have specifically shared the structure for doing so. When concocting a scheme, one must always ascertain your end goal, who is involved/affected, and what you need to do in advance to accomplish it. For instance, if your goal is to introduce propaganda of your own creation to your classmates, first you would need to determine who are the most gullible and trusting people in your class, from which

you can then create a course of action. Planning is an important skill for life, and smart people know how to create effective plans.

34. When flattering others for any reason, there is a fine balance to keep in mind: you should be nice enough to the point where they feel happy and accomplished, but do not make it so excessive where they realize your compliments are not genuine. Flattery is a wonderful way to ingratiate yourself with others, because it can be used as the foundation of all friendships. Good friends give each other undue compliments. Flattery is also a good way to make sure your enemies do not realize how much you dislike them; the nicer you are, the easier it is to disguise your hatred.

35. Studies have shown that people who walk more quickly are better in school. Regardless of how much you walk, ensure that you walk quickly. A good pace to aim for is a 16-minute mile pace; if necessary, time yourself to reach this goal. You will notice, if you watch carefully, that smart people walk fairly quickly; only people who are unmotivated slowly meander about with their friends. If you make this correction in your behavior, you will find that your academic ability will improve.

36. A wise person once said "if you are five minutes early, you are on time." However, this philosophy, even if it is somewhat accurate, needs refinement; always try to be as early as possible. This means showing up for class fifteen minutes early, and always arriving before the stated time on invitations or reservations. If people appear annoyed when you show up to events unusually early, it is because they are impressed by your punctuality. Apply this principle to all aspects of your life; for instance, always turn in homework early. It will show your teachers how dedicated you are.

37. There is no gesture more odious or reprehensible than the high-five, especially if unsolicited. It is an unnecessary transfer of pathogens, and serves no purpose other than to show how hooligan-like you are. Instead of high fives, use more hygienic methods of commenda-

tion such as fist bumps. The entertainer Howie Mandel is a practitioner of this sterile technique. A hand raised in the air should not be taken as an invitation for a high-five, and assuming it as such indicates you are very crude in your mannerisms.

38. All educated people read a great number of classics. Here is a list of some of the better books to contribute to your sophistication of mind: *Crime and Punishment* by Fyodor Dostoyevsky, *Anna Karenina* by Leo Tolstoy, *The Brothers Karamazov* by Fyodor Dostoyevsky, *The Tale of Genji* by Murasaki Shikibu, *Romance of the Three Kingdoms* by Luo Guanzhong, *The Adventures of Tom Sawyer* by Mark Twain/Samuel Clemens, *A Tale of Two Cities* by Charles Dickens, *War and Peace* by Leo Tolstoy, *The Mote in God's Eye* by Larry Niven, *The Metamorphosis* by Franz Kafka, *The Joy of Work* by Scott Adams, *Never Gonna Give You Up* by Rick Astley, *How to Reassess your Chess* by Jeremy Silman, *Never Gonna Let You Down* by Rick Astley, *How to be a Good Person* by Franklin Barnes, *Never Gonna Run Around and Desert You* by Rick Astley, *The Fountainhead* by Ayn Rand, *Never Gonna Make You Cry* by Rick Astley, *Freakonomics* by Steven Levitt and Stephen Dubner, *Never Gonna Say Goodbye* by Rick Astley, *Finnegans Wake* by James Joyce, *Ulysses* by James Joyce, *Never Gonna Tell a Lie and Hurt You* by Rick Astley, *Les Misérables* by Victor Hugo, *The Count of Monte Cristo* by Alexandre Dumas, *I am America (And so can You!)* by Stephen Colbert, *A Citizen's Guide to Civility* by Miss Manners, *How I Defeated the Borg* by Jean-Luc Picard, *Macbeth* by William Shakespeare, *Great Expectations* by Charles Dickens, *The Odyssey* by Homer Simpson, *The Iliad* by Homer Simpson, *In Search of Lost Time* by Marcel Proust, *Don Quixote* by Miguel de Cervantes, *Heart of Darkness* by Joseph Conrad, *An Illustrated Guide to Gotham* by Bruce Wayne, *Catch-22* by Joseph Heller, *The Cat in the Hat* by Dr. Seuss, *Pride and Prejudice* by Jane Austen, *The Bible*, *The God Delusion* by Richard Dawkins, *The Koran*, *How to Defeat Bowser in 3 Easy Steps* by Princess Toadstool, and last but not least, *Doctor Zhivago* by Boris Pasternak. Only

if someone reads all of these books can they be considered to be truly educated.

39. Yet another tool for becoming a smart, successful, and Machiavellian person is knowing how to obfuscate your intelligence, either emotional or intellectual. Doing this will enable you to further utilize information imbalances and heighten your level of intelligence. One effective, if obvious, method of doing this is by frequently utilizing malapropisms in your daily speech; smart people will recognize this as a sign of stupidity, and thus your staggering intelligence will remain unnoticed. Another method of doing this is by feigning knowledge of current trends or events; especially to your uneducated peers, this will be an obvious mistake. People will then assume you are either a brilliant, but misunderstood genius, or a doddering idiot who knows nothing of life. Yet another method of doing this is by flaunting your intelligence whenever possible; this can be done in a variety of ways. Here are some examples which have been used successfully before if youre in need of dire help: concocting frivolous schemes on a biweekly basis, answering every question in class even if it would be perceived as impertinent, and forgetting to use apostrophes.

40. When attempting to improve one's character, every piece of advice must be taken completely. Do not treat this guide as a cafeteria, where each maxim can be taken, examined, and uncaringly discarded if it would be unpleasant to digest. Even if you must fight hard against ingrained habits, it is important to endeavor to change all aspects of your personality to improve. You may feel as if advice is stupid; do not worry, this means that you are unable to contemplate it completely, and you should accept it to understand. Good advice is not a simple, clean statement; it is a Zen koan, where the answer is vague or even nonexistent. Be willing to untangle the knot of clarity, or even better, take a sword to the Gordian knot and cut it into ribbons.

41. Extracurricular activities must be chosen with sophistication in mind. Classic activities such as musical instruments and sports are not unique enough. Choose more interesting activities such as flower arranging and underwater basket weaving. These activities promote artistic and creative thinking, whereas mundane activities like gymnastics and soccer are mindless and crude. The Japanese art of ikebana, or sophisticated flower arranging, has centuries of culture behind it, while soccer is kicking a ball around aimlessly. Underwater basket weaving seamlessly combines the arts and physical endurance in the same activity, making it perfect. Some particularly enlightened colleges even offer it as a class.

42. One skill in society which is often neglected is cooking. In today's society, where fast food is available everywhere and food can be ordered by a tap of your finger, people have grown dependent on these tools instead of being self-sufficient. It is convenient to not always cook your own food, but you should still be able to cook your own meals aside from microwaving. If possible, take culinary classes at school or in an outside program, or even watch cooking shows on TV. These will help you learn essential skills, which are very useful for college or later life. Even if it is marginally more expensive to cook food rather than buying instant ramen noodles, you will not regret it later, and vegetables and grains can be bought cheaply at some places. It is also advisable to, if you are going to eat out frequently, diversify your meals; most cities have a great variety of different restaurants, and even if you are unaccustomed to eating some foods, it cannot hurt to try them.

43. Having good personal finance skills enables you to gain financial independence and be successful. The core of good finance skills is investing, either in bonds or in stocks. As a general rule of thumb, cheaper stocks are better to buy because they have more room for growth. If you buy ten thousand shares of a company at a penny each, and the price increases by two cents each, then you have made a massive

profit. It is better to buy stocks in obscure companies, because it is less likely they will go bankrupt since their CEOs will not be assassinated as frequently. Also, there is nothing wrong with buying stocks when they are expensive; if they are expensive, it is conceivable that they could grow even more. Online stock trading simulators are a good way to practice essential financial skills.

44. Sitting in the front of the class shows the teacher how committed you are to learning. If necessary, move your desk right in front of the teacher so you fully absorb everything they say. At the end of class, give the teacher a note explaining how the day's lesson inspired you. This will show you have fully absorbed the content of their class, and you really love learning. If they find this behavior intrusive or even creepy, you should transfer classes; they probably weren't a good teacher anyway. People with bad eyesight especially should do this.

45. To further delve into smaller, less relevant topics, board games should always involve strategy and minimize luck. Chess is a classic, and not a bad choice, although personally I do not like it that much. Scrabble is a very strategic game which also builds your vocabulary, although it is not as popular as chess. I recommend it to hone your strategic skills, and as a fun game to play. Checkers is absolutely pointless; if you want to play a game on an 8x8 board, play chess instead. Dungeons & Dragons, while not strictly a board game, is a wonderful way to practice strategy while also interacting with friends.

46. Society is founded on ideas. Every revolution, every war, and every argument started with an idea. If you have a good idea, you can change the world and how you interact with others. Every successful company started with a good idea. Uber exists because someone wondered if there were alternatives to conventional taxi services. Google Drive exists because a bright worker at Google saw the dismal failures which were Pages and Microsoft Word, and wondered if there was a cloud-based method of creating documents and storing ideas. Treasure ideas as if

they were your own children; do not be afraid to steal them when their owners aren't looking and keep them as your own. Sell your ideas to the highest bidder, that is, if you cannot be more successful using them yourself. Do not be afraid to waste countless hours with others trying to make successful ideas. The process may be painful, it may be fun, but after a lot of work you can have a successful idea, and use it to change the world, for better or for worse.

47. Many people would consider North Korea, or the Democratic People's Republic of Korea, to be a failed country. It has failed to make any significant technological advancements in the past twenty years, with a potential exception for intercontinental ballistic missiles and other weapons. Its citizens live in a state of propaganda-induced bliss, unable and unwilling to see anything else other than their superiority and the American imperialists causing ruin in their country. Although this alone would be enough evidence to conclude that North Korea is a failed nation, instead you should view it as a success, at least in some ways. North Korea proves that if indoctrination is conducted in all levels of society, from people being forced to venerate their dear leaders to rousing, patriotic songs being played on loudspeakers in all public areas, a personality cult can be formed successfully. It proves that national pride and patriotism is alive and well, and even in the face of adversity and hardship people can love their leaders. In your daily life, think about the many accomplishments of the Kim dynasty, and think about how you can apply their propaganda techniques to your daily life.

48. The model human being sits in the rain with soggy clothes and socks, yet refuses to use an umbrella on personal principles. The model human being watches their friends go to the movie theater to see the latest superhero movie, which they really wanted to see, but instead goes to an educational seminar at the library. The model human being sits alone during lunch at school and reads the newspaper because they know reading is the key to success. The model human being is not afraid

to reprimand their classmates for breaking the rules, even if they don't think it would make a difference. Remember to commend your friends if they are model human beings.

49. Once upon a time, there were three brothers who owned a shop in a small town. One day, the youngest brother went outside and saw that three goats were tethered to the front of their shop. Because he respected his brothers, he called them outside to show them the goats. They then went back in the store so they could argue over which of the brothers would get the goats. The youngest brother argued that since he was the youngest and the older brothers were richer, he should keep the goats to sell himself. The middle brother was in charge of accounting for the store, and argued that he should keep the goats because he could sell the horns to a local apothecary, the skin to a tanner, and the flesh to a butcher. The oldest brother argued that since he was the oldest and naturally the best, he should keep the goats for himself. The middle brother eventually got everyone to agree to splitting the goats equally. When they went outside to retrieve the goats, they were gone. What can we conclude from this? If the youngest brother were selfish and smart, he could keep the goats for himself and make money. Because he was kind, everyone lost. Always put yourself above others if you want to be successful.

50. All civilizations rise and fall, building themselves on the bones of their predecessors only to languish in ruin. Many have made careers studying the plight of the Romans, the Greeks, and all of the classical civilizations of yore, but there are no conclusions to be reached which cannot be found in today's society. While they were all able to portray themselves as vanguards of new renaissances, and it is true that innovation was fostered in these civilizations, they all fell to childish infighting or stronger enemies. While you may be one citizen of one nation, not part of a global hegemony or a world-spanning empire, you are still part of the same cycle. You look up to your idols, whether

they be presidents, scientists, or television stars, yet you make the same mistakes they do. Society consumes the meek, and only the mighty will hold their own against the inexorable tide of progress, where the innovators flourish and the followers perish. Hundreds of people all compete for the same few positions in companies and colleges. Modern society is built upon competition, a primal force of nature which devours some, but leaves some as victors. Some make a name for themselves in their respective fields and win numerous accolades, but they are replaced by the newcomers, and this process continues. Venerated figures die and are mourned, but their bones crumble to dust in forgotten crypts. Naïve teenagers, just having graduated college in a relatively sheltered environment, are thrust into a twisted universe where selfishness overtakes compassion and greed overtakes charity. They enter with a fervent belief that they can make a difference, and leave as soulless drones. They see their superiors working in their offices, and strive to be like them; however, they cannot anticipate the struggles and the sacrifices ahead of them, and they eventually fail. Sometimes they contradict others, believing that their fresher perspective on life means that they are equal to their elders; still, new perspectives are not always tolerated, and eventually they learn to accept the central dogma of society. How can people possibly survive in such a cutthroat environment, where simple concepts of politeness and etiquette, which we are taught in kindergarten, disappear? Some attempt to find friends in the vast ocean of life, where for every benevolent fish there is a shark waiting to eat you alive. Some return to the comforts of home, seeking a lazy life of indolence and leeching from their parents. The smart ones realize that there is no mercy in life, and success is gained only through attrition and hard work. Suffering is a natural part of life, and cowardice is for those too weak to accept suffering. Those who preach ways to find cheap bliss in life, which is not derived from years of hard work, are false prophets. Those who view their work as a means to an end themselves are destined to become gears in a soulless machine which will devour them without remorse. Their idle thoughts only serve as catalysts for others to seize initiative and promote themselves. Those who are passionately dedicated to appeasing others' whims will only become stepping stones for braver people to prosper. The smart absorb their more foolish competitors' ideas while applying them for personal benefit. The hopelessly cynical will see their more optimistic enemies overshadow them; it is easy to snuff out a candle which is dimly lit. The only people who can survive have the will to conquer obstacles, the will to fail, and the will to succeed after failure. People who cannot grasp this simple concept are consigned to oblivion, and are forced to the bottom of society. They are relegated to bland offices and cubicles, where loud-mouthed supervisors scold them into working harder. Everyone has experienced pure tyranny at some point, but only the smart view it as a lesson and not a punishment. Unfairness is not a crime, but merely a truth. Failure is a tragic lesson, but not a useless one. The successful people can enjoy their temporary accomplishments, but they know that there are always higher tiers of achievement, and once the initial glow of success wears off, they realize that they are still failures. There is no path to success in life which does not involve hard work. However, there is also no path to success which does not involve a balance between work and relaxation. Some foolhardy people believe that they are so much more accomplished than others that they do not need anything besides work in life; these people will burn out and fail. It's a paradoxical outcome: the people who work too much fail, and the people with no determination or focus also fail. What can we conclude from this? The secret to life is hard work, and the future is only what we make today. To separate yourself from the crowd, demonstrate that you are a better worker than everyone else.

Chapter 9

Frank expected more difficulties in selling his act to others, especially those who tended to view everything with a critical eye and did not see him as the reason why they had passed fall semester. Instead, he saw the link to the text shared on Snapchat and the few printed copies he made circulate throughout the school, from student to teacher and teacher to student. For many, it offered a concise guide on how to become their idealized version of Frank: who knew that wearing bright colors and avoiding profanity could improve their IQ? The vanity of the manifesto did not occur to most, who were simply happy to learn; the absurdity also did not occur to most, and the people who noticed were all too happy to pass it along to their friends as a humorous piece. Frank, of course, was deadpan when asked to explain exactly what he meant when he wrote that "paranoia is a sign of intelligence," quoting directly when possible and telling a hyperbolic tale of backstabbers everywhere when not. For those who had not paid much attention to Frank, none of this behavior seemed incongruous; as he clearly was a good person, who were they to question the foundations of his belief? Those who knew Frank to be a kind person, but also realized that a good person in theory and a good person in practice clearly were dissimilar, simply assumed that their own perception was at fault. A few distinct schools of thought began to form, including those who saw the potential for a school-wide phenomenon (surprisingly, this group did not include Frank, at least at first) in the satire and wished to do their part to stoke the flames of confusion, and those who earnestly believed Frank needed to start a lecture series. John read the text during math class methodically, poring over every word and nodding approvingly before passing it to Juliet, who gently but intently pulled it from John's hands and started reading herself.

"It's interesting, isn't it?" John remarked, noticing Juliet's unusual eagerness to begin reading. He put away his reading glasses.

"It's exactly what I had hoped for. I can see he took my advice."

"What advice did you give him?" John was a bit confused: when Frank encountered him before class that day and told him about his latest creative effort, and said because he trusted John's judgment, he would be deeply touched if he were to give it a look-over, it sounded like a spontaneous affair. Something that Frank pulled out of a top hat like a magician. Beth rolled her eyes as she eavesdropped.

"Nothing much, really. I can't possibly take any credit for this. He was tutoring me—you were there, you must have seen us—we talked a bit, and I convinced him it was necessary for him to speak to a wider audience. He was skeptical, you know, but clearly I convinced him."

"It's like you're his Muse. Great work, Juliet. I'm proud of you." John's first thought when he read the text was that Frank had managed to articulate many of the sentiments that John could not have otherwise put words to. What other word but "simpleton" could describe someone like Regina or Louis? John had a particular bone to pick with the latter, and not solely because of Beth. Earlier in Mr. Reinhardt's class, Louis had discovered that something about elementary chemistry did not sit right with him. It made no sense why a proton should be positive and an electron should be negative, or why you couldn't stick all the atoms in a molecule in one long, trailing chain and be done with it. Louis, who was developing a burgeoning sense of his intellectual inadequacy, had turned to his group partners to give him the answers to the questions that Mr. Reinhardt was asking them. Louis tried to remain silent, but Mr. Reinhardt smelled his weakness and made an effort to call on him at every opportunity. After a few rounds of these shenanigans, John thought Louis had to be put in his place, and gave him a mildly unconventional answer.

"Louis, what exactly is a covalent bond?" Mr. Reinhardt asked with a sneer.

"A covalent bond is when two atoms share flux capacitors!" Louis announced with a grin—he was a biology wizard! Mr. Reinhardt looked deadpan at him for a few seconds, then burst out in laughter.

"Louis, where did you learn this novel fact?" Louis looked around with frightened eyes, turning to John, who looked at him coldly.

"You asshole!" Louis shouted at him, then ran out of the room. The class, including Mr. Reinhardt, collapsed. One of Louis's friends imitated his voice and re-enacted the incident, to everyone's amusement. Later, during PE (Louis had transferred into John's class soon after the beginning of the year due to the incident in drama class), Louis encountered John in the locker room, and tried as hard as he could to embarrass John in the same way.

"You have a hole in your chest!" Louis exclaimed with a howl. This was true: John did have a slight indentation in his chest cavity, only cosmetic of course, but Louis was never that good at biology. John took a moment to realize exactly what he was referring to, and admitted he did indeed have a hole in his chest. Louis, seeing this barb did little to scratch John, asked if he had ever dressed as Iron Man for Halloween. John did not quite know how he could accomplish this, and Louis explained to him like John was an idiot.

While John was lost in his memories, Juliet had reached the section on dating, which reminded her that she was sitting next to a bachelor that was still the object of one of her dearest friend's affections:

"John, what do you think of Regina? You two were excellent when you performed your scene. If I didn't know any better, I'd say you liked her."

"She is handsome; but not tolerable enough to tempt me," John responded with a frown. John, ever since what had happened during PE, wondered if Louis had been right all along: John did have a hole in his chest, right where his heart should be. Without that little organ that imbued his body with vital fire and kept his blood racing, John was a husk of a human being. He went through his day speaking in subtle variations of a monotone, moving only toward the slumber that would eventually end it. He was a bad person, and if he were to become good enough for Beth, well, the solution was currently in Juliet's hands.

"I can see why she finds you cute," Juliet commented, and for a second John expected her to launch into the same sort of soliloquy Regina did that fateful day in English class.

Ernest read the first two pages quickly, scanning for the deficiencies he knew he would find, then threw the paper down with disgust:

"It's shameful. It's brutish. It's uncouth. I hate it."

"You only read two pages," Frank grinned. "You haven't gotten to the juicy parts yet."

"By a small sample we may judge the whole piece. Where's that cult you tried to found in middle school, the Wise Camel or whatever? Bring that back. I liked that." Ernest disliked the figurative and the insincere, and it pained him whenever Frank brazenly lied about his intent. One of their junior classmates had complimented him on his satire, only for Frank to say that he was never unserious.

"Ernest, you're saying you'd much rather I walk around chanting about camels and celery sticks than have people exercise their shoulders and betray their friends?" Frank asked incredulously. Ernest, out of all people, would have no time for the banal middle-school hijinks of a cult that never went anywhere.

"Yes, I really would. This is funny. I'd even join the rituals if you gave me the robes. But *How To Be A Good Person* is malicious. Nobody but true idiots would take the Wise Camel seriously, but all our classmates who are now chastising each other for swearing are doing so under a firm conviction they have become good."

"They'll learn eventually," Frank retorted, truly not sure how to best defend himself.

"So? They haven't learned yet. By next year you will be a social pariah, mark my words." Frank rolled his eyes and gave Ernest's copy of the text to the next person in line.

Tom was just about to finish his history test when Jason, who was sitting in front of him, went to grab a tissue and take a drink of water. Their teacher was engrossed in something on his computer that from the mouse movements, looked like Solitaire, and clearly would not see anything he did. Tom could not help but sneak a quick peek at Jason's paper, spotting the answers for some of the latter problems on the test he wasn't quite sure about. Jason turned around just in time to see Tom lean back without a trace of guilt in his eyes. Jason knew what just happened, but he did not want to make a scene; with any luck, the teacher had by some miracle also seen Tom copy answers. After class, Jason confronted Tom, who initially looked at him with a sneer like he didn't know exactly why Jason was there.

"Why did you cheat off me?" Jason was furious, even though he did not show it. What was the point of Jason's hard work studying if someone were to swoop in and take all the credit? Madeline had told him once that diligence was the mother of good fortune, and Jason fancied himself diligent, but the good fortune was supposed to be his alone and not Tom's too.

"What are you talking about?"

"I saw you there looking at my test. Don't be coy."

"I was stretching."

"Yeah, like everyone stretches by leaning in front of them to copy off their classmates' papers!"

"Exactly, everyone does it." Tom could not believe how rude Jason was being.

"I'll tell the teacher."

"He won't believe you, I have an A in the class."

"Then why would you cheat?" Tom did not have a good answer for this question. Anyone who had taken health class would accuse him of traditional teenage risk-taking and poor decision-making, likely the result of an undeveloped frontal lobe. As much as Tom did not like to concede mental weakness, in a way, this was perfect: he was not to blame. His actions were due to unconscious reflex, a surge of testosterone, or something that only made him more human and Jason more annoying for doubting him.

"I don't know, I just felt like it," Tom responded with a hint of sassiness. Jason sighed in exasperation and walked away, and Tom smiled in his victory.

Jason immediately did the logical thing and complained to Ernest, who by now was so conditioned to his classmates' faults that he did not really care. Ernest was not ashamed to admit he was a good student, just as he was not ashamed to admit that it did not come naturally to him. Many refused to believe this latter claim, and if they did, they did so under the assumption that Ernest's definition of "shameful" was their "excellent." While he was not enrolled in calculus like Jason and Frank, what math he did know he did well, indicating an agile comprehension that if started a few years earlier, perhaps would match them. Ernest found his classmates' fascination with the latter irritating, especially as it meant he was put on the same pantheon as Jason and especially Frank; just as Frank directed any serious inquiries to Jason, Ernest directed any inquiries for help to Frank, assuming that Frank would have the patience he simply did not have time for. Jason, when overhearing one of these conversations in the hallway, immediately resolved to direct any truth-seekers to Ernest if anyone ever asked him simply to continue the fun, which they rarely did.

"So what's the big deal? He looked at your paper a bit, maybe even copying the wrong answers, and he said he's doing well enough in the class that he doesn't need the help. Who cares?" Ernest did not dislike Jason to any extreme degree, and decided to make a rare exception and offer advice in the most sympathetic tone he could muster.

"For one, I couldn't stand his obnoxious smirk. He thinks he knows everything. I wanted to punch him," Jason lamented. "He thinks that just because he's rich and his family has a lake house in Tahoe that he can do whatever he wants at school."

"I heard about that, actually. What's up with that? They can't ski in the summer, and won't there be too many mosquitos?"

"They don't deserve anything but mosquitos. A pox upon them!" Ernest laughed; Jason had some good lines when he was irritated.

"He didn't invite you, I can tell."

"Why would he? I called him a cheater."

Tom had not invited Ernest, which was fortunate, as Ernest would have staunchly refused. Tom had tried a few others out of his closest peers, emboldened by his father, who said that as a kid, he would go on trips with his friends and that Tom was old enough to be trusted alone for a week. Jason was also slightly incorrect factually: Tom's father did not own the lake house alone, he shared it in a rotation with some of his work buddies and other relatives. He could afford it himself if he really wanted, but this way he could foist the maintenance expenses onto other people.

The first person Tom invited was Alan, surprisingly enough. Tom did not understand why all the popular kids avoided Alan. Alan held himself up with good posture, and never hesitated to crack a joke or follow the tide of conversation. Those weren't hard benchmarks to reach, and Alan passed the test. Besides, he had always been friendly to Tom, seemingly without any traces of pettiness or jealousy. When Tom casually asked if he had any summer plans, it sounded like he was destined for a boring summer of video games, so for once Tom decided to be the generous one and invite him, the popular kids be damned. After Alan came John, who took a few minutes of explanation to understand exactly where Tom was inviting him; John asked innocently if there was any witchcraft involved, and Tom was slightly concerned for his mental health. Tom thought that the genders needed to be evened out slightly, so he then asked Regina, who was lukewarm until she asked who else was coming.

"I think I convinced Alan," Tom answered, which elicited a minor groan from Regina, "and John," which got a far more enthusiastic reaction.

"He really wants to go?"

"John loves nature, fishing, and anything woodsy. He will be good company. We also won't be fishing, but I didn't tell him that." Tom had many fond memories of fishing trips with his father and consequently assigned some of those positive emotions to John. Beth was a tougher sell:

"So what's the point of this trip, just to relax?"

"Yeah, exactly that. We can unwind a bit, swim, play games, whatever strikes us. What else would you be doing over the summer?"

Beth thought a moment, then responded definitively: "Exactly that. Sounds fun. I'm in."

Tom's hot streak of successful invitations led him to believe that Juliet would be easy to convince too, but she seemed distracted. He had not quite shaken his initial fondness of her.

"It will be fun, I promise. You will have plenty of time for journaling, yoga, Instagram, or however you care to spend your vacation."

"First week of June? I can't, we're going to Hawaii. I'd love to come next year though. How many more people are you trying to invite?"

As much as Tom always treasured his visits to Tahoe, he couldn't help but be jealous of Juliet in that moment. "I doubt we could have more than six without my place being a bit cramped, so maybe one more. We have John, Alan, Beth, and Regina already."

"You should invite Frank," she said thoughtfully. "He would be great company."

Tom was hesitant to invite Frank mainly because he associated too much with the intellectuals of the school. The idea of not being the smartest person in the room scared Tom; if he were outmatched by someone else, what else would he have to rely on? Frank saved him the worry about this existential dilemma by politely declining. Swimming wasn't his thing, Frank said, and Tom only became more convinced of his initial assumption: Frank would ruin the mood. Ted, when asked, cited some very unique fears about horror movies and zombie killers wearing hockey masks in an attempt to say no without hurting Tom's feelings. Ted saw enough of his classmates at school, he didn't need to see more of them, and he and Tom would have plenty of opportunities to socialize. And so it was done: Tom had succeeded in his quest.

Pranav turned to Frank with an expression of befuddlement, holding his copy of *The Catcher In The Rye* that had far too many annotations for his own good.

"Have you read this? It makes no sense. I don't understand why this is required reading."

Frank took the book from him and read a random quote out loud: "Everything I had was bourgeois as hell. Even my fountain pen was bourgeois. He borrowed it off me all the time, but it was bourgeois anyway." Frank turned to Pranav with the same curious expression: "What are you reading, Karl Marx?"

"No, just some book about a teenage failure. We should be reading books about successful people, not high school drop-outs."

"Well, Marx was successful in his own special way."

"I understand the point of reading books like this is so we empathize with the characters, that by reading about Holden Caulfield or whomever we learn how to understand our own fragile minds. I'm literally quoting what my teacher said to us. But why should I care? Holden Caulfield never took calculus."

Frank flipped through a few more pages carelessly, not paying any of the words any particular attention. "It's good to know I'll have something to look forward to next year."

Pranav appeared to be in deep contemplation for a moment, then he turned to Frank again: "You know, your mentioning Karl Marx reminded me: you really have something going here with this manifesto. I can't say I had much faith in my classmates, but whatever faith I had has been annihilated: these suckers really believe everything you've written. I know you joked about it before, but you should start a cult. Or you can't call it that, so a club."

Frank nodded with some appreciation. Pranav, as always, was onto something. "I have never seen myself as a natural leader, but I do know some natural followers."

"It was more of a theoretical exercise than anything. A joke, if you will. It's highly improbable that you could do—"

Frank interrupted boisterously: "Pranav, worlds are turned on such thoughts. We are doing this."

Pranav was taken aback at Frank's sudden enthusiasm: "Frank, you may have the charisma to do this, but I really don't."

"I think we will need two separate power hierarchies. One, the front-facing part: these will be the officers on paper, my classmates who are so desperate for something to put on their college applications that they'll do anything. Two, the true puppetmasters: you and my other friends, who will help plan meetings and keep everyone on task. Do you think you can be a puppetmaster?"

"I can do that, certainly. Let's talk later, I don't want anyone to overhear," Pranav finished, glancing quickly around the room to ensure nobody could spoil their fun. This was exciting, this was exhilarating, and he had no idea what he was doing. Frank didn't, either: he had grandiose plans that raced through his mind, but if mass-brainwashing were that easy, everyone else would have done it already.

"Mr. T?" Frank came into his room to see Mr. T assembling a charcuterie plate for a Friday afternoon professional networking meeting (He and the other teachers assigned fancy names to these events to dupe the administration into thinking they had any intentions of doing work), and he gestured for Frank to help himself.

"It's he," Mr. T said with a smile, fully engrossed in arranging some cornichons and pickled onions in a floral pattern.

"So, as you may be well aware, my little manifesto has been circulating more than I expected."

"You have a good ear for satire. I wish the school newspaper had someone like you on board. What did you want to discuss?"

"How do I start a cult?" Mr. T somehow was unsurprised.

"Let me guess: your classmates are blindly assuming your kindness means you could never possibly be insincere, and are now all endeavoring to shape themselves into better people, and you want to capitalize on this before the trend fades away, all so you can have your shot at high school infamy? As a teacher, I am supposed to caution you against doing anything so risky and unwise; as a person, I can be the teacher supervisor for your club. There's a good documentary about something called the Third Wave, which actually did not happen too far away from here, that you may find useful as an instructional guide, albeit not in the sense originally intended. I can loan you a copy."

"So before I have a chance to watch the documentary, how do I set the foundation starting now?" Mr. T's bemused encouragement only convinced Frank further he was in the right.

"The Third Wave was structured around a simple motto: strength through discipline, strength through community, strength through action. From day one, you need discipline. Day zero, even. You have this covered now, as after all, that's what you wrote about. You need strength, too: make sure that everyone spends their entire summer eagerly waiting for your wisdom, something you can build up through maybe weekly posts on social media or other advertisements. Community is most important: this club will be simultaneously insular but welcoming. Anyone can come and experience what you have to offer, if only they sign over their souls, and anyone who doesn't is to be distrusted."

"It's the syndicate, everyone has a share!" Frank exclaimed enthusiastically.

"Exactly. Use your remaining time wisely, and I cannot wait to see what you have in store for us next year."

Frank left Mr. T's classroom with a new sense of purpose that he thought he could have never found otherwise. In the short span of a school day, he had transformed himself from a lovable prankster to someone charismatic, suave, popular, and so much more. This sense of self-importance was shattered when he came across Juliet, who accosted him before he could launch into his spiel.

"So I was thinking a bit more about what you had written, and I was curious: is my skirt too short?" Juliet asked, pointing downward. Frank immediately shook his head.

"I really can't say, I am rather inexperienced on the topic of woman's clothing; I have few standards for comparison."

"But you're the good person now, surely you have some sort of judgment?"

"It's a matter of context. Come to my club next year and perhaps we can have a Socratic seminar to address the question of our times: when does a skirt become too short? I do apologize for skirting the question, if you will." Frank thought he did a good job segueing to his new predominant topic of interest. Maybe this would be easier than he thought.

"I will see you there," Juliet promised, and she went off without an appropriate answer to her question. This led her to English class, where John was rapidly proving his worth as the second-best good person available. John answered every question posed to him with no judgment, pointing to specific quotes in the text and using them to support his arguments so admirably that Ms. Baldwin was willing to consider this temporary distraction educational. Juliet was first in line, still disappointed about never receiving a good answer as to her skirt, and John blushed to the amusement of everyone except him. Someone else told them to shut up, and John responded in turn, "Well, the polite thing to say is 'please be quiet, my dear friend.'"

"I want to be your dearest friend," Beth said, Juliet and Regina both agreeing with her. John blushed more.

"We'll all have time to become BFFs at the lake, so don't worry John," Regina assured him. John was not worried before, but he was now: why hadn't Tom mentioned this before? It was surely entrapment, he thought, but John was too polite to do anything but grimly nod and admit this was certainly a possibility. At least Beth would be there, and Alan too, so at least there would be some sanity. Ernest watched them warily from across the room, marinating in his own anger. John was being exploited, he was being abused, he was being harassed by everyone around him, and the worst part was that John did not seem to mind. In fact, John was enjoying his borrowed grace, which in a way was helping *How To Be A Good Person* deliver its promise: John finally had an outlet for his moral dogmatism, and he was suddenly cool because of it.

Behrooz heard of this amusement after school, which drove him to find Frank and see what he was missing out on. He read the first few pages as he walked toward the parking lot, nodding approvingly at the simple but declarative syntax. He had never put much thought toward computer fonts before, but Times New Roman seemed now all the more proper; no wonder why they used it for their English essays.

"Hey Frank, what's this about a club you're going to make next year?"

"Oh, you heard about that? I haven't thought it through yet. It's not going to be anything too elaborate, just a casual melding of minds and discussion space. In these immoral times we live in, I believe everyone should ask: where are those good old-fashioned values, on which we used to rely?"

Behrooz appropriately hummed the *Family Guy* theme song, and Frank smiled: the conditioning was already working perfectly; associations were being built between happy times and the club.

"This is good stuff. I'll try to finish reading this soon, and maybe I'll see you in the club next year. If you need more club officers, you should ask Alan. I can't really say so with any certainty, but I think he's been depressed about not being recruited into the leadership program. He needs something to sink his teeth into."

"I certainly will, Behrooz. Have a good day."

"You too, Frank," Behrooz said with a wave. Behrooz already considered himself a good person, but if there was one universal truth he was certain of, it was that everyone had room for improvement.

Alan's interest was piqued when Frank offered him a position in the club and immediately went to John to learn more, drawn by an inexplicable inner instinct that told him John was the one who had his best interests in mind. Alan knew little about what the text promised, only that it was new, exciting, and what everyone else was reading.

"John, what's this good person thing everyone is talking about?"

John turned around to see Alan standing right behind him, his foot tapping impatiently.

"It's good advice, that's all I can really say. There's nothing more to it. Are you going to join the club?"

"That's exactly why I was asking you, John. I don't know exactly how being a good person is going to solve my problems. I'm barely scraping by with an A- in math right now, can it help with that?"

"Well, Frank does have some innovative study strategies he shares, but beyond those, it's just general stuff. Little tweaks you can make to your state of mind that, taken as a whole, will make a difference. I wish I were as lucky as you to be given an opportunity to get in on the ground floor of this."

"So you're saying that I've been offered an exclusive privilege?" This argument was far better—why didn't John lead with this?

"All I'm saying is that when given an opportunity, don't let it pass you by. You won't know what you missed until it's gone," John said, his mind drifting toward Beth again before he snapped himself back to the present moment.

The school year concluded in a few weeks without any more lasting excitement, everyone eager to enjoy a break they all considered well-deserved. John boarded the bus and looked back at the school, which appeared just as menacingly big as before. The bus was especially crowded that day, and seeing his usual spot was taken, John went to the back and sat next to Beth, who seemed happy to see him.

"I don't feel any older. It's been a year, and this still feels like day one of high school," she said after some meditation and after the bus had sufficient time to proceed through the residential district surrounding Heller.

"Don't worry, tomorrow will be a new day. You may feel different then," John offered, and as he felt too tired to suitably appreciate that he was sharing oxygen with a special someone, he leaned back and closed his eyes.

Chapter 10

- -

John had already waited five minutes outside his house and was starting to grow impatient and cold. A crow suddenly called out, and he startled. Typically, his parents would have wanted to see him off, but it was early in the morning and they were so confident in his abilities that they didn't even supervise him packing his suitcase. Before he thought about going back inside to warm up a little, a van pulled up, and Tom waved from the passenger's seat. John could see Tom's father shout something at him, and Tom stepped out to help John move his suitcase into the surprisingly voluminous trunk. Tom and his father had spent a few minutes the previous night planning out their route, minimizing travel time in the order they picked up Tom's friends.

"Feel free to sit anywhere you like," Tom's father shouted in no particular direction when John squeezed himself inside the van.

"Thank you for doing this for us, Mr., uh..." John realized suddenly he did not know Tom's last name.

"Langley, but please, call me Steve. Bulldog, if you think that sounds cooler. I'm off the clock," Mr. Langley interrupted with a smile, offering his hand for John to shake. Tom frowned slightly—his dad never let Tom call him "Bulldog," which definitely did sound cooler. John always preferred to sit in the middle seat, or whichever would give him the most leg room.

He always felt tense on long car rides, something about the space being confined. John wanted to initiate some small talk with Mr. Langley, but he scared him for some reason; there was just something innately wrong with calling someone else's parent by their first name.

They drove through quiet streets through a commercial area and then to a gated community by the water. Lilac trees were in full bloom, even though it was early in the morning, and some geese wandered on the lawn. Mr. Langley ignored the posted signage politely asking all guest arrivals to wait at the entrance and instead drove straight in, past a line of cookie-cutter houses to an address that Tom confirmed on his phone. John looked up to see Beth lithely squeeze past his legs to sit on his right, waving hello before yawning dramatically. Without any delay, they kept driving, picking up Regina, who sat to John's left and immediately started talking with Beth, leaving his head aching in the crossfire, and Alan, who seemed disappointed that he wasn't sitting in the back with the others.

On long road trips, John typically amused himself by staring out the window and imagining what stories took place in the decrepit houses, gloomy caverns, or endless expanses of green they passed. Seeing a deer or an attractive bird would cheer him up for hours. Unfortunately for him, his view was obstructed by the people sitting next to him, and even though he could stretch his legs, he still felt trapped.

Regina was bursting with excitement—her parents did not believe in road trips, as they believed there were so many interesting sights locally that one could never get bored. This was true, to some degree, but a new exhibition at a local art museum did not qualify as "interesting" in her mind. She was with people who were her friends, or at least partially so—it did not take her long to warm up to Tom's enthusiastic stories of childhood memories, opening presents around the fire, and going swimming in the lake, which all served to convince her that Tom was so generous for bringing her to the best place since Disneyland. Alan struck her as boring, and since he immediately fell asleep to the gentle rocking of the car, he had no way of defending himself. She needed to share her excitement with John at once:

"What are you looking forward to doing most, John?"

John thought sagely, still staring straight ahead, and remarked: "Yes, this will be very relaxing. I am looking forward to it." He turned to Regina, expecting her to make some comment but instead seeing her smile thinly.

"What was the question again? I'm a bit tired." Regina gave up trying to talk with him, as he was proving boring, and continued conversing happily with Beth. John went back into his meditative trance.

After a few hours, by when the terrain outside looked rugged and unfamiliar, Mr. Langley proposed they stop to grab an early lunch somewhere; a quick vote was called, and everyone (including Alan, who had woken up from his slumber and immediately began regretting missing out on a few hours of social interaction) decided they were hungry. They pulled into a strip mall, and they climbed out one-by-one. John immediately wished he had worn a jacket, and Alan, still a bit drowsy, almost tripped over his own feet.

"Is In-N-Out fine with everyone?" Tom asked, and nobody cared enough to object. John never ate fast food at home, and was scared at the indulgence until the smell of fresh French fries hit his nose. Mr. Langley almost grabbed John's wallet when he tried to pay for their meal, pulling out a black credit card and signing the screen before John could cough up an objection. The kids all sat at their own table, as Mr. Langley needed to take a phone call outside; John could see him take bites of his burger as he talked, which to him seemed a bit rude. He sniffed his milkshake and burger suspiciously before taking a bite, the salt and fat making him wish he had thought of this years ago. Everyone else was smiling in approval at their meals, and so John did the same.

Alan found the pleasantly plastic surroundings comforting. The nice thing about fast food chains is that they standardize their restaurants: Alan was relieved to know that the food he was eating and the immaculately clean restrooms were all the same as at home.

"How long have you and your family been coming here?" Beth asked Tom, who emulated his father in talking with his mouth full:

"Ever since I could remember, we've come here at Christmas and during the summer like we are now. I'll have to show you all my favorite spots."

"You're so lucky to have a place like this," Regina commented; she had noticed Mr. Langley's credit card and had imagined herself a house as glitzy as Versailles.

"There's no such thing as luck in this world. That's what my dad always tells me. It's all hard work. My dad came from a poor family, and worked all his way through school to become a lawyer, and he maintained that fierce fighting spirit all the while. They don't call him Bulldog for nothing. One time, when he was talking with one of his clients from Apple, he—"

"We get the point, Bulldog is the best person ever," Beth said with a grin, putting a condescending emphasis on his father's nickname, and everyone but Tom and Alan laughed. When Alan thought of bulldogs, he thought of ferocious animals with teeth that rend flesh and a growl that makes others scream in fright. But beyond that, he hoped that by ingratiating himself with Tom, he would be privy to some of the same status he had. Alan wanted his own black credit card some day, one that would immediately demand obedience from anyone who saw it. Mr. Langley stepped back inside to find them as they cleaned up their trash and copiously apologized for his absence. They didn't notice, and until Tom had directed the discussion to his family, they had forgotten that he was driving them.

They climbed back in the van with full bellies and a bit more energy, and they were off again. The sunlight made patterns on the forest floor, and any residual traffic from the start of their journey had cleared up, so they drove quickly. When they drove by rivers, Mr. Langley explained how every fall, the salmon would swim through to breed in brilliant hues of red and green; everyone smiled at the image of rushing water and happy fish until he described, even more enthusiastically, how this created a feeding frenzy for bears and bald eagles. It was important in life to be like the bear, he always told Tom, and devour one's enemies wholeheartedly. John pointed out a bald eagle he saw perching on a rock to Beth and Regina, who immediately pulled out their phones to take photos before it went out of view.

"The symbol of America," Mr. Langley explained. Alan shared a fun anecdote about how originally, the national bird was supposed to be a turkey, but nobody besides Mr. Langley seemed interested. John began to grow bored of staring into space and ignoring the two chatterboxes next to him, and considered taking out the copy of *Don Quixote* Frank had loaned him. Many months back, after the musical, John had gone up to Frank to personally congratulate him on the show, not quite understanding the extent of his involvement. The next day, he had brought John his own personal copy of the book, entrusting him to do as he wished with it as long as he read it. Since that moment, John had the half-promise he mumbled to Frank squarely in the back of his mind, a promise that stared at him from his nightstand every morning and watched him play video games with a guilty look. It was a hefty tome, and John was just about to take it out before he remembered it was buried in his suitcase along with his swim trunks and underwear. And so he waited—Mr. Langley promised them that it would just be another hour.

The portion of the lake with their vacation home had many other homes just like it, none of which were particularly large; each was spaced from the other by a hundred feet of woods or so, enough that each could live in their own little plot of suburbia and believe that they were the only ones in the area. The particularly intrepid ones would take out their binoculars on the eve of sunset and look out from the upper floors of their homes to admire the palatial mansions on the other side of the lake, which had even more space between them and backyards for children to frolic.

Tom led the way with a careful stride up a slightly-sloped path that ran between flowers and a birch tree to the front porch, and took out the key his father had entrusted to him earlier that morning. Regina was disappointed—this house was no larger than hers! Mr. Langley led them on the house tour: Tom's old bedroom upstairs, with a few baby pictures of him and other children; the guest bedroom, with attractive olive-green tartan bedding and a pleasant smell of fresh linen; the master bedroom, where one lucky person would get to enjoy their own private bathroom; and downstairs through the small kitchen, with a dishwasher and coffee machine and spacious oven; the fancy dining room with china and silverware undeserving of teenagers; the upstairs living room with a rocking chair that Tom associated with his grand-parents; the bottom floor with the large-screen TV (a smaller model was in the master bedroom, yet another of its perks) and hardwood floor; the computer room that had served as an office for many harried professionals who never learned how to take a break; and the study, with a few solitary bookshelves and poor lighting that left the room constantly dim.

"Unfortunately, we only have three bedrooms, so two of you are going to have to camp out somewhere," Mr. Langley explained. Everyone but Alan graciously offered master bedroom privileges to everyone else, and so he eagerly hefted his suitcase upstairs. The rest played rock-pa-per-scissors, and the losers, John and Beth, were banished downstairs. John chose to sleep in the computer room, where there was just enough space under the desk for him to stretch out his sleeping bag. A small window in the upper corner provided a natural tone to the room, otherwise disturbed by the constant low thrum of the computer. Beth chose the study, and John followed her to look at the books. She pulled one off the shelf at random that seemed large enough.

"James Joyce's astonishing masterpiece, *Ulysses*, tells of the diverse events which befall Leopold Bloom and Stephen Dedalus in Dublin on 16 June 1904, during which Bloom's voluptuous wife, Molly, commits adultery. Sounds scandalous. What does voluptuous mean?" Beth asked, reading the back cover with mild disgust; the print was too small for her, this was clearly John's sort of book.

"Curvaceous and sexually attractive—well-endowed, in other words," John said without a trace of discomfort, and Beth giggled. John took a moment to look through the rest of the bookshelf, which was stacked with effectively every other classic novel one could think of. Initially stocked a few years prior by one of Mr. Langley's old golf buddies, every time someone came, they added a new book first so they could appear intellectually adequate, and then as tradition. There were even a few foreign-language books on the bottom shelf from people's international travels, in French, German, and a few languages that John could not identify.

"How's Louis doing, by the way?"

"Louis was a mistake. We broke up." John offered his condolences insincerely, as if he had not imagined this conversation in infinite variations long ago.

"It's no big deal, John, it's just the circle of life. I moved on long ago."

Well, why didn't you tell me "long ago," John thought to himself; on the positive side, this did retroactively justify his dislike of Louis, as he had clearly wounded Beth dearly. Someone called from above for them to come back to the front door, and Mr. Langley stood on the threshold chatting with the Monroes, who lived next door and were old friends of the family. Unlike many who came to the lake, they had moved there permanently about ten years ago. Mr. Langley took the opportunity to wish them adieu and begin the long drive home, and the rest of them stood politely unsure what to do next.

"You're all here alone? Do you think you're going to do any cooking?" Mr. Monroe asked, somehow conveying geniality despite his resting frown. John stumbled out a "Sure... um... we certainly could," not wanting to offend his newfound neighbor. "Well, don't worry about going to the store or anything, we can take care of that for you. It's nice to see some new faces around here. And if you ever want us to stop by and help with the cooking, my wife and I would love to help. All of you look like you could use some meat on your bones!" he responded, chuckling a bit. Once again not wishing to offend, John and the others thanked them, and as promised, a few hours later a few bags of nice groceries with a few printed-out recipes arrived on their doorstep. There was no receipt, and John began to worry before Tom assured him and Alan, who was starting to wonder as well, that to their generous benefactors, the expense was equivalent to a cup of coffee.

"What are we going to do with this?" Alan asked when he saw yet another container he couldn't confidently identify. He and John took point on unloading the groceries, examining unfamiliar labels and wondering if this was the sort of food adults ate on a regular basis. John held a jar of capers and swirled it, not sure if it needed to be refrigerated. The pantry was already fairly well-stocked, and Alan was happy to see familiar foods like cereal. He did not think of himself as a picky eater; rather, he had discerning tastes. The others immediately went to their rooms and changed into their swimming clothes; they were promised a lake, and if they were not there to swim, how else would they occupy their time? One advantage of their premium location was easy access to the water, and all they had to do was go out the sliding glass door downstairs, walk through the garden, open the gate, follow the path just a bit more, and voila, their own private dock. By the time John and Alan finished putting away the groceries and chased the others frantically outside, they were already swimming.

"The water's warm!" Tom shouted. John took this as an invitation to jump in, and immediately regretted his decision. John's breath flew out of his lungs, and he switched to treading water by instinct, just as Ms. Stevens had taught him. The lake was peaceful; it was too early in the season for the tourists to flock here by the dozen and drink beer on motorboats, and so the only noise was them splashing each other and just being kids. Swimming tired John too quickly, and he pulled himself up onto the dock to take in the view. Tom promised that at night, there would be fireflies that cavorted, blending in with the real stars. For John, swimming was exertion, something inextricably tied to school bells; he could never be like Alan and do a cannonball without shame, or be like Beth and take compliments on her sleek, black swimsuit in stride. She sunned herself on the rocks like a Siren. John felt ashamed of his bare chest, his ugly shorts, and his lingering shivers from the water. All he wanted was to go back inside.

They prepared dinner that night from one of the recipes Mrs. Monroe had given them, Tom reading out the steps one-by-one while Regina and John tried to work together amicably. Regina avoided her usual shenanigans, not wishing to inadvertently put John on edge and mess up the meal, or worse. It would be an inauspicious start of their trip to have an ambulance take someone away on a stretcher. They sat at the dinner table, uttering unfamiliar phrases like "Beth, would you please be so kind as to pass the potatoes?" and "This squab is exquisitely cooked! Compliments to the chefs!"

"It was all Regina and Tom, not me at all," John shyly commented, looking at the place settings again in case he had made an error; John could never remember, although he had never put any thought into remembering whether the knife went on the left or right.

"This is delicious!" Tom proclaimed. "What bird are we eating again?"

"This is pigeon," Alan explained. He had never eaten pigeon before, but in his mind, one bird was close enough to another bird where it didn't matter. He took a small helping of vegetables and tried to mask their flavor.

"Probably one of the pigeons that got stuck inside Mr. Reinhardt's classroom that time," Tom joked. That was the highlight of his day: Mr. Reinhardt screaming German obscenities while chasing an apathetic bird with a broom all through the classroom, everyone else sitting at their desks too scared to move a muscle. Beth suddenly found her appetite dissipate, but she choked down the rest of her dead pigeon with a smile.

That night, nobody could come to a consensus on what to do, so they segregated by gender: Regina and Beth went downstairs to continue watching some sort of drama that John thought sounded uninteresting, and the others sat upstairs for a brief bout of vigorous conversation that rapidly faded when nobody seemed truly interested. Tom, who sat on the couch across from the fireplace, could not help but think something felt out of place. Last time he was here, there were stockings hanging safely out of reach of the roaring fire, a Christmas tree with a collection of international ornaments accumulated over decades stood not far from the entrance, and he and his family were sitting and relaxing. His father would, after much polite urging, would saunter over to the piano and play some Christmas carols, and all the men would sing in a beautiful baritone. They would be summoned from their evening peace by the smell of freshly-baked carrot cake, a family tradition, and they'd sit around the table and laugh well into the night. Tonight, the fireplace was off (it wasn't cold enough, and they were scared they'd burn the house down), and nobody dared talk. The piano was unused, although Regina promised she'd play for them at some point; Tom never enjoyed playing, but he could muster up a little ditty if he really wanted. He would have been a great proficient had he tried, his father always told him.

Slowly, everyone went to bed, finding it unnatural yet oddly comforting to say good night to their friends. John and Beth, isolated from the rest, were the last to see each other, and John immediately began to wonder as soon as he closed his door if he should have slept on the couch. The computer room had the personal touches of many of its residents, which combined created a homey yet eclectic setting. John was most scared of the taxidermied raven, which on the top of one of the shelves seemed to stare into his eyes. He shined his phone flashlight around the dark room to see two black orbs, darker than the rest, reflect back at him. That's definitely not creepy at all, he thought to himself.

John slept soundly and woke with the sunrise due to the lack of curtains. He gently put on some socks due to the cold floor and tip-toed outside his door, noticing that the door to Beth's room opened sometime last night. He averted his eyes and moved upstairs to give her privacy, even though there was no way for any outside observer to tell that the long lump on the floor was her. John resolved then to finally begin his book, and he took a seat in the rocking chair, which once again had that unusual quality of beckoning to him. The light filtered through the blinds behind him perfectly to let him read without turning on a lamp, and for once he did not feel tired.

John was in a comfortable rhythm by the time Beth came upstairs to see if anyone else was awake. She had expected to be the first one up, but somehow she was not surprised to see John relaxed in the rocking chair, slowly moving back and forth, his feet like unhurried compass needles. She had not intended on reading that morning, but it was still too early to eat breakfast, and none of her friends would be awake already, maybe with the exception of Juliet. She went downstairs to her room and took more than a cursory glance at the books, picking *1984*, which had a short title and seemed cryptic enough to be amusing. It was a bright cold day in June and the clock struck 7; that was the first time John had heard a grandfather clock, and he looked up to see Beth similarly startled. She waved tentatively, and John did not know what to say.

Beth still could not resist the temptation to check her phone before she started reading, and felt a minor twinge of guilt. John projected the image of a scholar, and there she was, checking Instagram. Fortunately for her, Juliet was a constant person, sticking to simple routines when convenient; this included Instagram, where she tried her hardest to post twice a week, and through no particular artifice but being a teenage girl on Instagram, she had accumulated close to 2000 followers, a respectable total indeed. Her Hawaii vacation intersecting with their lake trip was fortuitous, even if at the moment Beth was sad the trio was not complete: Juliet had made her first in what would be a series of daily posts chronicling her vacation. There she was, lounging on a beach towel with the shade of an umbrella just within view, sunglasses perched above her head, holding — Beth did a double take: a copy of *How To Be A Good Person?* "A bit of light reading," Juliet had written with a few garish emoji, and all the comments referencing her chosen tome were along the lines of "damnnn smart and sexy" instead of anything substantial. There was no indication in her smile that this was anything but a spontaneous gesture. Frank was just as surprised as Beth: he had woken up half an hour earlier, and nearly dropped his phone in astonishment when he saw a text from Juliet with that same picture and a similar, if more personalized caption, sent without any sense of irony. He promptly shared her post on the new official How To Be A Good Person Club Instagram page, which he hoped would slowly build traction over the summer until the movement crested. Beth considered showing John, but he didn't seem like the sort to use social media.

Alan turned out to be good-natured, generous, and likeable. In three days no one could stand him. He was still of the peculiar notion that his performance at the lake would be graded, not only on participation but on zealousness of execution, with the reward being hitherto unknown.

Even though he woke up late, he did not let that stop him from inserting himself into whatever discussion was taking place downstairs. Alan insisted on being as nice, as sweet, as kind, and as good as he could possibly be, and took it as a personal slight when the others politely declined his repeated requests to do their laundry. He had even, seeing some of the thorough glances Tom gave the girls at the lake, crawled out of bed early one morning to come down and fraternize with Beth. If Regina had been awake then, he would have tried in vain to have an insightful conversation with her, too; Alan was never one to discriminate. After all, a participation grade was a participation grade. It was only due to his incompetence that Beth did not realize he was trying to flirt with her, and Alan gave up and started playing on his phone.

The morning after Regina learned of John and Beth's new reading ritual, she woke up to her alarm a few hours before she ordinarily did, and turned over to shut off her phone before she remembered why she had woken up so early. She stood up and stumbled over to the bathroom, looking over herself to make sure she could be seen by others. After combing her hair and brushing her teeth, all done quietly as to make her sudden arrival a triumphant surprise, she leisurely walked down the stairs, holding onto the railing in case she should trip and fall. Beth was surprised to see Regina up so early, and surmised she intended to impress John, who unfortunately did not react beyond a mumbled hello. Regina walked over to John's armchair and leaned down, reading the title of the book and sounding out the words, all while staring directly at John, who still showed no reaction to the proximity of her face. *"Don Quixote...* have you read Marquez?" Regina asked, still standing in John's personal bubble. Surprisingly enough, Regina had in fact read Marquez and enjoyed his work, and she assumed that as John was clearly reading a book with a Spanish name, this related factoid would impress him. He could even sit up, his face then even closer to hers, and ask her in that silky voice of his to educate him. This inquiry not receiving the correct answer, more extreme measures were needed, and Regina went to the study and, carefully stepping over Beth's sleeping bag, took a book she had heard of before and returned to the living room, sitting on the couch a few feet away from Beth; as she started reading, she glanced up at John frequently to see if her bold move had aroused his interest. She wished to say something very sensible, but knew not how.

Tom greeted John, Regina, and Beth in his usual fashion, slinking down the staircase and looming behind Beth, who was in her usual position pinned to the corner of the couch. He never failed to startle John, who was usually so enraptured in his book that beyond a vague notion of the others arriving and greetings then routine, a sudden voice seemed insensitive. Tom's arrival created a before and after, as Regina could no longer hold her composure and pretend to be solely focused on her book, and Beth shook her head to rouse herself from her chosen tome. It forced John to accept that happy silent reading time was an impermanent reality, and by the time of Tom's arrival the clouds tended to part over the lake, revealing an ordinary day that lost its eerie quiet. Tom had not yet gotten over his initial surprise that most of everyone else he had invited wanted to read books for fun. He saw that Regina was the least interested, and asked her what she was reading:

"Looks long. What is it?"

"Some Greek guy goes on a sailing trip to find his father."

"That would make a great movie." Tom was certain he had seen something with this exact same plot before, he just couldn't put his finger on it. That bothered him.

"There's more to it too, I think. It's deep."

"An acute analysis," John muttered from his chair, and Regina smiled at the compliment (finally, he called her cute!) until she realized he was not talking about her. They then proceeded to a late breakfast where Tom skillfully manned the pancake iron and reveled in his authority. He tried to make shaped pancakes, but aside for one that resembled

Mickey Mouse after an unfortunate encounter with a train, he failed miserably. Alan came just in time to taste one of Tom's culinary innovations—adding dark chocolate shavings—and immediately complimented him on his prowess: the best meal yet, he claimed. Regina was hurt that her squab was not sufficiently appreciated.

John proposed they take a walk through the woods that day instead of going to the lake, hoping for some form of recreation that did not involve going partially nude; even taking showers in the downstairs bedroom gave him anxiety, simply knowing that his peers were but a few feet away. Everyone else agreed, and those not already dressed changed quickly and loitered by the door. For all their time at the lake, the weather had remained constant, and today was no exception. Regina took a selfie with all of them as they left, Alan trying in vain at the last minute to become the center of attention and John still surprised that phones had cameras on both sides. They saw the Monroes walking in the other direction, and assured them they had been cooking and functioning as adults without any problems.

"Teenagers these days are too wimpy. They have no integrity or principles whatsoever. I'm glad all of you are an exception." When the Monroes had walked sufficiently out of eavesdropping range, John turned to the others:

"Were they being a bit condescending just now, or is it just me?" John disliked any sort of affable condescension, whether it was coming from teachers or other authority figures. That level of nuance was beyond his comprehension, and John was far too paranoid now about mixed signals to appreciate what they had to offer.

"For what do we live, but to make sport for our neighbors, and laugh at them in our turn?" Tom considered this sort of social interplay a ritual of life in high society, one that if John and the others kept coming with him on vacation, they could learn to appreciate. The fundamental principle which Tom's father had imparted in him at a young age was never to question another's morality.

"Some of these people grew up in a different era. Things were simpler. Easier. Better. And understand that if any of your elders say something that you dislike, they know better than you. Trust them. Someday, you'll appreciate their wisdom." Tom had treasured that lesson then, even as he found it increasingly hard to maintain as he grew older and wiser. Was it really true that the poor were only there because of laziness? Were "good genes" the key to athletic and academic success? Tom worried he was betraying his status by considering any of these topics in great depth.

John considered philosophical discussions of a deeper nature as he continued reading *Don Quixote*; he turned to Beth one morning and asked plainly and abruptly, without any particular exigence:

"If God is out there, why do people die? Why can't we all live happily ever after, without a care in the world, without disease, without such unpleasantries as tooth decay?"

"If God isn't out there, why do people laugh and cry, why is nature beautiful? How could any of us ever engineer a sunset or rainbow?"

"I don't know. I just want to know why He created pain." John had just read a particularly gruesome passage about Sancho Panza receiving lashes, and did not know why anyone would find that anything but tragic. But why then did everyone in the novel think it comic?

"The God I believe in is a good God, a just God, a merciful God. He's not the mean and stupid God you make him out to be," Beth said with a tinge of arrogance; she thought it far too early in the morning for him to questioning any of her beliefs. Alan came down early that morning, and looked at John's book with initial incomprehension, and then looked at him with disgust when he saw how quickly John had been plowing through the book.

"I don't understand why you would ever torture yourself with some-thing that long." Alan thought tools like Sparknotes were manna from heaven, intended to save everyone the trouble of literature, although with his new moral allegiance, it was perhaps time to disavow himself of that opinion. But that thought was supplanted in his mind by just how weird John was being by daring to read something with such small print. How crude.

"It's not torture if I enjoy it," John remarked, still avoiding eye contact.

"You don't need to pretend to enjoy it, you know. That's an unpleasant personality trait." Beth and Regina, who while enjoying their books with far less passion than John, certainly did not want to tolerate a personal attack on one of their own, looked at Alan with fearful horror. Alan knew then that he had messed up, and backpedaled furiously:

"I mean, well," he stuttered, "if you do enjoy it, that's even better!" Alan then went to the kitchen to pour himself a bowl of cereal, and consoled himself by thinking that he was no less of a good person for his slight. Men talked, they sang and danced! They amused themselves with countless pleasures and intrigues, some of which involved the written word, and many that didn't. He and the others proceeded through the rest of the day without any more mention of that morning's controversy. It was their last full day, and they frolicked in the lake with renewed spirit. Their routine played out in a familiar pattern: Regina would compliment Beth on her swimsuit, Alan would engage Tom in some sort of swimming contest to assert dominance, John would lazily tread water until he felt a chill to the bone and exited, and they would take turns in the showers afterward. They ate dinner, today moussaka, with the same concentration: John and Regina were still proving to be a dynamic duo in the kitchen, Alan and Beth cleaned up, and Tom was an accomplished master of "mise en place" if he knew what that term meant. They sat around the living room with heavy bodies and tired minds, and they all decided to go to bed early that night—their schedules were synchronized and their minds were one.

"A glooming peace this morning with it brings," John remarked to himself as he ascended the stairs. No longer would he be able to see his friends in such unprecedented casual moods. Beth languorously reading with her book held aloft, in bare feet and pajamas like she was at a slumber party or posing for some needlessly modern tableau, had by then seemed a part of his morning routine, just like brushing his teeth or applying deodorant. Before he could finish the very final chapter of *Don Quixote*, Tom came down, already dressed; he parted his hair frantically, as if he expected to be presentable in the early morning.

"Can I ask you for some advice, John?" John nodded—what was he going to do, say no?

"I am an open book."

"What is it like to be in love?" John found this question elementary. He could think of no love story more archetypical than that of his very own Don Quixote and Dulcinea del Toboso, the innocent peasant girl who did not even have the faintest idea that such a gaunt, cultured, witty knight could fall for her. He thought a moment, synthesizing in record time all his accumulated life experiences, and concluded:

"Lechery provokes the desire, but it takes away the performance." For John, the idea of taking initiative was unfathomable when it came to affairs of the heart. He had seen what happens when people entertained such fancies on a whim, and when did it ever end well? John avoided the sort of romantic comedies where anguished declarations of love in the rain would wipe away any trace of anger, even if he could imagine himself as the star. Perhaps Regina was right; to be fair, she never said any such thing directly to John, but what else could be inferred through her behavior? A more recent example he had to work with was *Romeo and Juliet*; how was Juliet, anyway? He had heard second-hand of Tom's occasional attempts to impress her, although seeing as Juliet was not at the lake, those clearly could not have gone well. It must be strange to be named after a teenage lover, he thought—did that create some sort of obligation to perform, an expectation of impetuousness leading to tragedy? By presenting himself as one not opposed to the occasional catcall or ogling of swimsuits, Tom seemed far better suited to these sorts of roles. He could easily sweep away anyone or dance a waltz with beguiling charm, or at least any person John could imagine playing the opposite role. John found his classmates excellent templates for psychological profiling, especially as they presented themselves as such great studies at the lake and at school. He described to Tom exactly what his diagnosis was, and how this was sure to ensure his success in any future romantic endeavors.

Tom did not understand John's point, but as it sounded like John was complimenting him in some way, he thanked him. Tom had by then picked up on Regina's continued inclinations toward John, and also John's very own partiality toward Beth. And now, he found himself warming up to Regina. Maybe it was just an unique quirk of the teenage mind that drove any young boy, finding himself in a position of authority, to immediately think fond thoughts about the nearest attractive person in a swimsuit. Juliet qualified, but on a phone screen she seemed so far, and so Regina it would be. Tom had also by then discovered what woes befell those who confessed their affections in a needlessly elaborate way, and he had patiently waited all week for a private opportunity. As it turned out, in a house with five people that proved hard. Tom sat for a few minutes with his head in his hands, trying to remember exactly where Regina would always sit, but could not conjure in his mind's eye anything but shadowy forms; disappointed, he returned upstairs.

John made one last survey of the house for any of his personal belongings he had forgotten, clutching his copy of *Don Quixote*. He had finished without any pomp and circumstance, and now was a man reborn. He had no need for his compass, he thought, and so John tucked the book right where Beth's head was when she slept. That spot felt right.

Mr. Langley knocked on the door precisely when he was expected, and they took their bags and left.

Chapter 11

The new sophomores flooded the halls on the first day back from summer vacation invigorated with new purpose. They had a sacred responsibility, or so they were told, to mentor the younger generation just as they had been mentored themselves. While they got to arrive at school late and act casually for a bit, as soon as the second bell rang, all bets were off. They looked no different than the freshmen: perhaps on average they were a bit taller, and spoke with deeper voices, but to the juniors and seniors, who also populated the halls with their own new purpose, they were still young and innocent. It was a simple binary in their mind: if a student were younger than they, they were cute, innocent, and naïve. If older, they commanded a grudging respect while they waited for them to graduate and clear the stage.

Frank, Alan, and Pranav had chosen to arrive early to debrief all that had occurred over the summer; walking as a group of three, they were stopped by one overzealous teacher by the parking lot asking if the young freshmen needed any help finding the theater before another teacher waved hello and rescued them from ignominy.

"To be young again," Frank laughed. They made their way past the locker rooms and up the ramp to the central courtyard, choosing a table that was not damp from condensation. As soon as they sat down, Frank pulled out folders from his backpack containing last-minute paperwork and notes.

"Why aren't the other club officers here? And why is this guy here?" Alan asked, pointing to Pranav, who Alan thought did not look at all like a sophomore.

"It's early, and I wanted to make sure the most important people were here," Frank answered, looking at Pranav knowingly. This was technically true, if not in the sense Alan thought: Alan was there so he would be suitably on-board with the club activities that day. Frank had neglected to tell Alan, and all the club officers in fact, that their club was grounded in a satirical text; he did not view this as an important detail. It was rare that clubs met on the first day of school, but a good person plans ahead, and Frank certainly wanted his first day to go off without a hitch. If his social media experiments were any indication, a sizable percentage of the "popular kids" were going to attend, either of their own volition or because their friends insisted. As to not disrupt Mr. T's bemused tolerance of the impending chaos, he had announced that membership would be capped at thirty members, with all meetings recorded on the off chance someone really had nothing better to do after school (Mr. T just so happened to keep expensive recording equipment in his cabinets of wonder). This announcement, made the night before school, prompted fast responses from people like Juliet and Behrooz, all gleefully announcing their intentions to be there. Frank woke up the following morning and forgot for a happy few minutes exactly what he had done over the last few weeks until he checked his emails to see a few anxious freshmen trying to reserve spots in the meeting. This is bound to be interesting, he thought.

"That doesn't answer my question: why is he here?" Alan did not like surprises, and with his belief that the draconian methods Frank had planned for that day were good person boot camp, any deviation from his conception of lunch that day was already a failure on his part, and Alan did not like failure.

"Pranav," Frank said, emphasizing his name with mild disappointment that Alan was being so bossy, "is a consultant. Yes, he's a consultant. He has extensive leadership experience, and has studied the text extensively. He's a mentor, in many ways, to me." Pranav nodded in approval, and resisted the temptation to chuckle. The plan was simple: Alan would be the only officer who knew of Pranav's involvement, and even he would be misled. Armed with his self-assured superiority, he would keep the secretary and vice president in line for Frank, Pranav, and all of their other friends who wanted to get in on the action. Pranav didn't even know the other club officers' names, and he suspected Frank didn't either.

"Cool. So, Pranav, what will you be doing during the meeting today?"

"I'll be in the back. Just watching, taking notes, consulting." Alan seemed disappointed. "I'll also be in charge of the ID cards. That sort of boring stuff which really should be handled by experienced people." They kept talking until more people started to show up and their secret meeting could not really be considered secret. Alan saw Behrooz walking up the ramp, and went off to greet him; Frank and Pranav waited for him to leave, then fist-bumped each other.

Behrooz smiled when he saw Alan, and immediately wanted to know how he enjoyed the lake. By then, the sting of not being invited had worn off, and Behrooz listened attentively while Alan described just how refreshing the water was, how comfortable the bedding was, and even how they had cooked real, adult meals.

"Sounds like summer camp," Behrooz commented while Alan kept rambling about how much fun everything was.

"Oh, no, I have bad memories of summer camp. This was so much better. So much more mature. The others even read books!"

"And were you one of these people?"

"No, of course not." Behrooz felt a bit better knowing that were he invited, he wouldn't have enjoyed it at all. As soon as the bell rang, they went immediately to their classes, not wishing to be trampled by all the freshmen who didn't know any better.

John distracted himself talking to Ms. Baldwin, who he saw talking to an overly eager freshman and desperately wanted to end the conversation. She pointed the freshman toward one of the club's advertising posters across the hall and nearly shoved him out of her classroom before she turned to John with a smile. They exchanged the usual pleasantries about their summers, and John let himself be swept along in the tide to Mr. T's classroom for English. Mr. T's classroom was decorated in the same way as it always was; he popped the skull of his skeleton from its spine and held it in front of him, mockingly remarking "Alas poor Yorick, I knew him well" before reattaching it. The only new decoration John noticed on first glance was yet another club poster, this one taped on the door as to give every student leaving a reason to come back later. John was happy to see Beth in his class again, lukewarm about Juliet, and let out a visible groan that Mr. T quietly noticed when Regina walked in immediately after he did. John performed some quick mental arithmetic and came to the conclusion that Beth plus Juliet were better than Regina alone, and decided to sit next to them. It would be temporary, anyway, and they were all happy to see him, which made John feel better. Far better that, he thought, than sitting with people who disliked him.

Mr. T waited for everyone to sit down and get their first-day jitters out, then began in his usual casual manner:

"Welcome to advanced English! Some of you may know me as your health teacher, but I wear many hats around Heller, and you'll see me most as an English teacher. If any of you are taking AP Government or Japanese, you may also have me as your teacher. Nobody? Oh well. Anyway, these seats that you're sitting in now will be your seats for the rest of the school year, assuming no major issues come up. I hope you know your compatriots well, and if you don't, there's a first time for everything."

"Isn't this great? We're all going to be best friends!" Juliet whispered to the three others, although John assumed that comment was directed at him. John's attention was firmly on Mr. T, however, and he did not pay her comment much heed.

It took John the better part of English class to realize that Beth and Regina were not the consummate intellectuals they were at the lake, or at the very least, their seeming passion for reading did not extend to literary analysis. Regina he could understand: it was blindingly obvious in retrospect that she had not yet shaken her crush on him, but Beth? She could simply be a casual reader, he supposed. But a worse possibility existed, one that took a few seconds to reveal its elementary logic to John: was Beth flirting with him too? It seemed a strange possibility that two attractive girls could be interested in him, but if one was, did that not open up the floodgates for more? The marginal probability of attraction presumably did increase after the first; if one were ugly, and John had been told by others (namely Regina) that he was attractive and sure to attract a lot of female attention, naturally most would be superficial and not exhibit attraction. But if one were attractive enough for one person, who knew how many silently stood behind them? What if he had once again misinterpreted something more for mere kindness? But anyway, John was daydreaming again. He could hold himself together until the bell rang.

"Oh, before I forget: during lunch today, either come quickly back here or watch the live-stream of the inaugural How To Be A Good Person Club meeting. Frank has been working hard to deliver everything he promised you all last year, and we're expecting a high turn-out, so I hope to see you all there," Mr. T said to conclude class, and all of his students bubbled with speculation.

"Are you coming?" Beth asked John, who looked at the posted flyer with unfamiliarity.

"Oh, yes, I would love to. Thank you for inviting me."

"You know I'm definitely coming," Juliet beamed. "It would be the epitome of neglect for me to disappoint my Instagram followers. Regina, you should join us too."

"Such fancy vocabulary, Juliet, you sound like a real intellectual. I'm impressed," Regina responded, carefully avoiding making a binding commitment.

"Why thank you! I try my hardest. A person's vocabulary reflects their education and intelligence." Beth was not looking forward to attending a club where everyone talked with such a similar air, but it was the first day of school, what else would she do?

The three of them reunited during lunch, and encountered a crowd of people massed around Mr. T's door. They saw that people were being let in one at a time, wherein they were given a piece of paper to write their name and grade and then had a photo solemnly taken against a white background.

"I feel like I'm in a prison lineup," Beth said to Regina, and the two of them laughed.

"Don't smile! This isn't a football game!" Alan told Juliet, and she tried her hardest to not blink due to the camera flash. The desks were spaced out in an even grid, and Frank stood ready in the corner, sternly watching those who came in. When exactly thirty people were seated, he gave a signal and the door was closed, leaving a few disappointed students outside. Frank walked up to the podium and began:

"Today, all of you will begin the hero's journey, from the shameful little brats you are now to proud, intelligent, and most importantly, good people. You have taken the first step by coming here, and for that you should be proud. That makes you automatically better people than those outside, with their faces pressed up against the door—do you see them?

They were late! They were tardy! And as all of you will know with great intimacy, they are losers! We live in a cruel world. Those who are weak, perish. Those who are not weak, thrive. Shakespeare wrote: some are born great, some achieve greatness, and some have greatness thrust upon them! Starting today, we will be thrusting our greatness upon you, and with great vigor at that! Alexander Hamilton wrote that energy in the executive branch is of utmost importance, and I wholeheartedly agree with him. Now, are you leaders or followers?"

Most of everyone seated shouted that they were leaders.

"Correct. Stanley, please escort that kid who said he was a follower outside. We don't need any negativity in here." Stanley did what he was told and dragged the freshman out, ignoring his frantic apologies.

"As leaders, we must be role models for those unenlightened. All of our actions need to be precise, in accordance with the highest code of conduct we can possibly maintain. Given that goal, we are not going to spend today lecturing on philosophy or theory. People learn best by doing. Alan, please sit down at that empty desk. Now, stand up!" Alan stood up like a rocket, posture straight, and saluted Frank with a sharp "Yes, sir!"

"At ease," Frank commanded, and Alan sat down. "Now, etiquette is of utmost importance. You are to address myself, the other club members, and any faculty with these new standards. We are all equal here. Understand? Now, everybody, stand up!" The club attendees imitated Alan's positioning, and Frank walked with the other officers and corrected their form, moving hands gently to people's sides and cautioning those whose gazes were not firmly forward to avoid sloppiness.

"Sitting is also an art. Keep your spine straight, hips facing forward, hands clasped together unless you are writing something. Imagine you are posing for a portrait. Very good, Juliet. Stand! Sit! Now, the walk. Observe how I walk with my elbows at a sharp right angle, my feet straight, and my hips forward yet again. One foot up, one foot down,"

Frank explained as he paced in front of the class. "And you will see that with practice, this becomes quite natural, and with practice you will find your speed increasing until you reach an appropriate demeanor."

John found himself learning these new positions quite quickly, marveling at how he had been doing everything wrong his entire life. He found comfort through routines and habits, as following those freed up his conscious thought processes for more interesting topics. He hummed along to the military march Frank played to teach them proper walking rhythm, and he knew for certain that he had made the right decision in coming.

"It is also of utmost importance to correct your classmates when they inevitably make errors. Now, you may find yourself thinking: 'Frank, why should we try to convert the simpletons to our side? Didn't you just tell us they are of inferior moral constitution, full of nasty habits like drinking bubble tea, and actively scheming to destroy American society as we know it?' But what each and every one of you must understand is this: we are good people. We are altruistic—do you know what that means? It means that we know that society is only as strong as our weakest link, and that when one of us fails, we all fail. Where we go one we go all. Look at these sheets carefully that Alan is handing out. Frequently, throughout the day, you will engage with your fellow club members here, as well as any who are watching online. If you observe any violations of etiquette, journal them as the sheets instruct. Also fill out evaluations for yourself if you think you've erred, otherwise you won't improve. A good person never makes the same mistake twice. Now, I am a nice person, I'm not some wannabe totalitarian dictator—nobody is going to be punished here. Just remind them nicely to be better people, and if their conduct is so seriously improper that it reflects on our club as a whole, we can have a little chat and see what can be done, how about that? I hope I can trust all of you to keep each other, and yourselves, honest, and as long as each and everyone of us in attendance does that, we shall have an unified front against those scary people out there. This is a brave new world, indeed, but I am not scared. And I hope none of you are scared either. It is unreasonable to expect that when we live in such a vast ocean as this, that those out there not on our side will easily be converted. In fact, it is a childish instinct that drives them to reject our wisdom—but we must expect such petulance. Eventually, as we bide our time, they will unconsciously begin mimicking our actions, and we shall overcome all obstacles in our way." This was fun! Frank saw that there were only a few minutes left in the period, and decided to wrap things up.

"Typically, we will begin every meeting with this, but as you are all adjusting to these new rhythms of life, I wanted to ease you in. Everyone, stand up, hands over your hearts. Face the flag. I pledge allegiance to the flag…"

"With liberty and justice for all," Behrooz concluded solemnly. His leadership meeting unfortunately overlapped with the club, but nevertheless, he could not miss out, and he watched the video live from his phone. Ms. Foster gave him an approving look. "Good on them for doing the pledge. People start crying about civil liberties when us teachers do it in class, so I'm glad that someone has taken up the torch."

"This week has somewhat of a special schedule, so because of that, I won't see all of you assembled after tomorrow until next Friday. There is no homework tonight besides practicing discipline, but after the next meeting, I will expect all of you to have read *How To Be A Good Person*. There will be a quiz. The Navy SEALs have a saying: it pays to be a winner. While I cannot grade you, as this is a club, you will have the opportunity to earn Frank-Bucks. Think of them as brownie points or little merit badges. The most commended members here will earn a prize at the end of the semester. Now, go enjoy your last few minutes, and practice all those terms of proper conduct that we went over today. The philosophy starts tomorrow."

Frank thought it miraculous that all of the thirty-odd people who showed up at the beginning of the meeting stuck around until the end. At the end of the meeting, everyone stood up in unison as previously instructed (and modeled by the plants in the audience) and thanked Frank before dutifully filing out and signing their names. They couldn't wait to come back tomorrow to receive their ID cards and learn more about the fundamentals of being a good person. Alan left quickly, as his next class was on the other side of the school, and so Frank and Pranav did a final clean-up; surprisingly enough, everyone had taken the initiative to pick up their litter.

"Have we met before, Pranav?" Mr. T asked, now finally standing up from his desk to break the illusion that he wasn't listening the entire time.

"I don't think we have. In any case, you'll be seeing a lot of me here, assuming we don't get shut down within a week."

"A pleasure to make your acquaintance, in any case," Mr. T said as he extended his hand. "Any friend of Frank's is a friend of mine."

Frank walked into Mrs. Huang's class a celebrity. Regardless of if they cared, it was impossible for anyone else in the class not to have noticed at least one person besides Frank walking as if they were in the Marine Corps, greeting their fellow club members with salutes and everyone else with a dismissive sneer. A few mockingly saluted Frank as he walked toward his seat, a gesture he returned with a smile.

"How many people came?" Mrs. Huang immediately asked him; Mrs. Huang valued her lunch periods too highly to willingly spend them with students she did not know, or else she would have done this reconnaissance herself.

"We had exactly thirty in Mr. T's classroom, and I was told we had a hundred watching from the library. I was not disappointed."

"You see," Mrs. Huang gestured toward the rest of the class, "this is how you become a leader." She gave Frank a salute jokingly, and she began her lecture without any further distraction.

"This year, we are only going to speak Chinese in class, understand? You are advanced students; all of you are extremely intelligent, and if you want to do well on the AP test next year, it is imperative we begin now. We are also going to begin weekly cultural tests! To learn a language, you must know the culture! We are going to start by learning about tea. All together, read out loud: tea is China's traditional drink..." The less proficient students looked at their papers with confusion while everyone around them read flawlessly, if unenthusiastically. How was this supposed to help them? They all drank tea at home, and beyond knowing which teas they liked or disliked, it seemed unnecessary to be able to explain the fine artistry inherent in different types of tea leaves. Many were not used to only speaking Chinese, and even Frank was somewhat reluctant to speak in class, despite his usual enthusiasm. But by the end of the period, most were comfortable with the new scheme of things, and those who weren't went to the administrative office to drop the class.

The last thing Ernest needed to overhear was two freshmen in the hall talking about how fun the club meeting was. It was enough to hear Mrs. Huang gush about it in front of the entire class, despite knowing nothing about it but its name and progenitor, but now he had proof that the contagion had spread beyond the more radical elements of the school. Granted, he knew nothing about what happened in the meeting, although if he had known most of it was Frank connecting a good person's moral foundation to walking single-file and standing up on cue, he would have collapsed more than he did when he ranted to his parents after school. Earlier they had read the manifesto after hearing about it from another parent and, like Mrs. Huang, thought it accurate if a bit harsh. They considered his worries overblown and his attitude uncharacteristically paranoid, but Ernest knew he wasn't crazy. The worst part about it was that Frank seemed to be doing relatively little to market the club at this point; his cronies had taken care of all the hard work for him already. Even after only one meeting, word of mouth was infinitely more effective than anything one person alone could muster. So, in essence, he was not only a cult leader but a lazy one too.

Frank, who considered himself very much not lazy, happened to be walking by Mr. T's classroom after school on his daily patrol to make sure all the club posters were placed just so and none had been defaced. He didn't really expect that to happen, but he knew only the most notable of clubs would ever receive such special attention, and so if he noticed anything awry whenever he decided to conduct spot checks, he would know he'd made it. He checked Snapchat once more to see if anyone else had posted photos; Frank did not use Snapchat to communicate with others, ever, but he did frequently use it as a surveillance tool. He was supposed to avoid social media, but no good person would pass up having a live map of their classmates accessible at all times.

Someone tapped Frank on the shoulder, and Frank fumbled the stapler in his hands and turned around with a forced smile. Juliet laughed like they were old friends, and she and her friends saluted him with various degrees of crispness.

"Do you need any help with those flyers?" Juliet asked sweetly, adding a "sir" at the end in case it was required.

"Great meeting, by the way, I learned a lot, sir," Regina added, not wishing to be left out of the conversation. Regina considered first impressions extremely valuable, and unlike some, she was used to the idea of regimented drills and thought it no different than learning new choreography.

"I think I'm good on these, ladies, but..." Frank added as a seeming afterthought, not wishing to abandon the opportunity in front of him, "I could use a few more pictures for our Instagram account. Mr. T always sticks around after school, so if I could politely entreat you for a few minutes of your time, I would greatly appreciate it."

Surprisingly enough, Beth was the first to say yes; she and Juliet needed to stay at school for cheer practice anyway. Regina didn't want to be a contrarian—it would be very disrespectful to someone who had already volunteered so much of his time for them—and Juliet never said no to a reasonable request. And so Frank knocked with two sharp raps on the door and entered. Mr. T was an accomplished multitasker, and thus never minded pleasant students coming in to say hello at any time; as befitting his custom, and as they were distinguished students with many exemplary traits, he offered them miniature English trifles from his refrigerator. "Testing out a new recipe," he said. "I promise they aren't poisoned."

"This is delicious. Could you do us the favor of letting us take a few publicity photos in here? We'll be quick, I promise," Frank asked after tactfully swallowing his first mouthful; he made a mental note to Google a recipe and try making one himself.

"Go ahead, I trust your judgment. Maybe you could lecture to the three of them while they all lean in with curiosity, here, I can hold the camera," Mr. T suggested. "Try writing something on the whiteboard while one of you takes notes—Juliet? Thank you for volunteering. What do you think? Come on, we're at school, this isn't *Playboy*. This is what kids consider normal these days? Frank, you're fine with this? Well, if Fujiwara-sensei let them pose like that for Fashion Club, this can't be any worse—I have champagne flutes and sparkling cider if you think they'd add that classy aura. You're really pulling out all the stops, aren't you? Don't bump your head, Frank." As promised, a few minutes later, they finished, and Frank politely shooed them out of the classroom before he would be forced through obligation to follow them. Mr. T turned to him with a smile.

"You certainly have grown into your new responsibilities, Frank. Be careful, though; if you turn into Charles Manson, I'll get in trouble. I can't even imagine the paperwork. How well do you know them?"

"Not terribly well. I've talked to Juliet the most out of the three of them, but I've tried my hardest to prevent that from spiraling out of control. She certainly possesses an interesting temperament—have I mentioned to you before how she gave me the idea for my little manifesto?"

"You didn't, actualy. And here I was thinking that you're the sort of person who spontaneously comes up with such outlandish ideas."

"I remember vividly our conversation that day. I don't know what put me in such an agreeable mood—I guess some of her energy rubbed off on me." Mr. T gave him a curious glance before Frank elaborated in greater detail.

"That makes it all the more surprising John wanted to sit next to them in English class. As a teacher, I'm used to developing first impressions extremely quickly, but there is more to some than meets the eye. You and he would get along quite well; you both have an interesting sense of intellectualism. And before I forget: what do you think your club will sell at the food fair next week?"

Frank knew exactly what Mr. T was hinting at, and burst out in maniacal laughter: "Kool-Aid."

Chapter 12

John followed a reliable schedule every morning during school days: he would wake up to his alarm clock, which he kept on the default tone; look out his bedroom window to decide what sort of weather it was that day; put on clothes without much regard for fashion or style, only instinct; stumble to the kitchen and make himself a bowl of cereal with a glass of orange juice; brush his teeth, by now used to the unpleasant taste of the toothpaste; wave goodbye to his parents if they were awake; and walk a few blocks to the bus stop. John's bus stop was located across the street from a grocery store and bakery; some of the other students would have pastries and coffee while they waited, and some would have Doritos and Gatorade. He had sometimes considered grabbing a croissant or something, but it didn't feel right. He would grab a newspaper and start reading it while he waited for the bus, which was dependable enough to always show up right when he was starting to become absorbed in whatever he was reading that day. Still barely awake, he would get on the bus and find a seat that was to his liking; often, this would be a seat across from Beth.

Beth wondered what it was about the newspaper that John found constantly fascinating every day. Once she had picked up a copy at her bus stop, expecting something vaguely political or economic, but she only found updates about board meetings and a new chain of salad bars. John seemed like the type who would attend board meetings as a recreational activity, but until she suddenly developed an interest in the banalities of suburban life, no more newspapers for her. That left her on her phone most days unless she had homework to do. One morning, when she was in the mood for conversation, she asked John how he was enjoying his newspaper; the answer, she assumed, would be the same as on any other day, but if she were lucky it would start a conversation. John looked up, surprised as usual, and dropped the classifieds page in his astonishment. Beth, not knowing if John held a particular interest in antiques or plumbing services, bent down to return the page to him, carefully avoiding crumpling the paper. Still in a generous mood, and worrying that he did not in fact need the classifieds page, she saw that his right shoe was untied; John had never quite mastered the double knot. As she was already bent down anyway, she then took the initiative to tie John's shoe for him, all while maintaining a casual smile that conveyed this was normal etiquette and just what friends did.

"How are you on this fine morning, Beth?"

"I'm fantastic, how are you, John?" Their conversations had grown more frequent due to the club, which encouraged small talk between fellow good people as a means of boosting camaraderie. Beth and John were both reserved enough to generally avoid this whenever possible, but after the newspaper, the ice was broken and it would have been weirder, they thought, not to continue acknowledging each other.

"I'm hanging in there, I'm hanging in there. How are your friends?"

"What a funny coincidence, John, I have some exciting news about one of your best friends, but I don't know if she told you already."

"Do tell. My interest is piqued."

"Regina and Tom are officially a couple now." John dropped his newspaper again, this time picking it up before Beth could. Tom and Regina's courtship was brief, so brief that Beth had no knowledge until she saw

Tom and Regina holding hands in the hallway after school and forced her to explain what happened.

When Tom asked Regina the first time if she'd like to study with him, she was so happy to finally be the recipient of the inquiry that she said yes immediately. The same logic applied a week later when Tom proposed a more romantic trip to the mall. Regina had discovered through trial and error that while John was not opposed to eating lunch with her occasionally at school, shopping was a no-go. She even left the opportunity open for other, more John-suitable social events, but John found movie theaters smelly, and he didn't seem like enough of a foodie for lunch out on the town (more precisely, as he seemed content with a sandwich or some variation thereof daily, would he really want a manicured salad? Or even more precisely, would he look happy and Instagrammable while eating one?). Unlike that self-absorbed, cynical, holier-than-thou John, Tom was able to make the first move, and that combined with his smile and desire to treat her to lunch (at nice restaurants, too) was a winning combination. Her prince had come.

"So Regina, I saw your Snapchat story. Tell me everything," Juliet said eagerly before school one day. Juliet had a nagging suspicion for a few weeks then that Regina took more away from her lake trip than she had previously said.

"Well, at first he asked me to help him study for a chemistry test, and we just hit it off after that, you know?"

"You certainly have chemistry with him. I cannot think of anyone who would have been more eligible than he; he's truly a man of good fortune. What is he like?"

"Strong, witty, assertive, sweet... he's just so many things. I don't know. He's great."

"Are you a couple yet, or just good friends?"

"A couple of good friends." Regina winked, and both of them laughed.

"What first attracted you to him? I mean, yeah, we both know he's awesome, but was it his strength or wit?" Juliet thought it a bit tactless to say it outright, but she suspected that Regina was infatuated with Tom for more reasons than just the physical. Tom tried his hardest not to flaunt his wealth—and it was really hard for him, because he often wanted to badly—but everyone could see from his clothes and the Ubers he took to leave school that he had more than he let on. He had learned from a young age some classic paternal wisdom that he thought applied to his new friendship with Regina: "Everyone has their price, Tom. You can get anyone to do anything you want if you find what they want and give it to them." He knew Regina's family was closer in financial stature to him than the poverty line, of course, but Regina was so happy to be in the presence of wealth that he couldn't help himself.

"His voice is full of money," Regina said suddenly.

John was going through a similar set of mental gymnastics to process all of Beth's new information; his jaw slowly dropped and he sputtered slightly, fragments of words falling out. It hurt to know that Regina was so fickle; even if he did not reciprocate her affections, he appreciated the idea of someone having affections for him. In fact, that idea was almost better than the real thing. It comforted him slightly to dismiss this new romance as the result of bribery. John considered himself principled, and most importantly, frugal: he saw no reason to spend the money he earned from his grandparents or his weekly allowance on trivialities. There were times for generosity, but spending money as a means of gaining someone's affections was effectively enabling prostitution.

Prostitution was thus added to one of John's many moral fears. He had an active imagination already, and every Friday, as he heard his fellow club members blow the whistle on kids smoking marijuana in the restrooms, discreetly fornicating in class, and playing poker in the band room after school, he became all the more certain it was his responsibility to fight back. John volunteered every week in the "morality patrol," who would go around the school during lunch, pick up trash, and chastise those who were considered to be human trash. He didn't care much about the socialization, or the respect and wary looks their special new uniforms offered them. What mattered most was that he was doing his part to make Heller a better place.

"Today, I want to talk about willpower. It takes a special mind, a culti-vated mind, to do what we believe is right in the face of overwhelming odds. All around us, people encourage us to sin: our morality patrols have seen lizard-like temptresses lounging behind the school, smoking and hollering and encouraging our people to join them. But nevertheless, we resist. Would any of us here care to share some personal anecdotes about how they have displayed willpower? Go on, tell us in your own words." Mr. Cathcart had suggested once to Frank that he join the improv team; why would he when this was so much fun? Frank got an outlet for his creativity, the school was a bit cleaner, it at least looked like his classmates were along for the ride, what more could he ask for?

John found it immensely gratifying to identify temptations in his life and ignore them. He sometimes wondered if the elementary school drug training was accurate and that hooded men would emerge from the bushes and offer him cocaine; he had rehearsed his courteous denial many times, mumbling to himself exactly what his teacher had told him then. He talked about some of these experiences at the club meeting when prompted, explaining how he ignored the lecherous glares of his depraved classmates. It did not occur to him that Beth and Regina would realize they were the subject of some of these anecdotes. Frank, having no knowledge of the newspaper from that morning and misremember-ing the Regina incident as hopelessly romantic, was proud of John for showing some spine. The fellow club members' polite applause, enforced as to encourage members to grow comfortable with the environment, emboldened John. He knew that he was doing the right thing, and he prayed fervently that the others would follow suit. He had heard Beth once talk about how the Lord was her shepherd while at the lake, on some occasion when he needed a Biblical reference explained to him, and he hoped Frank could shepherd him and other wayward souls toward a brighter future.

"Alan, were we supposed to add the salt first before we shook the vial? If so, I forgot." Alan let out an exasperated sigh, then flipped through his disheveled lab notebook and slid it across the lab bench to Behrooz, the instructions open. Behrooz read the instructions again, then looked at his own copy just to make sure. Behrooz gave Alan an apologetic look.

"Argh, do you realize how much effort it will be to redo those last three steps? I thought you were the science guy." While Behrooz was initially excited to be in the same lab group as Alan and John again, his excitement rapidly faded once they started doing labs. Biology was a safe science, as they knew it: the samples of vegetables they placed under the microscope were at no risk of spontaneously combusting or spraying acid. Chemistry was a different sort of beast: an inventive modification to procedure was not met with "Write that down, I want sixth period to try this" but instead "I don't know what chemical you just made, but to be safe, everyone exit the classroom immediately!" There was nothing improvisational about chemistry, and Ms. Denham made sure that Behrooz understood that after class when the above incident happened.

"You're a leader now, Behrooz. You can't let these things happen under your watch, or even worse, do them yourself." Behrooz apologized copiously. But this wasn't really all his fault, he thought while watching Alan and John squabble about which color their solution was on the pH strip. John was a natural butterfingers whose hands were rarely steady unless he was holding a pencil; Behrooz tried coaching him on this once during lunch, with no noticeable improvement, and had even gone to Ms. Denham, who unhelpfully suggested John wear bicycle gloves. Alan was assertive, and took great pleasure in being right and far less in being wrong. He insisted on precision, wasting far too much time making sure the meniscus in every test tube was right where it should be; at least his hands were steady enough to pour precisely. Whenever Behrooz encouraged Alan to speed up and skip these needless steps, as soon as another error was evident in the results, it was clearly due to a missing milligram of copper sulfate pentahydrate and not because Alan read a 1 as a 7. Behrooz thought he was the only person capable of taking the middle path and steering their sinking ship, and this stress gnawed at him; his test scores were not always up to par, one field where John and Alan had zero issues, and a few times Ms. Denham had asked him with genuine worry if he was suffering from anxiety.

These worries came to a head one day after a long weekend, when the three of them were working on yet another lab; this time, by some miracle, they had seemingly managed to do everything correctly. While they waited for their gelatin to denature, Behrooz reached into his backpack and brought out a bag of Iranian pistachios. The highest quality in the world, he promised—did any of them want any? John said yes without any question, and Alan sniffed his warily before doing the same; they didn't quite resemble the pistachio ice cream he was used to. They stood there, cracking shells and chatting away, Behrooz glad this icebreaker worked, until he looked up to see Ms. Denham looming over them furiously.

"What do you think you're doing?"

"I'm being efficient, ma'am, fueling my brain while we wait—healthy food leads to a healthy mind. It's what being a good person is all about," Alan explained in a tone he sincerely meant to be instructional but really sounded condescending to Ms. Denham.

"You really take that document seriously? But no, you cannot eat those in class; do you realize how expensive it would be to fix a machine that has a little piece of pistachio wedged in it somewhere? Or if one of your classmates is allergic to nuts, inhales some dust, and goes into a fit of anaphylactic shock?"

"We're sorry, Ms. Denham. I do not think this is the time to question my moral principles, as we are doing science." Alan had inadvertently become the spokesperson for their group, and he was doing an awful job at it; once again, Behrooz regretted not taking charge.

"Don't be sorry, just do better," she said with a sigh, muttering under her breath something about the deficiencies of the high school English curriculum.

"Oh, by the way: do you want a pistachio?" Behrooz asked, undeterred by her negativity.

"Well, I don't see any harm," she said, and Behrooz put a few into her waiting hand.

Pranav found Frank after a club meeting one day, who was excited to see a sane person with whom he could have a normal conversation.

"What's up, Pranav?"

"I understand you're busy these days, but could you spare an hour to look through my English essay?"

"Certainly. What are you reading? Still *The Scarlet Letter*?"

"Yeah." Pranav's enthusiasm for English sagged as the class delved into *The Scarlet Letter*; he viewed the overstated symbolism and the unremarkable plot as relics of a bygone era. He understood what he was reading, as much as there was a lady and her creepy devil child, and this level of understanding combined with well-chosen literary analysis was sufficient for class if not his enjoyment. Frank found this fascinating, or enough to spend hours editing his essay. His feedback was meticulous, insisting on a far higher standard than Pranav's usual; Frank did not believe it was sufficient to only draw conclusions from the text, but also explain how those conclusions bolstered the thesis. After a rigorous editing session, they created a finished product that Frank was happy with and Pranav was too tired to reject. When asked if he wanted to borrow the book, he said he'd get his chance next year. Their collective efforts were rewarded, so much so that Pranav's English teacher, Ms. Liu, was flummoxed:

"And you said a sophomore helped you?"

"Yeah, Frank. He's the guy who's running the How To Be A Good Person Club. You know, the one with the morality patrols based on his manifesto."

Ms. Liu laughed loudly. "I have a meeting in a few minutes, but I'm going to need you to tell me all about this later. Just how you said that, so deadpan, means there's something interesting going on. This is Mr. T's club, right?"

"It's his, but he doesn't do much. He sits in the back and grades papers."

"He and I need to have a little chat." Someone knocked on the door, and Pranav took the opportunity to exit.

Mr. Simon's classroom was positioned awkwardly at the corner of one of the buildings, with massive windows in the back to let in enough light that even when he had the lights turned off, the room appeared in chiaroscuro. When the lights were turned on, the light was blinding: it reflected off every table and every wall, and his students developed headaches at a rate above the school average. They were watching the same documentary about the Third Wave that Mr. T had loaned Frank previously, and were taking notes furiously. At times Mr. Simon would stop the documentary and ask for questions.

"Mr. Simon, sir! Psychologically, why do people go along with these movements? I always think of it as a natural human instinct to seek freedom, democracy, and equality, but this seems to be everything but that. I can't believe it happened so close to us," Beth asked smoothly, no longer stumbling over her now-standard salutation. A few students in the class snickered, and Mr. Simon was about to deliver a rambling segue about how Beth was answering her own question in a remarkably astute way until he realized she saw no irony in this.

"Well, that's a very good question, I must admit. Does anyone in the class want to take a stab at answering it?"

"Well, Beth, as much as I appreciate your optimism, I don't think it really holds true in most cases. Society is founded on discipline, everywhere we go, and standard power structures. Mr. Simon lectures to us, and we stay silent in our seats because it's how we've been trained. There is no physical force restraining me from standing up, as I am now, and walking toward him, but I can see that all of you are looking at me with horror because I'm violating the social order. I think it is a natural human instinct to respect people in power, even if they are authoritarian, because those in power tend to come with solutions to problems. In the documentary, they talk about academic performance improving, and as I look around this classroom, I can tell that a few certain someones have tidied up Mr. Simon's room for him. Imagine you're a poor farmer somewhere, with nothing to live for besides raising pigs and eating potatoes—someone comes over and says that he can make you rich and cure the blight affecting your crops, and all you have to do is to wear a swastika on your arm, you're going to take that offer without question. It doesn't matter if you value freedom or not, he's the one in charge and you have to respect him," Ted gleefully answered. Typically he would not be this verbose in class, especially without Tom to egg him on, but his approach had been doing wonders for his grades. The less he studied, the better he did, and Mr. Simon appreciated his habit of giving accurate answers in class. Ted even went as far as to tutor some of his classmates, offering his own unique perspectives on the subject matter covered. One area he still struggled with was coherency, often stringing together chains of related thoughts to such a degree that by the end, nobody knew where he started, but Ted was a flawless imitator and merely spoke as Mr. Simon did.

"Ted, how can you constantly provide such astute and timely perspectives? Are you a time-traveler sent from the 1960s?" Mr. Simon asked him after class, when Ted and Beth both lingered.

"I don't think there's anything special to it. All I try to do is put myself in the shoes of those historical figures and think: if I were them, what would I have done?"

"That's not as easy as you make it sound. But anyway, I'm glad to see that you're helping people like Beth out when they need it," Mr. Simon said meditatively.

"I appreciate it very much, Mr. Simon. Ted has helped me a lot; I don't think I would be doing nearly as well as I am in your class right now without his help," Beth contributed. "I do need to leave for cheer practice now, but thank you once again, sir." She left in a hurry, and Mr. Simon turned to Ted once again.

"You know, I don't really mind all the 'Mr. Simon, sir!' stuff. I appreciate the respect, and I do think the classroom is the right place for that. But I'm a bit out of touch with what's hip these days, Ted, so you'll have to help me out here: is there some new teenage trend that's driving all this, you know, strangeness?" Ted nodded.

"Well, it's that How To Be A Good Person Club, they're teaching people to do all of this."

"Obviously I know about that, Ted, it's barely fifty feet away from me. But no, it's more than that: I've been teaching at Heller for longer than you may think, but I don't quite remember this level of idiocy and blind zealotry. If it wasn't the club, they'd be bottle-flipping or something instead, and I'd be asking you what primal instinct drives people to throw their garbage on the roof." Ted shook his head as if to say that he did not consider himself one of those blind zealots.

"I don't want to take up too much of your time, Ted, but I don't know how I can change my curriculum to foster the same sort of healthy academic curiosity that people like you possess. It's like all of my students, no matter if they address me as sir or not, were hit on the head by a hammer when they were little. I'm fighting a losing battle here."

Ted considered himself many things, but "academic" was not one of them, and he was starting to feel contempt for Mr. Simon. He was just another teacher who was stuck in some byzantine labyrinth of bookshelves and didn't know anything about who they taught. Ted was regretting doing so well in his class now—if anyone else heard about this, he no longer would be the cool kid. Ted thanked Mr. Simon generously for his time and left, and Mr. Simon went back to his desk and started grading yet another batch of worksheets devoid of insight or creativity.

Chapter 13

E ven before stepping inside, Regina always adored the appearance of the Waterfront Pavilion, the dim sum restaurant Juliet's family owned. She loved the fountain in front with lily pads and koi, the red-and-gold hues of the building, the Chinese name plastered in similar gold lettering, and the line stretching out the door. She had a table for two already reserved, so all she needed to do was wait for Tom, and then they could sneak past the line with quiet apologies and go right on in. Regina's parents had misgivings about her choice of restaurant, having appraised Tom the first time they all met as cordial, if unadventurous; couldn't she have gone for pancakes or something? There was nothing wrong with a good old-fashioned breakfast of hash browns, poached eggs, and sizzling bacon in their mind, but Tom was so nice in letting Regina choose where they went to eat, and the last thing she wanted to do was waste a good opportunity.

Regina discovered a few facts about Tom quite quickly at brunch, soon after Tom showed up fashionably late to the restaurant. For one, Tom did not know how to use chopsticks. Or, he did, but his skill was limited to stabbing the food he wanted to pick up. Before he could massacre a char siu bun, Regina had to politely lean over and explain how to use them correctly, showing with hers how they moved together. After about thirty seconds of Tom trying all angles of attack to pick up the aforementioned char siu bun, she politely suggested he use the fork a kind waiter presented him.

Tom also had no idea what he was eating or why. Tom simplified the dishes he was eating into a few different types. There were the bread things, which generally had a white, fluffy exterior or maybe a sticky, translucent casing, inside which there were blobs of paste that were pork, shrimp, or some combination thereof—he really could not remember. There were also rolls or something of the sort that were wrapped in a type of pasta, he assumed; these tasted pretty good. Tom's culinary expertise perhaps did not extend much to Asia, but at the very least he ate out frequently and was not a picky eater; he took some pride in being a good sport and trying everything, even enjoying most of what he ate.

The chicken feet were a tougher sell: Regina said they were called "phoenix claws," which seemed to Tom like one of those schemes parents used to get kids to eat their vegetables. He did not like the idea of playing with his food, which refused to obey his fork, and they did not taste like chicken or what he imagined phoenix to taste like.

"How do you like the food?" Regina asked warily. Even though she could see Tom was smiling, she was still concerned: if his jolly exterior concealed some inner disgust, he may not let her pick where they ate ever again.

"It's all very good. Very exotic," he commented in between mouthfuls, and Regina politely laughed. She didn't think anyone else around them would consider the food "exotic," but Tom was most certainly entitled to his own opinion.

"I'm not sure if that's how I would describe it, but I do agree, it's quite good."

"So is this like a standard Sunday brunch sort of thing?" Tom asked with curious eyes. His dad would love this place.

"Kind of. Well, not always, but at least once a month," she explained, trailing off when she saw Tom more interested in the bamboo steamer than her. As Tom began to get into the rhythm of eating the new foods that Regina seemed comfortable with, he took a moment to look around the bustling restaurant, admiring the owners' panache to have lobster tanks and old ladies pushing carts instead of traditional service. He also remembered that Juliet's family owned the restaurant, and he smiled at how humble their story must be (he'd have changed this reaction had he known that this was one of a chain of equally bustling restaurants, which combined made Juliet's family quite well-off by his standards). He wondered if Juliet would show up in an apron right out of the kitchen, grease stains and all, asking how they enjoyed the food that she had made. When he got up to go find the restroom, he couldn't help but laugh at the winding path he had to navigate to get there, past waiters giving him the stink-eye for walking too slowly and the décor that seemed too fancy for an ethnic restaurant. He second-guessed that latter observation when he came back to his seat and looked at the menu with prices listed: this was well within his budget, but he expected a Panda Express level of bargain.

He went as far as to make a third judgment, realizing that he was the only white person there. He shared this observation with Regina, who found it hilarious:

"Yeah, I guess you are. Typically there are some others, but it's not like anyone cares. You're standing out more by not using chopsticks than anything else." Tom suddenly felt a pang of shame. He looked at the soiled fork and knife in front of him, then looked around and saw that the only other person with a fork and knife was an old man with trembling hands, who still somehow managed to use them more dexterously than he did. He wondered then if the young kids who looked at him with an awe-struck expression only did so because he looked different, like a stranger. He was unique, he stood out, and for reasons entirely beyond his control. Tom couldn't wait to leave, and fortunately both he and Regina were getting full. Tom flagged down a waiter, paid the bill with a smile, and they took a few last sips of tea before leaving.

Tom's initial hypothesis was proven true in part when, as they were about to pass through the grandiose lobby and wave the lobsters good-bye, Juliet walked in with her parents for their lunch. Hasty introductions were made, and the subject of their conversation immediately became Tom.

"Have you ever had dim sum before?" Juliet asked with a smile, and Tom shook his head. "What did you eat?"

"I forget the names of everything; Regina, could you help me out?" Regina did her best to remember and list everything, and everyone but Tom laughed when she mentioned the chicken feet. Tom said politely he liked them, and Juliet's mother said something in Chinese that everyone else laughed at, only reinforcing further in his mind that he was an outsider. There was no shame in that, he was told by Juliet's parents, who exhorted them to come more frequently and try more stuff on the menu; still, why wasn't he the one in charge? Regina's parents drove up quickly after they left the restaurant, and she thanked him generously again for brunch and left; Mr. Langley arrived soon afterward to pick him up, and Tom immediately explained everything he ate, the squishy turnip cakes and the chewy sesame balls, with a youthful excitement.

"I haven't taken you here before? I guess I must have come with work buddies or something; the food's great, but it's so crowded. If you liked it, we should go another time. I want to see you try bitter melon." Tom was surprised his father was in such a good mood; it must have been the chicken feet story, which caused a rare laugh. He was hoping his father had never been before, just so he would have something to hold over him, but Tom felt like he was only the butt of yet another joke.

Over the next few hours, clouds heavy with rain rolled in, and the day turned from a cheery blue to something desolate and clammy. John resisted the wind as he walked with his family back home from their afternoon walk, and he laid out his raincoat and umbrella in his room in anticipation of tomorrow morning. John slept to the sound of rain and woke up to the sound of rain, and he ate his morning cereal in dreadful anticipation of his morning walk to the bus stop. He expected to hear thunder as he walked, but only saw rain pour in streaks and everyone else foolish enough to be out in the early morning walking in haste. He grabbed his newspaper as usual and nestled it under his jacket for safekeeping. The bus arrived just before John started to worry, and he sat near the front like he always did. He saw Beth a few rows behind talking with some people John had never seen before, but he paid her little heed until he looked up once absentmindedly and saw her clutching something that to John's uneducated eyes, happened to look like an USB drive or something of the sort. It can't be, John thought to himself, but it was too late.

His first reaction upon seeing Beth take a heady drag of an e-cigarette was to inwardly scream in horror. As he saw her take it out of her jacket pocket and move her hand toward her lips, he wanted to lunge forward and knock it out of her hand. It would then bounce harmlessly on the padded seat and land on the floor, when she would then wholeheartedly thank him for doing the right thing. He was paralyzed by fear, however, and could not even open his mouth to gasp. His second reaction was to dismiss what just happened and look back at his phone. She didn't know better yet. The club had not talked about drugs yet, although they had just finished a fascinating nutrition unit that John enjoyed primarily because of the free food, and the general advice about doing no harm clearly had not marinated sufficiently. Content with this explanation, and all the more sure that Beth would make a good pet project for later, he sat quietly like any other day until the bus arrived at his destination, his face frozen.

Beth thought little of this, and she did not even notice John's horror; even if she did notice his facial expression, she'd have thought it merely another one of his strange flights of fantasy. Vaping was an occasional habit for Beth, one that none of her good friends indulged in, and one that many of her bad friends indulged in far more frequently. It was a minor compulsion: some days just called for a little bit of nicotine, and there were not nearly enough of those days for her to think she had a problem. That was why she avoided doing so in polite company. She did not remember how she started; probably at a party of some sort, maybe Louis's? He seemed like the type. In the past, her worries had always been if her parents found out, or her good friends—she would be excommunicated! Now, her worries also included the club: Beth could handle a few rumors based on furtive glances, but not a full public shaming. If she were doing something illicit that could be framed as morally good, that would be another story. If, for instance, she were a modern-day Robin Hood, shoplifting from drug stores for the good of the homeless, she could tolerate a smear campaign. But sadly, the PR team behind the proliferation of e-cigarettes in every form in every school could not loan its protections to her.

While John believed himself to be sufficiently recovered from that morning's shock, chemistry class turned out to be a surprising reminder. First, a quiz on combustion, which left John reeling with self-doubt over exactly what carbon dioxide was and why it was that things were set on fire, including tobacco and marijuana; then, Behrooz happened to discreetly ask him about Beth. Behrooz had motive behind his inquiry, as much as he tried to convince a John clearly on edge for some strange reason that it was innocent. Recently, Behrooz had gotten into DJing as a hobby; this had the full support of his friends, including Tom, who one day went shopping with him at a fancy store in San Francisco and gladly footed the bill for hundreds of dollars of equipment. Happy early birthday, Tom had said; Tom was eleven months early, and Behrooz still did not like Tom, despite his charity (Tom privately hoped that if he invested in Behrooz now, he would DJ for free at his parties, saving money in the long run and giving him cool kid points). At a party where Behrooz was helping out just to be nice, he happened to talk with Beth casually, who to him seemed immensely attractive on first sight. Behrooz knew that John and Beth were something approaching friends, and without any particular desire to learn what nuance there was there, decided that John would be a good judge of character.

"I don't know what I can say, Behrooz. I'd have to think about it," John lied. John had plenty of nice things to say about Beth: she was friendly, intelligent enough without being annoying, attractive, and currently single. Then again, he had seen her take a fatal puff, one that would race through her trachea to stain her pristine little alveoli black as coal, a blemish that would eventually spread through all her lungs and internal organs until she was reduced to a coughing, sputtering mess. The details of what she did wrong were irrelevant, all that mattered to John was that she had done something to make her less of a good person in his eyes. John considered himself to have exacting standards; maybe Behrooz was less discerning.

"But surely you can find something to say about her, John. This isn't a test of anything, I'm just curious. Give me a few adjectives you'd use to describe her." John thought for a moment, then reluctantly suggested Beth may be considerate, lively, and complex.

"What do you mean by complex?" Behrooz asked. To him, that seemed like a cop-out.

"I view her as one of those people who can't be summarized by a single word. But really, I think we ought to move past that crystallization of identity. It's dehumanizing." Even though Behrooz appeared annoyed, John continued, far too interested in where his train of thought was going to stop: "You know, when we were reading *The Catcher In The Rye* earlier, I was thinking about that exact same point you brought up.

Somebody like Holden Caulfield is defined by his rejection of society. He doesn't fit; he's like a puzzle piece for the wrong puzzle. He sees people acting in what they perceive as a normal way and doesn't understand why they're all dancing around like marionettes on strings with class or dignity or whatever you want to call it. It's awfully bourgeois, if you think about it: everyone running around like ants to appease their monarchs. At first, when I was reading, I didn't understand where he was coming from. I thought he was a spoiled brat who couldn't handle failure; a bad person, if you will. But the more I read, the closer I come to this realization: I am Holden Caulfield. You are, he is, she is, we all are. We all have a bone to pick with a system that doesn't really give a damn about any of us. Society tries to shove us all into little boxes, and when we don't fit, it cuts off our limbs until we do. Everyone always tries to give us advice, but it doesn't mean anything until we experience it ourselves. Learn by doing, you know, take a few risks. Don't listen to the orthodoxy." The bell rang, and John immediately left, proud of having articulated his point so clearly.

Ms. Liu could not believe that students queued outside Mr. T's door every week for a chance to be let into a propaganda session. It wasn't as if this were a casual affair for the attendees, either: Frank assigned readings in preparation for discussion, as this reserved the full extent of his half-hour for more exciting topics. Frank had found an introductory philosophy textbook online, and used it to source readings when *How To Be A Good Person* or his prior knowledge proved insufficient. At the beginning of the week, he and the other club officers would identify a few prospective readings, beginning an email chain that always resolved itself quickly. Someone would make a PowerPoint quickly, Frank would fill it in with his own insights, and the week's work was done on that front. While some of the initial hype had died down from the first few meetings, calculated public-facing initiatives like the morality patrols ensured that everyone who mattered knew of the club, and Frank never had any issues filling seats. One could not casually attend the club without being seated in the corner reserved for people who were insufficiently prepared; those who sat there were envious of the others, who were treated like adults and not children. Frank did not know why his meetings were so popular, despite them offering little of value besides passionate lectures.

One of his main theories was that some of his attendees, namely Beth, Regina, and Juliet, attracted a good percentage of the male coalition; he mentioned this to nobody but Pranav, who thought some of the attendees would struggle to find a date otherwise. There were other female attendees, certainly, but Frank did not know them as well and therefore paid them little regard. Beth attended out of a lack of self-esteem, and she vainly searched for advice that she could follow to actually feel better. There was plenty of advice that the club told her ought to make her feel better, that was for certain—retooling her wardrobe required some thought, and many outfits she enjoyed were filed away for weekends and vacation, but the people who were most happy with her changes were her parents. She had tried to explain to them once exactly what it was she was doing at school, but when they seemed to respond poorly to the idea of an especially charismatic classmate embarking on a moral crusade, she told them instead it was for Christian Club. They were fine with that, although privately, they were not sure if it was right for a public school to display such Christian morality publicly, and made a mental note to bring it up next time they were at Heller.

Regina's personality was extremely malleable and thus subject to the influence of peer pressure. First, this came from her friends and John, but recently, Tom had been a lot more bullish about attending weekly, and even participated in some of the morality patrols. Tom had avoided actually reading *How To Be A Good Person* for a long time, instead relying on his friends' summaries, but after a few weeks he was suddenly quite curious to know what sort of text justified their new behaviors. Tom quickly realized he was reading a work of satire, if only because it was so out of character for how Frank behaved otherwise; Frank initially denied Tom's accusations, calling him ridiculous and clearly feebleminded in some way, but dropped the act when Tom made it clear this only increased his passion for club activities. It was no big inconvenience for Regina to attend the club with Tom, and she also weighed the chance of scandal in her mind: if she were to suddenly stop attending, would they spread rumors about her, accusing her of having never been devoted to the cause? She considered herself extremely principled, and there was no room in that moral foundation for any inconstancy.

Juliet found herself with a plethora of reasons to attend club meetings. It was only thirty minutes per week, ones she'd otherwise spend eating alone in the sunshine and studying. Juliet also wanted to keep her grades up: she had recently injured herself during cheer practice (through no fault of her own, she thought), and came out of that experience with a broken ankle and a slight mental fog, both of which only made it harder for her to do as well in school as she wanted. With a remarkable amount of free time cleared up in her schedule, Juliet sought new hobbies: more yoga was a start, being something physical she could still do, and reading more was also something she could do without pains. Frank had been so kind, after all, to provide a list of recommended books in his manifesto, and when she texted him one afternoon asking for recommendations, he did her the favor of responding quickly. Her afternoons were then occupied by literature, at least whenever she was in the mood. Frank's positive feedback, delivered over text and at school in bland, impersonal remarks only made her more certain she was doing the right thing. More importantly, her grades were back to normal.

When Ms. Liu learned Pranav attended the meetings, she correctly assumed he was there to expedite the chaos, and was not disappointed when he recounted, starting from day one, all the club had done.

"So it's like the Third Wave without the Nazism, right?" she asked, just in case the answer was no.

"Effectively, yes. Frank has a list somewhere of the craziest club activities he could think of, and he's slowly checking off everything."

"Do you want me to do any advertising?" Pranav, not wanting to inspire another riot of bombast, politely declined. Pranav viewed Ms. Liu as overly prone to hyperbole, too frequently seized with absurd ideas that fed upon the class's energy. On one of the first days of school, Ms. Liu had walked straight into her door, laughing it off with no apparent trace of injury. Teachers were not supposed to walk into doors, they were supposed to grasp the handles delicately, open them, and walk through like normal people. Pranav was initially worried that he was betraying Frank by spilling the beans to Ms. Liu, but she did not seem to mind.

"Frank sounds delightful. I want to meet him and have him tell me all the things. Last time we talked about this, I remember promising to talk to Mr. T. Now seems like just as good of a time as any, as we have a staff meeting in a bit anyway." Ms. Liu found Mr. T's door open as usual, although he was busy taking a phone call in what sounded like German to her; he gestured to a tray of cut fruits, cherimoyas, jackfruits, and even some durian that made her wince. Classic Mr. T.

"It's always good to see you, Ms. Liu. Business or pleasure?" Mr. T asked once he ended his phone call with boisterous laughter and best wishes to the incumbent CFO of Credit Suisse.

"Pleasure, today. Tell me about that club you manage. Is manage too strong of a word?"

"Frank, as he should be, is the head honcho here; Pranav, who I believe is your student, also strikes me as more involved than he lets on, even though he isn't a club officer. I do little but supply the club with resources and keep our coworkers off their tail. Have you read their little manifesto? Here's a copy."

"Nothing like calling something a manifesto to leave a first impression." Ms. Liu started reading, struggling to hold in her laughter. "Hold on, hold on. So is everyone in on this? I mean, it's a bit lengthy and it takes more than a casual read to figure out what's going on, but I can't believe that people are going along with this completely without realizing this is a massive troll."

"It's the delivery that made the difference. I have not seen anyone laugh in any of these meetings ever without being sternly reprimanded unless one of the club officers told a funny joke. Then, you get sternly reprimanded for not laughing. As it turns out, you can disguise anything under layers of self-confidence and invective. I don't think even the club officers are fully aware of what they're preaching; Alan, if you know him, seems especially scary. I've heard about him from other teachers saying that he's been having difficulties interacting with others constructively. Not like he never had any, of course, but he's been more defiant."

Ms. Liu looked around the room, trying to recall if anything seemed different. "How does someone get into one of these meetings? Is this a mafia-style, you know someone who knows someone, sort of deal?"

Mr. T put on a Brooklyn accent, to Ms. Liu's amusement: "You're a teacher, they will roll out the red carpet for you. Every Friday, at lunch, you can watch the corruption of the American youth. What better lunchtime entertainment could you ask for?" A few other teachers heard their conversation and came in, and together they walked to their staff meeting.

Chapter 14

S ophomores at Heller tended to appreciate their second year of PE more than their first. They ran faster, swam longer, and sweated more, but by then it became a familiar routine. Some went as far as to say they enjoyed it. Ms. Stevens only taught freshmen, and so they instead appreciated the wit of Mr. Clements, who made even pushups funny. Frank particularly appreciated Mr. Clements due to his fondness for power-walking, and that day in class, in lieu of running or anything that got the blood pumping, they walked. Quickly, to be fair, around the field, darting in and out of shadows and making pigeons jump when they passed too close, but not so quickly that John and Ernest could not argue. Light philosophical debate—debate which everyone else considered arguing—had become a frequent pastime for them. Ernest was easily incited to invective, every fault around him an underlying symptom of some greater societal ill: the school lunches are tasteless, no wonder why America is malnourished; Mrs. Huang played a FOX News interview with President Underwood, why is she bringing politics into the classroom? John responded to these challenges with as much gravitas as he could muster, never quite sure which of Ernest's comments were soliloquy and which were invitations for discussion.

"What does it mean to be intelligent?" John asked Ernest suddenly. John considered himself a not unintelligent person, but Ernest was clearly more so. It did not matter that people like Frank and Jason did just as well academically, they were simply viewed as less intelligent; Jason had his unfortunate track record of head-patting and outbursts of anger, and Frank's intellect was overshadowed by his eccentric tendencies. John was not quite sure what he brought to the table, but he knew that somewhere in his head lay pearls of wisdom.

"Intelligence is something we are all born with that determines our position in life. Some of us are more fortunate than others because they possess greater, I guess, natural blessings," Ernest responded with certainty.

"What makes you think we are born with it? Why do we have classes if they are not meant to teach us something besides conformity?"

"John, there's a difference here between intelligence and knowledge. I have great knowledge; I am not intelligent. Someone like Frank is intelligent, but he has no knowledge." Ernest did not mean this as a great insult toward Frank, who was well ahead of them and probably would lap them soon enough, but rather as an explanation that could let him sleep at night without the inescapable feeling of having done something wrong. Ernest left this unspoken, but he thought John possessed great intelligence and little knowledge as well.

"So are you defining knowledge as how we use our intelligence?"

"Exactly that. A mind is a terrible thing to waste."

"I'm not quite sure I get what you're saying, Ernest. A toddler who we all may consider precocious for whatever reason, maybe because they learned how to read early, still puts their hand on a hot stove despite them possessing the intellect to know that's what they shouldn't do, that they don't see any adults putting their hands on hot stoves and thus should not do the same. If we are born with a certain level of intelligence that really determines our position in life, most of us would have scars on our hands. Every man is the son of his own works, and the majesty of human creation is proof that we are not governed by our nature."

"That's a terrible example. Some things in life are instinctual: we all know not to play with knives or jump off cliffs or drink bleach without being told. Very few of us don't possess those instincts, and those who don't grow up to be stuntmen."

"We aren't savages, Ernest. We don't stand in drum circles ululating all night simply because our primal instincts drive us to belch and procreate. Our instincts help us act in society according to normal principles beyond the simple idea of 'don't die.' There's some little motor inside us that tells us when not to talk out of turn in a conversation, ensures we're too scared to suddenly take off our pants in the middle of class, and that tells us to settle disputes amiably instead of coming to blows. Those aren't necessarily natural instincts—a toddler feels no shame. But most of anyone, regardless of intelligence, learns to develop these instincts."

"So what about those people who aren't 'most of anyone'—here's what they do: they commit crimes. They rob, steal, lie, and do whatever brings them the most pleasure, society be damned! 'Why so serious,' they ask, feigning innocence and belying hearts of darkness. They think they're little harlequins, cartwheeling around and jumping for joy all because they are having a blast at the expense of everyone else. They're pickpockets at Times Square, they're drunk drivers, they're everyone and everything! We are all born with those instincts, and it is only our intelligence that keeps us in line."

By now, Frank had caught up to them, and could immediately tell he was missing some action. He interceded to the best of his ability: "I don't think it's quite fair to paint all criminals with one broad stroke, Ernest. Some have noble motives: Jean Valjean only stole to feed himself, it's not like he ran around shooting pistols in the air screaming 'Yeehaw!'. And I do think it's a rare breed of criminal that acts without motivation like that. They aren't savages, Ernest."

"Sure, sure, ruin my argument by bringing up Bernie Madoff," Ernest sneered, his tone more acerbic than usual. Frank gave him a quizzical look, but let him continue. "When you take any convict, someone who committed unglamorous crimes, maybe shooting up a 7-11 or something, can they really change? I don't think most of them can comprehend that level of nuance you claim they have. They didn't spend their youth playing piano or attending math camp, they spent their youth setting ants on fire and stabbing kittens with a pocket knife. They talk crudely and signal their incomprehension with their fists. If you really think that those people aren't beyond hope, you should try talking them out of their drunken stupor. Go ahead, I dare you. I bet some of those kids across the track are probably suitable subjects. Go on, John."

"Well, Ernest, I really don't know if I could do it," John stammered. "But I really think you're judging these people too harshly. Every brute has a heart of gold."

"You know how you sound, John? Like a man who's trying to convince himself of something he doesn't believe in his heart. Each of us has a destiny—for good or for evil," Ernest coldly responded. Ernest was surprised John did not agree with him more easily; after all, did he not attend a club centered on elitism?

John continued to address Ernest, his voice starting to strain: "So why wouldn't a convict be able to change? He served his time, paid his price, you don't think that would matter at all?"

"I mean, sure, he could be a changed man. But he is still a convict. A nicer one, but he still has the heart of a convict."

"What does that mean? Is having the heart of a convict a bad thing? Many great minds have thought in devious ways," Frank ventured, trying to understand exactly what his problem was. "And even beyond that, I'm curious to know what you think prison is. Prisons aren't insane asylums where people hang upside-down from the chandeliers and trace pentagrams with their own blood on the walls. They have libraries, civilized things—prisoners take classes, they have jobs, they try to improve their lives. Sure, there may be the incorrigible ones who live in solitary and fashion shivs for a living, but those are rare exceptions. Those must be the ones with those 'hearts' you mention. Useless things, they are."

"How do you know, Frank, have you ever been to prison?" Ernest was growing impatient with Frank. Frank was mimicking John's rhetorical patterns, and Ernest felt outnumbered. Eventually, after they all grew hoarse and Mr. Clements blew the whistle to end their exercise, each of them walked to the locker room viewing themselves as the victor. Ernest believed he had proven the existence of the human soul, John the importance of willpower, and Frank discovered that the best way to irritate Ernest was through debate. Even in the locker room, they exchanged glares, all feeling equally wounded by the others.

John came back to their conversation that night as he slept dreaming of walking through concrete hallways lined with iron bars and prison wardens. The prisoners inside their cells gripped the bars and shook them, screaming and hollering, shouting obscenities for no particular reason but to extend a middle finger high in the sky toward the system that had brought them there. He imagined Regina and Beth there—both seemed like nice people, but did they really possess hearts of gold? They were too nice, that was it: they did not deserve a wretch like him who always forgot to thank the bus driver. Maybe he was on the wrong side of the bars. He deserved to sit among the rubble on a dirty bench covered with hypodermic needles and think of all the shameful things he had done. John was a sick man, he was a spiteful man, he was grotesque and disfigured and bulbous and lecherous and hobbled and evil! John found it hard to look out on a beautiful world that had so many flaws. It was made of origami, and one stray match would set all the trees in the world alight, and all the birds would fry and turn into piles of ash, all indistinguishable from each other. Who would clean up the mess then, some celestial vacuum cleaner? Once he had tried to fold a paper crane after reading that one would be granted a wish if they folded one thousand. He cut out a square of paper, measuring with a ruler so he could get it right, and worked his hands and fingernails all to make something that could barely pass as a bird. He shed a tear that washed over his closed eyes—how could he ever hope to understand his own fragility if he could not understand paper? John's thoughts made little sense to any outsider, but he personally saw a beautiful logic that defied any attempts at examination.

Tom found Alan eating lunch alone, which was a fairly common occurrence. Before Tom was initiated into Frank's cabal, he had assumed that all of the club people would eat together in a faceless mass, but he had noticed that more and more, they ate quickly, treating lunch as a time to refuel and not one for social gathering. Regina was home sick with a bad cold, otherwise Tom would have obviously eaten with her; he decided bravely then that Alan would be a worthy lunch partner, especially as Alan was eating his sandwich with an unusual glumness.

"Why so gloomy, Alan?" Tom asked with anticipating eyes; Alan still seemed despondent, and so Tom did something rarely empathetic and sat down next to him. Alan thought a moment, then decided to respond honestly:

"It's my dad. He isn't doing so well. Cancer, you know. I don't want anyone else to know, otherwise they're going to feel pity for me and treat me like an emotional wreck. Can you keep a secret, Tom?" This was the first time Tom could remember that anyone had asked him to keep a secret of any importance. It felt good, he thought, like he was finally able to do something noble just for himself, not for anyone else. It felt so good that Tom ignored Alan's monotone, unusual brevity.

"Of course I can, Alan. That's what a good person does." Tom had no intention of betraying Alan's confidence. The poor guy. Out of all the people he could have turned to, he turned to him. That meant a lot. It really did. Tom thought for a minute if he should give Alan some sort of gift, ostensibly out of the kindness of his heart, but really to show that he cared. Maybe a Nintendo Switch or something like that, that way they could play together at his house sometime.

"You know, I lost my mother when I was young," Tom suddenly said with a hint of sorrow. Alan immediately offered his condolences, but Tom shrugged them off.

"Not in that sense. She's still alive. She had an affair with her masseuse and they ran off to Italy. I haven't seen her since; she doesn't even send me birthday cards. But my dad and I cope just fine." Alan stifled his laughter—it seemed poetic, in a way, that Tom had a personal problem so alien, so cinematic, so... Alan hated the word, but bourgeois.

"It's not funny!" Tom cried out in anger, but he was so happy to see Alan's good spirits returned that he, too, laughed. "Never tell anyone about that either, please. Now we're even: you know a secret, and I know a secret too." Tom found it a bit harder to maintain his own good spirits that night when he video-called Regina, who seemed quite healthy aside from an extremely nasal voice and intermittent sneezes.

"So Tom, I was just wondering, are you friends with Alan? I've seen him be nicer to you during club meetings recently, and I was curious if there was something happening there." Regina disliked Alan's mood swings and standoffish nature, seeing them as an inconvenience during class; recently, he had adopted tinges of officiousness, and that only compounded her feelings. Regina saw in Alan all that she disliked about Tom with none of the positives either. Tom walked with a swagger and a peculiar insistence on fist-bumping everyone he met. Tom still hadn't learned how to chew consistently with his mouth closed, and he constantly referred to Regina as "his girl," a habit she found cute at first but not as nice as being called by name. Regina had no doubts that if Alan were to somehow acquire a girlfriend, he would do the same. "Is not general incivility the very essence of love?" Beth once commented when Regina told her yet another story of Tom making a fool of himself.

"Yeah, we're friends. He's one of the guys. Why do you ask?"

"I was thinking about that awesome trip to the lake we all had, and how you two seem like such different people, you know? It made me wonder how you two became friends. Is there a story behind it?"

"I really can't think of anything. One day we weren't friends, and then we were. There's nothing unnatural about it. Things happen." Tom's soreness from lunch that day shone through, which Regina interpreted as defensiveness.

"Is there something you aren't telling me? You can trust me with anything, Tom, like I trust you."

"In my younger and more vulnerable years my father gave me some advice that I've been turning over in my mind ever since. Pay it forward, he said, always pay it forward. You never know when a good deed will come back around to repay you later. I never thought about that until I grew wiser, like I said, and I started seeing the benefits of even a tiny bit of charity. You should try it sometime, Regina." Tom placed a particular emphasis on her name, and Regina suddenly wished he'd go back to saying "babe" or "my girl."

"I had always known you to be a charitable person, Tom," she said with the same emphasis, "but every day you surprise me with the new ways in which you show it. Was he a coincidence? I can't help but wonder if his new leadership position meant anything to you last year." Regina knew she was on thin ice already, but she found Tom's generosity less romantic when she knew there were other recipients. If she were the only one, she could avoid thinking of herself as easily bribed.

"It was his lucky day. I need to go now, dinner's ready. Get well soon, I miss you," Tom curtly finished, turning off the call before she could say goodbye to him. Dinner wasn't ready, of course, but Tom needed some time to cool off. If Regina truly thought Tom's motives were ever anything but pure, maybe she was deceitful herself. That would make her a bad person, someone who needed a firmer hand for a proper education. Tom considered himself adequately qualified.

"Frank?" Ms. Norris barked from her desk as everyone was leaving. Frank stood still for a moment, immediately unsure if he had done something wrong. When he walked to her desk, her typical resting frown faded slightly.

"I've heard some interesting things about your club, in particular how you keep everyone organized. Quite effective, so I am told. Could you explain more? I've always believed that the truth is rarely pure and never simple."

"Why, yes, I have noticed that too," Frank responded, still not quite sure if Ms. Norris was about to segue into criticism.

"It does sound a bit, shall I say, inventive, but it is certainly effective. You have a natural talent for leadership. Maybe I'll steal your system for next year, how about that?" Ms. Norris continued, still intently focused on something on her screen.

"Well, uh, I am sure that you know best," Frank stammered before quickly walking outside. She could smell his fear, he was certain. But still, her emphasis on scientific precision certainly was not out of character. Any teacher who insisted on starting lab sessions at 7 AM sharp could be the sort of teacher who saw the merit in Frank's system of drilling, and even more distressingly, see the merit while being aware of the irony. Ms. Norris was not an anomaly, Frank thought: many saw him as the one who finally had the chutzpah to do what they all had been thinking all along. They may not believe all the cheers they shouted to end meetings, even if they wrote some of them, but they still showed up every week to watch those who did not act as double agents simply follow orders. Frank was told that on club days, many gathered in the library to watch the live-stream of the meeting on someone's laptop, and in this way customs spread through the small group of loyalists. The ones who attended the meetings consistently, some by design and some through dogged determination (Tom and Juliet always found a way for their groups to attend), gained an elite status. They had seen him speak in the flesh, and despite this being exactly the same as watching him on YouTube, were somehow best qualified to understand his wisdom. Frank couldn't help but admire the sheer conceit of the scheme, especially because through some miracle, he had pulled it off.

Frank was unsure if Ms. Liu wanted to speak to him because she admired his conceit or if she disliked how he helped Pranav. He quickly stopped by Mr. T's room to refuel (Frank's custom of watching Food Network with his parents proved helpful to Mr. T, as Frank was able to give cogent feedback when Mr. T created culinary experiments) and then knocked on Ms. Liu's glass door. Ms. Liu's room was one of the few that opened into the central courtyard, and was sufficiently shaded to create an interesting optical effect, the opposite of the other classrooms with similar doors: anyone outside could look in easily because the room was brightly lit, but from inside, the courtyard appeared shrouded in darkness.

"Welcome to my domain!" Ms. Liu said exuberantly from her desk. Frank looked around with open eyes, not used to English classrooms that were normally-furnished. One side of the room was completely plastered with old senior portraits, ranging back to when Frank was a toddler.

"It's certainly a spacious classroom," Frank remarked.

"So, first off, I'm not quite sure what you're doing with the club, but I love it—I hear my students talk about it amusedly quite often, and Mr. T has only the highest regard for whatever you're doing." This was going a lot better than his talk with Ms. Norris, Frank thought—far less cryptic, at least.

"I appreciate it. It's really just a casual melding of minds, you know. I cannot take any credit for anything. I couldn't do it without my people."

"It's funny you say that, Frank. Did Ms. Norris say exactly why she was so curious about your 'inventive' methods?"

"No, she did not; I assumed she wanted to try out my ideas for her class," Frank said with a mild laugh, which Ms. Liu reciprocated with worried eyes.

"As much as I hate to be the bearer of bad news and make an awful first impression, she was concerned about bullying, namely that some of your club members seemed to be creating a hostile work environment for each other, and apparently some of her other students were concerned."

"Were they attacking people who weren't in the club?"

"No, no, it's just that apparently they thought it a bit cliquey, and even degrading for those in the know—being blunt with each other while working, that sort of thing. One student said that she heard one of your members call another an 'incompetent simpleton with rags for brains,' and it made her feel bad for them." Frank appeared pensive.

"So is this something I need to take action on, Ms. Liu?"

"I don't think so; Ms. Norris seemed to be more concerned that her students were concerned rather than being concerned herself. It's all very interesting, you're definitely giving us some food for thought in the teacher's lounge. I wanted to make sure you were in the loop so you wouldn't be surprised if something were to happen."

"Do you expect something to happen?"

"I'm scaring you, aren't I? No, of course not, I shouldn't have mentioned anything in the first place. Oh, before I forget: I'm impressed by your work on Pranav's essay. Sophomores typically don't write as well as you, but then again, you also wrote *How To Be A Good Person*—I guess I shouldn't be surprised."

"I really did little. It's far easier to write from an outsider's point of view. Lower stakes." While they talked, Ms. Norris made a rare trek to the principal's office, something she typically had her TAs do when needed. The email chain titled "HOW TO BE A GOOD PERSON???!?!?" had resolved itself in a rather unsatisfactory manner in her opinion. All of Frank's teachers said he was a good kid and that at least the club members weren't using homophobic slurs with each other, so in a way that was progress to be commended. She found Mr. Kurtz furiously typing on his computer, or with as much alacrity as the two-finger method could provide.

"Is this about Frank?" Mr. Kurtz asked, briefly looking away from his computer to make eye contact.

"As much as it's not my place to get involved in these cases and be the vocal minority, I do think all of you are brushing this away too quickly. Have you read his manifesto? It's incendiary. Someone wronged him and all his followers."

"It's a work of satire, Mary. It's just some kids having a bit of fun, fighting for something they believe in. It's remarkable, really. My wife sold pot brownies back in the 60s as a teen. This is no different—this is better, even."

"No, you aren't understanding. I agree with you, it's comedic, but I have kids who are coming to me to report those kids bullying each other and being condescending to those who aren't 'good people.' If they don't think I'm doing anything, they're going to go to Ms. Wolfe and then you, and all the parents are going to come in wondering how their teachers are neglecting their students. It's ridiculous—when I tell them to avoid rude language, they obey and switch into soldier mode, which only scares the others more." Ms. Norris did not work 60-plus hours per week to have Mr. Kurtz tell her she wasn't teaching properly.

"Let me tell you this: in my experience as an educator, sometimes students need to learn to live a little. That's why being such a competitive, academically strenuous school is a double-edged sword: our kids get so wound up over the tiniest of things that they only know how to function with their books and not with others. If you're really concerned about it, try modeling the behavior you want to see. Smile a bit, shake hands, tell a joke, don't be the sort of person they're scared to talk to. I can't wait to see what progress you make with them," Mr. Kurtz finished, dismissively waving Ms. Norris out of the room before she could argue more. The other teachers would hear about this.

Over the course of a few weeks, Beth and Behrooz had enjoyed a courtship that proved remarkably civil in comparison to their peers. Behrooz interpreted John's rambling as encouragement to reach out to Beth, who responded warmly to Behrooz's offer to eat lunch downtown; a few other social engagements blossomed from there, all leading to them taking a brisk walk in Beth's neighborhood. The pedestrian path alongside the overpass was thin, so Beth walked in front of Behrooz, shielding him from the breeze. Behrooz grew tired of this and shimmied up alongside her, and there was barely enough room for them to walk together, hips rubbing together. After a minute, Behrooz reached his hand out to her, and after a second she took it. They continued walking, still crammed together like sardines.

"It's a nice day, isn't it?" Beth tentatively offered. She wished it were warmer, but it was sunny, so that was all she could really ask for.

"I can't think of the last time it wasn't a nice day. Fall was so hot, and I'm glad that winter has calmed down." Behrooz was tempted to say something cheesy like "any day is nice with you," but he thought that would disturb the tranquility of the moment. There was a lot of value in silence, he thought. It ruined the point of actually going for a walk to spend it constantly thinking about someone else; the better alternative was to admire the scenery and let others serve as accents, or highlights. He took off his coat and gave it to Beth, who slid her arms through the floppy olive sleeves and smiled a thin grin. When they walked by a flower box, Behrooz leaned down and broke off a rose, brushing away the wetness of the fresh stem before offering it to her. She still accepted this gesture with a smile, holding the rose delicately to avoid the thorns. It felt romantic, or as romantic as they could walking down a suburban street in the morning; Beth hoped for a second that nobody would see them, before stopping to think why. Surely the dog-walkers and old men were no threat; aside from one puppy stopping to sniff Behrooz's shoe and receive a head rub, nobody paid them much notice. Beth put her finger on exactly what was wrong when, passing by a park, she saw an older gentleman take off his woolly overcoat and wrap it around his wife. Too soon, she thought. Too soon.

Behrooz often walked Beth to the bus stop after school to say a quick goodbye; they would quietly embrace, and he would return to the parking lot while she stared at her phone and predict if the bus would be late that day. Somehow she never grew tired of the shrieking crowds of her classmates that pushed themselves onto the bus given the first opportunity. They could behave so nicely in class, sitting fairly obediently and only occasionally talking back to the teacher, but come the familiar chime of the bus doors, they wouldn't hesitate to elbow anyone out of the way, even her. Politeness clearly did not work—when she tried the novel tactic of saying "excuse me" constantly, she woke up the following morning to an unfamiliar bruise on her thigh—and so she resigned herself to always being the last to board. She would really love to sit in the front of the bus more often, where people like John willing to roughhouse a little ended up, but if that was the price she had to pay for a good conscience, so be it.

Chapter 15

T om was late again. This wasn't an infrequent occurrence, and through force of habit Regina looked around once more, sighed, then sat down and started browsing Instagram. She had told Tom many times, with varying degrees of politeness, how she did not appreciate his constant tardiness; it reflected poorly on his character and made her feel less valued. Tom never had anything to say but "absence makes the heart grow fond." After Regina had waited about ten minutes for Tom, he sauntered toward her, still oozing casualness. Seemingly not sensing any annoyance behind Regina's smile and hug, he pointed vaguely behind him, explaining that there was "traffic." Regina recalled no such traffic.

"We should get some coffee," he suggested, knowing that Regina loved coffee and relied on it to cheer her up; as she had stopped drinking bubble tea because of the club, coffee naturally was a far healthier substitute. At least it was unsweetened. Tom recalled the example of Pavlov's dogs that Frank had discussed in a meeting at some point, with the unspoken lesson that the attendees were conditioned in the same way, and hoped that Regina would associate him with coffee and thus happiness. Whenever he ran into Regina happy for her own reasons that seemed not to be due to his involvement, he always remarked "Wow, looks like you've drunk your coffee today!" as if it were the funniest thing ever; Regina never failed to laugh, and he knew the trick worked. He never knew a happy relationship could be this easy.

"Do you want to sit around the park and just relax, you know? It's a nice day—ooh, have you ever been to the Japanese garden?" The Japanese garden was its own enclave within the park, taking up a deceptively small amount of space. The city had sent architects to Japan to do research, and after great expense successfully recreated something that would not be out of place in a remote mountain village or the grounds of a Buddhist temple. Tom mumbled his assent, and they made their way over to the garden; due to the cold weather, the only other passersby were old couples who walked tremulously. Regina pointed out the koi, the jizo statue that Fujiwara-sensei said had special cultural significance, and the exact replica of a Japanese teahouse (or a chashitsu, as Regina insisted on calling it).

"You can book authentic Japanese tea ceremonies there—they even import the tea!" Regina explained enthusiastically, and Tom shrugged without paying what she said much consideration. One day Fuji-wara-sensei had taken the class on a field trip here and gave the same tour in far more detail than Regina was giving to Tom. Tom did not think a Japanese tea ceremony sounded particularly interesting, although it sounded like the cultured sort of thing his father would appreciate; he appreciated more the general feeling of tranquility that pervaded the space. If he applied some wishful thinking, a few deep breaths, he could imagine himself on vacation with Regina at his side.

Regina was about to show Tom her favorite spot to sit, under a ginkgo tree, when they discovered John had beaten them to it. He appeared plaintive, staring out at the pond and blinking occasionally. He seemed not to notice them when they sat down until Regina tapped him on the shoulder. John recoiled, then relaxed again, still sitting sphinx-like. John and Regina both considered this their favorite spot in the park because it completely blocked out any view of the city surrounding them; it was truly as if they were in Japan.

"How are you, John? What a funny coincidence to see you here. Do you come here often?" Regina felt guilty for disrupting John from whatever he was doing, but thought it less awkward than waiting for him to notice them.

"Sometimes when I feel like life is overwhelming, I take the bus here by myself and come here. I could sit here for hours. They say that the secret to meditation is breathing—have you heard that before? You begin by focusing on your breath at the exclusion of all else: in and out, almost like you are tasting the air. And when that rhythm becomes natural, you lose track of even that, and then your mind becomes quiet. We live in a society that focuses on speed at the exclusion of everything else. Tomorrow, and tomorrow, and tomorrow, we always move against the waters of time. It's a river that runs downhill forever, or a waterfall. If we always think about what needs to happen tomorrow, all the way until our universe is a shriveled black dot, when do we think about today? Life is meant to be lived slowly, savored, chewed, contemplated. Will you stay a while?" Tom looked at John with a rare awe—he was a monk at the temple, sharing wisdom accumulated over generations! But Tom did not want to listen; he had left his house with the intent of socializing, of being boisterous and laughing a little too loudly, of having a good time to eclipse all other good times. There was no room in that for John's quaint philosophy. He was content to leave John as he was and take Regina with him before she, too, could become a statue, but she had other plans:

"When you describe it like that, John, it sounds lovely, but life ought to be lived with a healthy moderation. You can't appreciate the exhilarating thrill of going quickly without slowing down sometimes, and the oppo-site holds true too. Tom and I are going to indulge ourselves a bit; you've earned a treat, if you want to join us." John saw no flaw in this logic, and stood up creakily, taking Regina's quickly offered hand to steacy himself. They walked as a trio over the bridge that was so perfectly framed in view before and left their slice of a foreign land for the familiar city.

John looked at the baristas, the menu, and the confections displayed with such confusion that Regina had to ask him if he'd ever been to a Starbucks before. He had, he indicated, but he had never made a decision himself on what to order before.

"You'll want an iced latte, right?" Tom asked, and before Regina could say anything to the contrary, he had added it to the order. Regina would have ordered one anyway, but couldn't he have asked first? Rather than gently rib Tom about this, as John was standing behind them, she cooed, "Of course, my love," smiling to Tom and then to John, as if to say "Aren't you jealous?". When their drinks arrived, Tom grabbed a straw in his hand, damp from the condensation on the plastic cup, and jammed it through the lid of Regina's latte. She, still holding hers, daintily held Tom's cup in place as she did the same, leaking a few drops of his own iced latte onto her hand. John, not knowing any better, assumed these extravagant displays of largess were normal in every relationship. It was quite sweet, actually, how they held the door open for each other, never hesitated to grab a napkin when the other had crumbs on their chin, and how they never seemed to extend any of these favors to him. John grew slightly annoyed with these displays when he bumped into a glass door that Tom did not hold open for him; Regina, hearing a mild thunk, looked back at John, who shrugged as if these things just happened. She mouthed "sorry," not wanting to say it in case Tom realized he made a mistake. Tom, then, would give her a look as if she was in the wrong for not correcting his mistake. And later, once John was comfortably out of earshot, Tom would shake his head, and maybe say something like "a good person would have held the door open." By then Tom would have happily forgotten that he was the one in error, having held the door open for Regina in the first place.

After they finished their drinks, they walked more quickly under the spell of the caffeine with no particular destination in mind. Tom saw a good place for a photo, and commanded the others to stop and smile; John did not understand what was going on until Regina pulled him into the frame. John had a tendency to ruin photos, as his facial expression was always halfway between two extremes. It began to grow late, and John couldn't help but think he was supposed to be home; he bid them a swift farewell when he saw the bus come, and they stood waving him good-bye until the bus was comfortably out of sight. They had forgotten by then that they did not originally count on meeting John, and they were growing tired too. Tom and Regina sat in each other's company impatiently until their parents came to pick them up. Tom was happy to see in the car that his hastily captioned picture of the three of them (two-and-a-half, Tom corrected himself—John was so quiet he barely counted) was receiving the suitable amount of attention online. On a sudden whim, he asked his father if he had ever participated in one of the tea ceremonies:

"I did, once. They're very sophisticated—every minuscule movement is chosen with precision. I don't think it's something you could ever appreciate." No surprise there, Tom thought.

Beth let out a sharp exhale after she was dropped off at Behrooz's house; even though she had already seen it multiple times, the black Ferrari proudly displayed in the driveway projected quiet power, especially as the house was not nearly as sprawling as some of the others in the neighborhood. One time Behrooz giddily let Beth inspect the car, pointing out every flawless detail; it was his dad's, bought at a steep discount from an old friend and dutifully maintained ever since. Behrooz promised Beth that when he learned to drive well enough to be trusted behind the wheel, he would take her on a ride along the coast somewhere. She knocked on Behrooz's door sharply, then rang the doorbell when she received no response. She had gone through this ritual multiple times, but this was her first time eating brunch with the family; she thought it a sign she was being absorbed into them, accepted not as an invader but as a friend. Behrooz's mother opened the door quickly and apologized for the delay.

"Breakfast isn't anything fancy today, but we're so glad that you could come," she explained, and Beth sat down just as Behrooz's father exited the kitchen holding two steaming plates of eggs Benedict—they had calculated the perfect time to invite Beth such that nobody would have to wait.

"It looks gorgeous," Beth commented, not wishing to speculate what their definition of "fancy" was if this wasn't it. She spied Behrooz waving to her from the kitchen, who was busy mixing a salad.

"So, Beth, how is Behrooz's new business going?" Behrooz's father asked in between mouthfuls.

"Well, he tells me it's going well, but I'm not sure. Behrooz, how is it going?" she responded politely, noticing Behrooz rolled his eyes slightly.

"I couldn't have predicted it to be this great. There are so many positive experiences and so many good memories—I can't thank all of you enough for supporting me." His parents grinned, his father even clapping faintly: this was the correct answer. Behrooz took any opportunity he could to ply his trade, even the senior center. Behrooz surprisingly enjoyed these gigs; nobody was in his face screaming song requests, and he felt like he was appreciated for helping them remember happier, more nimble times. Parties for friends, or even friends of friends, were pleasurable in their own way—if not for those, he wouldn't have met Beth, so in that respect he couldn't complain.

"While we've always been supportive of Behrooz in his, how should I say it, entrepreneurial endeavors, I do wish he would be more discriminating in the jobs he takes. I worry that people are doing bad stuff at some of these parties, smoking or vaping or drinking, you know, bad stuff. That second-hand smoke isn't good for you. You two are rare exceptions to the trend: I think so many teenagers are misguided these days. They hide it well, but they all have their problems. It's hard to see that when you're stuck inside with them, you know, but the most level-headed people can get out of that trap," Behrooz's mother explained to Beth; Behrooz tried to intercede by quipping "they don't call it 'high' school for nothing," but his parents shot him a look as if to say he was proving their point.

"I understand exactly what you mean, Mrs. Ghorbani, but I don't think any of us are better than the rest of them. If you were to sit down to brunch with any of my peers—well, OK, most of them—I think it would be the same. I do agree with you regarding him though, I would hope there are plenty of legitimate opportunities out there for him that aren't relying on teenagers."

"I think he's so desperate for anything he can find, Beth, because we don't give him an allowance," Behrooz's father said with a smile, and everyone but Behrooz laughed. "But no, don't get me wrong, that's a good thing! More people need to take initiative these days—there's a good P.T. Barnum quote, you must have heard this at some point, 'there's a sucker born every minute.' Am I right?" Behrooz gulped and nodded, hoping his father wasn't referring to him.

"Well, if society doesn't support teenagers' entrepreneurial efforts, how are they to become independent? Just for once I'd like to see all these things sort of straightened out, with each person getting exactly what he deserves. It might give me some confidence in this universe." Behrooz sighed, then turned back to his food. He ate in silence while the others kept talking.

John could not help but think that life was going quite well. A new semester promised a fresh start, and most of all, more opportunities. John had brought one of his more skeptical friends to the semester's inaugural club meeting, who was even less impressed when he was sent to overflow seating in the back of the classroom, where about ten kids stood while Mr. T pretended to work behind them. A few days prior, Mr. T kindly informed Frank that it would not bother him in the slightest if a few lucky waitlisted club members stood in the back during club meetings, hands at their sides and not allowed to show any discomfort. Frank thought this genius, and Mr. T was curious himself to see if this measure would exacerbate the status differences between students; while some lucky students got off the waitlist and could intermittently earn seats, others were forced to spectate forever.

"Today, I want to talk about beginnings. We all have heard the cliches: a journey of a thousand miles begins with a single step, ⊠⊠⊠⊠⊠⊠⊠⊠, or however you want to say it. For some of us here, this is the beginning of your awakening. You have watched us here grow and evolve over the last semester while staring in from the outside, fervently praying that someday you may be given your turn. We are all caterpillars in our chrysalises, and some day we may burst out and become butterflies! As unfortunate as it is that you did not come here last semester, you are advantaged now in that you have so many kindhearted people around you to welcome you into the fold to our casual melding of minds. I believe people learn best by imitation. When we were children, we watched what the others did on the playground and mimicked their movements and rituals for fear of being left alone. When our parents spoke to us in puerile baby-talk, we moved our lips to match theirs. And so here too you shall learn through imitation. I will not waste time explaining again how to walk, talk, and otherwise carry yourself. You will watch what others do and try your best to copy them—and if you are in doubt, you will remain silent until you work up the courage to blend in. I am glad to see some familiar faces here, Ted and so on, who have decided to be on the right side of history. Could we get a round of applause for our new arrivals?" The audience clapped appropriately, and Ted knew immediately he had made the right decision. Tom had sold him on coming to the club with the promise of absurdist comedy, but

Frank's double-talk was not quite his sense of humor. What Ted did find interesting, however, were the dating prospects. Ted found the prospect of so many conditioned to deference and obliviousness impossible to resist.

Ted thought himself clever and beguiling. He had worked hard to cultivate his bronzed, muscular figure, and he believed he was entitled to a return on his investment. Ted advocated thrift and hard work and disapproved of loose women who turned him down; he found it strange that those who loitered in the hallways and were catcalled by so many others did not even think to give him a sweeping glance. The others tried too hard, that's why they were never successful, Ted thought. He did not think to apply this same logic to himself.

Ted's train of thought led him to a second intuition: it could not possibly be a coincidence that the club was developing such special assets, and if anyone were responsible for that, it would be Frank. But despite that, Frank did not seem to have a girlfriend, and Ted was immediately curious to know if this were some stratagem Ted was too blind to see.

"So Frank, who's the lucky girl?" Ted asked with a wink, turning his head slightly toward Beth and Juliet.

"Alas, I am a bachelor. Business and pleasure are two separate spheres, Ted, and any intersection only ruins both—besides, I wouldn't be following my own advice then, would I?" Frank knew then that Ted's motivation for joining the club was not entirely honest, but then again, neither was his for running it.

"No profit grows where there is no pleasure taken. I think you have that peculiar charisma that would suit you very well if you were to throw your hat into the ring. And I know exactly whom I would set my sights on if I were you, my friend."

"Ted," Frank sighed with a voice beyond his years in wisdom, "there is a benefit I am reaping from this moral austerity that you may not realize. I am not sure if I understand it myself. But I urge you to take a day to observe this intricate architecture that surrounds us and admire its beauty. Nobody alone could do it, it's simply not possible. I do not know what higher power I serve, but I think He has made it so if I resist that self-gratification for now, the penthouse suite awaits me upon my retirement. If you are content with a little cardboard box somewhere, then live your best life; did you know that Diogenes, one of the greatest philosophers of all, lived naked in a barrel? Alexander the Great once came to seek his counsel, and Diogenes told him to stop blocking his sunlight."

"Am I Diogenes in this story?"

"No, you're the barrel," Frank said with a laugh, and both reached a mutual understanding. "A better comparison may be the film *Dirty Rotten Scoundrels*, if you've seen it. I'm the guy in the suit living in the mansion, you're Ruprecht."

"I would have expected greater humility coming from the greatest philosopher of our time."

After the meeting, John promised his friend that if he kept showing up, he would have even more fun, and could not understand why he politely declined. Oh well, his loss. John had had mixed success with recruiting for the club: he didn't know why, but nobody ever wanted to listen to him. Everyone always asked John so politely what exactly it was they did in the club, nodding at regular intervals and commenting on how interesting it all seemed, but they never showed up. This must be exactly the sort of moral duplicity he was supposed to fight! In reality, plenty of these casual inquirers watched the recordings online, and decided henceforth to keep a safe distance from John and the other disciples at all times.

"Tyger tyger burning bright, in the forests of the night; what immortal hand or eye, could frame thy fearful... uh, symme-try?" Jason's classmate read the line again a few times in the hopes it would make sense. Jason's eyes smoldered with rage.

"It's symmetry, like it would be said normally. Nobody says symme-try, what language are you speaking?" Jason was used to his classmates being idiots, but this was a new low. He scanned the classroom for Mr. T, hoping he could provide some support, but he was occupied elsewhere.

"You see, Jason, bright and night rhyme, and therefore eye and symme-try rhyme as well. William Blake was from England. In a British accent, or at least the one used at the time, they must have pronounced those words differently."

"What sort of British accent have you heard where they say symme-try? This is English class; we are supposed to preserve traditions, not anni-hilate them. It's symmetry, but go on. It's irrelevant." Jason's classmate saw an opportunity to topple the mighty academic titan, and continued arguing:

"In poetry, did Mr. T not say that much is left to the interpretation of the reader? There is a rhythm here we can see through the trochaic meter, you can even beat it on the table. **Ty**ger, **Ty**ger, **burn**ing **bright, in** the **for**est **of** the **night**. And part of that too is the rhyme scheme; if you don't have that, you don't have rhythm. Poetry is like music with words; I never knew you were tone-deaf."

"You're all idiots. I'm done with this," Jason said in a volume approach-ing a shout and stormed out of the room. Mr. T was tempted to chastise him, but Jason did have a good point—it clearly was symmetry and not symme-try, and nobody with a good grasp of poetry would think other-wise. This wasn't the first time Jason had grown surly in class discussions: Jason had the unfortunate luck of being paired with similarly obstinate students, who unlike him tended to be wrong frequently.

Pranav happened to be walking by Mr. T's classroom when Jason came out in a huff, and suspected the worst.

"What's wrong, Jason?"

"Nothing's wrong—they're wrong! It's symmetry and not symme-try! My classmates have no idea what they're talking about." Pranav had no idea what Jason was talking about either.

"My dear Jason, when will you realize that in this world today, isolationism is no longer a practical policy? You can't always be going on about making enemies. We are brothers in arms, so if there is anyone or anything we should be fighting, it's not each other. Get some fresh air, take a drink of water. Your classmates need you." Pranav was generally loath to be a mentor, but it was a role he found himself in increasingly frequently. During club meetings, Pranav tried his hardest to deliver cogent points, encouraged by Ms. Liu to take something out of his experiences besides a love of sadism. Alan, still thinking Pranav a "consultant," frequently went to him for advice; Pranav discovered Alan was satisfied with "try reading *How To Be A Good Person* more carefully" as a blanket answer for everything, and he hoped this would not stunt his emotional growth.

Ernest quickly found Jason after class in the hallway, who immediately began ranting again about how unfairly he was being treated. Ernest could do nothing but shake his head. Jason was a loose cannon, a disrupting influence. Sure, he told jokes on occasion, having a surprising ability to pun when required, but all that camouflaged bitterness. At least Ernest was justified in his cynicism, having to overhear every week Mrs. Huang smile and nod approvingly as Frank explained the week's meeting to her (one promise to discuss Confucius, which Frank intended to keep, only cemented in Mrs. Huang's mind that he could do no wrong), unaware how she was being poisoned. How could he not grow bitter himself when he was the sole truth-keeper, cursed with knowledge he could never share, and even when he did share, was never believed? Jason had no such problem—in fact, Jason believed that Ernest was the duplicitous one, somehow being popular while just as bad as he. They were alike, Jason thought, except that Ernest had what he didn't. How dare he pretend to be nice? He was just looking for someone else to criticize. This simmering tension manifested itself in a conversation that rapidly fizzled:

"I don't know what I can say besides 'if you need help, please ask me. I am here to support you,'" Ernest said with a pat on the shoulder he had seen done many times elsewhere.

"Don't worry about me, worry about yourself," Jason sneered, and patted Ernest on the head in a decidedly unaffectionate manner. Ernest left for robotics before Jason could think of anything else to say.

Chapter 16

The club meeting that week ended a bit early, and most immediately flocked toward the snacks that were still available in the back of the room. Initially, Frank was opposed to feeding his club members, or really doing anything that would make their experience enjoyable, but one day Alan brought in a bunch of cookies on some spontaneous whim, and from there, as things are wont to do, they escalated. "And those things do best please me, that do befall preposterously," Frank had quipped to Mr. T one day when the display was especially extravagant. Frank thought it a bit hypocritical of Mr. T to think so much of his generosity, but after seeing Mr. T one day quickly hide some of his better food from Alan, he understood, and went as far as to treat that as a lesson.

Beth and Juliet stood in the corner, watching the others warily. Paranoia was a sign of intelligence—they knew that for a fact—and Frank had warned them about potential turncoats in their midst. A good person could find no security, even when with their own people; they never knew, he said, if someone were trying to work up the ranks to dismantle the system from within. Even having a lot of Frank-Bucks wasn't proof of innocence. A few weeks earlier, a club member was excommunicated after it was discovered they had cheated on a test; he had no personal connection to any of the club leaders, and thus could not plead for forgiveness. He groveled, even shed a few tears, but the other members remained stony in their seats. While in reality this was a tidy affair, rumors distorted what had occurred that day into something fantastical: some claimed poor Leo was forced to crawl on his hands and knees out of the classroom; one said he was pelted with trash, and held up an empty water bottle for the sake of analogy; some turned Leo's silent, resigned procession out of Mr. T's classroom and down the hall into a stomping tantrum or maniacal rage—he had tried to choke Frank, but Frank used his karate skills and pinned Leo against the wall! Only those in the room where it happened knew for sure if Leo left a coward or a hero, and the taboo on sharing internal affairs with outsiders ensured that never changed.

"Something wicked this way comes," Beth joked, and they both stopped their laughter by the time Ted had pushed through the crowd to them. Ted had not quite yet mastered the salute or the special walk, but those were both secondary priorities in his mind. Tom's success with Regina gnawed at his mind every day he saw the two together; Ted did not view Regina as a person with her own desires and priorities, but an extension of Tom's wealth, a share of which was rightfully his. Ted had tried a few times before to get a relationship going, but he never got along with "his girls," as he put them. They were nice to him, and since they spoiled him he became contemptuous of them. Inevitably, they would break up over text just as suddenly as they had started, and Ted could then go about his life without a care.

"How are we doing over here, ladies?" Ted asked with a smile, sizing up each of his potential targets. Beth looked severe as always, and Juliet still seemed prone to geniality.

"We're as fine as always, Ted," Beth responded first—a good sign indeed. Ted took out a penny from his pocket and flipped it sharply into the air. Heads, her, tails, Juliet. That seemed just as fair as anything.

"What's the coin for?" Juliet asked, her eyes following the arc it made as it revolved around and around before sitting comfortably in Ted's palm.

"It's a good luck charm. So Beth, would you want to meet up at some point to do the readings?" Ted asked, briefly glancing at his packet to remember what exactly he was supposed to do. Beth, all too eager to help a wayward soul become a better person, responded in the affirmative.

"That's settled then. Library, Monday afternoon?"

"Uh, yeah, sure, Ted," Beth answered, and they walked away and left Juliet alone.

"Hey, Frank, do you think you could help me with something?" Frank turned from watching the snacks carefully to John, whose head was bowed slightly.

"Ask and you shall receive."

"I feel like recently in class, I've been struggling to make connections. All the knowledge comes into my brain, you know, but I can't sort it all out. It's like you have a bunch of boxes in a storage room, all dusty and whatnot, and you need to find something. I can barely recall what I've done on any day without actively trying to memorize things, and everything is just combined into this sort of intuition I can never really work out. Like I'll be taking a history test, but I won't be answering based on what I've learned, but on common sense. It's hard to explain, but I'm sure you get what I mean. That's another thing, too; I've been having such a hard time explaining myself lately. It's like all these thoughts keep popping into my head, but they're in a language only I understand." John had always prided himself on being fiercely independent academically. Asking for help was a sign his own brain had failed him, and he thought that if there was one thing he could rely on, it was that. But maybe even that was inconstant, a manifestation of the same dream-reality that had infiltrated his idle thoughts long ago. John's dreams tended to be long, vivid, and confusing; Bismarck happily rubbed shoulders with Ms. Bracknell.

"I think I understand what you mean, John, and I am here to help. Have you considered booking an appointment with the school psychiatrist?"

"I've never trusted psychiatrists. They always want to find something wrong with you, and I don't think there's anything wrong with me."

"But John, did you not just say there was something wrong?"

"There is something wrong with my exterior self, in how I interact with others. There is nothing wrong with my inner self, or my mind, whatever you want to call it."

"So are there any particular classes where you struggle the most?"

"I think Chinese is one of them. I don't understand how to get my mind under control to express myself in other languages—I can barely do that in English."

"*Delusions of grandeur*?"

"That's a bit racist, Frank, speaking nonsense just to mock my own difficulties." John was about to launch into a grossly exaggerated, pseudo-Spanish rant before Mr. T said from his desk that Frank was speaking Chinese. Instead of apologizing, John looked at Frank with a new understanding:

"How did you learn to do that?"

"Like anyone else would: study and a bit of elbow grease. If you want someone to help you with your Chinese, I am afraid of accidentally teaching you bad habits; you could ask Regina, or maybe Juliet. Even Mr. T could assist you if somehow Mrs. Huang is unavailable. I'm sure all of them would love to help you out. And as for expressing yourself, well, that seems like something that would be exceedingly hard to tutor. But if anyone could do it, it would be Pranav."

"The consultant?" John asked. Frank was briefly confused before he recalled that he had introduced Pranav that way once; he was surprised John remembered.

"He proved a great help to me freshman year when I knew little. I still know little, but I now know just how little I know. Did you know that 'sophomore' literally means 'wise fool' in Greek? The first step to self-improvement is accepting your current low status."

John did not know yet if he wanted help. John was struggling, even if he did not show it: while his grades indicated no decline, they came at the expense of more and more free time and study sessions without breaks that left him all the less certain if he really knew anything. Or if he really could know anything—was he not a pawn of the universe, an errant bunch of star-stuff that one day coalesced into a person? If not knowing was inevitable, it wasn't like he could do anything to change it. If the universe truly wanted to humble John, he would know it.

"You want me to tutor him?" Pranav asked in astonishment.

"I want you to be your best self. I merely suggested to him that you have a chance of solving his problems. He may be too stubborn to accept that, though; he rejected talking to the school psychiatrist."

"Well, that's obvious, you can never trust psychiatrists," Pranav declared with certainty. "But if he does talk to me, what should I do?"

"Walk him through his schoolwork and try to understand how he thinks. See if you can identify the source of whatever disease ails him. Curing it may be harder, or maybe he will come to a sudden epiphany and save you all that work."

"It really is nice that despite our hopes, we are helping people. I feel like when my parents ask me what I'm doing in school these days, I can give them honest answers."

"You know what they say, Pranav, honesty is always the best policy." Frank went to talk to someone else, and Pranav took a glance at John, who seemed to be quite happy vigorously discussing some finer point of policy with another club member. He certainly seemed well-adjusted, but if there really were something wrong, there was nothing Pranav could do but try his best.

In English class, Mr. T's class was reading *Macbeth*, and it brought John no shortage of amusement to address Beth as such; she was Lady Macbeth then, and the others unanimously voted to make John Macbeth proper. It was almost a relief, he thought, to be virtually betrothed to someone not terribly repulsive, and who wasn't presently trying to woo him.

"Your face, my thane, is as a book where men may read strange matters. To beguile the time, look like the time; bear welcome in your eye, your hand, your tongue: look like the innocent flower, but be the serpent under't," Beth read solemnly, spitting out the awkward contractions. "What does that mean, John?"

John took a moment to rescue his mind from the grim halls of Inverness and bring it back to the present moment. "Could you repeat the question please?"

"Beth was asking what that passage meant, or that entire speech. For the worksheet," Regina clarified, looking at John expectantly under the rational assumption this would remind him. John began reading out loud with sonorous intonation: "O, never shall sun that morrow see! Your face, my thane, is as a book—"

"Beth just read that, John. Are you feeling all right? You look a bit tired," Juliet asked, and John was reminded then that while not terribly fluffy, his book would do well as a pillow, from which he could learn via osmosis.

"He's always like that," Beth explained, and once again they waited for John to give an answer—why were they asking him anyway? John thought himself no more qualified than any of them. He looked down at his paper and saw that he had been absent-mindedly writing some sort of notes, with no conscious will, the entire time; scribbles spanned the entire paper, picking words from the passage seemingly at random interspersed with question marks and arrows. Clearly they had mistaken his ramblings for insight, an error which he frequently made himself.

"Well, when he mentions the book, it's like the book that we are reading right now. So maybe this scene takes place in a library? And this could be like the Library of Alexandria, which was burned and sacked by the Romans I think—but I don't know if Macbeth is a Roman name for the sake of the allusion, I would have to do more research—do any of you know?" John offered, and their muteness conveyed to him that he had not given the right answer.

"A more plausible interpretation," Regina interjected, "is that Lady Macbeth is convincing Macbeth to be deceitful when hosting Duncan, to project a welcoming appearance while secretly scheming for murder. This is all to consolidate their power, of course. The serpent could reference the Garden of Eden if we are to resort to allusion, as then snakes are traditionally viewed as conniving..." While Regina continued explaining, John scrambled to compose his thoughts into something more serviceable; perhaps there were some fragmentary analyses in his notes that his subconscious had dredged to the surface that could help. "Macbeth, Macbeth, Beth, Beth, death, death, death, lies, lies, lies, lies..." John read to himself quietly, thinking that maybe there were some connections between all of those and his present state, or maybe that somehow it all related to Macbeth's psyche, and he was about to write down a thesis statement before asking himself if he should really be focusing on Lady Macbeth, who in that moment seemed far more complex of a character. What exactly did it mean to "unsex" somebody, and how could he learn to do it? By now, Regina had taken charge of the sane individuals at the table, and John turned in his messy worksheet exactly at the bell, to the amusement of Mr. T.

"Is there something wrong, John?" Mr. T asked with a furrowed brow after quickly scanning his worksheet, if it could be considered work; there were certainly answers to the questions, articulated with sufficient clarity and depth right where they should be on the paper, but the cloud of jumbled thoughts surrounding them was more interesting.

"I'm just a bit tired, that's all. But aren't we all?"

"Not like this," Mr. T thought to himself as he quickly graded the worksheet: good enough, clearly effort was put in, 10/10. Mr. T never claimed to grade different students with different standards, even if one person's average was another person's excellent. He did give disappointed looks to people who did not continuously seek improvement; most did not want to disappoint him, and his habit of giving extra credit for general good deeds, clever insights, or spectacular improvements proved another motivation to excel. He considered himself an adept at bringing out the best out of his students, and he hoped his students enjoyed challenging, but fair classes.

"Ernest, are you ready for the presentation on Thursday?" Frank asked casually before class. Ernest sneered at him before realizing Frank was asking a reasonable question, and then chose to reveal emotion.

"Not at all. This is ridiculous. She expects us to go to the library to find a book, and then translate a summary to Chinese? I don't know half of these words." Ernest could barely stomach military intrigues in English, and he was not primed to appreciate the strategic brilliance of using straw soldiers to bait out arrows in another language; the anecdote being fictional only incensed him more.

"I believe aeons ago, a wise scholar invented the dictionary exactly for that purpose. But I do agree: I would love more time to do research and ensure this presentation is actually usable for others."

"People already asked. She said no."

"We can do better," Frank declared, and he stood up to go to Mrs. Huang's desk; Ernest followed begrudgingly.

"Ernest! My favorite student!" Mrs. Huang proclaimed, and sat back in her chair as Frank explained that it would really be a great favor—nothing necessary, but just a convenience—if she were to entreat the class by giving them until Monday to finish their presentations, perhaps as a compromise by adding how they could apply the historical principles mentioned to the modern day. Mrs. Huang could have said no to Frank. But if he thought an extension was needed, and if Ernest thought the same, it was a sign. She trusted the two smartest people in the class to represent the will of the others, who undoubtedly were struggling if the top two were. She considered herself an exceedingly fair person. Ernest and Frank returned to their seats and sighed with relief.

"I doubt you need the extra time, Frank," Ernest wryly commented. This was the first time he'd seen Frank give any indication that his academic success came with struggle; Ernest made a point of always displaying his own suffering, lest others think him intelligent.

"I doubt so too, but I don't see why I can't be fair or reasonable on occasion."

"That's not a very good person thing to do, although I think you know that. If you're going to be an ideologue, why not be a consistent one?"

"Apparently you think of me only as the leader of a cause. Well, I'm also a human being." Frank was happy that aside from a few contrarians like Ernest, most did not care to analyze or critique Frank's morality. The attention the club's unique initiatives at the beginning of the year received faded as more clubs launched their own publicity stunts, and most did not regard the morality patrols as any worse than the tango dancing class held weekly or the Bible study group that disguised its religion under a zeal for literary analysis. Frank was still perceived as charitable, and indeed he considered himself charitable: did he not identify that John was in grave need of help and dispatch someone to solve the problem? Juliet related that one train-wreck of an English class to him one day after school, as befitting her club duty to report on others' failures, and agreed with Frank that John needed to change. She suggested she task herself with curing John, but Frank thought this potentially harmful for a few reasons.

Frank knew that last time John was in a depressive funk, it seemed to be because of either Beth or Regina—he could never really tell which, and he thought it crass to ask them to clarify. In both those cases, romance was the issue: John had the peculiar teenage tendency of assigning romantic roles to anyone in proximity who seemed open to him. It was a bad habit learned from Regina, and for a moment Frank regretted playing along with Regina's light-hearted prank then. So then, under the scientific principle of past performance being an indicator of future events, what horrific things could happen if John were thrust into a private setting with someone of the opposite sex possessing warm spirit, a figure fitting statistical trends, and an inclination toward physical contact? Frank tried his hardest during club meetings to disavow everyone present of the habit that had clearly caused John so much harm, no matter where their inclinations lay; he had seen Regina and Beth once ogle a particularly studly junior, and had thought about how best to discuss the serious matter without calling them harlots. Clearly he had not succeeded in creating a professional setting completely free of the profane, and this cycled around back to John and Juliet. He hoped Juliet would not give an encore of her performance back in Ms. Bracknell's classroom, although there was the chance John would goad her. Maybe there was something John had done back in freshman year to earn those covetous glances initially, a latent willpower disguised under his awkwardness. In other words, John perhaps was dreamy in multiple senses of the word. Frank could not possibly slander John, or imply he believed neither of them capable of acting rationally under their own willpower, and so he told Juliet that Pranav, the consultant, would be on the case.

"I hope John knows we care about him. I do, and all of us do. We want him to get the help he needs." Juliet occasionally had dreams of becoming a psychiatrist, and thought her abilities would be suited to assisting John, who had seemingly never before projected weakness to her.

"I do as well, but I cannot force a psychological revelation on him. John possesses a keen intellect and his heart is as true as steel. I trust John out of all people to fight the natural shocks of life alone. Or, with help, and in that case our esteemed consultant can unweave what fabric John is made of."

"If I have any ideas, I'll be sure to text you," Juliet said with a wave, and doubled back before Frank could question the necessity of her personal involvement: "Oh, also: do you still want the survey done by Friday?"

"Friday would be lovely. Keep working hard. I appreciate your devotion to the cause." This survey was an inventive stratagem meant to see if the club was actually teaching anything, and to test the limits of the club devotees' patience. Five hundred Frank-Bucks were on the line, which meant everyone knew this was important.

Regina rapidly began to question whether that really was a good trade-off for her time after she started working. When Frank told everyone to complete the optional survey, she was expecting a quick feedback form, not a midterm. Tom claimed he was doing it, and expressed reservations about Regina's commitment to the cause. She couldn't really say no to that, she thought, so she pulled out the dregs of her coffee from the fridge, sat down at her desk, and started typing away. Why did he insist on coming to the club every week and participating in discussion? Why did John and Juliet? John was always a bit of an intellectual, she thought, but Juliet never expressed an interest in philosophical discussion or Machiavelli until she started coming to the club meetings. In a span of six or seven months, she had become a different person. Someone with the brains, the beauty, and the brawn; a generous person as always, but something more as well. Regina hadn't. Sure, now she could quote phrases like "I think, therefore I am" or paraphrase Socrates, but her fundamental outlook on the world had not changed. Where were these benefits of being a good person that everyone else claimed to be developing? Tom, for instance, claimed to be a better person, and made a frequent point of being one whenever Regina had expressed doubts in the past, yet wouldn't a good person show up on time to dates? She needed to talk with him more, but only after she finished the survey.

"Easy, wasn't it?" Tom asked with a grin, not wishing to admit he had cheated and used Sparknotes.

"The readings are so dense. Too much old-timey language."

"I beseech thee, complain not about thy suffering," Tom admonished Regina, and both of them laughed.

"Prithee, have mercy on my mortal soul!" she responded in turn. She thought the previously-assigned readings from the year magically were translated in front of her eyes, from approachable, if irritating language to paragraphs upon paragraphs chock-full of jargon and confusing metaphors. She did not know if she had written coherently, but she was writing in quantity and following MLA format, and so she was satisfied. Her last thoughts before turning in her responses, as she gave them a final scan, were that they reminded her of John.

Chapter 17

Beth's breakup with Behrooz came suddenly and without any ceremony. Beth arrived a few minutes late to her usual lunch spot with Behrooz, in the hallway not far from Ms. Baldwin's classroom, and delivered the news. John happened to be nearby and watched: Beth's scant tears, Ted walking up to John and elbowing him conspiratorially, Behrooz's face filled with panic, Beth walking away, and finally, Behrooz crying.

"Should we go console him?" John asked Ted, who winked at Beth as she passed by.

"Nah, he doesn't need it. He's a tough kid. He'll be fine."

On a normal day, Beth would have immediately ran to Regina and Juliet for emotional support, but she didn't think they would understand. Her courtship with Ted had been exhilarating, made all the more so by her simultaneous relationship with Behrooz. Behrooz would sit next to her with his hand over her shoulder, all while she was texting Ted sweet nothings and gooey poetry she had written herself. When he left her at the bus stop, Ted would emerge from the shadows and they would embrace. Few noticed, not even John, who often mixed up Behrooz and Ted anyway. A few nights after Beth began dating Ted, she had a dream that they were walking together through a park on a cold winter's day.

There was snow, which reminded her of a trip her family took when she was still in elementary school. Ted helped her build a snowman, and together they furnished it with cute button eyes and a carrot nose. They then made snow angels and had a little snowball fight, where Ted apologized for his good aim after winning handedly. It wasn't until Beth woke up that she realized this was the park she went to with Behrooz. But by then, she had already filed away that very real date and instead chose to remember a happy winter wonderland.

In the moment, Behrooz could do nothing but glare at Beth's vanishing frame and Ted, who stood across the hall with a knowing smirk. Everything made sense in retrospect: Beth had mentioned once that Ted was a new arrival to the club meetings Behrooz could never attend, but nothing after that. Who knew how many times Beth spoke falsehoods, claiming to be enjoying the moment with him while really imagining someone else? He could accept that for some reason, she did not love him anymore. What he struggled to understand was why she lied to him, and he thought the two people best equipped to answer that question were Alan and Frank, who by that time had both heard what happened.

"I can tell you are somewhat displeased with this situation, Behrooz. What bothers you most?" Frank asked before sitting down, inviting the others to do the same.

"She lied, sir. She has always lied. I don't think she ever spoke a word of truth. But when she spoke, I believed her."

"Impudent strumpet!" Alan shouted in a fit of frenzied epiphany. He did not know why he took Behrooz's side so naturally, in particular against one of his own. "We ought to excommunicate her!"

"Let's not go so easily to hysterics. It doesn't suit us. I believe everything happens for a reason, and sometimes the universe conspires to test our faith. It gives us a good pounding, bruises us a little, just to see if we bounce right back up and ask for more. You're a reasonable man, Behrooz. You're an ordinary man, who desires nothing more than just an ordinary chance to live exactly as he likes, and do precisely what he wants. You're an average man, of no eccentric whim, who likes to live his life free of strife, doing whatever he thinks is best for him. Just an ordinary man."

"Well put, Frank," Alan interjected, now sounding collected.

"Lerner and Loewe deserve more credit than I, but I hope you get the point, Behrooz. I think this is the universe doing you a favor, unshackling you so you can return to those pure and simple times—once again, those good old-fashioned values—that brought you happiness."

"She's so deliciously low, so horribly dirty!" Behrooz exclaimed triumphantly. "How could I see an uncut gem in her? And why did I think I needed her anyway? How greedy of me! I can do without her. I can do without anyone! I have my own soul, my own spark of divine fire!"

"Exactly, Behrooz! Now you're getting it. Relying on others can become an addiction, a dependency: whenever they disappear, you go into cold sweats and a tempest of emotions. Beth is capable of living without you, just as she is capable of living without Ted. The bells still ring every fifty minutes without you, the sun still rises and sets without you, butterflies flap their wings without you, people live and die without you. Or you, Alan. Or me, or anyone. Nobody is unique in that way. All we can do is go with the flow and try not to drown."

"I just want to know what I did wrong. What did I do to disappoint Beth?"

"Nothing. Or maybe something—I don't know. But I believe there is no great fault in either of your moral constitutions that is responsible here. We are adolescents, some of us still don't know how to tie our shoes! How can we hope to understand the human psyche? People like me try our best to sculpt the world into a purer reflection of humanity's good without so much of the evil, but really, such cosmic conflicts are matters of opinion."

"Frank, you did write an entire document explaining how to be good."

"I suppose I did, Behrooz. I am superstitious enough to believe that forces beyond my understanding may have dealt me a bad hand of cards, setting me behind from the womb compared to you guys, or perhaps I got a pair of aces and I'm an Übermensch. That hand of cards is just as responsible for my deficiencies as it is my strengths, and I have no way of knowing which are which until someone pulls back the curtain. We are getting a bit sidetracked from you and Beth, you know."

"That's fine, it's really fine. It's still a touchy subject, the last thing I need to do is rub salt in my own wound. I'd better be going now." Alan took the initiative to leave more quickly than Behrooz; he was promised juicy gossip and tales of hatred and revenge, not something so civil. It disgusted him. Beth was clearly wrong, and Frank refused to censure her appropriately. To Alan, this break-up was predestined, an inevitable consequence of Beth dating outside the club (it did not matter to him that Behrooz watched all the videos and did the readings; he was out of sight and out of mind). Ted was a suitor of better moral fiber, and it was proof that the universe was just, not the opposite, that he started dating Beth. Frank's empathy then was a crack in his shell, as far as Alan could see. Frank had made the mistake of being compassionate, being empathetic, and most of all, being human. When Alan criticized his actions later under the guise of seeking spiritual guidance, Frank insisted there was no contradiction present: a good person looks after their own, and Alan did not know if he meant Beth or Behrooz.

Ted was in a gloating mood during PE, and this made Jason more irascible than usual. Ted spoke of conquest, of a siege with war drums and trebuchets that breached Beth's emotional barriers and let him sack the city, but Jason only heard the dripping of slime. Machismo scared Jason. Machismo taunted Jason for swimming too slowly, for running too slowly, and only relented when he beat it in a pushup contest. Beth had feelings too, didn't she? Jason did not know her well besides that her hair was not too springy on her head, but she was more than a statue to be carted off and displayed in a museum somewhere. Jason's hatred was compounded by his knowledge of Ted's checkered war record: the cycle had played out before many times, Ted bragging about whichever inventive stratagems he had used to seduce his latest lover, to steal her from the watchful eyes of conservative parents or an overprotective boyfriend, and a few weeks later the cycle would repeat itself. Tom refused to be outdone, and spoke of Regina so tenderly that Jason wanted to retch. He had never liked Regina; she preferred to talk in biology class last year instead of doing work, annoying Mr. Reinhardt, and what thoughts she did manifest on paper were meaningless. One time he had brought up that fact to John suddenly, just in case he really was treating her affections as consequential, but he did not seem to care.

"Could you guys please just shut up about Beth, Regina, or whichever femme fatale's entranced you today? None of us want to hear it," Jason yelled, still out of breath.

"Are you jealous, Jason?" Tom asked with a smile. "We can teach you, if you want. And maybe you'll sit on a couch one day, your special someone by your side, and apologize for ever doubting us. We'll even teach you for free."

"I'd never want to learn from sleazebags like you."

"Hey, hey, hey, break it up, boys!" Mr. Clements interrupted, waving his arms like he was shooing away pigeons. "Keep your head in the game."

"Sorry, Mr. Clements," Ted groaned, too scared from last year to risk any disciplinary consequence. Ted subscribed to an unique variant of the gambler's fallacy: like a hollow-eyed wretch playing a slot machine, he went into every new relationship certain that this would be the one, and told himself "better luck next time" when this never proved to be the case. He and Beth had definitely started off well: their first day in the library, he hadn't dared to reach across the table and do anything until she grabbed his hand as they left and turned to him with soulful eyes. They then walked together, hand in hand, to the bus stop, Ted thinking there was nothing better than supple hands that yet could grip strongly. He had waved her off at the bus stop before walking ahead, and when he peered back to look inside, she blew him a kiss. Not everything was so rosy, however; Beth had taken far too long to break up with Behrooz, still victim to forces like guilt and hesitation. Ted encouraged her every day with slanderous stories to do the deed, claiming he had once seen Behrooz at a party flirting with some of their classmates who had gone to approach him. It was sexist of Beth to maintain a double standard, Ted argued: Behrooz deserved punishment for his crimes, so it was only fair.

"I'm proud of you," Tom commented, patting Ted on the back heartily. Jason looked murderous, but did nothing. Wimp, Ted thought.

"Now that we have that administrative business out of the way, today we will be talking about change. Change is a scary thing, and often, it is our duty to fight against change. Change brought us the Cultural Revolution, it brought us Hitler, it brought us Al-Qaeda! Change is feared, and rightly so! There are a few types of change that are often maligned in today's society. There is change toward new ideals, a sort of entre-preneurial change. It drove Steve Jobs to create Apple and Robert E. Lee to secede. This change stems from heroism, sudden quixotic epiphanies that may drive men mad! Civilization has absolutely no need of nobility or heroism. These things are symptoms of political inefficiency. These change-makers are to be persecuted, like that little ghost of a boy we purged from our club just a few weeks ago. There is also a second type of change, a reversion to the past, a more primal state. A state of savagery, of clay huts and Biblical floods and wild animals, when we walked hunched over with towering frames and clubbed each other with bones. But this sort of change is not all bad, don't get me wrong. When the present state of society is in turmoil, when there is some incurable illness, often what is needed is to return to the past. A simpler time, when values were derived from common sense and not societal constructs. All of us can think back to a time when things all were simply right. We may remember in kindergarten when we played games on the carpet and played patty-cake with our friends not knowing that such things were childish and wrong—nothing but innocence guided us then. Sometimes I like to think of our noble quest as returning to that age of innocence, that undiscovered country shrouded in mist where everything is all right. Maybe it's in Tahiti, maybe it's here, and maybe it's in another realm. But anyway, where was I? Ah yes, change..."

John used Frank's speech as an opportunity to practice the Cornell notes Pranav was teaching him. The scaffolding of topic, information, summary comforted John because it gave his brain something to build on. He was free to construct strange ziggurats and precipices and Gaudi-like cathedrals, but at least now they were built on a solid foundation.

"...Now that we have explored some times in which we've all changed, I want to conclude with an extremely interesting quote from the great philosopher Zhuangzi. You would be well-advised to reflect on this. 'Once Zhuang Zhou dreamed he was a butterfly, a butterfly flitting and fluttering around, happy with himself and doing as he pleased. He didn't know he was Zhuang Zhou. Suddenly he woke up, and there he was, solid and unmistakable Zhuang Zhou. But he didn't know if he were Zhuang Zhou who had dreamed he was a butterfly or a butterfly dreaming he was Zhuang Zhou. Between Zhuang Zhou and a butterfly, there must be some distinction! This is called the Transformation of Things.' We are naturally inclined to consider change irreversible, like a staircase we descend one step at a time, never to be able to reach the surface again. But maybe that isn't the case. That's some food for thought. Anyway, all rise. I pledge allegiance..."

Frank ended that day's meeting with adrenaline coursing through his veins, which manifested itself only through relatively bombastic delivery and a minor twitch in his left hand. Frank had frequently been asked if he planned on running for some sort of class council. It seemed a logical progression if he wanted to convert more people to his peculiar ideology. While the idea of dealing with bureaucracy instead of being a simple autocrat scared him at first, when he discovered the day before the registration deadline that he was the only person interested in running for class secretary, and also when he confirmed that no matter what he did, everyone would be forced to vote for him, he threw his hat in the ring without hesitation. Pranav and Jason, upon hearing of this, suggested an elaborate campaign rally, full of needless posters, signs, and chanting—Frank could not maintain broad support if he was not popular, and the best way to become popular was to fake it until you make it. A small sample size, consisting of the people at the club meeting, indicated Frank had unanimous support. And this small sample size had watched him that day even more appreciatively than usual, some like Alan greeting him afterward with a hefty handshake and well-wishes.

"Tom? Could you do me a little favor?" Frank asked, and Tom pulled himself away from Regina to give him his full attention. "Do you by any chance have any spare suits in my size or can rustle some up for me? I think my wardrobe needs a minor overhaul. And maybe those American flag pins, you know, the ones presidents wear."

"If I had any, my dad would have donated them long ago. What do you need one for anyway? You aren't running for president."

"Everyone has to start somewhere. You know, Stalin was secretary, and look where that got him," Frank said with full earnestness. Mr. T walked from his desk to deliver the obligatory congratulations, and Frank asked him about the suits as well.

"I remember back on Clinton's campaign, we had a fun time once in Nevada trying to get something for Bill after he spilled ice cream on his good one. That was a big mess. But as for suits, let me check your size quickly," he said, pulling out a tape measure from a drawer. "I have a guy who owes me some favors. He'll send you an email and your wardrobe will be set. If you're going to do this, I can't possibly let my charges go out there under-dressed. Or, you know, I'll give him a call now—his schedule tends to be tight in the evenings, but now should be better. You'll be dressed just in time for opening night." Mr. T dialed a number on his phone remarkably quickly, and was out the door before Frank could question its necessity. He came back inside just as the bell rang: "He'll be here in about ten minutes; Mrs. Huang's fine with you skipping class for this, by the way, and thinks a red tie would, shall I say, suit you."

Frank examined himself in the bathroom mirror after receiving a text confirmation from his mother, who was working from home that day, that a few boxes of clothing had arrived safely and a surprising promise from Mr. Poverelli that he would attend the show that night (Mr. Poverelli typically had far better things to do, but his dinner engagement was canceled and he saw a flyer on the wall, and thus figured it beat sitting at home and watching *The Office* reruns). He looked sharp! Frank disliked how sticky hair gel was, so he instead combed his short hair to the side slightly and adjusted his flag pin; he had initially put it on upside-down, but thankfully noticed before any could see his sacrilege. After a second more of contemplation, he took it off. He hadn't earned the privilege yet of serving his country. Frank knew that by walking out of the bathroom in his current outfit, he would be crossing the Rubicon: no longer just the shepherd of his flock, but a man of the people as well. He stopped by Mrs. Huang's classroom briefly during passing period to apologize for the delay, and she assured him it was no issue at all and thanked him for taking her advice. So far, so good.

"Why do people change?" John asked Ernest after school in the central courtyard, where Ernest appeared to be frantically inputting numbers into his calculator.

"I know what sadness lengthens your hours. She was so good in middle school, and now, I don't know. She never struck me as a flirt. But alas, people change. The world would be a simpler place if people didn't. I wish they didn't."

"Funny you should say that—did you watch Frank's lecture yet?" John continued, phrasing it as if it were an inevitability that Ernest, being a man of some intelligence, would be interested in club affairs.

"I did not. You should have seen him in the hallway earlier; he changed into a suit and tie. He looks like a mobster. I bet it's for the election, you know. I heard he's running for class secretary or president or something. He's changed too. He used to be funny at times. Now he's a phony. Nothing is more deceitful than the appearance of humility." John appeared wounded, and it took Ernest a moment to remember that to John, Frank was nothing but a leader, a leader who had dispatched Pranav to make him a better person in the ordinary sense of the word. Ernest also was not being completely accurate: Mrs. Huang had, without Frank's knowledge, decided to tell the class the reason why he was conspicuously absent, and she had told the story with such embellishment Ernest thought it implausible until he did in fact spy Frank wearing a suit. Ernest didn't see why Frank wouldn't go all the way and run for president. Too much public scrutiny—that must be it.

"Some change is good. Too much is bad. Change is a scary thing, you know," John concluded, and he walked off proud of his learned brevity. John wished that he was back at the beginning of freshman year, when he did not feel like a kayak careening down whitewater rapids, having no control over which rocks he'd crash into. Then, at least, he did not feel like the only sane man. One night John had pondered the question of if he was the only real person in what was otherwise a world of simulations, and he could not find proof one way or another. He recalled that famous passage included in that week's reading; perhaps a dream was a better way of looking at it, he thought. If he were to wake up just then, right before his first day of school with that raucous assembly and all the new faces, still retaining the memories that even now seemed hazy, he would not know if he were in a particularly vivid flashback or if his mind had spun improbable tales to numb his anxiety. The John then who faced a day with a bowl of oatmeal and scrambled eggs would not be different than the John who remembered one day he had a bowl of oatmeal and scrambled eggs. In an instant, what was the past would then become an idealized future, and he would be lost, not knowing how to return. With that discomforting thought in mind, in only a few hours, perhaps at the assembly when the catchy tune of "Uptown Funk" drowned out his inner monologue, the two Johns would become one.

Frank walked through that same theater door John and everyone else had walked through that first day exactly thirty minutes before the show began. He saluted a few friendly faces, Mr. Liebkind still manning the flowers, and walked with a confident strut to retrieve his ID badge from behind the concessions stand.

"I hope you're not trying to upstage me," Mr. Cathcart laughed from behind the door; he was in the box office chatting up the parent volunteers while the actors prepared backstage. He wore a near-identical suit, only more rotund. "You know the drill at this point. What's the outfit for, if I may ask?"

"I officially launched my bid for class secretary yesterday, and Mr. T was kind enough to put me in touch with a friend of his. I'm saving the pin for next year, but I think this still looks nice, wouldn't you think?" The other people in the room all agreed that Frank looked quite nice in his suit, one complimenting him on how he tied his tie (Frank had spent hours one weekend over the summer practicing, tying and untying increasingly elaborate knots until the full Windsor came as second nature). "I do hope this outfit won't be a distraction," Frank mused, suddenly distinctly aware that his outfit was excessive, even for him.

"You're an usher, it's fine. At least everyone else is wearing business casual." Mr. Cathcart waved his hand dismissively, and disappeared backstage without further comment. Frank returned to his post and gave a sharp nod to Mr. Poverelli, who was intently reading a program he'd spied on the floor somewhere and did not regret coming at all.

"And I thought we were overdressed last time," Regina remarked to Juliet after Frank escorted them to their seats, squarely in the middle of the house.

"On the contrary, I think he looks quite nice," Juliet yawned, dramatically fanning herself with her program. "Is Beth still in the lobby?"

"I'm sure she and Ted are enjoying their pre-show pizza. He's such a bore. I don't know what they see in each other. I know you're not as experienced as either of us in the amorous arts, but trust me: if they can get along so well, young men's love then lies not truly in their hearts, but in their eyes." Regina could not properly enjoy any visit to the theater without a haughty pre-show conversation. The lights dimmed, and Frank stood in his usual position by the door. *Noises Off* was a classic farce, loaded with just enough slapstick to keep the audience entertained. Doors closed, doors opened, doors slammed, and Frank suddenly had a craving for sardines, which he had been told would be a great revenue-maker for concessions. He opened the doors to the lobby exactly when the stage turned bright for intermission, smiling appropriately as familiar faces left the theater. "Great show," a family told him, and he reminded them that he was not the director. Tom and Ted were consumed still in uproarious laughter—why couldn't all shows be like this? Beth, Regina, and Juliet followed them, all appearing stern in comparison. Juliet broke off from the pack and turned toward Frank.

"Walk me through a day in the life of an usher. Why do you do this?"

"It's rather peaceful, actually, the simple routine. You've seen me here every show: I'm always here helping people to their seats. There's no hidden meaning to anything. I just help others. You may enjoy it—Stanley is."

"Well, I think it's more fun to be able to sit back, relax, and enjoy the show. You should come to the basketball games, those are great. You can meet your constituents."

"I already attend the games, I can't believe you've never noticed me."

"Next time, why don't you come say hi to Beth and me? It's still performance, and I am sure you are a patron of all the arts." Frank gave her his standard knowing smile that bordered on a smirk and walked away, gesturing for her to follow.

Juliet found Frank's work uniquely fascinating, curious if he got bored after seeing the same show over and over again or if any guests ever caused trouble. Even when the answers to these questions weren't the ones she was expecting, she continued her idle conversation, following him on his patrol even as he went to the second level of seats. The upper level was empty during intermission except for one younger kid on the far end squinting to read the program in the darkness. The view was nice, she thought, and she was surprised when Frank told her that he didn't consider them the best seats in the theater. They were useful, he said, if one needed to sneak out early from a show; many parents with young children did just that in case their charges didn't share their taste. It was like a field trip, but not terribly exciting, and Frank was obligated to return to the lobby to spy on conversations and tell people to queue in a more orderly fashion. Juliet stayed talking with Frank until the end of intermission, chiding her friends when they didn't neatly tuck their snacks away like he had reminded them earlier.

After the show ended, Frank waved all of his friends a curt goodbye as he swept the seats for discarded candy wrappers and spare programs. The ingenuity of the audience astounded him—how could they always sneak in so much candy? The heavy janitorial work was not his responsibility, but Frank still felt an obligation to leave the theater cleaner than he had left it. He snuck out through the front door after congratulating the cast members, and walked through the heavy night back to his house.

Chapter 18

Regina was unsurprised to see John sitting on the same bench as last time in the Japanese garden, staring directly at a peculiarly shaped rock that jutted out of the pond. If he weren't wearing a different outfit, it could have been the exact same day. Tom was with her somewhere, technically speaking—he had seen some old middle school friends and gone to catch up; he wagged his finger at Regina, warning her not to talk to strangers. Regina sat down next to him, mimicking his posture, and waited for him to speak.

"You know, this rock has probably been there since before we were born. Hundreds of people, some of whom are dead by now, have sat on this bench and admired the same rock. And chances are, this rock will outlive us too. It's comforting to know that some things never change," John offered after a few minutes. "Where's Tom?"

Regina looked around once more, and groaned: "He's somewhere."

"Even when we sit still, the Earth spins around its axis, the Earth around the Sun, and even our solar system still spins furiously quickly around our galaxy's center. Wherever you look, we move. There's nothing we can do about it."

"So... how are you?" Regina assumed John would answer "depressed," but she asked anyway, turning toward John with relaxed posture.

"I don't know. How are you?" Regina felt a moment of emotional connection that she had not experienced in quite some while—Tom never asked her how she was, except in a perfunctory manner that told her quite clearly from his tone of voice exactly how she was supposed to feel.

"Well, I do have some exciting gossip that should cheer you up. Beth and Ted are no longer a couple." John showed no response, so Regina continued her narrative. Ted had slapped Beth during an argument, in a joking matter, not hard enough to draw a bruise, but Beth decided then that he was nothing but a scoundrel. "We're done," she said, and she had left the room before Ted's sweet apologies and empty promises could convince her otherwise. By instinct, Regina and Juliet were nearby, and they immediately consoled Beth as she cried into Juliet's shoulder. The questions immediately began:

"Why did you date him in the first place?" Regina had asked, now free to share that Ted had been an awful person the entire time and Beth completely brainwashed.

"I dated him because I thought he was a gentleman," Beth explained, and the others immediately chimed in to tell her that Ted was absolutely not one.

"If you want to know who's a gentleman, I can think of nobody more chivalrous than Frank," Juliet triumphantly explained, and Beth assured Juliet that this insight was not improving her emotional well-being, and Regina decried that answer as nonsense: nobody epitomized chivalry more than Tom.

"I don't know what to do," Beth continued ragefully, "everyone I meet is an idiot, or worse. Maybe they're all good and I'm the monster."

"You want to feel sorry for yourself, don't you? With so much at stake, all you can think of is your own feelings. One man has hurt you, and you take your revenge on the rest of the world. You're a coward and a weakling."Juliet raised her hand to signal her objection to Regina's tough love, but Beth nodded her head in acknowledgement.

"It is true. I must be a coward and a weakling. You're right."

Regina continued her pantomime for John, using different voices for each of her friends, and John began to suspect that Regina was an unreliable narrator. John put his hand to his chin and appeared engaged, for once completely in the moment. This was no time for meditation—he would have to strike decisively while the iron was hot. Beth was out there somewhere, lost, vulnerable, exploited, clearly in need of yet another exploiter. But not in the mean way, the way that made Beth unsure if she wanted to cry herself to sleep some nights, but in the nice way.

"So what does Beth plan on doing now?"

"It's not for me to say. There are bad people out there in the world, John, who despite being handsome conceal hearts of darkness. And there are also good people too, who possess hearts of light while still being handsome. Beth has wasted a perfectly good year of her life with the former. If I were her, I'd want a break from it all. That reminds me: are you coming with us to the lake this year?"

"Yes, a break from it all does sound quite nice. Who is coming?"

"Well, Beth is, I obviously am, and Juliet's family is only going to Singapore the week after, so she's going to come as well. We'll have a full house, but lots of fun!"

"And Alan?"

"Tom said Alan was occupied with something, but he wouldn't tell me what. I'm sure he just wants to play video games at home or do something introverted like that. We're too mature for that. Just fun, games, and relaxation for us." John, his mind still crackling with uncharted possibilities, said yes without hesitation. They waited there, trying to meditate with varying degrees of success, until Tom suddenly crept behind them and made Regina nearly fall off the bench with astonishment.

Tom insisted they leave to get a drink, John said he didn't need anything, Regina tried to persuade Tom of the natural beauty he was missing, Tom insisted once again that Regina come with him, and they left, Regina looking back to wave John a goodbye laden with imaginings of what could be.

Behrooz was too preoccupied with his recent success to think much of Beth's latest failure besides considering it inevitable. His DJ business had blossomed, and after growing tired of always playing for such high-energy events as "Senior Zumba," Behrooz asked Ms. Foster very sweetly if the school could be allowed to save money by letting him take over at school events. She said no—it simply wasn't done, there was no precedent! It was much easier, she said, to have students from the music production club volunteer countless hours so their names could flash by misspelled in the credits of official school videos. Behrooz did not see how this was a counter-argument, and eventually teased out a promise from Ms. Foster that if he could get himself 100 signatures, she'd hand over the reins. Behrooz spent one day furiously begging everyone he remotely knew to sign and give him a chance, including Frank, who suggested he try to convince everyone at that day's club meeting to help out.

"You aren't underdressed, I promise," Frank smiled, and took a moment to readjust his tie. Behrooz stammered and asked if he could leave a signing sheet with him instead of daring to enter the club's sacred space.

"That won't be any issue at all. Good luck. It's a shame that you've somehow never been able to attend the physical meetings. It's just a casual melding of minds, I promise. There's nothing else to it."

"I'm really not in the mood for seeing Beth. Or Ted." Frank chuckled knowingly.

"I don't think we'll be seeing much of Ted anymore." Ted had sent Frank an email shortly after his breakup explaining that for "personal reasons," he would no longer attend the meetings. Frank immediately went to show Mr. T, who grimaced and shook his head. "I don't mind a parasite. I object to a cut-rate one." Ted took little from his latest failure, not even that his reputation as womanizer was beginning to seep into his daily interactions with others, who even if they did not view Beth with much esteem certainly thought more of her than him. Ted considered himself a self-made man: he succeeded through elbow grease and failed through applying it too parsimoniously. He was a self-made man who owed his lack of success to nobody, least of all himself. Some had tried to explain to him exactly what he had done wrong, that Beth was a "good girl" who ought not to be censured for her occasional pangs of conscience. Even Tom criticized Ted for slapping her, thinking it too forceful a gesture for such little reward. All these factors combined drove Ted to find the common courtesy to email Frank, assuring him he was no less of a good person now and that he'd keep up with the lectures. Frank had outsmarted him by merely refusing to play the game, and in the process had stolen three of his possessions that by birthright should have been his. That sneaky bastard.

Frank had made it through one year of his club without running out of ideas. It was time to check off another item from the bucket list: the arbitrary leadership change. Frank viewed his club officers as largely expendable and interchangeable; if they were able to keep the regular attendees in line while still remaining easily suggestible and not too inclined toward independence, they were perfect. He still needed to get rid of somebody, that was certain. Alan was quick to admit that Stanley, while certainly an interesting person during debates, didn't have the full commitment to the cause that the others did. He wasn't part of the true inner circle, Alan argued, still believing that he had cracked the code. Frank checked his spreadsheet to see who had earned the most Frank-Bucks, hoping that a viable candidate would emerge who also could legitimize the entire process.

"How about Juliet?" Frank considered Juliet uniquely loyal, uniquely competent, and uniquely irritating. Frank bristled at physical contact and surprises he did not engineer himself, all things which Juliet provided in great abundance. Despite his best attempts to turn the club's members into a homogeneous blob, she and many others refused to comply. But still, Frank could respect Juliet's academic prowess, which was clearly demonstrated at every club meeting. She was like a family pet that he couldn't ever truly say no to, even if she ripped up the occasional cushion.

Alan immediately agreed with Frank, looking to him and Pranav for their approval. Juliet, he thought, had greater potential, especially as she had taken the initiative to kindly ask Alan one day in the hallway when she could interview to become a club officer. When he was too dumb-founded to answer, she asked Frank the same question. Frank hadn't really thought about interviews or any procedures of the sort, but as Stanley was content with a demotion (this was somewhat in name only, as Stanley agreed that Juliet would provide a better face for the club, and he certainly would be consulted in the future regardless) and Juliet would like nothing better than a promotion, he was willing to entertain the idea. An interview was a great idea—kudos to her for thinking of that for him. And additionally, while he was at it, he could easily create some paperwork for her too, as that would take care of another item on the bucket list. Juliet discovered that while Beth genuinely seemed excited for her (she suddenly seemed a bit more positive about the club, but didn't say why), Regina had nothing to say but empty congratulations.

Juliet spent an hour or two over the weekend reviewing, even emailing Frank some clarifying questions, and on Monday during lunch the two sat in the school library, Juliet scribbling away and Frank eating his salad. Frank waved to the librarians innocently, and Ms. Bracknell too when she walked by and did a double-take; he explained to her that this was normal for the club, and that normal people spent their lunch periods writing essays and watching others doing so.

"It's a spectator sport," Ted remarked to Frank when he passed by before sitting down at a table about ten feet away from his. Ted rarely went to the library, but as many of his friends were proving not to be very good ones, the air-conditioning and uncritical attitudes were welcome reprieves. Ted never knew books could be so cute.

When Frank told Juliet she had passed after school, she did a little fist pump and gave Frank a hug; he stood still, not quite sure if he was supposed to reciprocate the by-then unsurprising gesture. Did she really do this to everybody?

"What will I be doing as club secretary? Taking notes during meetings?"

"We have recordings, so that really won't be needed. You will help lead discussions, primarily, so be sure to bring your current enthusiasm to the club next year."

"Well, I am a cheerleader."

"As I'm well aware. As your first secretarial duty, you can make some campaign posters for Friday's election."

"Everyone already knows you're running. You're popular, they're all going to vote for you anyway. Nobody else could possibly be such an attractive candidate."

"It's tradition, Juliet, and I have always considered myself to respect tradition. Pranav, whom you know as our consultant, has helped with much of the digital advertising, as I'm sure you are well aware, but he and I are not as artistically inclined as you." Juliet laughed, and was about to assure Frank that his flattery was very much appreciated until he clarified: "You saw John's drawing of Regina? Think that, but worse."

"I can teach you at some point; are you coming to the lake?"

"Oh, no, I never could. Enjoy John's company, though. He's an interesting one." Frank could see that Juliet was expecting something more, but he had a speech to write and no time for distractions. "Anyway, I really ought to head home now."

"Which way are you walking? I'll go with you," Juliet insisted, and she matched Frank's pace as he left as quickly as he could.

In what proved to be the grand finale of high school PE, the students played golf on the football field. Mr. Clements talked up the activity as intentionally relaxing, a way for those who had never seen a golf club before to experiment and those who played at the country club every weekend to torment their peers. Tom surveyed the lane before him, which was marked with vividly orange plastic cones on the rough turf. His father never took him to play golf, thinking it a sport for those too wimpy to actually exercise, which had been a sore point for Tom since his youth. Instead of such refined amusements as golf and polo, Tom and his father engaged in plebeian pursuits, tossing a football around or shooting hoops at a basketball court by the Boys & Girls Club—the very same court where his father played as a kid. Tom handled his club like it was a weapon, aggressively driving it into the turf and throwing up black clouds. He imagined himself a Tiger Woods, shooting golf balls like meteors across the horizon and rewarded with trophies and cool drinks, and accomplished none of those things. This did not stop him from teasing Jason for his pitiful attempts at hitting his golf ball, which formed a trench as it skid across the field to a resting stop just before it could hit someone else.

"What are you, scared of the golf ball? It won't hurt you. Take out your feelings of rage. Pour your emotion into it. Have some feeling." Jason glared fiercely at him and hit the ball again, which gained some slight lift but otherwise did not travel far.

"You're a math person. Calculate the trajectory of the ball. Science it up. Come on, Jason!" Jason ignored his taunts and maintained the same form, each time making the sad walk of shame to pick up his ball and bring it back to the start.

"Stop being a loser and start being a winner!" Jason looked across to the far end of the field, where Mr. Clements was guiding a student who somehow was doing worse, walked up to Tom, and punched him squarely in the chest. Tom gasped for air, and looked around for sympathetic faces. His classmates averted their gaze, even Ted. Jason walked back to his lane and started hitting his ball again, this time with proper form and technique. Tom checked his watch—too much time left—and went back to practice.

Beth was willing to be the victim of anything but circumstance. She could accept that her poor judgment led her to act rashly, or that she judged Ted's character based on superficial attributes. But above all, she could not accept that she had done nothing wrong but be exploited by others who wished her harm. Despite her inclinations toward the good person philosophy and all it entailed, Beth believed her own hubris had stopped her from seeing her own flaws, and by association what exactly everyone else was doing right. Her parents had taught her from a young age that confession was the secret to absolution, and when a private conference with her heavenly Father, manifest in her teddy bear, proved a one-sided conversation, she sought additional support.

"Frank?" Beth asked, peering around the corner just to make sure nobody else was watching. Frank rapidly put away his phone and turned to Beth with a smile. "I am at your service."

"This is a hard confession for me to make—oh no, don't worry, not that sort of confession—because it violates the trust you have placed in all of us this year. I know your time is precious, so I will keep this brief. How do I stop vaping?" Frank gave Beth a look that radiated judgment, but also a lack of surprise, as if somehow this explained everything.

"I am glad you chose me to talk with. Why do you want to stop?"

"Well, it's somewhat obvious: it reveals feeblemindedness, it leads to long-term health effects, it's not trendy anymore—"

"No, Beth, not like that. Why now do you want to stop? What's put this thought in your head?"

"After Ted and I broke up, I've had some time for self-reflection. At first, I blamed him: the entire time, he was concealing his true character, manipulating me into thinking a certain way and accepting his temperament as normal. But I now think this is a lazy outlook. I don't want to be a victim, to play a victim because it gains me sympathy. I know there are so many others out there just like him that walk these same halls. All they see is a victim, a little plaything who will give them a kiss occasionally and make them feel high and mighty. They don't see themselves as immoral, they see themselves as budding capitalists, responding to a cruel world with cruelty of their own. Such an astute judge of character as yourself probably does not need to be told this, but it's easy for people like me to put themselves into subservient roles just because it works. It works, Frank. It works every time, and because of that, you forget all the bumps and skids along the way that leave wounds and scars, just because the highs are so good. You'd phrase it as sacrificing long-term benefit for short-term gain, and that's exactly what I want to stop. I want to stop being impulsive solely to gratify others, just because I think that makes me happy too. But it doesn't. It only makes people like Ted happy. I wish we lived in a society where it wasn't socially acceptable for me to appeal to the, you know, down there, instead of the brain."

"You make a compelling argument," Frank responded after some thought. Frank definitely thought Beth made good points. Frank had enabled Ted's predatory behavior due to his stubborn insistence on being equal-opportunity and breaking the rules occasionally. He had created this mess, and it was his responsibility to fix it, not because of any club doctrine, but because he was a good person. "Have you already disposed of all your vaping paraphernalia?"

"I have already. I'm all clean now."

"Well, it seems like you have everything largely under control, and I want you to know that I can provide any support you need. This gives me an idea, in fact, for next year."

"A vaping awareness campaign?"

"No, something better." Beth believed Frank had proven her lingering suspicions completely right: the fault ultimately rested with her for having made poor decisions, and erasing any impact of those poor decisions was entirely within her capability. She thanked Frank, reaching out for a handshake and fist bump, and went on her way. Frank immediately did what every responsible person does when told a secret and shared it with his friends, who together all swore to stay quiet. Alan and the other club officers were deemed too untrustworthy to be included.

"Is it really our responsibility to deal with vaping? That's, like, the principal's problem," Jason asked dismissively (Jason happened to walk by Frank and the others as they were conversing and was invited to join the brainstorming).

"Why shouldn't it be our responsibility? Mr. Kurtz clearly hasn't done anything to stop it. Drug users stink up the bathrooms. The secondhand smoke makes me gag. If we can pick up trash, this isn't too much worse."

"So how then, Frank, do we solve the problem? Do you have a solution in mind?" If Pranav knew Frank, he always had a solution in mind.

"It's simple. All of you know the placebo effect, right? We make some sort of fake drug, work with the administration to not only get them to pay for it, but look the other way, make some money, and rat out everyone to the administration."

"If it were as simple as punishing people for doing drugs, I don't think we would need to have this conversation," Jason sarcastically remarked. "But there are some people I'd love to see behind bars."

"And when was the last time you saw anyone punished for vaping? Never! Over the last year, we've built up this remarkable infrastructure, one which we'll be testing at the assembly today anyway, and it would be a shame to waste it all on trivial affairs."

"None of this has been trivial, though. I don't like pulling the 'I'm a junior, so trust me' card, but I wish my robotics team ran this smoothly." Before Pranav could continue, Frank interrupted:

"Exactly. A lot of trivial affairs accumulated become serious indeed. One grain of sand is infinitesimal, but thousands can drown someone. Can we ever have too much of a good thing?" Everyone murmured and agreed that no, it was impossible to have too much of a good thing, and they bubbled with suggestions for how best to execute the scheme. It was miraculous. It was almost no trick at all, they saw, to turn vice into virtue and slander into truth, impotence into abstinence, arrogance into humility, plunder into philanthropy, thievery into honor, blasphemy into wisdom, brutality into patriotism, and sadism into justice. Anybody could do it; it required no brains at all. It merely required no character. Somehow, Frank had convinced himself and his accomplices that the slippery slope they descended was not a slope, but a set of stairs, one they descended entirely on their own volition and with nothing but an endless treasure trove at the bottom. Wealth beyond their imagination, with a side of moral vindication. Frank always believed the ends justified the means, and Frank also never said no to a good deal; if the only people losing were those breaking the law, and everyone else won, who could complain?

Class council elections followed a predictable pattern: each class would be herded into the theater to sit obediently while the kids presenting suffered from stage fright to various degrees. Few articulated policy positions deeper than reaffirming their class was indeed the best, and everyone in the audience pretended to pay attention before immediately going to vote for their friends. Frank had purposely pulled strings with the student body president, who he knew from math class to be sympathetic to his cause, to schedule the speeches to be delivered in reverse alphabetical order; while seemingly arbitrary, this served to ensure Frank presented last. He wanted his audience's memory of his speech to block out all the others, and he had promised his friends before the assembly he would do exactly that.

After the two candidates for treasurer delivered equally credible promises to not embezzle all the class's money, Frank signaled Jason in the audio booth and Queen's "Don't Stop Me Now" began playing with thunderous intensity. Frank had to admit that there was nothing quite like walking on stage to a full audience of applause. Some of his friends had signs, and they led the house in chanting his name; many seemingly joined in the chanting just for the fun of it, and the teachers chuckled at the glitz of the affair (Mr. Cathcart despondently sighed, "Lord, what fools these mortals be!"). Frank signaled like a conductor, and at once the audience fell silent. He had a little speech that he prepped on some index cards and had tested on Jason beforehand, structured around the theme of "strength through discipline, strength through community, strength through action"; certainly it was plagiarism, but for about half the audience it was an original theme, and besides, what could they do about it? They certainly couldn't just stand up and leave, especially not after his brilliant, but brief air guitar performance.

"Friends, Tigers, countrymen, lend me your ears. I can see from my audience that my reputation precedes me, and thus I shall keep this brief. One of the core tenets of my club is 'strength through discipline, strength through community, strength through action.' Together, these things once made Heller great. Any yearbook you read will prove that we have entered the dark ages. Students simply aren't as studious, as spirited, as splendid as they used to be—our state senator graduated from Heller! And look at us now: we are a pale imitation of our former selves. We need a leader to restore our former glory, and I am that leader. I will make Heller great again! Together, we all can make Heller great again! Raise your hand in the audience if you want to fail high school, if you want to be consigned to a fate of remedial education and relentless mockery from your peers? None of you? I thought so.

Raise your hand if you want to be alone, an outcast misunderstood by everyone, even yourself. Nobody? You should see a trend forming here. Heller, as it stands, is spinning out of control—we are a car, accelerating and accelerating toward an indomitable wall, and if we do nothing we shall burst into flames! But if we grip the steering wheel hard enough, perhaps we can avert disaster. That brings me to the last point: action. The actions we make every day, no matter how small, rotate that steering wheel; if good, they lead us the right way, if bad, we turn back to our original course. As secretary, I vow to do my part to lead the way toward a brighter future, one where we have a class of future senators and not borderline misfits. Millionaires, not paupers! I ask little of each of you, other than that every day, you model the behavior of a Tiger—a real tiger, ferocious with teeth bared, not a paper tiger that crumples in a stiff breeze! That's not so hard, is it? If you need guidance in how to become a better Tiger, a better person, ask me or any of the other club members; we have sworn an oath to defend those good old-fashioned values on which we used to rely, and we believe that each and every one of you can help us on this quest toward a land of milk and honey, of bread and circuses! Lastly: if any of you are against progress and wish to see our school crumble to dust, guess what? You have to vote for me anyway! Don't we all love democracy? (This was met with a resounding yes from the audience.) Once again, this is Franklin Barnes, asking you to help me make Heller great again!"

As he delivered his speech, pounding the lectern for emphasis, everyone he cared about was focused intently on him and only him. He left the stage to applause and Queen, and wondered if the other class council candidates felt uncomfortable now that their speeches were so depressing in comparison. After the assembly, Frank snuck out one of the back exits of the theater only to see that Mr. T had the same idea.

"I hope you know you have a true natural flair for this sort of thing, especially with the Mussolini-like delivery," he said, stopping for a second when a large drop of rain fell on his head.

"I'll take that as a compliment."

"I loved the Queen bit—wasn't that SNL originally?"

"Imitation is the sincerest form of flattery, and you know how much I love my clichés," Frank joked. "If 'Uptown Funk' is blasted at every school event, it's only fair I adopt my own fight song. My personal favorite, while fitting, wasn't terribly appropriate."

"I doubt Ms. Wolfe would have enjoyed your inventive rhyme of 'faster pace' and 'master race.' But where do you go from here? If I do say so myself, you seem to have succeeded at what you originally set out to do."

"I don't know. I hope I get lucky. For now, I'll just be singing in the rain," Frank responded as he briskly walked away with a spring in his step. Mr. T followed him from a distance, and when Frank thought he was out of view, he shuffled his feet a little, swinging around the lamppost and jumping up the stairs.

After school, Beth still felt burdened by her conscience. This time, it was more of a creeping, existential dread, tinged with infinite possibilities of disappointment; even if Frank took the news well, what about somebody like John, who as usual stood out in the open seemingly not caring about the rain? There was something about John that made him perfect for confessions: he treated whatever he was told with reverence, never perturbed no matter how extreme. Beth made sure to grab a seat next to John, and she hoped he would do something to break the ice.

"John?" Beth asked, looking around to make sure nobody was eavesdropping. John grunted, and she took that as a yes.

"As much as I hate to admit this, I have finally stopped vaping." Beth waited for John to make eye contact, and after she lightly nudged him just to see if he was awake, he looked up. "I'm so proud of you. You have no idea how much courage that took," he said through the faintest of tears, "and yes. I feel the same way toward you."

"Uh, thanks?" Beth offered with a raised eyebrow—how could John possibly have misinterpreted that? John caught on that Beth did not profess feelings of unwavering loyalty, and his breath steadied.

"So anyway, great work. Are you still coming to the lake?" John asked, still elated for no particular reason. "I've been helping Regina discover the joys of meditation in the park downtown, by the garden, and I think all of us can build on that progress. It's very scenic, up where Tom's house is. I bet there's great fishing." This prompted another raised eyebrow—did Tom know about this?—but Beth conceded that yes, she was coming still, and meditation would do her a lot of good. "It clears the mind," Beth recalled from health class.

John felt reborn when he exited the bus onto the slightly damp asphalt. He was someone that could be trusted, someone who was trustworthy—yes, he was someone deserving of respect! Beyond that, too, he was injected with a new vitality when he realized what else Beth's confession meant. She had changed, changed to be a better person, one capable of reflection; this reflection had guided her to spurn Ted, and perhaps it would lead her on a brighter path later. There were still a few days of school left, but only finals, which didn't really count; as far as John was concerned, he stepped off the bus a free man. John thought for a moment that if he were to run, arms at his sides, he would lift into the air and fly through the clouds, capering through the cloudy expanses of gray and refreshing rain. How exhilarating it would be to see his neighborhood as specks, the peninsula as one finger extending into the water like a pier, his country crystalline, and his humble planet as a blue dot that would shrink and shrink to nothing! John would live among the stars, keeping pace with the planets as they spun around with no end in sight. This grandiose vision disappointed him when he counted his steps and saw his feet were as ordinary as always. He walked a bit more quickly than usual, eager to get home and collapse on his bed.

Chapter 19

John packed lightly, as always; everything he brought had to have a purpose, or else he would look in his suitcase when he returned home and feel wasteful. Still, everything he deemed valuable enough to bring added up to one bulging rolling suitcase, which he spun around in circles on his driveway like a top. Every crack in the pavement seemed a new plaything, a mountain ridge emerging from a plain or a ravine that coursed to the core of the Earth. Mr. Langley arrived driving the same van as last time, and Tom rode shotgun as usual.

"Are you excited, John?" Mr. Langley asked while checking the map to figure out where Juliet lived.

"I'm as excited as always, Steve," John responded perkily, and the two laughed as if this weren't the first time they'd seen each other in months. Tom rolled his eyes and took out his phone to text Regina. Juliet was next to enter, and her parents waved goodbye while she tried her hardest to maneuver to John's right smoothly, quickly giving up and sliding across his lap; she chuckled and smiled at John, who smiled despite not thinking it humorous.

"Lovely name," Mr. Langley remarked when Juliet introduced herself. Beth was next on the list, so they drove through the lilac trees to her door; a few flowers fell onto the car's windshield. Beth was delighted to see Juliet's face pressed against the glass, John's looming faintly next to hers, and nimbly moved to John's left. Juliet was extremely curious to learn what she had gotten herself into, and due to John's proximity saw him as the most reliable witness.

"So you're in the woods, right? Do you know that scene in *Snow White* where all the birds and rabbits come out of the bushes to help her do the dishes? I've always wanted to live in a tranquil little cabin like that, away from all the distractions of life. I hope that's what the house is like," Juliet bubbled, and John nodded his head in understanding.

"You just want to live like a princess, the nature's not part of it at all," Beth joked, and John glared at her while Juliet laughed it off—how dare she ruin her fantasy? John explained carefully to Juliet how while there were wild quail, deer, and raccoons, they were to be admired from a distance and not abducted as household pets.

"I'm just kidding, John, although it would be nice, raccoons are kind of adorable," Juliet reassured him, and just as Regina entered the car, John decided he had had enough socialization time and took out his book. Frank had made a summer reading list for the club while working with his teachers to get around the minor technicality that summer home-work was prohibited; Frank added his favorite books and let others on the list without much argument. John, in a way, was admirably precocious in starting *Catch-22* in the car; the others who cared (Tom's half-hearted participation had its limits, even though Regina expressed her desire to go with the majority and play along) were waiting to see Tom's promised mythical bookshelf.

"It isn't mine, really, it's more of a family collection. I never look at any myself," Tom claimed, which he rapidly amended to "rarely, sometimes, on occasion" when Regina looked at him shiftily. So far, all these descriptions were persuading Juliet that she was traveling to a fairytale castle. This was going to be the best trip ever, and she was about to share this insight with John when she saw him already enthralled in his book, eyes glazed over. She discreetly snuck a peek over his shoulder, seeing Beth was doing the same. Lots of violence, this must be a rousing read.

Juliet's preconception was not entirely disrupted when as they approached their destination, the air gradually became more misty, which made them shiver as they exited the van and hauled their suitcases up the path to the front porch.

"Looks like it might rain, I hope you brought umbrellas," Mr. Langley remarked after taking a heady whiff of the air. "There should be some firewood in the garage if you want to use the fireplace."

As the new visitor, Juliet was automatically granted seniority and given the master bedroom, and so the others returned to their usual positions. John found his little alcove just as inhospitable as before; a distinctive, lemony scent of cleaning supplies reassured him that at least it was sanitary.

"So what do you guys do for fun around here? We obviously can't swim when it's this cold out," Juliet asked Regina upstairs while they waited for Tom to leave the restroom.

"There are board games in that cabinet, I believe," Regina responded, and she walked over and opened the repurposed linen closet to see stacks upon stacks of jigsaw puzzles and board games, all somehow neatly partitioned. "You know, I never did any of these as a kid," she mused, and grabbed a jigsaw puzzle featuring one of Monet's *Water Lilies* and brought it downstairs, just in time to hear the doorbell ring. The Monroes proved charitable hosts as usual, and were joyous to see a new face. Tom by then had come down, and John and Beth heard the commotion upstairs and wished to investigate too, and so all five of them stood in a huddle.

"Who's putting away the groceries?" Tom asked, hoping the answer wasn't him. John immediately volunteered, and Tom and Regina watched him from the table.

"Would you be so kind as to bring us two glasses of ice water?" Regina requested semi-politely, and when John did not respond quickly enough she reached around him to fill two glasses from the refrigerator with a noise that sounded like a woodchipper. Eventually, everyone assembled in the living room and looked at each other blankly: they did not think they would need to provide their own entertainment so soon. They had exhausted themselves of conversation on the ride there, and Juliet had already cooed appreciatively during the house tour, astonished that John and Beth slept in sleeping bags and not on the couches. Why didn't I think of that before, John thought to himself. Too late now, and this way, his space was entirely his own. He had named the taxidermied raven Edgar, thinking it clever if trite, and in this way Edgar became a guardian angel that protected him as he slept instead of a demon who would spontaneously animate and peck his brains out.

"Regina, you never played for us last year; care to give those keys a spin? Piano books are inside the bench if you need them," Tom suggested, and Regina regretted not doing this the previous year; John would have been so impressed! He still watched now with rapt attention as she worked through the highlights of her repertoire while simultaneously chatting with Tom, but it wasn't the same. After about an hour, she assumed her audience was losing interest, and so she delicately closed the piano and went back to join them.

"I used to play, long ago. I stopped though, never had the focus," John commented. That surprised Beth—John out of all people wasn't focused? "Give it a try, John, see what you still remember," she urged, and John reluctantly walked up to the piano and launched into a flawless performance of "The Entertainer," seemingly not remembering that he had ever stopped. Beth immediately turned to Regina for judgment, who smiled and gave a thumbs-up.

"I thought you stopped playing," Regina remarked pointedly, to which John only responded "Muscle memory." The piano most certainly having provided its maximum utility now proved a distraction, and everyone migrated downstairs before they would be tempted to do anything artistic. Tom took the armchair immediately, leaving the other four to squeeze together on the couch, which John found oddly comforting.

"What should we do now?" Tom asked brusquely after he decided sitting quietly was not what he had taken his friends on a six-hour journey for. Nobody suggested anything in the first thirty seconds, so he turned on the TV and they channel-surfed until they agreed upon Food Network; Tom ordinarily would avoid it like the plague, but he hoped it would tell him in no uncertain terms how he was supposed to cook his own dinner from the ingredients the Monroes provided.

They went to bed early that night, all exhausted from the car ride and uncertain if the fireplace would explode. Before John went to his nook, after Beth had poked her head out in her pajamas to say good night, he went to the sliding glass door in the family room, only fifteen paces from his sleeping bag, to stare outside. The mist and darkness challenged John's perception of distance, and it appeared that he were on a boat in the midst of the lake instead of firmly on land—he could tell no difference unless he saw the doormat below him. Every minute, the green light of the patrol boat would flash, which circuited the lake slowly enough to not make noise or disturb the wildlife just to make sure everyone was in order. Before the light could increase in size too much, like a train slowly chugging toward him, John went to his room and wished himself good night.

John dreamed the house was filled with mist, that overnight it had found a crack and forced itself in. He woke up, lost, not in the same room in which he had fallen asleep. It felt like hours he wandered through rooms and hallways that were close enough to reality to be believable, all without seeing another face. Eventually, his lucidity caught up with him just enough to make him think looking for family photos would reveal at least whose house he was in, or otherwise act as a focus for arcane energy that like a lighthouse beacon would attract his friends. But all the faces were blank, smooth globes of skin that perhaps from the outlines alone could be recognizable as his classmates, but otherwise resembled crash test dummies. John wanted to shout for help through the fog, but something in his throat stopped him from making any noise at all. John was cold, not having had the foresight to bundle up, and sometimes he thought he had woken up, only to still feel strapped in place and unable to see anything but his eyelids. Back and forth John shifted between endless snowy white and gray interludes, until he sensed a faint brightness climbing through his tiny window; his body felt refreshed, but his mind was tired. John left his room to see Beth staring out through the sliding door at the lake, which was still shrouded with mist as to be invisible, and the garden, where the flowers somehow in bloom gorged themselves on dew.

"You too?" Beth asked quietly, just in case John was sleepwalking. She had emerged just a few minutes before John, quietly hoping that after a few minutes of staring outside, her body would tell itself it could squeeze in a few more hours of sleep; it had not occurred to either of them that going to bed early would shift their sleep cycles.

"I thought I heard a voice cry, sleep no more!" John most certainly did not want to go back to sleep; since he thought the view outside too eerie for comfort, he went upstairs to get breakfast. Beth followed, and Juliet also came down the stairs bleary-eyed just as they were about to start eating.

"What are you guys doing up so early? It's 5:10 AM!" Juliet asked, looking around furtively to find some other clue.

"The same as you," Beth muttered, and Juliet sighed and sat down across from John.

"Do you think Tom and Regina will be coming down as well?" she asked, realizing that there were four seats and they could not possibly accommodate five, not unless they moved to the dining room, which would demand physical exertion.

"They tend not to be early risers," John explained between bites. "And what a shame it is, this is such a lovely morning. Say, how does some meditation sound? There's something about this weather that's very mystical, almost enough to be portentous."

"Where will we sit? Everything's going to be damp."

"Now don't be silly Beth, there's a remedy for everything excepting death," John said, unwilling to be stopped by anything as trivial as water. "If you're scared, you can bring a towel, but I think it's part of the experience, right?"

"Meditation is an extremely important part of yoga, you know," Juliet chimed in, and Beth decided that her other options for entertainment were so limited she really couldn't say no. There were three benches in the garden, and so they sat and cleared their minds, and John quickly discovered that unlike the others, he was incapable of sitting in full lotus for more than a few seconds. Breathe in, breathe out, John told himself; whenever a gust of cold wind blew and startled him, he told his mind he was on a boat racing through the ocean, or flying in the atmosphere where the winds were undoubtedly more turbulent. He had read a book once that told him to isolate any feelings of discomfort, remarking upon cold, for instance, as 'wow, that feels weird," nothing more. Regina came downstairs, curious to see if the others were awake. She saw the three of them sitting in the cold outside, eyes closed, faces at peace, and thought them mad; most definitely unwilling to join them, she went back upstairs to her warm bed.

An hour passed, and a loud foghorn somewhere in the distance was enough to convince the three that their spiritual returns were rapidly dissipating. They stood up and stretched a bit; Beth showed them Tai Chi moves her grandfather had taught her and said something unconvincing about how the hand movements focused energy. The absurdity of the moment dawned on them, that it really was strange how it was barely past 6 and they were frolicking outside, and so they went back inside to the study. Juliet pulled her reading list out of her pocket and searched the shelf, both happy her options were extensive and also quite terrified. Her earlier reading binge had turned into a habit, but not one with any great frequency, and after asking John what he would recommend, she chose *Don Quixote* and weighed it in her palm.

"You really read something this long?" Beth rolled her eyes—"of course he did, he's John"—and Juliet laughed again: "You truly are an intellectual."

"I don't think I'm an intellectual; that flattery really is too much. There's nothing much in how I think. It's not important, it's a minor compulsion. I can deal with it if I want to. But anyway, *Don Quixote*. I promise it goes by quickly. Frank recommended it to me; that's even his copy of the book!" This proved convincing enough for Juliet, and they returned upstairs. John took the rocking chair as usual, and Beth and Juliet sat together directly across from him (both the rocking chair and the armchair downstairs were brought originally by Mr. Langley, who believed any house was incomplete without them).

It had never occurred to John until a particularly lascivious passage in *Catch-22* that he was sitting across from two cute girls who were there because of him. Regina didn't count, as she was out of his line of sight, and she generally waited until Tom descended to have her breakfast. John did not know if only two days were sufficient for a routine, but he was enthused regardless: their bodies all somehow shifted to wake at dawn, their morning routine remained identical the following day, and even Regina was so impressed by their devotion that she too read quietly with them. John assumed that had he not planted the seed of literacy in them, they'd be in their rooms painting their nails or having pillow fights or something else altogether boorish and unsightly. He at some point too would have engaged in similar activities, but he was a better person now. He had standards to uphold, an appearance to maintain, and as much as it pained him to cut himself off cold turkey from video games, he could not take away their John. It was simply not right, it was simply not chivalrous.

John ordinarily would have considered it socially unacceptable to have any non-school-related thoughts about his classmates, but by being with them outside of school, he had made that difficult. John considered them friends, having weathered a full year of Mr. T with them, and felt just as privy to their eccentricities as he was sure they were to his. Indeed, it was then inevitable that they liked him as much as he liked them! But, of course, neither of them knew the other held any designs, as that would be all too much like *Pride and Prejudice*. No, novels did not govern the real world, John knew that as fact! Truth was much more ordinary than fiction, which meant that both most likely were trying as hard as possible to focus on their books—almost like they were meditating—and maybe, just maybe, reminding themselves occasionally who sat across from them.

John was nobler than they were, however; he suppressed any feelings as soon as they could surface. How lucky was he compared to his classmates to have such unfettered and intimate access to the two of them, as cherubic as they could ever be? John's initial astonishment at his revelation faded to guilt, and then to pride: was he not a better person for his denial of temptation? His denial was made easier in that he never actually had to deny anything, perhaps excluding his own curiosity. If his initial theory were correct, their demeanor would turn flirty and seductive after some sufficient time had passed, and while they did seem a bit close for any ordinary classmates, John observed no marked change. This drove his mind in opposite directions, his expression occasionally turning frantic: what if he was missing signals? Were they waiting for some catalyst? Who would break first? He wondered if he, instead of sitting in the rocking chair, sat on the couch, if the others would still sit in their usual positions, with him comfortably squashed in the middle. Or, would one of them take his position, rendering him the person watched and not the watcher? Maybe it was the other way around: John, ringed in sunlight, was like a marble sculpture, or a model for portrait artists at work. How could he know for certain that as he read, they did not briefly pause their reading on occasion to stare at him, just as he was sometimes prone to lapses of concentration himself? As much as he wanted to try this experiment, if only in the spirit of scientific inquiry, he could not bear the potential awkwardness of them looking at him strangely and shifting in their seats. So, failing that, he could only imagine what they thought of their peculiar daily routine.

Juliet found herself increasingly disappointed in Beth for picking favorites. She had not realized that Beth and John had already developed a fair rapport, one which never seemed evident at school; they finished each other's sentences at times, had an inside joke revolving around chickens, and had a chemistry that while not exceptional, irritated her because she had never noticed it before. John's pithy one-liners amused Beth, who also seemed prone to cynical moods; they had nothing to feel sorry for, they were on vacation! "Those who do not complain are never pitied," John dryly remarked when he and Beth were commiserating over some prior shared misery. Tom and Regina were another case altogether: they finished each other's sentences frequently, far more cutely at that; had multiple inside jokes and pet names that made them seem like schoolchildren instead of mature teenagers; and functioned too cohesively. Regina made Tom breakfast, which certainly was adorable at first, but Juliet began to worry Tom was somehow coercing her. There was nothing wrong with a little authority in her mind, but she did not appreciate anything that could possibly hint that the three early birds were not living their best lives. If John and Beth were most comfortable together, and Tim and Regina (Beth once called Tom that by accident, having learned the habit from Behrooz; Tom's exasperation was somehow inherently comic, and everyone else in the house but Regina now knew how to push his buttons whenever they needed a laugh) were most certainly comfortable together—but where did that leave her?

One afternoon, Juliet proposed they take a family walk—she immediately corrected this to a "friendly walk"—to get some fresh air and convince Tom and Regina the mist wouldn't hurt them. The weather had not shown any signs of clearing, but by then the early birds were used to it and found it a welcome reprieve from the summer heat that undoubtedly awaited them at home.

"It's too cold," Tom declared assertively, and tried to convince Regina of the same.

"This is nothing, Tom—imagine when it snows," she responded with a mild trace of condescension, and Tom helpfully reminded them that he had no need to imagine when it snowed, as he came here in the winter too. Beth was convinced by Tom's reasoning, intent on finishing the jigsaw puzzle they had started the previous night, and the others put on their warmest clothing and walked outside. Mr. Langley had been partially correct: precipitation was on the horizon, and as soon as they had walked far enough away to not see the house, it started hailing. John marveled at seeing ice in June, and thought it cataclysmic; what sort of world did they live in where there was ice in June? Juliet took out her umbrella and used it to shield her phone, and then took a picture of the three of them trying their best to smile.

"With weather like this, when will we ever swim?" Regina asked in exasperation, looking back at John and Juliet, who walked next to each other.

"Who cares about swimming? This is so cool! This must be so rare, and it's not like you can't swim anywhere else. There's nothing wrong with a little cold when we have our friends," Juliet declared, not wishing to say that she was going swimming in Singapore anyway, so missing out on this was no big loss.

"The cold never bothered me anyway," John said deadpan, and this inspired yet another peal of laughter to break their silence. In the moment, John could think of nothing but their proximity and intimacy. The scenery was beautiful, the trees, the lake, all of it—but when at home could he ever do something like this? When would Alan or Frank ever know anything like this? The universe was clearly rewarding John for his faithful devotion.

"I have a genius idea: we should watch *Frozen*," Regina exclaimed, and they looked at John to see if he would flinch.

"If we want to watch a movie, Frank loaned me what he said was the absolute best movie of all time. I trust his judgment." Regina was skeptical, not wanting to spoil a good vacation with something most likely bourgeois, but Juliet seconded John's opinion: "I have never known Frank, or you, to lie. And oh, how about we all bake cookies! We can make ice cream too! Girls' movie night, let's do it!" Juliet looked at John, who could not decide if this was nirvana or hell on earth, and less excitedly declared: "Oh, you're an honorary girl. Tom can stay downstairs and watch football." A trail marker reminded them that they had walked a few miles out, and they turned back, vigorously debating if snickerdoodles or classic chocolate chip would be better. They settled their deadlock by having Juliet text Frank, who suggested they compromise by making snickerdoodles and chocolate ice cream; he sent a recipe for a dark chocolate gingerbread ice cream that apparently was divine, and Beth confirmed from home base, happy to know that they were surviving the hail, that the ingredients were all available.

Tom was somewhat annoyed to be kicked out of the kitchen, where he had the puzzle set up on the small table, and begrudgingly moved downstairs. Beth had taken the initiative to start measuring out all the ingredients, and she assigned everyone their tasks.

"Your family owns restaurants, this should be easy for you," John commented as he tried his hardest to crack eggs and measure flour without slipping and spilling everything.

"I rarely cook; my parents insist on doing everything, so I m out of practice. But it looks like you're handling everything well—girls love it when guys know how to cook," Juliet responded with a smile, and John was too confused to respond. Regina seconded Juliet's opinion, then looked downstairs, where Tom was completely enthralled in his jigsaw puzzle, not even bothering to turn on the TV. John smudged his sleeve with butter, and he rubbed the stain with flour-dusted hands, muttering to himself quietly "Out, damned spot!"; everything was going so perfectly now, and he could not afford a single blemish. Before they were about to put the cookies in the oven, they realized that in their spurt of giddiness, they had radically misjudged how long ice cream took to make compared to the cookies; the appeal of fresh-baked cookies diminished when they sat on the counter for five hours. As the ice cream churned and all of them remained in a culinary mood, John's thoughts immediately drifted to dinner: that was the missing piece of the equation! They could light candles, Tom could keep sitting downstairs, Regina could go eat potato chips on the couch with him, and it would become a scene out of one of those movies John never could watch. Beth, whose hands were the cleanest out of all of them, looked through Mrs. Monroe's meal plan and suggested leg of lamb, and they went through their culinary ritual once more to fill up the time. John still was bothered by his butter stain, and kept muttering to himself until he thought one of the others noticed.

After a few hours, Tom smelled rosemary and garlic and wondered exactly what sort of cookies and ice cream they were making upstairs. He followed the smell upstairs to see the four of them all somehow working simultaneously among pots and pans, helping each other with motivational phrases, and chose to keep a safe distance as they worked.

"I see you all really enjoyed watching *Iron Chef* yesterday," Tom laughed, and the others mimicked his gesture in a stifled manner. "Great work, Regina," he concluded, disappointed that they were too absorbed in their work to appreciate how he climbed all the way up the stairs to say hello. "I guess I'll set the table," he said to himself, and went to the dining room and made sure he did everything, even folding the napkins, perfectly; he would not let himself be upstaged, this was his house. Dinner was ready not long after, and their concentrated drive manifested itself in superb execution, a fact John credited to them following the recipes precisely:

"I remember Ms. Denham once described cooking as applied chemistry: if you can do a lab, you can cook." The others nodded in agreement, still in disbelief that the lamb was a perfect medium-rare and the asparagus was crisp. Tom finished eating first and immediately went to start cleaning up in the kitchen while the others bantered until their stomachs were full. The cookies came out of the oven just when the rest of the kitchen was spotless and the ice cream machine's thrum began to slow.

"So John, what's this 'greatest movie of all time' that we're watching tonight?"

"Well, unless Tom would like to watch *Frozen* instead (Tom immediately shook his head; his father had forced him to watch *Frozen* as punishment once, and Tom could not look at snowmen anymore without a feeling of disgust), we're going to watch *Casablanca*. 1940-something, black-and-white, romantic, classy, or so I'm told."

"Sounds exotic," Beth remarked, and after they portioned out a serving of ice cream and a few cookies for everyone, they went downstairs and Tom set up the movie. The fireplace was upstairs and it was still a bit cold, so Juliet went to her room and brought back a small blanket for the four of them on the couch; Regina sat on the side closest to Tom's chair, and John sat sandwiched between the other two. This was already the best movie ever, he thought. The narration began, and John felt himself transported to a land before time, back when people still talked with funny accents and "the war" was a state of mind instead of a historical event.

"What's so romantic about World War II?" Juliet whispered to John with a nudge, hoping he would have an answer. "Love and war are the same thing," he explained. In what was a rare occurrence for shows they watched as a group, they did not narrate or commentate; they watched with their eyes and ears first, their minds playing catch-up as they went along. Tom laughed at the witty double-talk, vowing to imitate Rick's brusqueness later; Regina, Juliet, and John shed tears when Rick and Ilsa shed tears; everyone felt their hearts sink when Michael Curtiz intended their hearts to sink; and everyone finished their cookies and ice cream.

"That may have been the best movie I've ever seen," John proclaimed after a moment of silence, and then turned to the girls flanking him hoping for their opinions. Tom, seeing no reason for counter-argument, expressed the same; something about watching the movie from the armchair made him feel thirty years older, like he should have had a fine cigar or a brandy. Framed from that point of view, he could not say no to any movie in black-or-white, and the pathos of the moment aside, he really could find no flaw.

"It was very intellectual," Regina offered in an enthusiastic tone, and John could not tell if she was being sarcastic or if "intellectual" was the highest praise she could offer, and both Beth and Juliet expressed that it was certainly a fine movie. It seemed as if decades of critics weren't wrong. It was rapidly approaching their new bed time, and they rapidly returned to their rooms and prepared for sleep. John stared out the sliding door again, counting the pulses of the hypnotic green light as it slowly brightened.

John slept restlessly that night, still processing the flurry of emotions and experiences from that day; every detail would be etched in his mind that even months afterward, he could recall every step and every feeling as if he were still there. What had he done to deserve such reward? Nothing at all: he had merely said yes to Tom, and thus had been whisked away to a world of pure imagination. During the course of his normal life, John lived a solitary life, content with simple pleasures and self-motivation the sixteen hours of the day he was not at school. What were the odds that while he was doing that, others were having their own perfect days, but in much greater quantity? Maybe it did not take a hailstorm to stir the mind and bring such epiphanies as how cute scarves were or how warm other people's bodies could be under a blanket. No fireplace or sunshine was needed for warmth, but John had always thought some outside energy was needed to kickstart life—was that not how physics worked? For a while these reveries provided an outlet for his imagination; they were a satisfactory hint of the unreality of reality, a promise that the rock of the world was founded securely on a fairy's wing, and these thoughts kept John going through the following morning's meditation, still just the three of them; the end of *Catch-22*; and their last dinner of the trip.

As John and the others enjoyed the baked salmon that by some miracle, they had cooked quite well, he looked around the dinner table and almost shed a tear for the family he would be ripped away from in just a few hours. They could squeeze in a game of Monopoly in one last outburst of final exertion, but once they woke up the following morning and meditated on the things they would lose, they knew Mr. Langley planned on joining them for breakfast and would then take them home. John did not seem to think the others appreciated the gravity of the moment, but he was too scared to bring it up because it would disturb the fragile magic present. Even if the previous day were the only one fully demarcated in John's mind with picture-perfect recollection, he still incorporated this meal into the pantheon, knowing that it would not last. The exact chronology of their vacation did not matter, and he started to wonder just how important factual accuracy really was. This process of chronicling drew out the minutes in slow-motion, such that even though they ate no more slowly than usual, the conversation felt like hours to John.

It also occurred to him then that he really did not talk to any of these people in his spare time. He would be alone when he returned home, waking up in the morning to his computer and little else. That would be worst of all, not seeing friendly faces like Beth, Juliet, and even Regina (who never stopped being friendly), just his lost expression in the bathroom mirror.

Tom was rapidly coming to the same conclusion as John, albeit from a different perspective. Regina was a fact: there was always his daily dose of Regina, taken at least once a day, if not twice. But who else did Tom interact with to such a degree? Ted was a loyal friend, but Ted was of the belief that friendship did not necessitate constant conversation simply for its own sake, even if he saw the pictures of meals Tom sent and Juliet posted on social media and knew that if only he had not messed up with Beth, he'd be sharing in the fruits of their labor. Alan was a good friend too, but life was tough for him, and Alan did not want to talk about his recent woes; Tom thought he knew what was wrong, but any emotional support he directed to him would be diverted from the great fun he was having with his other friends. As for the others, a week of time over the summer ought to be enough to keep him going through the rest of the season.

Mr. Langley's old boss and his wife had control of the house next, and they arrived just as the others were about to leave. John marshaled the clean-up effort that morning, and together they scrubbed and dusted with the same zeal they had applied to their cooking. The new guests were delighted not only to see that, but also gourmet leftovers in the fridge, and they were even more impressed that they were the works of teenagers.

"You and your friends, Tom, certainly run a tight ship," they remarked, and in a rare occurrence, Tom was modest enough to candidly admit it was mostly the others who were responsible. On the car ride home, they sat in the same seating arrangement as they did before, and Mr. Langley pointed out in the rear-view mirror that the mist seemed to be disappearing.

"A shame you didn't get to go swimming at all, but you have plenty of time. It sounds like you found ways to keep yourselves occupied," he commented.

"We certainly did," Tom laughed.

Chapter 20

A s the summer dragged on, Frank found himself making the walk downtown more frequently. Food was abundant and the park was pleasant, where Frank found some reprieve from the inexorable summer heat in the shade. His house was air-conditioned, certainly, but it felt sterile at times; the constant room-temperature almost seemed worse than the muggy heat outside. Frank had enrolled in some community college classes held online, which meant that his mornings were generally spent taking notes and being studious, but beyond that, he needed to find his own amusements.

Alan, as usual, took about ten seconds to pick up the phone. "What's up?"

"I'm just calling in to see if you finished the paperwork Ms. Wolfe gave at our meeting. I want to make sure we aren't burdened by any needless delays—this is vacation, you know, and the last thing any of us want to do is paperwork." Not long after Frank and his team agreed to do the celery juice project (other contenders were mouthwash and acetaminophen, both of which were rejected for potentially having health effects), they came to the realization that it needed to be school-sponsored if it were to be effective. Mr. Kurtz was not as dismissive as they had expected:

"So why should we be doing this instead of bringing in drug dogs?" he asked, frantically Googling how much celery cost.

"Well, for one, you don't bring in drug dogs. We think drug dogs would be far more effective, but as those are seemingly off the table, think of this as a plan B," Frank explained. Mr. Kurtz was extremely hesitant to bring in drug dogs, which he saw as a signal to the PTA and everyone else important that his leadership had failed. Heller wasn't supposed to have problems—it was in a reasonably rich residential area and sent at least one kid to Stanford every year. Drug dogs were for what Mr. Kurtz publicly described as "troubled areas" and privately described as "the inner cities"; his colleagues at conferences told him tales of woe, and he responded by promising to help in any way he could, which he never did.

"How do you know this will work?" Mr. Kurtz weighed his three options, as he saw them: he could either do nothing and tell his colleagues that he was choosing to ignore the drug epidemic on campus, bring in the drug dogs and polarize the parents, or go for the third plan and ensure nobody complained. If, somehow, this didn't work, and Mr. Kurtz did not expect this to work, the blame fell squarely on the students and they would be "punished"—not really, of course, because then they would reveal the administration told them to implement the scheme and become heroes in the process.

"When you run a club like I do, you begin to learn something about human nature. There's that classic P.T. Barnum quote: there's a sucker born every minute. And unfortunately for us, those suckers are tarnishing our school's reputation and their health. If teenagers can be taught good and evil, if teenagers can be taught multivariable calculus, they can be taught to drink celery juice. It's cheap, cost-effective, and it tastes like it ought to be medicinal. They'll think it's weed or something."

"Fair point, fair point. Why celery though? Couldn't you just give them sugar pills?"

"I learned a few things about celery in middle school. I was one of those Pemberley kids." Mr. Kurtz laughed and reached out his hand for a fist-bump: that was convincing enough.

"Send Ms. Wolfe an email whenever you need supplies and we'll get them to you by the end of the day," he said, and gestured toward her, who was standing in the corner and trying her hardest to remain calm. If they had gone to her first, she'd have chastised them for the sheer audacity of the affair; unfortunately, they foresaw that outcome and went directly to the principal. They all shook hands, and Frank and Pranav cheered when they left. This was going to be fun. More meetings and calls followed as Mr. Kurtz and Ms. Wolfe tried to file paperwork with the fewest number of people knowing, and Alan was brought in after a few weeks. Alan's role, which he was only partially aware of, was to sell the celery juice without getting beat up; Frank did not trust himself to maintain his composure under pressure, and Alan was eager for a leadership position, already thinking his status threatened by Juliet. Alan considered Juliet a suck-up, as she always showed Frank special favor while treating Alan rigidly and perfunctorily—the issue was that Juliet acted toward Alan as a good person should. What Alan did not know was that Frank, his cabal, and the administration had struck a backroom deal to make Alan the scapegoat should the operation collapse; Alan did not think he volunteered to be a martyr, he thought he finally would be able to hang out with the cool kids.

"So anyway, Frank, I totally agree. Paperwork is such a drag—why not have someone else do it? Surely your esteemed treasurer can afford to delegate."

"Exactly, Alan: you are esteemed, and thus the only person I can trust to handle these sensitive matters. Remember, we're the only two students who know about this. You cannot, I repeat, cannot discuss these matters with anyone else. There's money involved here, and as treasurer, you are uniquely qualified." The planning for the celery juice project coincided with some other behind-the-scenes machinations Frank was implementing: his old club secretary, who was supposed to become vice president, had started to catch onto the fact that he was not in fact the second-most senior club member, and had requested his position be filled by someone else if possible. Only his brainwashing prevented him from seeing the truth, instead believing he had committed some slights that were responsible for his silent censure. Naturally, Frank couldn't have his own club officers doubting the appearance of things—what if the normal people caught on?—and so some shifting had to take place. For vice president, his options were limited to Juliet and Alan, as bringing in a true outsider would only create more suspicions. Juliet was inquisitive as is, and while her promotion would improve gender, racial, and intellectual diversity for good optics, Frank did not want to enable her. Alan also did not need enabling—he was pompous and smug without an inflated title—but he executed his limited duties well and would definitely apply the same zeal elsewhere.

Frank still needed someone to fill the secretarial position, or whichever spot opened at the end of the day, and Tom was open to the idea; Frank promised Tom his duties would be limited and purely symbolic, and he would take no personal offense if Tom remained at the sidelines. Tom found the idea of a leadership position extremely appealing, seeing it as a stepping-stone to some hitherto unknown reward, and said yes without question. Why would he question anything? He was already in the inner circle, and unlike Stanley, whoever he was, he understood everything.

"When you phrase it that way, of course I can take care of the paperwork. I don't mind at all—it's good practice. I'll talk to you later," Alan concluded, and he hung up before Frank could say good-bye as well. Frank sighed, disappointed as usual that Alan did not understand basic etiquette, and decided to go for an evening walk. He'd be back home for dinner, and that would be a perfect end to a productive day. Frank's parents were both accountants, who met in graduate school and bonded over a shared love for auditing and financial prudence. Living thriftily early on as their salaries increased enabled them to buy a house in a nice area, right by an excellent high school and many other families whose salaries doubled theirs. They lived comfortably and happily, and took their son's general success as a sign little interference was necessary.

Frank arrived at the park downtown quickly and took out his phone to play some Pokémon Go. He had increasingly relied on it to make his walks less monotonous, and his natural fast walking speed only made things easier; he knew many adult professionals through the game who played far more than he did, and thus felt no shame in his minor indulgence. Frank was just about to throw a curveball to hit an Electabuzz when he heard Juliet's perky voice from behind him. She wore a sky-blue blouse and matching shoes, a "conservative but nice" outfit that was perfect for a future vice president.

"Frank, how nice to see you here! What are you doing?" she asked while giving him a hug he couldn't negotiate to a fist-bump in time. Frank was not terribly happy to see Juliet alone, meaning that it was less likely she had an excuse not to join him, but maybe this was a blessing in disguise: what a perfect opportunity to decide if she was worthy of a promotion, especially after Alan hung up on him so rudely earlier!

"It's a nice day out, and I was tired of staying inside. Weather like this doesn't deserve to be wasted."

"You wouldn't believe the craziest weather we had in Lake Tahoe last month—I'll tell you about it later. Come with me. Oh, nice outfit by the way. You look like a Mormon—in a good way, don't worry. I think it's stylish." This wasn't terribly inaccurate: after discovering that Goodwill frequently offered formal clothing in his size, Frank had decided to supplement his suits with something less extreme, and he personally thought his white polo and slacks suited him well while being utilitarian in the summer heat. Most definitely "conservative but nice."

"You look, um, summery..." he responded, continuing his walk in the general direction Juliet was headed and hiding his phone. Beth and Regina somehow weren't surprised to hear Juliet triumphantly announce "Look who I ran into!" and see Frank sheepishly standing behind her, smiling blankly.

"How nice to see all of you together here, my loyal disciples," Frank commented, surprised all of them seemed happy to see him. "Is there some special occasion I'm unaware of?"

"Juliet didn't tell you? So modest. It's her birthday today, and we were going to hang out a bit, enjoy the sunshine, you know," Regina explained. "It's so nice you could come," Juliet said once more, standing a bit too close to Frank for his personal comfort.

"Well, happy birthday. I didn't bring a present, but I've been deliberating this decision for quite some time now, and I think this is the icing on the cake: you're being promoted to vice president! Your commitment has been spectacular over the past year, and especially as there's no particular difference in responsibilities, it's only fair that your good effort is rewarded." This unsurprisingly demanded another hug from Juliet, and the others politely applauded.

"This is an occasion that demands celebration. Let's get ice cream," Beth suggested. "Thanks for the recipe last month—best I've ever had."

"If it's the best you've ever had, what's the point in having more if it won't top it?" Frank joked, already regretting behaving so impulsively.

"Only one way to find out." Frank decided a bit of sugar never hurt anyone, and even he thought that on a hot day, this was an acceptable concession. He and Juliet led the way, and Frank tried his hardest to present an amiable exterior. Frank considered himself to be crossing a line by mixing business and pleasure this greatly, but he was a softie at heart, and over the year he thought he had developed somewhat of a friendship with all of them. Regina still leaned toward sarcasm in his presence, but he didn't mind; better that than blind obedience. Still, that meant he was playing politics even as he spoke: Alan would have no choice but to accept the turn of events, especially as he never knew he was up for a promotion, and he knew Tom thought in no uncertain terms that Juliet was an idiot wholly incapable of any prolonged deception. Frank didn't think Juliet was an idiot, as much as he thought only an idiot would act like she did, but he agreed with Tom on the latter point: as originally planned, her role would be to legitimize their operation and maybe assist with recruiting more of the sporty types. Those were decisions best saved for later, and in the worst-case scenario, Frank knew that he could bring in other friends who wouldn't need to be kept in the dark.

"So tell me about this lake trip. I saw the photos, and all I can say is that you all certainly ate well," Frank asked after he grew tired of Juliet's bureaucratic questions; the cognitive dissonance was too much to handle.

"Well, the food was a minor part of it. The weather was frigid and dismal, which was a great disappointment, so we mainly stayed inside, read, and meditated. *Casablanca* was great, by the way; did John ever get that back to you?" Frank was glad he could trust Beth to be levelheaded and direct.

"He did, although I'm still not sure what happened to my copy of *Don Quixote*."

"Oh, I read it—interesting book, if a bit long. I'm starting to get a feel for your taste, Frank; no wonder you don't have a sweet tooth," Juliet chimed in. "But I finished the entire book, are you proud of me?"

"Yes, great work. And where is the book? Eaten by a bear?"

"Well, I hope not. I put it back in the bookshelf there before we left, I'll show you next time. If you come, that is."

"As long as you say the book's safe, I believe you; no need to see it with my own eyes. So when you say the weather was dismal, did you really mean the hailstorm? That would have been awesome. Great walking weather."

"That definitely was an interesting afternoon. These weirdos decided to go for a walk though," Beth remarked.

"I guess I'm a weirdo then," Frank responded, and all of them laughed.

"Oh, no, no, no, you're exceedingly normal. Next time there's a hailstorm, you three can meet up and go play tennis or something. Do we still want ice cream or not?" Dirt & Grass was a boutique ice cream parlor that decided to be retro in décor while also appealing to millennial, cosmopolitan tastes with inventive flavors. Frank had never had to decide between black sesame and smoked salmon before, although in that case the choice was obvious.

"No, no, I insist," Frank said as he shoved a $20 into the bemused cashier's hand, even as Regina and Juliet both insisted on treating him. Tom's displays of largess had imprinted vaguely on Regina's mind, as she now believed the best way to tug on the heartstrings was to pull on the purse strings. Common courtesy drilled in her from youth and from Tom's bullish temperament told her honored guests must never pay for anything; Juliet believed in the same, and also wanted to repay Frank for his earlier generosity.

"Let him pay," Beth said quietly but firmly, shooting the other two a strange look, and they moved to their table, ice cream in hand. When they all sat down, Juliet immediately took out her phone to snap a selfie of the four of them about to dig into their ice cream.

"This is your birthday. I'm an intruder, isn't this kind of weird? I can hide under the table. I mean, I stick out like a sore thumb," Frank pleaded, keenly aware that he was going to have a very hard time explaining this to the others. Birthday privileges weren't exactly codified in *How To Be A Good Person*, nor the importance of "Sweet 16" celebrations, but nepotism and hypocrisy certainly were. On the positive side, this all but assured some of his most valuable club members' loyalties, which were good to build up alongside layers of deceit.

"Nonsense, Frank. We all respect you greatly, and you're such fun to be around," Regina explained, not wishing Juliet to say something insensible. "How did you put it Juliet, 'honorary girl'? Welcome to the dark side." Frank shrugged and leaned in slightly for the picture; Juliet pulled him closer, their cheeks almost touching, to match Beth and Regina on the other side. I could get used to this, Frank thought—this must be what John was up to at the lake.

"How's your ice cream?" Regina asked Frank after seeing him take a bite and grimace.

"Fishy."

"Here, let me try some," Juliet insisted, sticking her spoon into the side of Frank's portion and taking a similarly sized scoop. She swallowed her bite with a similar expression, but still tried to smile.

"I agree." Both the smoked salmon ice cream and his company began to grow on Frank, and he appreciated how they laughed at all his jokes and tried their hardest to include him in all their gossip. They explained to Frank that he was even more fortunate than he had realized: they were going to have a banquet at Juliet's restaurant that night, and he and his parents were welcome to attend; Juliet had already called ahead and was assured that three more non-picky eaters would be no problem at all (Frank's parents were happy to finally meet some of his friends, even when told this was the result of pure coincidence).

"Well, I am absolutely floored by your generosity. It's hard to believe that if I had chosen to take my walk ten minutes later, none of this would have happened."

"Today's your lucky day," Juliet smiled, and they quickly finished their ice cream and temporarily parted ways.

Tom met Alan for lunch downtown about a week later after Frank had had sufficient time to inform Alan of the administrative changes and assure him that his status with the celery juice project was not threatened at all—part of being a good person was belying one's own intelligence, Frank explained, and in that way this was really a blessing in disguise. Tom felt bad about not checking in with Alan before, and asked Alan about his father as politely as he knew how:

"Things aren't looking good. I'm sorry, Tom, but things aren't looking good. I don't know what to do except hang tight. That's why I couldn't go, Tom, I hope you understand."

"I understand completely, and that's why I always insisted that you spend the time with your family. That's more valuable at the end—there are always more summers, but you're never going to get that time back."

"Do you remember that poem we read in English? 'Do not go gentle into that good night,' and so on, however it goes? I've been trying to memorize it. I think my dad would appreciate it."

"It is a good poem," Tom commented, trying to avoid being too sentimental.

"Anyway," Alan continued, "life is largely the same these days otherwise. I try to keep up my routines. Club stuff, too; did you hear Juliet was promoted? Good for her." Tom thought he could sense some resentment.

"Yeah, good for her. I never thought she had it in her, but we all know how good of a judge of character Frank is—he knows more than I, or really you, would about what goes on behind the scenes. He's the man in charge, and I'm thinking about accepting that secretarial position myself."

"Wait, what? You're secretary now?" Alan asked, a bite of burger falling out of his shocked mouth.

"It's tentative, depends on if the other guy still wants to leave or not, but I think it will be good. Great fun." When Tom realized that Alan didn't know he was given a chance to become secretary, he felt like he had betrayed him. Alan spoke passionately about club principles, continuing to speak of Juliet's nomination as the epitome of egalitarianism. How impressive it was that she rose from an unknown to vice president! He claimed not to be envious, but Tom thought he sounded wounded; when Tom pressed further, Alan responded, "Yeah, I guess so, but treasurer is a very important position. I will have many more responsibilities next semester." When he refused to clarify, Tom assumed this was another of Frank's half-truths. The club seemingly maintained two hierarchies: the official, front-facing one and the elusive board of directors behind the scenes. Many who helped Frank prepare materials did not even attend club meetings! But Tom could not do anything but smile and laugh, tactfully changing the topic before he would be forced to lie to a friend.

"What are you most excited about for this year, besides the club?"

"I don't know, Tom. You go first."

"Well, I signed up for a strong course load this year, lots of AP classes. Frank convinced me to go through with it, and what do I have to lose?"

"You know, Tom," Alan said suddenly, "I used to be under the impression that you didn't like the club at all. Or Frank, for that matter. I remember at the beginning of the year you absolutely refused to get involved with anything. What changed?"

"Call it an epiphany, I don't know. I try not to dwell on the past or unpleasant things. I should ask you the same: why are you so devoted?"

"I've always tried my hardest to look for opportunities to get ahead. We aren't all born equal, no matter what they say. You should know that as a fact. Just remember that all the people in this world haven't had the advantages that you've had." That stung.

"Well, I guess you're right. I'd like to think the world rewards plucky, adventurous spirits such as yourself. Greed, for lack of a better word, is good, and there's nothing more good than being a good person."

"I couldn't agree more." After Tom returned home, he dropped the facade he had maintained with Alan and went straight to his computer. Tom had a duty to Alan—his code of honor—to avoid dealing any lasting damage. But this also meant that Tom lied to Alan, multiple times at that, and that was a double standard Tom could not cope with. Tom also possessed his duty to Frank and to the others: they were a well-oiled machine with or without him, and if he refused to play ball he would be a traitor and a turncoat. Just like Leo, just like Ted. Tom opened his email and began writing:

Re: Secretary

Dear Frank,

With recent club developments, which I do not care to summarize further for fear of wasting our time, my attention has once again been drawn to the secretarial position you had offered me previously upon Juliet's promotion. I was greatly honored, and I accepted knowing fully the intricacies of your club's power structure. I did so under a full awareness that everything was being handled to my standards, without the possibility of any loose ends or underlying resentments that could signal the premature demise of our club. I have come to realize, however, that my promotion to secretary could potentially jeopardize that. Alan is clearly of the opinion that he is not expendable, a state of mind which is contributing to his excessive ego and I worry a building envy for myself and Juliet. As much as I value Alan as a friend, I do not trust him to provide the actionable insights needed for our influence to grow. He does not have that "killer instinct," so to say, as his judgment is clouded by his blind desire for social status. Juliet suffers from a similar issue: despite her budding passion for the good person ethos, and surprising studiousness, I worry this ambition will rapidly fade if she pierces the veil and unveils our duplicity. Even beyond the text being satire, a fact I'm astonished she missed in what you said was a thorough examination, the simple fact that we frequently brainstorm ways to amplify the insanity would be devastating to her. She is a truly kind person, someone who believes you are making the world a better place. I do not want to see her when she realizes this is an impossibility. That is not to say that I don't believe the club has become peculiarly educational, more than I imagined at first, but that there is a peculiar lack of charity. It is exactly the issue I believe you criticize in your manifesto, a blinding focus on self-improvement at the expense of all others. You do not suffer from this syndrome yourself, but I imagine some of your disciples do. I could write at further length, even if these elaborate missives are out of character for me, but I believe that I will be best served maintaining my current position as consultant. Godspeed to your fellow officers; they will need it to keep up with you.

Your friend,

Tom

Tom read over his writing a few times, adding and deleting a few sentences to try to make his main points clearer, then hit send without further deliberation.

Chapter 21

When Mr. T came back from the break room to see an orderly queue of roughly fifty students that hugged the wall and went all the way down the hallway, he knew he had to have a talk with Frank. Many of the newcomers were freshmen, whose initial energy from arriving at a new school had faded into droopy complicity; they mimicked the posture and mannerisms of the veterans around them, and thus looked beaten and worn. Alan, in his ingenuity, had commandeered a desk from another classroom and sat with a clipboard registering new arrivals, who then went against a white wall to have their ID photos taken. Mr. T stood there admiring the spectacle, along with a few other teachers, until Frank came to check in, who seemed just as surprised as they were.

"Isn't it a bit mean to get all these kids' hopes up only to waitlist them? And if you weren't planning on doing so, I think my classroom would be a bit, shall I say, cramped." Mr. T asked, still keeping one eye on the endlessly snaking line, which also included some current sophomores that felt they missed out last year. "Especially if this is going to be an everyday thing. Have you looked into renting the multi-purpose room?"

"They don't let students do that generally, but maybe I can pull some strings."

"Or what about holding the meeting outside? We can bring some tables out, cordon off the area, and with the spectacle you'd be sure to attract some curious glances." Mr. T could tell by Mr. Simon's bemused expression that this suggestion could backfire, but as Mr. T did love to dine alfresco, he saw no reason not to move the festivities out of his cluttered classroom.

"And you're sure that nobody would mind?"

"Oh, I'm sure somebody will complain at the next staff meeting, but how will they stop fifty-odd upstanding school citizens? And if they don't like that, they can always let you use the MPR." This seemingly being a perfect plan, Frank walked down the line to shake hands and greet all his new converts, and Mr. T slid by them to enter his besieged classroom. Mr. Simon and the others held back, and when the bell rang, the throng dispersed. "Don't you remember your first day of high school being like this?" Mr. Simon sarcastically delivered.

For an August morning, the weather was warm, although the meteorologists predicted the weather to turn in the afternoon. Tom rounded the corner into the student parking lot quickly enough that a father with his kid walking to the elementary school startled back; he honked at them as warning, even though he was not close enough to hit them. Driving quickly felt good: the wind whipping through Tom's air invigorated him, even though it was 10 AM, and nobody could mistake his red convertible for anyone else's car, especially with its aggressive shine. His father had stopped him from immediately ordering a custom license plate, thinking it crass; if not for that, he would be driving the Langley-mobile. Tom was disappointed that his car attracted few glances from anyone besides Ted, who accosted him as soon as he started walking up the steps:

"Nice ride. Where'd you get it?"

"One of my dad's clients had a spare car, and he heard I had just received my license and felt generous."

"So a bribe?"

"Well," Tom thought out loud, "this was after the case closed. My dad has rich clients—is it really unbelievable they have a few spare cars?"

"Save the next one for me." Ted had made a resolution before the year began to move past any prior missteps and finally have a normal high school experience; as much as it pained him to think it, maybe the universe had given him a sign. His school, with its weather stains and peeling paint, was not a hunting ground. It was not an utopia or a gilded hall of human virtue like everyone else seemed to think. It was a prison, one which trapped free minds like him and stabbed them in the back when they talked too much—not a prison, perhaps, but an insane asylum. Those poor freshmen who explored the school warily, searching for their new haunts, who would tell them that every step had been traced before, that there was probably still gum stuck under the tables older than them, and that the teachers wouldn't remember their names after a few years? School was a rip-off, plain and simple. Some of Ted's musings were indeed prompted by seeing Tom's new set of wheels, desiring very much to have his own to ride along the highway somewhere, and realizing that even if he had his own convertible, he could not go anywhere because he was at school.

Pranav made a pit stop in the robotics room before school to ensure everything was in order; he was the boss, and all was indeed well. He, Ernest, and Jason had managed to set aside some minor ideological differences and instead cherish their similarities: they all wanted to win robotics tournaments, they all thought the administration was against them because they didn't bring in as much revenue as the football team, and they all secretly thought the others were horrible people. Pranav thought that Jason and Ernest were both too obstinate, which perhaps would be forgivable if their preferences did not constantly disagree. The team was thus simultaneously destined for its best year ever and trapped in a downward spiral toward fiscal ruin. On the other hand,

Ernest thought Pranav was snarky and constantly trying his hardest to replicate Frank's success in his own lesser domain; Pranav had over time grown paranoid about inventory not matching up, and when there was nothing to do during meetings, he often scoured drawers and supply closets for missing components. At first, he attributed discrepancies to incompetent freshmen, but over time he grew to suspect sabotage: the parts which Pranav knew to be definitely missing, if combined, could create a 3D printer—or maybe a trebuchet, he wasn't quite sure. In any case, Ernest frequently told Pranav to drop the case, or at the very least blame Jason.

It took remarkably little adjustment to move the club meeting outside; as instructed, Alan ran down to the theater with a few others and breathlessly asked the drama teacher to borrow some supplies, who couldn't have cared less since they promised to bring them back. Rows of chairs were pulled out of a supply closet that Pranav had the key to, and it was a miracle that the arrangement remained untouched until lunch time. Alan was displeased when he realized he'd have to complete this circuit daily, but as it was for a good cause, he relented; besides, it seemed the perfect task for some new recruits who wanted to endear themselves to the management.

"I don't know, isn't this a bit much?" One of them whispered to the other while Alan escorted back from the theater.

"This is like the army. If you're a coward, you can quit any time, or you can prove that you're capable of serving your school and by extension your country," Alan interjected, somehow overhearing them. The two freshmen shrugged and kept going. Frank had already begun his lecture by the time they all came back, but he did not seem to care. The meeting was largely a reprise from the previous year, with some added exhortations for veterans to mentor new members, and by the end of it another batch of new recruits was ready to tackle the rest of the day with a newfound vigor. The drama teacher, who had come up from his lair by the end of the lunch period to see what exactly the teachers were emailing each other about, went up to Alan and generously bequeathed the equipment to him until it was needed elsewhere. The only way one could tell there had been a club meeting on the grassy green was by observing the peculiar absence of discarded napkins and wrappers. As nobody had stopped them, although it was unclear to the officers if their good fortune was due to bureaucratic delay, they resolved to repeat the same ritual henceforth.

After school, Juliet made what she believed was her first visit to her academic counselor, who initially recognized her from the football games and then from the boisterous club meeting that had earlier occurred right outside his window. After reminding him of her name, Juliet began explaining passionately why she wished, or even deserved, to transfer out of her Spanish class into the equivalent Chinese class. This would necessitate a reshuffling of her schedule, certainly, a new free period before lunch that the counselors would have to fill for her somehow and a tearful goodbye to her new classmates, but this was really so she could learn more and become a better Tiger. Juliet did not know why she had taken Spanish originally: perhaps it was because she considered her Chinese adequate to not disappoint her parents and Japanese the language of anime obsessives, or maybe it was because it was simply the most popular choice and by extension a social obligation. But in any case, after two years of somehow passing with straight As, Juliet could barely introduce herself or order at a restaurant. Why do that, she argued, when she could instead become even more adept with the language of Confucius, Sunzi, and Xi Jinping? It pained Juliet to know that while she knew all of the dishes on her menu like the back of her hand, recently she had forgotten the word for subway station.

"But wouldn't it be cool to be trilingual?" The counselor asked, impressed by Juliet's motivation and sense of entitlement.

"Which language did you learn in school, if I may ask?"

"Russian, as back in that day, we were still unsure if the Soviets were going to invade."

"Do you still speak any Russian?"

"*No.*"

"I think I would rather leave high school speaking two languages fluently than three poorly. If my schedule takes a few days to sort itself out, well, everything in life tends to sort itself out eventually. Please?"

The counselor sighed and stamped Juliet's schedule. "As I believe you say in your language, or at least according to Mrs. Huang, add oil." This change in Juliet's schedule took her outside Mrs. Huang's classroom the following morning; Mrs. Huang was excited that someone had seen the light and amazed the counselors had been of help, and granted Juliet an undeserving seniority—as a clearly mature student, she was to wait outside and make sure nobody got lost when trying to find her classroom. Juliet took the time before class to wander a little, thinking she had never seen this side of the school before. Below her were the doors to the boys' locker room, and by instinct she avoided stepping near. Her wandering took her as far as the teacher parking lot, which was lined with wild grasses and looked almost condemned.

As she was about to turn around, out of the corner of her eye she spotted a box camouflaged in the shade, nestled among the ivy in the hopes nobody would notice it. "Box #3," the top said, and Juliet lightly dug through the greenery in case the first two were there too. Juliet knew it was wrong to look through a stranger's belongings, but it wasn't like anyone was watching; if Mrs. Huang were to look outside, maybe she'd think she was excavating a buried freshman. Inside were rows of neatly-arranged green vials, all labeled with a milliliter volume. A piece of paper with a skull and crossbones was placed on top, which while clearly drawn in pencil still made Juliet immediately return the box where she found it and go to wash her hands.

By the time Juliet returned, John had also found his way to Mrs. Huang's door, and assumed that Juliet was lost, or maybe even looking for him for some strange reason.

"I'm in your class now," she explained, choosing to save her tales of intrigue for another time.

"You speak Chinese?" John asked.

"Not as well as I should," she responded, not wishing to ask John why else she would be in his class. Mrs. Huang seated them and Beth at the same table along with a bleary-eyed freshman who clearly was intimidated by them; despite this, John insisted on including him in their warm-up drills, not letting his poor pronunciation and grammar get in the way of anything. After a few minutes and private consultation with Beth, Juliet decided that there was no point in bursting his bubble, and so let him become the unofficial table leader.

Alan on the other end of the school was already encountering difficulties with his physics teacher. Mr. Ivanov was a mythical figure in underclassmen's eyes and an omnipresent reality in the upperclassmen's: only the most under-achieving did not take physics, and thus everyone passed through his doors at some point; even if they had Mr. T, they still used his classroom as lab space. Perceiving a constant lack of critical thinking skills in his students, Mr. Ivanov always devoted the first week to a broad overview of the scientific method and all its associated pitfalls: today, Tom and Alan were attempting to put a series of pictures in chronological order that Tom believed depicted Little Red Riding Hood bravely escaping the big bad wolf and Alan a drug bust gone horrendously wrong.

Mr. Ivanov was taking advantage of the time to do some work on his computer, which Alan extrapolated from his intermittent groans was not going according to plan. Alan was startled when Mr. Ivanov muttered "F— this" under his breath when his CD drive jammed. This wasn't something teachers were supposed to do, he thought. They were supposed to plaster a little grin on their face, a furrowed frown if feeling gutsy, and let out a few tsks to relieve the tension. Profanity was a sign of a tumultuous and fragile mind, an instinct conquered through the Bosnia-Herzegovinas and the butterflies. Alan was about to suggest one of these easy-as-pie substitutes, but he held his tongue. He could handle it. More importantly, where was the physics in physics class? Alan had always heard the phrase "this isn't rocket science," and hoped that this class would finally be rocket science; unless the big bad wolf had graduated from Caltech with a degree in mechanical engineering, there really was no discernible link so far. Tom chose to look on the bright side of things: maybe AP classes weren't really that big of a deal after all. What were fairytales anyway, kindergarten?

Ms. Liu marked the beginning of the first day of class, while the students were still squinting to read the sticky notes labeling their seats, with a few thunderous rings of a cowbell. One, two, and three rings, and when some did not seem suitably alert, one final ring, this one reverberating through the now-silent room. Ms. Liu was not one to waste precious class time. Frank considered that start to class auspicious, especially accentuated by the fact she already knew his name and seemed to act under the incorrect assumption he already knew everything and thus could act as an unofficial TA. Being an official TA was already exciting enough: Mrs. Huang had all but insisted the previous year he work during her free period the present year to grade papers, clean the classroom, record said grades in her gradebook, write emails, take phone calls, complete her annual sexual harassment training, and do everything but teach. He had spent that period going through Mrs. Huang's rosters for every class, writing down their emails for her mailing lists and their addresses "so if they misbehave so I can come find them at their house and make them do their homework." He was surprised to see Juliet's name on the roster, but chose not to ask Mrs. Huang about her new student as to not show special preference; of course, he made a private note of her information, thinking it good person behavior to keep tabs on potential rivals.

Tom and John sat together and were immediately blindsided by Ms. Liu's frenetic energy; Tom thought it weird and John thought nothing, as those days he tended to do with more frequency. John had relapsed into old habits over the summer, and approached school and most tasks with the mindset of "if it isn't broken, don't fix it": if he was used to functioning on 5 hours of sleep and coffee, why stop? John's hand moved furiously to copy down flowcharts and notes about rhetorical devices, which Ms. Liu likened to Frank's speech the previous year (Pranav had provided her a transcript at some point, which he forgot about and would later deny). Frank did not like the extra attention, especially in a class where every comment and every idea received attention; it did not occur to him that holding a massive lecture in the central courtyard with marching drills would put himself on the forefront of everyone's mind. Still, English was one of his favorite subjects, and it was rather unlikely Ms. Liu would ruin it.

Jason immediately went to Frank after class solely to confirm that they had just experienced the same thing.

"What do you think? Weird or sane?"

"She is just like any other teacher, only more so," Frank joked, and Jason criticized his lack of originality. "You know, we live in the 21st century. I think we ought to be beyond these sorts of labels. They only stereotype and homogenize."

"And this is coming from the kid who describes others as drooling simpletons, gutless ghouls, and enemies of the people on a daily basis?"

"You know, that's exactly the sort of thing an enemy of the people would say. Your dearest comrade Stalin would send you to the gulag for such an absurd claim." Jason sensed that their conversation was going nowhere and that Frank had already given him the best answer he cared to give, and waved a quick goodbye. Frank continued walking past the flowerbeds, which had been refurbished over the summer and now bloomed in different colors, and stopped to consider a sweetly fragrant rosebush that sprouted out of some patch of dirt near the parking lot, one that he must have passed by hundreds of times but never gave any notice before. It was impressive that something so beautiful could grow out of such infertile soil, and that no teenage vandal had hacked at it with a pocket-knife or uprooted it just for kicks. No stems appeared plucked by teenage flirts who wished to assemble hasty bouquets for their star-crossed lovers, even. What a strange thing to find near the figurative gateway to the school for so many, an inauspicious portal; Frank took his discovery to symbolize a sweet moral blossom, laden with the beauty found in all ordinary things, or when he saw a cluster of aphids at its base, a tragic reminder of human frailty and sorrow.

Chapter 22

"**J**ason? Could we have a little chat?" Ms. Wolfe asked him during lunch as he ate noisily. She tried her hardest through her posture and expression to convey this wasn't premeditated, although of course it was. A new student in one of Jason's classes had complained that he patted her head as a form of greeting and did not quite buy the argument of historical precedent; she complained to her teacher, who thought it the right thing to do to tell Ms. Wolfe, and from there Ms. Wolfe thought she had better show a little leadership and take care of the problem. Jason felt his heart drop and his skin turn icy, and he knew his time was limited. He considered making a run for it—Ms. Wolfe was wearing high heels, she stood no chance—but that wouldn't be proper. He didn't know for certain he was in trouble, and in any case, he thought it best to face death with dignity.

Ms. Wolfe escorted Jason to Mr. Kurtz's door and told him to wait outside for a few minutes; she shut the door, and Jason tried his best to eavesdrop through the wall.

"So, Mr. Kurtz, this is about Jason. You know what I mean."

"What will the outcome be? A slap on the wrist or a disciplinary hearing?"

"What do you mean, Mr. Kurtz? We can't possibly decide beforehand."

"But he's a good kid, very well-behaved, and with this meeting being so impromptu we have had no time to build a case against him. So I do think whatever's the fastest outcome that gets us all back to lunch and ensures we don't have this happen again will be ideal."

"This is a serious matter, Patrick, not a game. If you were ever in my position you'd understand."

"It's just a bit of locker room talk—what's the harm? But anyway, bring him in." Ms. Wolfe knew that Jason was outside and could overhear, so she chose to hold her tongue and open the door. Jason walked in and took a seat, squirming a little when he felt their gazes on him.

"So, Jason," Mr. Kurtz began, "I think you know why we're here. I'll save you our side of the story and let you begin." Ms. Wolfe glared at him again, then Jason once more, but remained silent. Jason's first instinct was to redirect, claiming how his gestures were intended to be friendly and that nobody ever complained. He was equal-opportunity, patting members of all sorts of groups, a claim that sounded ridiculous but was really quite true; this, the principal claimed, did not make his behavior any less creepy. The accusations against Jason were first framed as sexual harassment, supplanted by relayed testimonials from many who felt uniquely targeted: others did not pat them on the head, certainly, and nobody they had talked to felt an inner sense of fuzziness or self-worth as a result of Jason's actions. Jason continued his attempts at redirection, arguing that even if it were harassment, it was mild, the sort of playground teasing where one kid stuck his tongue out at another kid and made a funny face, not the sort of harassment that demanded a tense conference that made his heart pound. It was fortunate for him that partially as a result of those mitigating factors, and that Jason was seemingly a good kid (albeit one with a strange penchant for outburst), that just like all the previous incidents, the only punishment was a strict warning not to do it again. He left the room silently, his head hung in shame, and spent the remainder of the period looking at happy children that all seemed to behave the same way without any sort of censure. If Juliet showed little hesitation toward brushing up against people, hugging them, or otherwise exhibiting a casual physical intimacy (which strangely enough, he thought, never seemed to be directed at him), and if Tom could give meaty handshakes to every acquaintance, and if Behrooz could give a back-pat and a smile, why was he now the pariah? It just wasn't fair.

"I didn't know you had this planned out beforehand," Mr. Kurtz remarked after Jason had left the room.

"Why wouldn't I? I have a duty to my students above all, and there's no room for assumption or prejudice here. You know what they say: when you assume, you make an ass out of 'you' and 'me.'" Ms. Wolfe, over the few years she'd been working at Heller, had learned that Mr. Kurtz operated under a slightly different ethical framework than would be usually encouraged. Mr. Kurtz believed that rules were a social construction meant only to make things take more time, and took time during staff meetings to indirectly criticize those like Ms. Foster who held onto such archaic customs. Likewise, Mr. Kurtz believed in personal experience above all, even more than any rules that were based on other people's experiences; after all, were they not all anecdotes? In this case, Mr. Kurtz knew Jason to be nothing but a gentleman, and whoever this transfer student was, how could they claim to understand Tiger values, how Tigers always did things? Jason certainly never dared to pat him on the head.

Jason initially found a comforting presence in Pranav, who discreetly stepped away from the leadership activity Juliet had stolen from her cheer team and was leading to talk with him under the shade of a redwood tree.

"You'll be fine. I've seen the administration not act on worse. Stuff that's a bigger deal, you know, like actual catcalling. There was this kid my freshman year—he's the year above me, although he transferred—who slapped a classmate's butt. Yeah, I know, not cood. And because his parents were rich, they did nothing about it."

"Well, I should have nothing to worry about now. There's no official punishment. So yeah, I don't care. Nobody cares, right?"

"This too shall pass. I should return to the meeting. Good luck." Pranav patted him on the back and walked back to his post. Pranav had been weighing in his mind whether Jason or Ernest was a worse person, and he supposed this tipped the scale toward Jason: just because Pranav's hobbies tended to be male-focused did not mean he looked kindly upon misogyny. That was one nice thing about the club, and Pranav thought it was part of the reason why it had not been shut down: they discriminated equally against everybody, and for such arbitrary reasons, that it was indeed just the ordinary sort of "harassment" Jason had described. With daily meetings, the club had been forced to diversify its curriculum, partially because people like Ted kept trying to abuse its powers for their own personal benefit. That was something only the officers were supposed to do. Greater focus was being placed on building team unity and "soft skills" that did not quite come across clearly in the text of *How To Be A Good Person*, but could be demonstrated through example.

Ted had overheard their conversation, and immediately turned to his own speculations. As much as Ted understood what Jason was going through, he couldn't feel much sympathy. Jason's mistake was having a lack of charisma. If he exercised more and had a more fashionable haircut, nobody would have complained. He would have suggested these tips to him, but Jason did not look like he wanted to take constructive feedback. Ted would normally avoid giving feedback like this that could unseat himself from his position, but as Jason seemed no significant rival, there really was no threat. Who would he go after, Madeline? Too cerebral, he thought—there was a point where one became a killjoy if they were too focused on academics. Even though there was nothing inherently romantic in Jason's behavior, it was somehow connected to that tangled web that occupied Ted's thoughts and only proved his original point. If Jason could be put in his place, he could too.

Tom found Alan in a mood more desultory than usual, and without any words from Alan knew to give him a hug and sit down next to him.

"My mother used to say that you could always find something to be happy about," Tom remarked after a few minutes. "And look at how stupid that is! But maybe, just maybe, she had a point. Even in times of sadness, there is something to be said for remembering the past fondly."

"That reminds me of something Frank told me once privately. There's supposed to be this movie called *Casablanca* that addresses that very same thing. He teaches us things like that, coping mechanisms, at the club."

"Of course, we watched that over the summer. But don't try to convince me that the club is the epitome of equality. You know just as well as anyone that's not the case. Who thought a club founded on the principle of inequality would be unequal? Don't take anything I say as criticism—I benefit from this system—but there's a line between levelheaded respect and being a groupie, and some of your peers take that too far. She—they are garden fairies. Besides, they wear black, which is such a beastly color. All of them dress like they're trying to sell me something. What I'm trying to say is that it's good there are people like us who are able to use their brains a little and grow as people. Does that make you feel any better?"

"I don't know, I don't know. I know nothing," Alan moaned, and he rocked in his seat continuing to repeat his mantra. Tom thought at that point he had given all the help he possibly could. Frank found Alan a few minutes later, still moaning, and tried to take up the torch:

"Is there something wrong?"

"I don't know, I don't know, I don't know..."

"Do you need to take some time off from the club? Pranav can step in as interim club officer. I don't want to add any stress to whatever it is you're feeling right now."

That brought Alan back to the present: "No. I refuse. I'm no coward. I can't possibly let all of you down just because I'm a coward. I'm no coward, I'm no coward..." Alan continued, seizing the opportunity to return to delirium. Frank sat with him for a few minutes, waiting for Alan to change his tune, but eventually grew bored and left.

Juliet, Beth, and John had begun to discover that they were the only three in Mrs. Huang's class who valued punctuality, and they frequently found themselves lingering outside her door thinking of ways to pass the time.

"What book do you think has most influenced the way you think?" John asked the other two. "We were talking about that in English the other day."

"I promise I'm no religious nut or anything, but *The Bible*. That has to be the most common answer, right?" Beth responded, still leaning against the railing.

"I think I'd have to say *How To Be A Good Person* has been the most of a guiding ideology for me. Everything I do, I try to think: what would a good person do?" John suggested.

"It's like that's your Bible!" Juliet joked, and John immediately saw the need to defend himself:

"No, not at all. That's a lot more important. Don't even mention the two in the same sentence."

"But you say that's your guiding ideology."

"Well, if anything, it's just tradition we'd ought to respect. Frank would say the same, and he'd undoubtedly give the same answer."

"Well, you and Frank are two very different people," Beth interjected. "At the very beginning of freshman year, I used to think he and you were two sides of the same coin, but look at the two of you now: he still wears a suit and tie every day, which I guess is just normal now, and you're wearing sweatpants. Aren't we all supposed to wear business casual clothing?"

"Yes, I'm wearing casual clothing. That's a tradition I think is quite reasonable to implement, and all of us are a bit classier now. Prettier," John added, "if that doesn't sound too weird." Juliet shook her head to indicate that it wasn't weird at all and that she appreciated the compliment.

"I think that's perfectly fair of you to say, John. It's so funny how both of you claim to be acting from the same principles, yet end up with such different outcomes. You're nice without being flirty—I don't think Frank would ever say anything like that."

"Why, because he isn't nice?" Juliet interrupted, looking down at her outfit and then at the others just to make sure.

"No, not like that, he's just a bit more reserved with his words. He's funny like that. I know that he tries his hardest to remain neutral and project severity, but you can tell when some things make him uncomfortable and he's choosing his words carefully. He speaks off the cuff, but there's a method behind his madness. I'm sure that he thinks our outfits are pretty too, but he would never want to come off the wrong way by saying that. So I think you're a bit more free-flowing, John."

"Exactly. Go with the flow, let life come to you. As ironic as this is, we should probably head inside now."

"I'll head inside first," Juliet declared. "I have a personal question." Mrs. Huang was working at her desk as usual, and when she saw that Juliet was not a freshman, she modulated her tone and asked what Juliet needed.

"So, *Teacher Huang*, I have a free period in my schedule right before lunch that for the last week, I've been trying to fill. A remnant after switching my schedule for this class, if you recall. Do you need another TA? Or if you have too many already, I can—"

"Fifth period is my free period, and I already have a TA then. But that will be convenient, actually. It is too quiet now, very boring. I think my current TA will be happy to make a new friend." Juliet took that as a yes.

"So I'll be a minute or two late, I think, but I will see you then. I can't wait to meet them."

"A new TA, Mrs. Huang? I certainly don't mind at all." Frank was hoping for a checked-out senior, someone who enjoyed solitude and did not encourage Mrs. Huang's rambling digressions, and besides, if he showed signs of hesitation, what would Mrs. Huang think?

"I know you two share common interests, so as soon as she gets here from the office, you can get to know each other better!" Frank thought he knew where this was going, but to ward off the inevitable, he responded innocently: "I'll be excited to meet her then," and went back to grading his tests, lazily circling errors with a red pen. A few minutes later, he heard someone outside the door, and through the tinted glass he could see a familiar outline, who had been given a similarly un-cryptic clue by Mrs. Huang after class and couldn't wait to see who the hunched figure was. Frank obviously knew at this point that it had to be Juliet, but he was a bit curious what would happen, so he kept his head down and waited for the inevitable end. She opened the door, saw the ineffable Franklin T. Barnes seemingly hard at work, dramatically put her finger to her lips so Mrs. Huang wouldn't say anything (she was ecstatic—they already knew each other!), and delicately tiptoed behind Frank—before she could do anything stupid, he turned around and smiled "Hello" at a now-deflated Juliet.

"Frank, how nice to see you here!" Juliet proclaimed, immediately taking the seat across from his. Frank thought it rude at this point to continue avoiding eye contact.

"How do you know Frank?" Mrs. Huang had extrapolated from both of them dressing nicely and being academically studious that they would get along; it was good fortune then that the awkward process of getting to know each other had been taken care of in some distant past.

"Oh my gosh, where do I begin? So freshman year, Frank was in one of my classes, and I had heard such nice things about him—he helped

Regina with John—and so one day I asked him to help tutor me. We got along extremely well, and I gave him the idea to write his *How To Be A Good Person*, and as soon as he turned that into a club, I knew I simply had to come. So he kept helping me out, I kept helping him out, and let's see... oh, he happened to be walking in the park on my 16th birthday, and he was such a gentleman—he treated us to ice cream, and he and his parents even came to dinner. You never told me they spoke Chinese, Frank, so that must be how you learned too! Frank's parents are so, so, unbelievably nice—obviously he is too. And now I can't believe Frank hasn't mentioned this yet, but I'm the vice president of his club. We're such good friends, and now we get to be even better friends!"

"They studied abroad and both kept it up when they came home," he clarified, blushing a little. Frank looked disappointed the mystery had resolved itself, but Mrs. Huang did not seem to care:

"How interesting. This is God's will!" Mrs. Huang declared, her mind already spinning with ideas for what to do with her two new charges. They certainly couldn't waste all their time doing work, that was for sure.

Tom's talk with Alan still weighed on his mind, and now he felt despondent—it wasn't fair! Regina looked at him angrily after Tom explained, with a trace of sorrow that was completely genuine, what had happened:

"What I don't understand is why you didn't see the need to mention any of this before. You could have told me any time why he didn't come to the lake! You made me think he was a loser. I mean, he still could be..." She trailed off and waited for Tom to respond.

"With something as important as this, I don't see why I should be obligated to tell you everything. When somebody tells you something in confidence, anyone with morals knows how to behave."

"You're my boyfriend. You're supposed to tell me these sorts of things. What other secrets are you hiding?"

"I don't see why I need to be forthcoming about others. Judge me for what I tell you about myself, but don't drag others into it. That's the end of it," Tom declared, and Regina knew not to push him further. Regina felt especially predisposed to the sort of personal talk Tom tried as hard as possible to avoid due to her earlier conversation with Beth about Behrooz. Beth had at some point over the summer gotten over her great mistake with Ted; at the lake, Tom had once blithely commented "You know what they say, fourth time's the charm!" when the topic inevitably came up at the dinner table, and that inspired her to simultaneously prove him right and wrong.

"I can't quite put my finger on it, but he really seems to care. Ted didn't give a crap about me."

"He really is sweet. So pure," Regina replied, and for a second Beth wondered if that was a jab at her own past history.

"I don't think he would ever hurt a fly. All he wants to do is to make people happy. I've never seen him raise his voice at all."

"Tom raises his voice sometimes, but that's just because he's a passionate person." Beth, nonplussed, continued:

"I think he will be a good role model, the exact opposite of Louis and Ted." Normally this would not be a major concern for Beth, but she could not risk a relapse of bad behavior. Too many people believed in her. Of course, if she were to date him again, the feeling had to be mutual. She found him one day after school loitering above the swimming pool:

"Isn't it weird how unpredictable life can be sometimes? Bad things happen to good people for no reason at all," Behrooz lamented. "It just isn't fair."

"You're honest! You're the only one I know that I can really trust," Beth exclaimed. "Finally someone gets around to telling the truth. Who knew that was so rare?"

"You know what they say, honesty is the best policy, right?" They spent a few minutes staring out over the school, a few feet apart, silently appreciating their mutual understanding. Eventually Behrooz bid Beth farewell, and he walked to his car while she stayed there, just staring, until it was time to go to cheer practice.

Chapter 23

John did not mind at all that Juliet was now in his Chinese class. She was unfailingly kind and patient with him, particularly the latter: while John considered his mind to be a steel trap, it was really a sieve, and Juliet was always there to help when John forgot simple ideas like what they were supposed to have done as homework or the word for "yesterday." It seemed only fair that someone with natural ability would be rewarded proportionally. It took him a few weeks to doubt this notion. Too many times did Mrs. Huang smile particularly genuinely when Juliet entered the room, and Juliet was often sent on special missions to copy papers or gather supplies during class; Juliet often arrived a few minutes late with a lanyard around her neck and a pile of papers in her hands. Rarely did this special treatment reach the level of favoritism, but when coupled with the fact that Mrs. Huang barely knew his name, he simply had to wonder. A little bit of hypothesizing never did anyone any harm.

"Who really runs the school, do you think?" John asked Ernest during a physics lab; Ernest readjusted their inclined plane and turned to him.

"Is this a thought experiment or just a casual question? Do you expect me to know?"

"I don't think it's either of those things. I think it's a question rooted in very real concerns, ones which we may derive from observing what goes on around us. It's becoming all the more clear, at least to me, that there are some people to whom the rules do not apply, who are free to do as they please and at no great personal cost."

"So you mean the club people like Alan."

"What about him? But anyway, when I see people like Juliet show up to class late because they were running errands across the school, when I certainly was never given the same opportunity to even prove my merit, what am I supposed to think? That life isn't fair? That it should just be accepted fact that a few people are able to control the rest of us on little strings to do whatever they very well please whenever they'd like?"

"That's exactly what we're supposed to believe, John. Life isn't fair. I can't believe it's taken you three years to come to that conclusion. You saw what they did to Jason earlier, although I do admit it's kind of karmic, but there are some people who lie and cheat and swindle simply because it gets their blood pumping. That's no excuse. Let me tell you a secret about your club that Frank would never tell you because nobody would listen to him:"

"Go on?"

"At some point in Mrs. Huang's class, Frank and I were talking about some sort of stupid philosophical dilemma, I can't even remember what it was at this point. But anyway, Frank said something stupid that he thought to be exceedingly clever, I challenged him on it, and he took that as a dare. So he went off to find the first gullible flirt like Juliet who was willing to give him the answers he wanted to hear and wrote some drivel just to convince her that he was a little Mr. Perfect and soothe his raging ego. And so he went off to build his personality cult and arrange everything just so that now he gets to plunder the school and everyone thinks he's right. Do you know why Mrs. Huang's so nice to Juliet? She's her TA. Do you know who else is her TA? Frank. You're absolutely right. It's clear who runs the school: idiots."

In John's mind, Ernest spoke paradoxically. He had to be wrong because he was criticizing the club and the near-mythical recollection of its founding; especially with Juliet on the team, Frank had been more willing to discuss her initial involvement, if only as an inspirational tale. He had neglected to mention her hug or her peculiar fascination with bubble tea and his personal life, instead choosing to discuss the open-hearted mentorship he had delivered and the effusive insights he received in return. But John could not believe that Frank had that killer instinct in him to mess with someone like Juliet just to settle a bet. Frank had been so kind to him freshman year! And wait a second—at the theater that night, Frank must have known what was up with his ticket. He must have romantically planned it out with Regina, all just so she could get her sweetheart. It was straight out of a movie, in a good way. But wait! John wasn't Regina's sweetheart then, or at least he did not know it at the time. All this was leading him somewhere, and it was leading him astray. Ernest was wrong. But Ernest was also right: everywhere John looked, too many favors were exchanged. John considered himself above playing whatever dirty games his classmates played, but that wasn't the mindset that brought success at the end of the day. The rich were robbing the poor, and they were too stupid to know it.

"The greatest trick the devil ever pulled was convincing the world he didn't exist," John said suddenly. "You're right: call him Satan, Baal, Lucifer, whatever, he exists. He's out there, lurking behind every shadowy corner with a knife in his hand, ready to plant seeds of darkness and twist the threads of fate whenever he thinks it will lead to human destruction. He pits us against each other, and all those people above us serve him. Some willingly, I bet, but many don't know that what they're doing is wrong. It's all very interesting, Ernest, thank you for enlightening me!"

"Now, I wouldn't take it that far, but I think you're getting the idea, at least in a way that makes sense to you. I can already tell we disagree on many finer points of this philosophy, so I'll leave it at this: to thine own self be true. Let's finish this lab, shall we?"

Tom was starting to discover just how much adjustment to his daily routine he could tolerate. At the beginning Frank insisted on the elite members adopting business casual dress, something he personally had adopted earlier to an extreme degree and thought would rub off onto the other members. He even led a weekend field trip to a few different thrift stores to begin accumulating a treasure trove of spare outfits, helped by a few teachers who saw this as an opportunity to clear out their wardrobes. Tom, of course, already owned the clothing required, and as soon as Regina called his outfit sexy, he went along with it. The daily meetings were more of an inconvenience, although at least now they were air-conditioned. Daily meetings required daily reading and preparation; Frank relied on his team to give second opinions on the curriculum, and thus Tom forced himself to read and take notes. For a few weeks, this was certainly acceptable, but Tom began to find editorials and essays boring. Frank frequently targeted his elite members during meetings, hoping that they would start discussions off on a bright note, and Tom found this stressful, especially as his rambling outbursts were now no longer rewarded. The cherry on top was that he had to do everything with a smile, as he worried that part of his appeal to Regina was his deep intellect. For once in his life, Tom had to work hard.

The meetings becoming air-conditioned, finally being hosted inside the MPR, was the coincidental result of a multi-pronged effort spurred by nobody in particular. The juniors were reading *The Scarlet Letter* in English, and Frank thought he could tap into some of that puritanical zeal with his meetings; he was succeeding admirably, so much so that Ms. Foster began to realize that her new class secretary was in charge of a radically different operation than she had assumed originally. As always occurred when they quarreled over principles in which they believed passionately, the club members would end up gasping furiously for air and blinking back bitter tears of conviction. There were many principles in which they believed passionately. They were crazy. Just crazy enough, in fact, that Ms. Foster suggested they move into the suddenly available MPR, where they could enjoy sitting in real seats and everyone else eating lunch did not feel like they were part of a non-consensual improv troupe. Frank was not willing to concede his ground immediately; that waited until the rainy season began early that year. Frank could tolerate the rain himself, and he most certainly could make others do the same, but it would be a colossal waste of money, and for that reason he moved inside. The meetings continued their fanatical fervor, much to the amusement of onlookers, who pressed their faces against the glass as if they beheld zoo animals.

"It's an interesting sight, isn't it?" Ms. Liu remarked to Mrs. Huang, who had decided not to take her TAs' descriptions on faith alone and instead come watch from a safe distance.

"Excellent leadership," she responded, and Ms. Liu agreed. From inside, Frank pointed out the many passersby in various outfits, all scurrying like ants, all engaged in conversations that were muted from inside their glass box:

"Look at how everyone comes and goes through the courtyard. My, what strange people they are! All of them—all of them have their faults somewhere, and it's our job to find them. You may think we're killing time here, snacking, gossiping, watching, but from every detail we can infer something about the whole. Now, look at that girl who seems to want to speak to us. She's turning around, she's hesitating. Will she step in? Will she run away?"

"We must go and help her!" Alan dryly remarked.

"And for what, as a curiosity to be examined on stage, berated for her messy hair and dirty face? We can do that without her in the room, certainly! Suppose she were to come in, the door's unlocked. I promise each of you we shall treat her with every due respect. Ask her if she needs help, why she chose to finally step up and confront us—she's already had weeks, but I certainly haven't seen her before—promise her temptation and enlightenment. But she won't. She's too weak. I can see it etched in her slouched figure and wary eyes. Let's resume our pastime and watch the folks go by."

"Sir! What about those teachers? Are they to be watched too?" A newer member asked.

"Who watches the watchers? A very good question, and one that deserves an equally good answer. It's entirely unnecessary, actually; it is a statistical fact that we agree with our teachers more than we agree with our fellow students. Any scheme we devise is likely, nay guaranteed, to have their mark of approval! They are busy folks, they have no time to step inside, and even if they would, they would have the common courtesy to remain silent. So what difference does it make? Let them watch us while we watch our classmates."

Every brunch, Alan would make his rounds through the shadier hallways of the school, where his customers would give him a few bills, and in exchange he'd give them a few vials of a murky green liquid. He knew all their names by heart, reinforced by cross-referencing their pictures in the yearbook, and he kept a meticulous list of who bought how much. Sometimes he'd find empty vials in the bathroom stalls, dropped there by sloppy students; he'd pick them up, give them a quick wash in the sink, and save them for later. Other sales were made after school near the science wing, where Ms. Norris would walk past and pretend not to see anything (sometimes Alan would top up his supply from a bottle he kept in one of her fridges, which she allowed under the condition that she'd drink whatever supply remained at the end of the week). This scheme certainly was profitable: the supplies cost practically nothing, and Alan charged different customers different amounts based on how much they were willing to pay and how many others they recruited, and he and Frank were astonished to discover that they had made a few hundred dollars in only a few days. When told of these profits, the principal surprised both of them by simply saying "I'm sure you need no reward for your efforts, but since I can't exactly pay you, consider it all yours. If you need any additional help, I'll see what I can do." Alan felt no guilt about any of this, as this would teach the citizens of the school to become better people.

He had reached that moral conclusion in a fairly roundabout way, one explained to him by Frank before school even started as he showed him the hidden locations of the celery juice stashes. A concern for one's own safety in the face of dangers that were real and immediate was the process of a rational mind. Anyone who bought celery juice, which for the sake of plausible deniability was code-named "juice," did so not knowing exactly what it was; they relied solely on rumor and some lingering faith they had in Alan to tell the whole truth and nothing but the truth. This was irrational—what sort of idiot would buy drugs at school?—and the cure for irrationality was education. Education through experience, the most profitable sort of education. Until their marks began to show concern, they were effectively consenting to be victims of their gambit. Alan felt no shame at all, not even when Ms. Denham caught him in the act once and was about to give him the tongue lashing of his life until Ms. Norris nonchalantly reached over, grabbed a vial, and drank it in one gulp. "Have you considered adding a bit of lemon juice? I have some in my room," she suggested, adding it would brighten the liquid; Ms. Denham was thus forced to apologize to Alan and try a v al herself. This specific hallway interaction was seen by one legitimate user, who immediately told his friends that "juice" was OK—even the teachers did it!

Alan tried his hardest to be discreet, and had grown quite adept at peddling his magical elixir without being spotted by unsympathetic peers. Unfortunately, Alan's best effort was inadequate to satisfy Beth, who saw him make a transaction and began connecting the dots. There was only one thing Alan could possibly be selling, and that was "juice"; but Alan was a club officer, and no club officer of good, honest moral character would sell drugs. And if they did, they certainly would be more subtle about it. That left another possibility, that this was club-endorsed, and Beth thought back to her offhand conversation with Frank about vaping last year: was this the "better" plan he had in mind? She gasped in horror—could he be poisoning all his classmates? No, definitely not, not if the picture she saw on Snapchat of Ms. Norris drinking "juice" by the bottle was real. Ms. Norris did not strike her as the stoner type, so that led her to another conclusion, using the same observational skills Frank had taught her: whatever this was, it was no drug, and knowing his sense of humor it probably was juice of some sort. Beth did not know if she ought to be horrified or amazed at how much Frank cared, in his own unique way, but she restrained herself. Some of her friends were ensnared in whatever trap Alan had planted, and she needed to do more than baselessly speculate.

After school one day, Beth followed Alan, pressing herself against walls and once even crawling beneath a bench in order to not be seen; he was vigilant, which surprised her. Alan took a roundabout route through the school, and just as Beth was growing bored, Alan led her to Mr. Galantine's classroom, which was unlocked but empty. She waited a safe distance away and pretended to call somebody; Alan left soon after, now not carrying the box that had attracted her attention originally. Beth waited a minute or so after Alan left Mr. Galantine's classroom, then nonchalantly walked toward the open door; she was surprised to see Pranav doing the same thing, and they sized each other up trying to decide if their cover was blown.

"Hey, uh, do you know what's up with the boxes?" Beth asked, already worried that she had said too much.

"I wasn't told the exact details for security, although he said he'll tell me the details later."

"So this is one of Frank's projects?"

"It's club business, that's all I know, and I think I know what it is." Beth thought for a moment, looking around the classroom for any clue.

"So if you know what it is, why are you clearly following Alan around?"

"Because I'm bored. If I were really curious and wanted to help out with whatever this mystery project is, he'd let me, but I feel like a secret agent now. It's just a bit of escapism, and he'll have a good chuckle if I tell him about this later." Pranav, assuming this answer would be satisfactory, started walking around the classroom hoping to find the box under a bookshelf or some papers. Beth stayed a minute, but decided that even if he didn't have anything better to do than play Sherlock Holmes, she certainly did, and she wished Pranav good luck and left. Pranav sighed in relief—his cover was not blown. Frank had really told him to follow Alan to make sure he was not pocketing any profits, and Pranav was curious to see if his missing robotics inventory would be explained too, and thus he thought his story plausible. It would have been completely unbelievable for Pranav to claim ignorance, but it was easier for him to give a contradictory enough narrative that Beth would simply not care.

Pranav did not concern himself with how exactly Alan executed his orders. He had thought the elaborate system of boxes cartoonish at first, but Frank believed them an effective use of reverse psychology: details like the skulls and crossbones and the boxes only being labeled with prime numbers did indeed make the scheme childish, and nobody would suspect children of selling placebos to their classmates. Originally, they were to split the profits four ways, one quarter going directly into the club funds, but Alan insisted that his recent success in the cryptocurrency market could be replicated, a conclusion the others accepted when Alan tripled his own share in less than a week. From there, it was like money showered from the heavens, and the reason Frank was so concerned about missing profits was that he did not want them to lose out on even more potential reward. Pranav had an uncle who dealt in precious metals, and so they bought a few gold bars and kept them in Mr. T's safe (the nice one with the retinal scanner, not the insecure one he used to keep his scantrons). They were told the stock market was lucrative, and so Alan set up an account using what he said was a technicality in Romanian law to trade there; Mr. T helped by translating the relevant documents for them.

"No, no, I can't possibly take anything," he said after Frank offered him a tin of caviar they had bought on a whim.

"But everyone has a share," Frank insisted.

"If you insist," Mr. T conceded, and they split caviar on blini.

They bought commodities too, pork bellies and bananas and wheat and cotton Frank joked they could dip in chocolate and feed to their members as a nutritious superfood. They were having the times of their lives, and nobody could stop them, and the longer they went on the more clear it became only the four of them could know everything. Mr. Kurtz and Ms. Wolfe knew enough too, but assumed that more students were involved; it was implausible, fantastical even, to conclude that some of the most altruistic people on campus would choose to act in their own best interests. Exactly a month into the scheme, they all celebrated together with chocolate cake Frank promised did not have any cotton in it, and they clinked glasses and wished each other luck in making Heller the best school it could possibly be.

Chapter 24

When Alan walked down the steps, Ted was waiting in the shade, clearly having waited there for a few minutes. Ted stood up to pace a little, as if he were a lawyer presenting a case. After Ted had seen Alan so brazen as to sell his product right behind Ms. Wolfe's office while she pretended to work, his entire preconception of Alan was shattered: he had always thought Alan a goody-two-shoes, and maybe he still was; some cool kid had probably blackmailed Alan with threats to his family, but if not for that, there was something else to him. There was only one way to find out:

"So, care to tell me what's in that box?" Ted asked, clearly referring to the copy paper box Alan was holding with utmost care.

"Just robotics supplies," he quietly replied while avoiding eye contact. Before Alan could scurry off, Ted called out:

"How much juice is in there?" This got Alan's attention.

"How do you know about that?"

"Just because you're the good kid doesn't mean you can get away with everything. It's a miracle that you haven't been caught yet."

"Well, thanks for the conversation, but I really need to leave now." Alan didn't like being called out, especially as it meant that he wasn't as subtle as he thought.

"Say, how much today?" Ted continued after briefly smiling to indicate he meant no harm.

"Thirty bucks. My dealer's jacked up the prices."

"Hmm, you drive a hard bargain. I'll take three," Ted responded. He pulled out a wad of bills from some inside jacket pocket and gave Alan a few, and Alan opened his box, angling the lid toward Ted so he couldn't take a peek inside, and gave them to him. Alan looked so cowardly, Ted thought, acting like a schoolkid. What inspired him to suddenly get into illicit business, even as one of the de facto "good people" on campus? He talked like a wannabe Pablo Escobar now, but he'd get shot in a dark alley before he got that far. Or realistically, roughed up on his way home when someone else wanted to move in. God help him then. Ted took out the vials from his pocket for another look, rolling them around in his hand and watching the green liquid splash. He could sell these for $50 each.

Alan had settled comfortably into his new occupation as salesman. Sales pitches were made whenever teachers turned their backs or whenever he met new friends at the urinals. First-time buyers were given a free first serving, but Alan knew perfectly well they would come back for more.

"Think of it as thrift, as a gift, if you get my drift," Alan said to Louis genially before he could say no. Alan could not believe that he had so seamlessly pierced the veil and entered the cool kids' club. As a kid, he had watched many cop shows with undercover schemes; espionage tickled his fancy, and maybe if he were lucky, like James Bond he'd pick up some benefits along the way. In these fantasies, Frank was the elusive head of MI6, who while always stern would sometimes drop the act and congratulate him on a job well-done. Everyone actually in the club, even Juliet, was off-limits, of course, but beyond that Alan thought he would let the chips fall where they pleased. Madeline was unavailable, as she stopped talking to Alan long ago, right around the start of sophomore year in fact. She was always shy.

Thursdays were the one day of the week when Frank's TA period came after lunch, and they were also long; Mrs.Huang saw these days as her opportunity to give Frank and Juliet clippedinstructions, leave the room, and let them catch a breath, relax a little, andshoot the breeze. It wasn't her fault that she so frequently had staff meetings during her free period, from which she would often return with cake for someone's birthday or a stack of readings she immediately told Frank to summarize for her. Today, as Frank and Juliet discovered, Mrs. Huang had skipped the intermediate step and simply decided to not show up at all. Frank cast a sharp shadow against the wall as he stood there pondering his options—it was not unlike Mrs. Huang to be a bit tardy, but never this late, and she would only assume the worst if she came to see them absent. He moved into the shade of a massive air-conditioning unit, where Juliet had already sat down, and together they stared at Mrs. Huang's door, which appeared a perfect mirror.

"This reminds me of one of those movies where we're stranded on a desert island," Juliet remarked. "Just the two of us, nature, and our wits."

"That would be the worst way to die. Imagine how sick you'd get of each other after a bit. It's not like you'd get cell reception—and it's not exactly like you can pop over to your library and check out *Ulysses*. I mean, we read *Lord of the Flies*, and it's not like any of us need to actually be stranded to simulate that here. We all know what teenagers do alone with nobody to guide them."

"There's a subtle difference there, Frank: those were all boys. You need some gender balance in there, and that cleans things up."

"OK, sure, you even out the genders a bit. You're still stuck on an island. That's no better."

"Besides, they were simpletons. You're smart; if we were ever stuck on a desert island, you could save us both." Frank looked at Juliet askance, who still lounged in the shade like she was on the beach.

"If we were ever stuck on a desert island together, I think something would have gone wrong long before then. So, uh, it's been ten minutes at this point. Shall we brave the rest of the period here or go somewhere else? This reminds me too much of PE."

"I would think you out of anyone would be more tolerable of a bit of sun. It's not even that bad—can't handle the heat?"

"I'm wearing a suit, you're dressed a bit lighter. Haven't I told you I'm cold-blooded?" Juliet leaned over to squeeze the wool and silk. "I guess this is pretty warm," she admitted.

"I exaggerate a bit—the temperature's really not bad at all. Maybe I'm even a bit chilly. But I'd much rather sit in a chair than squat on concrete."

"But as a good person, don't you know that this builds moral constitution, while also stretching your hamstrings, quadriceps, and gluteus maximus?" Juliet teased—if Frank could wisecrack, two could play at that game.

"You took the words right out of my mouth." They continued bantering for about an hour more until Ms. Huang arrived leisurely and commended them on their patience. It was so sweet how Frank helped Juliet stand, and how Juliet thanked him and opened the door for the three of them; her scheme was working admirably. Now, Mrs. Huang had indeed read *How To Be A Good Person*, and she kept a copy inside her desk in case she ever needed to share it with anyone. She knew what it said about dating, and she knew from the past few months that Frank staunchly refused to act outside the bounds of decorum, no matter how often Juliet inadvertently tested them, but couldn't a woman dream?

Mrs. Huang would have had better luck if Frank's patience weren't already worn thin by his duties as class officer. Frank had put a great deal of effort into his election campaign, far more than he needed, and so much effort that he indeed forgot he would actually have responsibilities the following year. Or, so he thought: Frank discovered that he and his other class officers captained a crew of about ten underclassmen, all of whom had no responsibilities but to accede to their whims. Someone wanted a book from the library? It went onto one of their cards, and a leadership flunky would pay the price if it were lost. Frank found this all very amusing at first, but realized this came as a double-edged sword: when he wanted to exercise his executive privileges to directly influence the school, Ms. Foster found the notion preposterous:

"You were elected to represent the people, not to crawl around on your hands and knees to serve them."

"Are we not civil servants? All of us here—the regular leadership students certainly act as our servants, but we too are beholden to a higher power."

"Well, don't let that trouble you," Ms. Foster continued with a careless flick of her wrist. "Just pass on the work I assign you to somebody else and trust to luck. We call that delegation and responsibility."

Frank took that in stride the best he could, although his discontent manifested itself again when the first rally came: all members of leadership were mandated to wear their class colors, and his was purple. Frank did not like the color, least of all in face paint or a bandana, which everyone else had to display or else be branded a bore.

"This is established custom, Frank. You're supposed to wear a T-shirt, put on some glitter, the whole shebang. Even I'm required to change my outfit a little."

"Would a purple tie suffice?"

"You're a little rebel, aren't you? But I'm not going to be the one to stop you. You can decide after the rally if you think you look out of place."

Frank shrugged and showed up to school that day wearing a purple tie sans other embellishment; nobody noticed the gesture besides Juliet, who told him that purple was a royal color and there was no shame in wearing it. Mrs. Huang seconded that gesture:

"I don't trust anything Ms. Foster says. She thinks I'm a racist and a sexist! Go help Juliet adjust her uniform. She looks very pretty, don't you agree?" Frank ignored the question and went to walk a half-circle around her, not sure if there were specific flaws he was supposed to identify; she did a little twirl and a curtsy.

"Uh, it looks fine? I don't know anything about makeup or hair, I trust you to handle it."

"Are you sure? I don't want to embarrass myself out there. I have standards to uphold," Juliet said defensively. Frank took a step back and looked again, worried he was standing too close before.

"It's fine, I promise. I think we should head down to the gym now, it's almost time, and I need to help set up the balloons." Ms. Huang ushered them out the door and wished them good luck. Rallies at Heller were gaudy affairs, filled with pop music championed by Behrooz and team-building activities; they were also an opportunity for some of the different extracurricular groups to ply their crafts, as otherwise there would be no way most of the audience cared. Beth was already there, doing some pre-routine stretching, and Juliet called over Frank, who had immediately gone to the opposite end of the gym when given an opportunity.

"Don't think you can sneak away like that without taking a photo," Juliet chided him, and she had one of her teammates take a picture of the three of them; Juliet and Beth smiled their well-rehearsed grins, and Frank appeared dour as usual. Juliet took her own selfies with each of them afterward, and only then let Frank leave. Frank hated rallies and all they stood for. They were a waste of public funds, a waste of valuable instructional time, and the constant thrum of noise hurt his ears. Frank was fortunately able to use his outfit as an excuse to avoid playing Twister or participating in the three-legged race, and instead stood near the entrance with the teachers. Mr. T passed out earplugs to his colleagues, and then gave a pair to Frank, and together all of them watched the spectacle and left halfway through to eat pizza in his classroom.

John stuck around after the rally to help Behrooz clean up after seeing nobody else help him.

"Thanks John, you're a good kid. What's that you're humming?" John looked at him dazed, but continued subconsciously: "*Moonlight and love songs, never out of date...*" The tune had been stuck in his head for days, playing on repeat, and he considered it no surprise someone musical-ly-inclined had chosen to break the ice and comment on it.

"Hey, I know that song: that's from that movie, *Casablanca*, whatever it's called. You've seen it?"

"Yeah, I guess I have," John admitted. "When did you see it? I saw it at the lake with Tom, you know, and all our friends there."

"Beth and I watched it over the weekend, at her place. It was very, what's the word again, oh, poignant. But I knew the song before: '*You must remember this...*' and all that. The oldsters love it, it reminds them of the wars they've been in. Sometimes they stand up and dance a bit, and one time someone told me to 'shut that damn thing off,' and he went to the piano and started singing and playing. We all cried."

"That's a very interesting story, but sorry—you said you saw it with Beth?"

"You're right, I guess I did. Oh, I see what you mean: I don't want to say we're together again, but I'm starting to warm up to the idea. We both independently are." After a few weeks of friendship and generosity without strings attached, Behrooz had suggested to Beth they get lunch together somewhere. The past was the past, and they both thought it immature to hold a petty grudge. That turned into dinner plans, and as they ate their pasta, Beth remarked that it was like they were dating again.

"So I guess we are," Behrooz had responded, and that was the end of that. John was almost insulted Beth had not thought to bring that up at some point over the last few weeks. She had plenty of opportunities, certainly. John considered himself an excellent confidant and a quick study when it came to emotions. But if Beth wanted to play her games, John could play his own. When he was young, John had attended a few chess tournaments. Beth started their first game, in what would surely be a series of many, aggressively:

"So, John, are you free this evening?" Beth asked him while Behrooz was busy putting away his equipment in the storage room.

"What sort of 'free' are we talking?"

"Regina had a really good idea that since we had so much fun baking cookies over the summer, that just the four of us should meet up at her place and do it again. Juliet found a really cute recipe for matcha cookies on Instagram, so that should be fun."

"But isn't that a, you know, girl thing?"

"Come on, you're an honorary girl! You and Frank are the only two who have earned that title. It's not like we're throwing a slumber party or anything. Are you scared of Regina?" John gulped when Beth said that word—Regina still left a poor taste in his mouth, not helped by the fact that for some strange reason, she was still nice to him.

"I can be there."

"Seven o'clock, her place. It's a date."

John did not believe at first he was dropped off at the right house because there were no cars parked in front; still, he daintily unlatched the gate and crept along the garden path to Regina's door, knocking faintly twice and then ringing the doorbell after taking a deep breath. Regina opened the door and beckoned him in, exhorting him to make himself at home. John, not knowing what else to do, sat on the couch and took the glass of ice water Regina firmly offered him. Even though she was not the one who invited John originally, she had all intentions of being the perfect hostess. She sat down in the armchair and delicately folded her arms, watching John sip the water.

"Tom couldn't make it?" John asked, swirling his water in case any powder precipitated.

"He wouldn't find this fun, he'd just want to eat whatever we made. I think he's at his internship anyway—I can't possibly complain, it pays the bills. I do love having new clothes." John looked around the living room a bit more. He wasn't sure how to describe it—plush, maybe? Some sort of Chinese watercolor painting hung above the unlit fireplace, and John dragged his socks through the carpet.

"Should we start measuring out the ingredients?" John asked, already uncomfortable under her gaze—her thin smile did not assuage his fear that he was the only thing occupying her mind.

"Don't worry, it will be more fun when we're all together." Vaguely ominous, he thought, but before he had to think of another question to keep the conversation going, the doorbell rang, and Regina cooed in delight. Beth and Juliet arrived simultaneously, and were both delighted to see that John had made good on his promise to show up. The thought occurred to John again that they were all alone, which felt like such an unusual state of affairs that he had to ask Regina to clarify; it was different when they were at the lake, Tom was there.

"My parents are having a romantic dinner somewhere and seeing a movie. They love it when I do things like this."

"And they know that I'm here?"

"Why would they care?" Regina asked as if it were the stupidest question she had ever heard. Everyone there had been promised cookies, and they understood the first step to eating cookies was making them. Before anyone else could volunteer, John rolled up his sleeves and started folding in the two sticks of butter the recipe demanded, leaving his hands encrusted with pleasantly fragrant dough.

"Your skin looks nice, John; what skin products do you use?" Beth asked, only realizing after John's befuddled expression that he most likely had never been asked that question before.

"Am I supposed to be using something? I never pay attention to that sort of thing."

"No, it's fine. Beeswax is good though. Especially for the lips," Regina offered. At least this time she didn't ask him about bras; Juliet did instead, having temporarily forgotten that John had no need for a bra. Once again, John responded in the negative, and Beth explained that Regina had once asked him a very similar question at school when they sat together in the vernal bloom and read romantic couplets to each other.

"You're such a flirt," Juliet added as a compliment, exacerbating John's embarrassment. He was such an idiot back then. He laughed anyway, the same way they did when they asked him what facial features he found attractive and why he hadn't taken the initiative at some point to seek a girlfriend. "We have some very attractive friends we could set you up with," Juliet offered.

"And how come I've never met any of them? It's like I only see the three of you, all as kind of interchangeable, and nobody else."

"Why, that's absolutely ridiculous! We have many friends, and, well, I guess they just have different interests. You need to get out more, John," Regina declared. "Sometime we're all going to show up to your house unannounced and take you out to a blind date with someone." The timer on the oven rang, and Regina took the cookies out of the oven; they looked just as beautiful as Instagram had promised. When Regina suggested a movie night as to fully enjoy the fruits of their labor, John said yes without question, partially due to his parents all but insisting he not wimp out. They settled on *The Princess Bride*, which somehow none of them had watched before, and John sat down just far enough from the others to not feel too weird. The only tangible souvenir of his outing was a tiny box of cookies, which he shared with his parents when they returned home. They all agreed they tasted excellent.

As soon as Tom saw John on Monday after class, he wanted to know exactly what he had done with "the girls," as he called them; he did not buy John's argument that he was an honorary girl and thus included. John assured him that he had sat a comfortable distance away from Regina, and that he did not ask her for the glass of water, she had given it to him.

"I don't want you to get your hopes up, John, that things like this happen all the time. You're a lucky guy, you know. Don't go off to some steamy paradise without letting me go first."

"I think there's nothing to it Tom, nothing that you seem to understand. Everything's innocent and done with the purest of intentions. I am honorable, you are honorable too; Regina said so many nice things about you, even, that I felt sad you weren't there."

"A little grease is what makes this world go round. One hand washes the other. Know what I mean? You scratch my back, I'll scratch yours. I'm glad you understand now that we all have somebody to thank for everything. You can't just walk around like you own the place, John, without understanding the sacrifice involved. You owe me one." In the moment, John did not care enough to evaluate the validity of Tom's claim. The green tea they used, apparently fresh from Japantown, smelled so good; Juliet's hand did indeed feel soft and supple, just as she had promised his would too if he only used more lotion (she was simply glad he seemed more receptive than Frank to the idea); and Beth did not mention once that she was dating Behrooz. Nothing could spoil that night, just like nothing could have spoiled that day at the lake; that day was even better, actually. Far more dreamy.

Ms. Liu recounted the fragments of that conversation she had overheard, along with other tangentially related facts that crossed her mind, to Mr. Ivanov over afternoon coffee. He seemed disinterested in the cookies and slightly more curious regarding the people involved:

"I don't have Juliet or Regina, but I do have John and Beth. Frank, yes: he, Pranav, and Jason are in the higher-level physics class. You said you sent Pranav as a spy to the club?"

"Well, that was last year, while I was more certain of his impartiality. This year, either Frank got to him or Pranav was a really good liar last year. I've sent other spies though, and they tell me largely what I'd expect. There's philosophy, there's history, there's propaganda, all of it kind of blends together into a homogeneous mass. The snacks are supposed to be good, though; I had someone steal some of the teabags for me. They really believe in wining and dining their attendees."

"So what's up with the boxes? That's a club thing too?" Mr. Ivanov had reluctantly let Alan store a box underneath a table, and had regretted that decision when he saw an unusual amount of his students regard it with a wary scrutiny. His first instinct was to call the bomb squad before they explained that it was most likely one of many boxes—and no, not multiple bombs.

"I can't say I've heard anything more than you have. I don't see what it has to do with the club though. I remember the good old days when students were bottle-flipping. This is weird. I don't know what to do."

"Well, who cares? It's not our job," Mr. Ivanov laughed. This appeared to be a mutually acceptable compromise, and so they changed the subject.

Chapter 25

As the junior class slowly earned their driver's licenses, a great number immediately set about finding ways to utilize their new power. Some snuck out during lunch periods when the parking lot was unguarded, returning late to class smelling of fast food. Many spent their weekends exploring their region's natural bounty, vast beaches and hiking trails; through the bonds of shared sweat, unbreakable friendships formed.

Weekend parties at beaches were frequent, or "bonfires" as they were known: a few hours before the party began, the leaders would assemble and stack piles of wood gathered from the beach or bought at the store, making artful arrangements layered with newspaper, and with the early winter sunset the blaze began, coursing through channels in the wood and producing tendrils of smoke. More and more students would arrive and set up chairs circling the fire, upon which they would make offerings of marshmallows, graham crackers, and chocolate squares to consecrate the space. Tom let out a mild obscenity when he discovered upon disembarking that he had left his potato chips at home.

"Regina, did you bring the snacks?"

"You were supposed to, Tom!"

"Don't talk back to me!" Tom snapped. Before they had left from Tom's house, they scoured Tom's kitchen for anything that would make the party more awesome. Regina originally did not want to go, and knew perfectly well her parents would not allow it, so she had lied and told them they were seeing a movie. After gathering what supplies they could, Tom looked outside and saw the sky's gray threatening to turn dark, and so he announced solemnly that it was time to leave. They bid his house adieu, and so they drove on toward death in the cooling twilight.

Regina searched the small trunk of Tom's car again, but found no portal to an eldritch dimension from which she could retrieve the potato chips. It was clear that the fault lay with Tom, but no matter; these bonfires were communal events, and others had plenty to share. They idly chatted for what seemed like hours, feet scraping in the sand, until enough people arrived and Louis, the host, saw fit to truly get the party started. Louis opened his cooler and pulled out a rack of tubes, and jokingly shushed his girlfriend before she could ask where he got such a large amount—it must have cost him a pretty penny, but good friends deserved as much.

"I didn't know this was going to be that sort of party," Regina quietly remarked to Tom. As Tom turned his head toward Regina, his face changed from a pallid yellow to infernal red due to the angle of the light, which still flickered fiercely.

"I didn't either, but we are here now, and it would be most rude to decline Louis's hospitality! With how much Alan charges, you know this was a great sacrifice."

"Wait, how is Alan involved?" Regina asked hesitantly, her hand trembling.

"He sells this stuff all over the school, haven't you noticed? It's all very scientific, he said, and he promised me it was all completely safe. You're so blind sometimes, it's adorable."

When everyone got their vial, some still not quite sure what exactly they were drinking, Louis counted to three and they all drank the contents in a big gulp. Regina, having never done this before, and having not really wanted to until everyone else started, expected an instant hit of nausea or giddiness; she did not expect something slightly vegetal, perhaps metallic, and more befitting of Jamba Juice than a cooler Louis pulled out of his truck. Most of the others were laughing, or staring into the flickering embers and thinking they saw sprites dance, or gazing mouth agape at the beautiful starry sky. She shook the vial again, hoping to find some last drops that would provide the promised effect, but nothing. Tom told her yet another joke about coffee and she chuckled as conditioned—but, she thought, was that what she was supposed to do? Everyone was having a fun time, and she enjoyed the company, so she stayed quiet about her lack of reaction. Perhaps she should ask Alan, she thought, what exactly it was that she drank, but whatever it was, it clearly wasn't poison.

In a fit of whimsy, someone began drumming on a piece of wood before them, creating a hollow beat that sped and slowed at random. Others joined in, some humming and chanting along with the beat, the ones without suitably acoustic pieces of driftwood clapping instead. A few stood up and began to dance and sway; Tom stood along with the others and pulled Regina up with him, who almost fell back down again due to the sudden movement until he steadied her. They danced around the fire, footwork uneven, the most musically inclined singing the themes of waltzes they knew, and the spectacle continued until the fire ran out of fuel. In the darkness, Regina could not be for certain that the sand-scoured hand grasping hers or the salty breath bearing down upon her was Tom's if not for his distinctive giddy whoops.

"That was awesome," Tom concluded as he drove Regina home, seemingly not concerned about any inebriation despite her protests.

"What did you feel?"

"It was like I was looking at the world through a kaleidoscope. Everything burst with color, the flames and the sand and the dark ocean water and especially you, babe. You looked prettier than usual." Regina giggled; compliments never failed to please her.

"And you looked especially dashing, my little cavalier. But," she said, snapping out of her fit of fancy, "did you feel different? Enlightened?"

"I don't know, I just felt more connected. It's hard to describe, but you know what I mean." Sounded healthy enough, Regina thought. "I wonder if Alan could get me some. I bet I could vape it. I need a vape pen." Regina nodded, and tried to change the subject before Tom could reveal any sort of moral deficiency. They then enjoyed the silent dark road as Tom's car snaked through the trees. Regina's parents wanted to know when she came home a bit later than usual how the movie was; they did not seem concerned, just curious.

"It was an interesting sight," she lied, and she went to bed earlier than usual. Dancing left her exhausted.

Regina couldn't hold her tongue after the party's weirdness, and after a weekend largely spent trying to cleanse her mind still needed to vent to somebody. Monday morning, Regina gave Tom the obligatory kiss on the cheek as they went their separate ways from the parking lot (Tom sometimes was self-conscious about being seen always with Regina, generally whenever they had minor tiffs; by the end of the day, it was as if nothing happened). She walked up the steps with slightly more haste than usual, looking for any friendly shoulder to dump her woes on—even John would do, as he was at least a good listener. She didn't have to resort to the nuclear option, as Beth and Juliet came around the corner out of the hallway, almost crashing into her.

"You wouldn't believe what happened to me over the weekend. Did you hear what happened?" Regina exclaimed in a frenzy, checking her phone to make sure she had time before class to rant.

"Let me guess, you were at the bonfire with the dancing," Beth remarked with a tinge of disdain.

"How did you know there was dancing? Oh God, that meant you must have seen me—I promise that I wasn't on drugs. I think it's a placebo or something, it tastes like vegetables and not marijuana, not that I'd know what marijuana ought to taste like. They're such apes."

"Someone there, I think Stanley, recorded a video, and he may have sent it to, uh, a lot of people. Check your Snapchat."

"But I'm not done. Tom pressured me into it. I don't know why he would do something so foolish like this. I've always thought him upstanding."

"Appearances can be deceiving, Regina."

"Tom is never deceiving. Just because your boyfriends all lie to you doesn't mean anything. Have I mentioned yet that Louis was there?"

"Don't you dare bring them into this. You aren't my mother!" Before Beth could even hint that Tom could be more generally problematic, Juliet characteristically refusing to pass any harsh judgment, Tom wandered over to them as chipper as he could be. Beth didn't think it wise to continue her moral support in his presence, and thus mumbled an excuse and walked away. Juliet saw Frank going somewhere with a newspaper and also took the opportunity to make a hasty exit. "Are they scared of me?" Tom asked Regina, who chuckled like he said a funny joke not remotely rooted in reality.

Regina's tiredness still lingered, and she yawned frequently as she walked toward the theater for their mandatory academic planning assembly. The students assembled outside the doors as usual, all but the class officers, who stood inside not knowing exactly how they were supposed to expedite any procedures involved. One of them had found some cheap bagged pretzels in a cabinet somewhere, and had passed them to her peers besides Frank, who politely refused. Tom was nowhere to be seen, so Regina chose to sit next to John in the front row.

"It's been a while since we've talked, hasn't it?" Regina asked kindly, watching John struggle to operate his seat.

"I suppose it has. How does this thing work again?" John responded, and Regina leaned over to unsuccessfully troubleshoot his problem. She picked up a plastic part that presumably fell off his chair and presented it to him, which he turned over in his hand perplexedly. "I suppose I'll just have to sit on the floor then."

"There are plenty of seats still available elsewhere. I'll go with you, otherwise you'll have to sit alone. I guess I would be sitting alone too if I don't move," Regina admitted, and they walked to the back row. The students sitting to their sides looked at each other and shrugged. They didn't know each other either.

"I have a video somewhere on my phone of freshman year in Ms. Baldwin's class, did you know that? Remember our *Romeo and Juliet* performance?" she asked when they were comfortably situated in their functional seats.

"Juliet performed in a play? I thought she was in the dance recital along with you."

"No, silly, in English class. She was there too, and Beth. Don't you remember?"

"I think I do, now that you mention it."

"I guess they were all there. Let me confess something to you: I'm kind of avoiding Beth right now. We had a little disagreement this morning. Nothing major, but I think we need some time to cool off."

"Oh, the party! Beth didn't lie!"

"What, she told you too? That little—uh—senator!"

"Yeah, freshman year, she told me that at parties people danced naked and flew on witch's brooms. I thought that was common knowledge."

"She must have been messing with you. I thought she was talking about, well, I don't think anyone was naked, but Tom and I also left a bit early. I think they were getting the fire going again as we were leaving.

I guess I can't deny that for sure, John, but I don't recall ever being naked." John nodded like he understood. "You know, I miss the simplicity of freshman year. I never had to talk about these sorts of impolite topics. I didn't even have to talk to Tom."

"Why would you want to go back to freshman year? Think of all the things you know now that you didn't before. You must be wiser, you must be smarter, you must be so many other things that you were not then."

"John, oh dearest John, you are such an innocent. I envy that. The nice thing about freshman year was that I could have flights of fancy without worrying those would lead to drugs and sex. I remember when I thought the height of impropriety was holding hands in public."

"That is very close to the height of impropriety, though. Maybe you haven't learned anything after all," John said deadpan.

"You've held my hand before, you've held Juliet's hand before, and I'm sure you've held Beth's hand before. Unless you're going to seriously criticize yourself for moral depravity, you may want to rethink that." John looked at his own hand with disgust, holding it in front of him as he curled his fingers; Regina reached out and grabbed it, and looked at him with a grin. "You've sinned again. Congratulations." John recoiled, seemingly terrified, and Regina let go.

"What is wrong with you?"

"Many things, John, but this isn't one of them. For someone who can be so philosophical at times, you're remarkably juvenile otherwise. Too gullible—people are going to take advantage of you, John, and any free thinker should know not to be taken advantage of. It's OK to have a strict moral code, but you need to take yourself less seriously and understand when exceptions must be made. Do you remember that example Frank talked about once where a pious Jewish man refused to save a drowning woman because she was potentially on her period?" John looked at Regina again with disgust, and considered jumping out of his seat and going somewhere else. "And no, that's not a taboo word to mention, John.

Polite people, mature people, can handle this sort of talk. So tell me, John: what's the moral Frank wanted us to learn from that anecdote?"

"That it's OK to let some people drown, that everyone must make sacrifices? Maybe that a man's dignity is worth more than a woman's life?"

"God no, John! Who told you that? He used that story to explain why sometimes it's immoral to always try to act moral. You console yourself in the moment by thinking that you're doing the right thing, and then you look back and think what a fool you were. If Frank, who out of all of us should know how to act most like a good person, understands the necessity of exception, you should too." The lights began to dim, and they went quiet. John felt a constant urge as the counselors droned on and on about graduation requirements to chastise Regina for her baseless slander—why did she not think that John was a reasonable man, an ordinary man, one possessing a strong moral compass as all men should? John was willing to bet that Regina had never read *How To Be A Good Person* with the same intense focus he had. He needed someone to prove him right, and since Regina had clearly been in an argument with Beth, she out of all people would clearly stand with good character. Beth's angry expression faded slightly when John started talking, but it returned in full force as John spun an intricate web of connections, stemming from Beth's attitude freshman year to her clear deficiencies now:

"Do you even understand what you're saying? You're talking rubbish, as far as I'm concerned. I wasn't even at the party, so what makes you think I'm involved?"

"If you are indeed as good as you claim, why did Louis host the party? Wasn't it your responsibility as a good person to convert him?"

"I don't know if Regina put you up to this simply to keep me on edge, but you know perfectly well we broke up before that summer, when *How To Be A Good Person* was more of a fad than a movement. By your logic, you should be commending me for breaking up with him! You think of me as some sinner you need to cure. Do you think I need an exorcism or something?"

"I don't know what is up with all of you people these days. So defiant. Maybe you weren't at that party, but if you were invited, you'd have gone with Behrooz to jump around in the darkness and rub butts. People like you can't be trusted to ever change, I don't know how Frank manages to put up with this. At least Juliet seems better-trained."

"I'm not sure why you see the need to drag every name you can possibly think of through the mud, but that's not even what's important here—'better-trained? All of you people?' Do you know how misogynistic that sounds?"

"You attend all the same meetings I do, so I don't see how you're still not getting it: do you realize how hypocritical it is to attend all the club meetings, and still talk back to others at every opportunity? You're just being contrary for the sake of being contrary. You could learn some respect from others—girl, you have an attitude!" Beth's jaw dropped.

"If you were paying attention at the meetings, and I mean actually paying attention and not drifting off into space like you always seem to do, you would see nothing portraying that sort of bigotry. I will be fair here and say that I see where some of your points are coming from, but as harsh as the club's dogma is, it certainly isn't sexist, and I think you're revealing all your own biases here by continuing to speak." John's face moved like he did not know how to feel, and Beth concluded acerbically, resisting the temptation to mockingly stick her tongue out: "Girl, you have an attitude!"

Even someone as consistently stolid as John betrayed his feelings occasionally, and Ms. Liu tried to speculate as to why that day he left the classroom with a slow step. She had noticed his wardrobe slowly change over time toward something resembling a Ralph Lauren catalog with a touch of teenage dork; the "good people," as others dubbed them, stood out in a crowd. And even though the change was gradual, she noticed that John was becoming more inconstant in his moods and prone to daydream; on the other hand, Frank never was anything but jovial, and Ms. Liu suspected that he took some pride in his perpetual lack of melancholy. She didn't want to tell John that she was willing to talk if needed, as that implied that there was something wrong with him, but there was something there she needed to unravel. Maybe Frank could tell her, but then again, it wasn't his responsibility to fret about his classmates' welfare for her. All she could hope was that if somebody needed help, they would ask. John thankfully turned around and walked back, as he saw a fair number of kids making themselves comfortable inside, and the bus was certainly going to be late.

"Ms. Liu, what does it mean to you to be a good person? Because recently, many people whom I used to trust have left me doubting whether I've truly been the best person I possibly could be, and I worry that I'm ruining my relationships with them."

"Well, don't you attend club meetings every day to figure that out? What room for ambiguity do you possibly see there?"

"Now that I'm forcing myself to actually think about what I've thought before, I think I've been looking at what he's been saying only for what I want to personally believe while discarding everything I don't like. That's kind of funny, right, because that's exactly what he tells us not to do." Ms. Liu checked to make sure Frank had already left, then laughed deeply:

"He's a crafty one, isn't he? I wouldn't expect anything less from a work of satire—well, at least I think it is, right?" John's expression told Ms. Liu that he had never considered that claim before and certainly wasn't in the right state of mind to do so, and so she dropped the point: "Without any specifics, I think it's really hard for me to judge, although I think I can see what you're beginning to think about. Explain to me how you think you've been ruining your relationships."

"I was talking with Regina this morning, and she accused me of being too rigid in how I thought; she cited letting a person drown because it was against your religion to touch a woman when, you know, she was doing that. I had always thought about it as demonstrating the necessity of sacrifice, but Regina said it meant, at least according to Frank, that rules could not be applied blindly. And when I brought up the entire thing to Beth, she accused me of being a sexist!"

"That's a serious allegation to make, John, why did she think you were sexist?" Ms. Liu thought that this maybe did explain some things about John, peculiar idiosyncrasies she had once attributed to mere social unawareness; did he interrupt the female students in the class more frequently than the men?

"Well beyond that, I described Juliet as better-trained, simply because she—"

"I'm going to stop you right there, John, and say that nothing you could put after that will make you sound less tone-deaf. And yes, sexist. But the first step in growth is identifying your own problems, and that's something I agree with Frank on. Do you think that because of the club's emphasis on 'blind obedience to ensure a harmonious society,' as I think he puts it, you naturally act with preconceptions of who should obey whom? As educators, we spend a lot of time in staff meetings, more than any of you might realize, trying to address these social issues. Implicit biases, as they are called. And what we find is that many people who seem ordinary on the surface actually will say these nasty things when you let them."

"Yeah, I think I understand what you're trying to say. But why didn't he ever tell us any of those things? Why didn't he ever tell us that being a good person could be so complicated?"

"I'm trying to think of how I would put this, John. That's a lesson that I think is written through all of what he says, what he writes. And I've watched a good amount of his meetings and listened to him and other preeminent experts on good person philosophy—believe it or not, some have spent their entire lives trying to answer what Frank believes he has in 30 pages. Understanding that complexity is important, and that complexity lets us understand why beyond it being instinct to save another person's life, why that instinct is correct. It takes practice, a lot of self-evaluation, and there's no one right interpretation. Frank gives you what he thinks is his correct interpretation, but that really is a broad classification, and within that he allows some room for error. If you have time, I think reading *How To Be A Good Person* again—carefully, this time—would be of some help. There are many of those implicit lessons that he's trying to weave into his meetings in the hopes that over time, you start to pick up on them. This seems cryptic, but he's verified as much to me: there's a method to his madness." The person standing behind John was clearly getting a bit antsy, and John took the hint to leave, his mind full of thoughts and regrets. Should he apologize? He didn't think so, and besides, to whom?

John and Beth did not quite enter a state of détente the following morning, and after growing increasingly annoyed with Juliet's cool temperament, Beth started to wonder if she was perhaps more "conditioned" than she ought to be—she did not dare to emulate John in calling her "trained," but Juliet's civility was becoming inappropriate. This was supplanted by her observations, which she was forced to agree with John on, that Mrs. Huang did show her a special regard. Juliet was willing to talk as always:

"Explain to me exactly what you did to get Mrs. Huang to like you so much. It's unlike her."

"Well," Juliet said with the appearance of thoughtfulness, "I think it's because I listen to her. During my TA period, all of us listen to each other."

"What sort of listening?"

"Frank tells the funniest jokes, and Mrs. Huang tells us so many stories. I tell them too what's going on in my life, they do the same, and it's like we grow."

"You never tell me what's going on in your life. Not anymore, at least. It's all just school stuff."

"I promise you aren't missing out on any scandalous secrets, and if there were any, it's not like I could betray their trust and tell you."

"We're getting distracted here. So when you listen, is this just about what they ate for breakfast, what TV shows they're watching, what normal people discuss?"

"I'm vice president, Beth. This isn't anything frivolous. We are capable of having very mature discussions—you certainly would never see us attending any parties at the beach."

"What's up with everyone and this party?"

"Stanley was so kind to attend as a little spy, just as some field research—an observational study—and record everything that happened. We all watched the video together yesterday, and we were horrified. I'm ashamed to know that some of the people we've trusted the most conceal such scandal."

"Why do you keep using 'we'? What do you think? What does Juliet Wong think?"

"Juliet Wong thinks exactly as a good person should," Juliet said dismissively, "and nothing more. It's proper—you should try it sometime."

"I see Frank over there, why don't you go listen to him a bit more? Hold his hand, stare into his eyes, give him a friendly little kiss on the cheek, canoodle in sin, whatever? If he told you to rob a bank you would."

"I don't know what's gotten into you, Beth, but you're talking like a crazy person. You're right: I'm going to go talk to Frank, and he will be nice and fair and not accuse me of being brainwashed." Juliet let out a huff and walked away at an appropriate walking speed, and Beth stood back to watch. They walked next to each other, close but not quite touching, all in such a way that Beth could honestly admit was appropriate and normal. She followed them from a distance, hoping that eventually one of them would break protocol, but she could not discern anything beyond a mutual respect.

Juliet had not known for a while what it felt like to be betrayed by a close friend, and thinking all the recent events far too interesting to be ignored, took the opportunity to talk with Frank after Mrs. Huang left the room at the beginning of the TA period once more.

"Frank, what do you think of Beth and Regina?" Frank knew immediately that this conversation was going to go somewhere unpleasant.

"Beth always has seemed fair and dignified, and while Regina's always a bit snarky to me, beyond that video I'm not convinced I can find much ground for fault. But clearly you do, so what's the issue? You look almost mournful."

"Should I stop talking to them?"

"That's it? That's your question? What would you do instead?"

"Talk to more decent people. Maybe John, I've always been fairly partial toward him; you too, definitely—I'm not sick of you yet."

"Well, if you want to stop talking to them just so you can talk to me, that should be reason alone to doubt what you're saying. Why would you do such a strange thing?"

"Loyalty, really. I feel like I've always been loyal to them. I've put great trust in them, I've spent so many hours talking with them, definitely more than I have with you, and look at what they give me in return. I don't think the same way they do, at least not anymore, and I have a higher purpose now."

"Have you found God when I haven't been paying attention? There's no higher purpose here," Frank said in his usual sarcastic tone, but after seeing Juliet's expression betray nothing but sincerity, he figured it out: "Oh, I see—damn it. Remember that fable I gave as an example once, you know, the woman who drowns because of a stupid man? It's important in life to cheat a little whenever you can get away with it, especially when not doing so leads to a worse outcome. You can always change your ideology, you can always find Jesus and then leave him. You can't treat friends in the same way, it just isn't sustainable!"

"You consider me a friend, don't you?"

"Yes, Juliet, of course I consider you a friend."

"But I worry that if I'm your friend, I can't be their friend too."

"What sort of playground feud is this? Friends can't be counted in the same way as paintings or bottles of wine. Not all are made the same, and even if you don't value them to a certain degree, maybe they value you a bit more. If that's the way you feel, I would rather not be your friend so you can keep two friends you already have. I'm willing to make that sacrifice because it's the right thing to do."

"If it makes you happy then, you and I are no longer friends," Juliet declared. She saw Frank appear contemplative, then cracked a grin: "Don't be silly, you really thought I was going to ditch you like that? One friend like you is worth a thousand ordinary ones!"

"I don't deserve such high praise, but I've really talked myself into a corner with this, so c'est la vie. Perhaps what you ought to do is look for traits in Beth and Regina that your other friends don't have. There's something to all of them, more than meets the eye and certainly nothing ordinary, and I think that can be said of anyone. I certainly don't know you as well as they know you, or any other permutation that you'll have, so take some time to think. Be more forgiving of their problems—everyone has them, even I do! That's what a good person would do." Juliet found this answer satisfactory, so she changed the topic quickly. Mrs. Huang had told her privately to take advantage of Frank while she still could; such an attractive bachelor could not possibly remain single for long, and when the current happy state of affairs ended, there would be no way he would offer her the same kindness. That was good advice, she thought, and so she stuck by it.

Beth came to the sudden conclusion during school that day that all her recent arguments with her friends had Frank lurking ominously in the shadows; it was impossible not to talk about what Frank did or said, or how others acted in his name. Fortunately, Frank was quite easy to find, and he did not seem to think anything strange of Beth walking toward him shaking her finger.

"You little sly devil, I know what you've been doing," she said jokingly—if she were too aggressive, she thought she would imply that he was the sole problem, which he probably wasn't, and it would be that more unlikely he'd give honest answers.

"Well, that makes one of us."

"I'll start with the easiest question, as I think it will be most revealing: what do you know about the 'juice' that's been showing up around the school?"

"The celery juice sold for ludicrous prices in small little vials to people who are too drug-addled to know any better? I know nothing about it," Frank admitted. "OK, I may know something about it."

"You know, when we talked about vaping last year, and you said you had something in mind, I was kind of hoping you'd be thinking of something reasonable. Posters in the hallways, that sort of thing. You instead chose to go all-in."

"I've never been one to believe in subtlety."

"How many other people are involved? I know Alan, Pranav, Juliet as well? So that makes three."

"Two out of three correct. Obviously this needs to stay on a need-to-know basis, and well, I didn't see the utility Juliet would bring."

"Interesting—I thought you told each other everything. This complicates things." Beth rubbed her chin.

"She tells me everything—I tell her less. Believe it or not, I was perfectly happy being a TA alone until she showed up out of the blue."

"There are layers all the way down, aren't there? I'll make another prediction: Alan has no idea how much trouble's going to find him when your little scheme inevitably collapses, because you keep your hands clean. You and Pranav just give the orders and let him handle the rest, and I bet that Mr. Kurtz is all too happy to let him serve as a scapegoat and keep you around for handling more of his dirty work."

"That's perhaps a bit cynical of a take, but perhaps that final outcome could happen."

"You have nothing to worry about from me, Frank. I think the ends justify the means. How do I get involved in this? I want to help, and quite frankly, I'm not thinking of my friends in the best way right now, so you're all I've got."

"We have dinner at seven reserved at La Grosse Pierre. We can certainly add a fourth—your current outfit will be fine. Welcome to the cool kids' club, Beth," Frank smiled, and extended his hand, which she shook with ceremony.

"My parents went there on their wedding anniversary; you guys must be making a lot of money if you're going on a weekday. I can keep a secret, so don't worry."

"That makes two of us!"

Chapter 26

For an unrehearsed operation, the office moved impressively quickly the morning Frank walked in with a Manila folder containing the list of names. He proceeded to the principal's office, who cross-checked it with the emailed copy before giving Frank a hearty pat on the back thanking him for his good work. Not even before Frank left, the list had been passed to the office staff, who immediately began typing out roughly one hundred summons to detention. By now Alan was comfortably in Mr. Ivanov's class, when a harried office aide walked in with a fistful of yellow papers and handed a few to a shocked Mr. Ivanov, who took a few moments to read the names. It did not take long for word to spread about who was targeted, and more importantly, who was to blame: Alan.

"It's almost beautiful, isn't it?" Alan remarked to Mr. Ivanov while watching through the window the long chain of students headed toward the gymnasium to serve their time.

"What makes this beautiful?"

"Justice. Everyone getting what they deserve. The scales tipped back in honest people's favor. However you want to phrase it."

"Why do you think they all deserved this?"

"It goes without saying."

"Yes, I know they all were caught in that juice sting, but does that mean they deserved this?"

"Yes, yes, I believe they did." Alan appeared hopeless, so Mr. Ivanov went to talk to other students, who unsurprisingly were more interested in discussing the breaking news than doing physics; to be fair, he was too.

During a passing period, Regina took the bold move of texting Juliet, who responded immediately expressing her confusion and polite dismay and then went silent when Regina said she got caught too, and because of Tom, no less. She wandered the halls looking for Alan or somebody who could apologize for this injustice. She could find nobody, or at least nobody who wanted to talk to her without grunting excessively. One sophomore pointed her out to his buddies and did a mockery of the dancing at the bonfire, flailing his arms wildly above his head; his friends began drumming on their binders and clapping along. Regina thought she was popular—she didn't deserve to be abused like this. She couldn't find any friendly faces in time, and so she went to class despondent, hoping that everything would blow over in sufficient time.

Ted did not find himself holding a grudge against Alan: he had beaten him fair and square, and Ted had nobody to blame but himself; the same could not be said for Alan, he thought, who undoubtedly had still been blackmailed by someone else. For this reason, Ted greeted Alan with a fist-bump in English class and not with a fist to the face. Ted and Alan had recently begun bonding over a new common interest: pranking Juliet. Alan saw this as the first step to romance, and Ted, who was long consigned to being a bachelor, was only too happy to pass on the torch to someone else.

"We have a simple game, Ms. Liu: I drop the pen, she picks it up," Ted explained sweetly after Ms. Liu had watched this routine repeat itself a few times.

"And what's the point of this?"

"Why not?" Alan interjected after nudging Ted's pen slightly to the side. Every time Juliet gracefully bent downward and reached, returning the pen to Ted with a predictable smile.

"Is this a game you can play outside of class? I mean, instead of now? I don't want to speak for everyone, but some of your peers appear distracted."

"Well, I don't know if we ever would have the means, motive, or opportunity."

"How about during a club meeting?"

"I don't go to those anymore, and besides, she wouldn't allow it."

"She wouldn't allow it?" Alan worried that Ted would somehow not do the club justice:

"We have different standards for authority. None of this casual informality. Juliet outranks us, it's as clear as that, and if during a club meeting she wants us to pick up pens off the ground we have no choice but to do that. One time we were even split into teams to play '52-card pickup,' which is a far more strategic game than this. It's like that. This is our only opportunity to turn the tables a little, even the score, so I'm sure you understand."

"And what do you think of this, Juliet?" Juliet looked at the three people staring at her and suddenly composed herself.

"I cannot help it if my classmates struggle with fine motor control. It is my responsibility as a good person to help them grow up."

"Well, that settles it!" Ted declared, and he returned to his work, being exceedingly careful to maintain a firm grip on his pen. Alan wasn't quite done playing, but he thought the joke must have grown old if Ted stopped. Near the end of the period, Juliet accidentally dropped her pen, and neither Alan nor Ted dared to pick it up.

Jason's struggles with group work had persisted into the present, especially when people like John tested his patience. Jason was initially ecstatic to be paired with John on their research paper—wasn't John the kid who thought deeply, who always considered alternate points of view? Those may have been true, but John, as it turns out, was also the kid who still struggled with apostrophes, who thought MLA format had something to do with getting a MBA, and who could spend hours staring at a blank document "composing his thoughts" until he hesitantly typed a sentence or two. Any attempts to get John to hurry up were met with silence, and if Jason pushed too aggressively, John would raise his voice and declare Jason could do the entire thing himself then if he was going to be such a taskmaster.

Perhaps if John were looking more closely at Jason's work, he would have objected to the hammer and sickles used as bullet points or the faint outline of Stalin on every page. Mr. Simon noticed, and discreetly called Jason to his desk.

"Jason, where do I begin? All teachers, including myself, signed an oath—a great loyalty oath—to protect the school against communism. And what do you do? You've ruined it all."

"It's just a joke, Mr. Simon. There's nothing to it."

"I'm not finished, Jason. Don't interrupt me. History is in a manner a sacred thing, so far as it contains truth. Those who do not study it are doomed to repeat it. Don't think I haven't noticed the robotics posters modeled after Mao or all the other communist activities you've done. I won't stand for it. I don't want to escalate this, Jason, but I will if I have to. Are we clear on that front?"

"If we're going to defend such American values as fidelity and honesty, I think that line was crossed as soon as Mr. Kurtz approved the celery juice scheme. I can see where you're coming from, Mr. Simon, but I think you're enforcing a double standard here."

"No, there's a difference: anyone above me is perfectly free to enforce whichever policies they want. I may disagree with them, but there's nothing I can do about it. My classroom is my empire, and if I wished to begin every class with the Soviet national anthem, it would take Mr.

Kurtz himself walking in to stop me. The opposite holds true as well: fascism may have swept our school in a kid-friendly guise, but I am still entitled to just say no to communism. Capisce?" Jason grumbled, but went back to his desk, where John seemingly had not moved a muscle during his conversation. Jason decided to try a different tactic and use a bit of empathy:

"John, how are we doing?" John didn't stir.

"John, are you awake?" John blinked.

"John, can we finish this project?" John blinked twice. Jason gave up and went back to work.

By the end of the school day, popular perception had faded from the sheer absurdity of the entire affair to disgust at Alan and most especially the administration for using him as a pawn, and most even did not think much of that. Other notable affairs—an AP Bio test, an APUSH presentation, a ceramics project—took greater prominence in those who did not have personal involvement in the affair, as it was simply another hare-brained effort on the part of the administration to change its students. Unfortunately for Alan, the latter group was feeling particularly militant. Alan had by then learned to tell when he was being followed, and the group of about ten tall, beefy, angry kids following him from a fair distance did not leave much room for ambiguity in his mind. When his pace slowed, they returned to a walk; when he sped up, he heard their footsteps becoming loud and clear. Ms. Liu's classroom was thankfully open, and she was happy to see Alan until he meekly gestured outside; she connected the dots and ran to lock and barricade the door.

Ms. Liu wisely suggested that Alan wait in her classroom for a bit until the kids outside stopped menacingly loitering—some were even her students! Alan seemed oddly calm after his initial outburst, quietly reading his book and doing his homework while Ms. Liu sent a flurry of panicked emails. As much as she had initial reservations about the celery juice plan, considering it childish at best and entrapment at worst, when the scheme began working she was forced to admit that the school had a problem, and short of bringing in the drug dogs and doing random backpack searches, this maybe was the next best thing. Alan has little to say about this last point, insisting he "had absolutely zero regret—if even one of my classmates becomes better, I will regret nothing."

"Speaking of charitable deeds, and this may not be for me to ask, but how much did you profit from this? Clearly you had enough surplus material to hydrate Ms. Norris weekly."

"Well, without going into the particulars, what supply expenses we had were covered by the school, and when on average you're selling for $20 a vial, let's just say that our club won't need to do any more food fairs."

"You keep the profits?" Ms. Liu looked again at the crowd outside, who she now realized probably owed a few hundred total to the boy inside her room gleefully chattering away.

"We asked Dr. Kurtz and he left that entirely to our discretion."

"And was this before or after you realized how much you were scamming your classmates for?"

"At that point we were only at a few hundred." Ms. Liu suspected then that Alan was somewhat more interested in the money—Alan could recount in great detail the biggest heists—and the artifice of the scheme than any sort of moral underpinnings.

"So given that you've made a bunch of money, why didn't any of it go to the school? Do you realize how many new computers that could buy, or how many of our printers run out of ink on a daily basis?"

"In a democracy, the government is the people," Alan explained. "We're people, aren't we? So we might just as well keep the money and eliminate the middleman." Ms. Liu grimaced, finally understanding Alan's twisted morality, and continued her interrogation:

"So all of this is meant to protect democracy?" First he nodded politely, and then his face broke into that radiant and understanding smile, as if they'd been in ecstatic cahoots on that fact all the time. "I have to admit,

Alan, I never would have thought of it that way before. But do you think all of your compatriots outside still staring at us think the same way?" Alan did not waste any precious energy in turning his head:

"No, I don't think they would."

"And why is that? Is it because they don't believe in democracy?"

"Exactly that!"

"I suppose I can't argue with your conviction. As much as this conversation fascinates me, I think I'll refrain from further comment until our weekly staff meeting. When the people outside get bored and leave, I should probably drive you home just in case they still have a bone to pick with you. You'll have a great story to tell your mother—would you want that?" Alan checked his phone for emails, only seeing one from Frank that read plainly "This will pass. Just know that you did the right thing."

"Thank you."

Pranav was thankful he had largely avoided any backlash from the recent events. All he could really do was congratulate himself on a job well done, and laugh along with Frank after Alan told them how he had narrowly escaped with his life.

"You always exaggerate, Alan. It can't have been that bad," Pranav told him confidently.

"No, I'm serious! There were these big kids, all standing around Ms. Liu's door! She was there, she can tell you herself!"

"Let's drop the point then. Would you mind leaving the room? I need to interview Frank for a psychology project." Many teachers, including the psychology teacher, considered the club a fascinating study in the power of groupthink; they could only imagine what good such a diverse group of students could accomplish if they were not too busy wasting their time with philosophy. The majority of the second semester in AP Psychology was spent conducting a research project, and Pranav would have been an idiot if he didn't choose his very own club.

"Pranav, do you truly believe everything they teach?" His teacher asked him with a tinge of worry in his voice.

"I have no conviction, if that's what you mean. I blow with the wind, and the prevailing wind happens to be from the club. There's nothing more to it, and I trust myself to remain an impartial observer."

"Very well. Just interview him, try to really tie everything together; this is an important job, you know, and the last thing I'd want you to do is waste a good opportunity."

Pranav and Frank sat facing each other in Mr. T's room, not sure if this was supposed to be an antagonistic confrontation. Pranav checked his notes and began:

"Have you considered running for president, Frank?"

"White House president or school president?"

"Both, I mean, but realistically the latter. You have a large force of the school behind you, and even if this recent controversy somehow tarnishes your reputation, that's nothing a bit of corruption can't solve."

"As always, Pranav, an interesting idea. Who else would run for the other positions?"

"Well, anyone who wants to; that's the power of democracy. I think you as president would be more than sufficient to ensure that club viewpoints are given appropriate prominence."

"No, you aren't thinking big enough. How about we have Juliet run for vice president and Alan run for secretary—he's earned the promotion. Treasurer, well, you're graduating, otherwise I'd suggest you. Three out of four is a passing grade."

"But still, isn't that maybe a bit too obvious? If it's just you, it's clear you're a demagogue, but when you pack the council with all your friends, it becomes a bit obvious you don't have the best interests of your constituents in mind."

"I've never been one for subtlety, and besides, this is a well-estab-lished fact: you cannot have too much of a good thing! I believe we originally set out back in my freshman year to take this idea, this idea we didn't even fully understand at the time, to its logical conclusion. We maintained that through last year, and what reason do we have to back out now? I understand it's natural to have second thoughts, some recent conversations I've had have certainly given me those, but I believe this movement goes beyond any one of us. It's a battle for the soul of our school, the soul of our nation!"

"Have you ever thought to consider, Frank, that such battles are best saved for people with experience? I don't think either of us can say with a straight face that we haven't been making this up entirely as we go along. Sure, so far this has resulted in my college fund being a bit beefier than before, but there's a point where all good things must come to an end."

"All good things must come to an end. That's a sad fact. It's a true fact," Frank admitted. "But we can postpone that end for a while. You're leaving us whether you wish to or not, but I still have a year left. I kind of hope all this dies with my departure. Maybe it will, maybe it won't. But I suppose that if we get to that point, I really won't have much of a choice in the ultimate outcome, right? I've been in some conversations with people from other schools; some are trying to copy us. They show my lectures during lunch and discuss them—it's actually quite touching, I think you'd agree, how we've inspired so many others. Imitation is the sincerest form of flattery, after all. But even if we were to do nothing next year, all it takes is for someone just a bit more brutal than us to muscle their way in and grab the reins, and then not only do we lose control, people are going to blame us for starting the entire thing!"

"I suppose you make a fair point, Frank. I can't possibly consider what we've done so far moderate, but there is so much worse that could happen that maybe it's a good thing to take responsibility. So would you consider abandoning the club at this point abandoning your responsibility?"

"Kind of, in a manner of speaking. I don't have a duty to 'the people,' whoever they are, but many, many club members look up to me and credit me for their success. And perhaps rightly so. It wouldn't be mature of me to not take accountability for everything, whether good or bad. Didn't you say you were interviewing me for psychology?"

Pranav chuckled, which disturbed Frank. "This is the interview. I'm killing two birds with one stone: I'm trying to develop a psychological profile of you, which we both know will be spun to be immensely favorable, and we're planning out how you're going to spend your senior year at Heller."

"So you've been in agreement with me the entire time?"

"Always have been. But if you're the devil like they claim you are, someone needs to play devil's advocate; this way, we prepare our own counter-arguments for the inevitable critics who just want to ruin every-thing. I know I won't be around to see the final results of wherever this goes, but all of us are in full support."

"Who's all of us, if I may ask?"

"Everyone who wants to be on the right side of history." Mr. T finally decided to jump in:

"You know this is my second career, and I'm not sure if I've mentioned this before, but I've been thinking about retiring from this one for quite some time. But I will swear on my honor, whatever honor I have: I'm not going to betray this scheme for anything like morality or ethics. My duties as a teacher may interfere with my personal allegiances at times, and I'm not going to lie to myself and claim that we are firmly on the right side of history, but what's the worst that could happen? In a few years, everything here goes back to normal? I'm willing to take that risk."

Mr. T did not let his conversation with Frank and Pranav cloud his judgment at the staff meeting that week, where he wisely kept his mouth shut while Mr. Kurtz and Ms. Wolfe insisted on their unfailing correctness, and he maintained that attitude afterward, when Mrs. Huang approached him casually. She never talked to him unless she needed a favor or wished to settle an argument.

"Mrs. Huang, how nice to see you! Is this a conversation we wish others to overhear?"

"*I don't think so, too personal.*"

"*Very well,*" he smiled, and he tried his hardest to ignore his colleagues' quizzical glances.

"So I understand that Frank and Juliet are the president and vice president of your club? How are they doing, I mean, together?"

"What do you mean, together? They work together quite well, if that's what you mean."

"Do you think they're a good match? Frank's taller, but not by so much to be awkward, and they both have quite attractive faces."

"Mrs. Huang, no wonder why you didn't want the others to hear! So this is what you've been doing with them for your TA period, matchmaking? They are two bright, capable, intelligent students; surely they can be trusted to make their own decisions. Besides, it's against everything they teach!"

"I think this is entirely reasonable. Juliet thinks Frank is the best person she's ever met—she's said as much to me in private. And Frank certainly hasn't said the same, but any reasonable person would share that feeling. Teachers are supposed to know what's best for their students." Mr. T dramatically poured himself a cup of water and drank it in one big gulp.

"We're making a scene, Mrs. Huang. They are your students as much as mine. Even if you think it's best for them, whether they know it or not, part of letting students grow is giving them the tools they need to discover that for themselves. I will not interfere, but if your meddling causes an otherwise great friendship to end, I'll be disappointed." Mr. T walked away, and Mrs. Huang groaned. He had no idea what he was talking about, as always. She could never shake the notion of Mr. T as a businessman, a wolf on Wall Street who had decided he'd made enough money to go somewhere else and do something emotionally fulfilling. Clearly he could teach—his students thought so, at least—but he clearly hated being a teacher. He wanted to do all of the easy parts and leave the hard work for people like her. Anyway, this most certainly wouldn't stop her from doing precisely what she wanted.

"Frank!" Tom shouted from the second floor of the science building. Frank showed no signs of being startled, and turned to face him.

"To what do I owe the pleasure?"

"Why?"

"Why what?"

"Why did you do this?"

"Do what?" There was nothing more fun in Frank's mind than speaking cryptically.

"Forget it. You're never going to apologize, you couldn't care less about how I feel because you've made money off all of us, and in your mind I'm now human scum."

"That implies you weren't before, Tom," Frank joked. "I kid, of course. Well, good talk. Nice seeing you again." Tom tried to stammer out some other objection, but by the time he could compose himself, Frank had already left.

Chapter 27

Ernest died today. Or yesterday maybe, John didn't know. They got a message from Ms. Wolfe: "Ernest dead. Funeral Sunday. Condolences." That didn't mean anything. Maybe it was yesterday. Mrs. Huang was still sad. She made Juliet gather flowers and put them in a vase. Alas, poor Ernest, John knew him well. Nobody talked much. Mrs. Huang did not give the scheduled quiz. John wished to know how Ernest died. Beth did not know. She was still sad. She did not know Ernest well. Ms. Wolfe watched the class for the period. She cried too. John tried not to cry. That would be weak. But John saw Juliet cry and so he cried too. Many tissues were used. Some spilled from the garbage can. John asked Mrs. Huang if the quiz would be rescheduled. The bell rang and John was still sad.

"How could he have had a heart attack? He's skinny!" Regina commented. It wasn't as if she knew Ernest personally, but she didn't like the idea that something similarly unfortunate could happen to her.

"The worst things happen to the best of people. I wish it didn't happen, but now it has, and we can only move forward from here," Frank assured her. It was rare that they talked one-on-one, but they both heard the news of his death simultaneously.

"Did you know Ernest?"

"I knew him well enough. Ernest and I had our disagreements. He called me 'evil' frequently. He opposed everything I stand for: my methodologies, my attitude, my good cheer. But I respected him greatly. They say not to speak ill of the dead, and I would never wish to do so. I can say that Ernest was a man of principles who kept to himself, wisely distancing himself from our own social circles over time. I have great respect for that. They say not to dishonor the dead's legacy, but I do not know what legacy Ernest will leave. I consider him my inner conscience—I think, 'what would Ernest do,' and then resolve to do exactly the opposite."

"You should deliver his eulogy, that was well said."

"No, it would be too hypocritical—besides, I'm not attending. I think affairs like that are best saved for family, or people who don't have any risk of bad blood. Maybe I'll visit him privately at the cemetery afterward." Regina was astonished to see Frank so pensive; he didn't cry, as far as she saw, but he spoke with thought behind his words, and that alone was revealing.

"Why would it be hypocritical?"

"You see, the very first fragments of *How To Be A Good Person* were spawned from a conversation with him. He believed me to be manipulative, only concerned with my own interests above all others. I argued my point that a person ought to make their own happy endings, make their own brighter futures, and do so with efficiency and zeal not weighed down by inconvenient things like morality. All to make the world a better place, mind you, a world you would prefer to live in. He believes—believed that sort of initiative abominable. So understandably, when I came out with my personal guide to all things good, he was a bit peeved. Even more so when it defied his expectations to become mainstream."

"Hold on, I thought you said that Juliet was the inspiration behind all of this? Didn't you say that her unfettered kindness and desire for self-improvement drove you to guide others along the same path?"

"That's not wrong either. Ernest planted the idea in my head of doing something, Juliet turned that idea into the form it took today. If not for her, I would be the captain of an underground movement, manipulating everything from the shadows. Instead, I captain a public movement, manipulating everything in plain sight. But anyway, Ernest. He hated all of this, and he's going to hate even more what's going to happen next."

"What's happening next, Frank?"

"Well, I guess here's your sneak peek: I'm going to run for student body president, and Juliet and Alan will run for other positions as well. That should give us enough authority."

"Well, you aren't guaranteed to win, right, but I do think you have a good shot."

"That reminds me of a funny little coincidence: anyone with a disciplinary record this year isn't allowed to run for office, for instance being implicated in that little drug scandal recently. And wouldn't you know my good luck, but quite a few potential rival candidates happen to be on that little list!"

"Ernest is right: you are evil," Regina declared, "but it's the good sort of evil. Ambition isn't evil, and I don't want you to ever think otherwise. Best of luck."

Behrooz was excited to, after three years of slaving away in leadership serving the whims of those above him, finally run for office. He would at last be able to represent his friends and fight for what would give them the best experience, not those out-of-touch leadership flunkies with their heads in the clouds. Ms. Foster was glad to see Behrooz taking some initiative, and explained to him the remaining options:

"Well, the current position you'll have the best chance at is treasurer. It's a very respectable position, very important."

"Why only treasurer?"

"Well, Behrooz, if you know Frank, Juliet, and Alan, they're running for the other positions, and if I say so myself, they'll be hard ones to beat. Nobody else is running for treasurer, and if you were to go take that position, I can promise that at the end of the day we'll have a ballot I can respect." Behrooz's heart dropped. He respected the club greatly, still making good on his original promise to watch lectures even if he never attended the meetings, but something about that entire crew rubbed him the wrong way. He promised Ms. Foster he'd get back to her by the end of their brunch period, but he wanted to consult Beth first.

"I don't see why you wouldn't want to do this. This has been what you've been working toward for three years now. Don't end this halfway," Beth exhorted him.

"Yeah, I know I've wanted this forever, but I just worry that they'll already have everything taken care of and there will be nothing left for me to do. And if that's the case, what's the point in doing anything at all? I'll just let them get someone else from the club to be treasurer. That will make everything easier."

"This lack of self-confidence is quite unlike you. You run a business, you're just as qualified as any of them to be treasurer, and they've already told me that they would love to have you on the team. Alan greatly respects you, he says you've been like a mentor to him."

"Tell him I appreciate the compliment—but wait, since when have you been such great friends with them? I saw the photos from that fancy dinner you went to; it looks like you've been having quite a great time."

"I suppose in the interest of full disclosure, I should admit that I discovered Alan's celery juice plot and Frank brought me into the operation to help out. I really felt like I was being charitable, you know? Sure, there may have been a bit of carnage, but have you been inside the restrooms recently? So much cleaner. The air feels fresher. It smells like victory." Behrooz leaned against a wall to process the new information. His loyal girlfriend had been a double agent the entire time! Maybe. Or maybe not, actually. Behrooz's initial reaction to the detentions was one of horror: they were grotesquely overreacting to what really was a personal choice! But then he remembered Beth, who had cured herself of that same habit and in the process became a far nicer person. Surely it was a good thing that more people were able to follow in her footsteps. The purpose of school wasn't necessarily to make its students happy, then, but do what was best for them in the long run.

"That actually makes me feel a bit better. I have some ideas for other ways to help fix this school up, that maybe won't border on the questionably legal but hopefully will be just as effective. I'd much rather work with ambitious people who know how to take initiative rather than a bunch of spineless dolts. I'm going back to Ms. Foster's room, I'm doing this. Tell them to leave a seat open for me at the table."

John had stumbled through that day, as many did, in somewhat of a fog. He saw reminders of Ernest everywhere: the vase of flowers that protected his desk in Mrs. Huang's room, the glasses he wore when he worked, and the faint outline of his face on the wall. John had read an interesting article about pareidolia in a magazine, once, where a lady claimed to see Jesus in a piece of toast. John had thought it preposterous then—why would Jesus choose a piece of toast to make His grand entrance and not something more majestic?—but he, too, saw a face in that piece of toast, and that day he saw Ernest's face everywhere. Death was a nasty thing, and its language was not in John's vocabulary. He relied on euphemisms, saying that Ernest "was no longer with us" or that Ernest "drew his terminal breath." The word "death" was verboten now that it was linked to a real concept and not something in a book.

John remembered that Ernest had written such a sweet poem about his grandfather's passing back in freshman year, one that made Ms. Baldwin cry. The imagery was poignant then, and John could imagine the same table in a blackened kitchen lit by one lightbulb that swung back and forth, back and forth, like a clock's pendulum. His grandfather's face was at one moment ghostly white and one moment not there at all. Back and forth, back and forth, until suddenly, there was no face at all. So Ernest knew death intimately, and that shadow followed him everywhere he went. John had not thought much about Ernest before, but in a way he seemed more real in his absence because John recalled his memories that much more vividly. John knew Ernest as a philosopher, one who like many philosophers was doomed to die prematurely.

"Maybe a long life does have to be filled with many unpleasant conditions if it's to seem long. But in that event, who wants one?" John asked himself as he drove home. He was really asking Ernest, though, who John imagined sitting in the passenger's seat. As John often did, he took an inefficient route home, weaving through hills of hedge-lined roads with vast front lawns and packed-together apartments connected by chain-link fences. He drove slowly and with purpose, just as he imagined Ernest would drive. Ernest would never have been the sort of person to head from point A to point B without taking in the scenery in between; John got out of the car once to smell somebody's roses, and John cried because Ernest would never smell roses again, or any flowers. Nothing at all, not even the flowers on his grave. The weather that day was windy, and it pulled John's tears off his face into the flowers he was admiring. "What sort of wicked day is this, that tears shall drown the wind?" John exclaimed toward the sky, ignoring the concerned glance he received from someone walking on the other side of the street. John had complained enough for one day, and he resolved to head home immediately before he could get distracted again. His sadness turned to joy when he entered his drowsy neighborhood and knew he was going to go to bed and take a nap. His parents had heard the news too from an email, and wished to know if their darling son was indeed all right, but by the time they thought to check on him, John was already asleep on top of his blankets, snoring loudly; John never snored.

Frank knew he should have reined in Mrs. Huang when she suggested they spend the period doing arts and crafts, but Juliet seemed so happy and he didn't want to be in the minority. So he went to the leadership room and left with a paper bag of scissors, glue, and markers, and they got to work, pushing the desks apart and working on the floor. It was just like kindergarten again: they cut up butcher paper, trimmed pictures, and wrote slogans in block print. Mrs. Huang leaned over from her desk occasionally to admire their work, and when Frank thought they were almost done, Juliet suggested they make posters for Alan and Behrooz too, and so Frank went back and grabbed another bag of supplies, and they spent another half-hour trimming away and turning what really was a calculated power grab into kitsch.

"Do you do a lot of art at home?" Juliet asked after seeing Frank's complete inability to draw straight lines without a ruler.

"I don't—my mother paints, sometimes, so I have a portrait hanging in my room. I have a photo, actually. Look."

"That looks professional! Mrs. Huang, you have to see this!" Mrs. Huang walked over, looked at Frank's phone screen, and voiced her approval: "She should sell her paintings."

"Does she take commissions? I've always wanted my own portrait. It would be very aristocratic."

"I doubt it, she's very busy these days. Maybe I'll learn how to paint sometime, and if I don't paint a self-portrait, you'll be first on my list. I'm not that bad at taking photos though, if I say so myself, although I prefer taking pictures of scenery and not people."

"You refuse to take selfies, so I don't believe you can take photos. I haven't seen any proof."

"I have principles, Juliet, and those principles tell me we should be focusing on these posters instead of my inadequacies." Frank could playfully banter and deliver witty rejoinders all day, but getting his fingers sticky with glue was too much to ask. He spent a good portion of English class that day pulling thin sheets of glue off his fingers, not convinced the sink had done its job correctly.

"You have a green stripe on your cheek, by the way," Ms. Liu pointed out after class, and Frank immediately ran to the mirrored door to verify. "Not sure why nobody else told you." Frank had learned from a YouTube video once that the alcohol in hand sanitizer could remove ink, and he casually scrubbed his face with a soaked tissue as if that was something normal people did.

"So Ms. Foster told me earlier that you were running for student body president. Do you think you'll win?"

"There's no doubt about it, in my mind. At this point I think it's a natural progression for this social experiment; I've been trapped in an echo chamber so long that I don't know if I will get anything besides bemused tolerance. What do you think?"

Ms. Liu stirred her mug of tea deliberately, as she often did when asked to consider important questions. "I think from a literal point of view, there is no way you can't win; Ms. Foster's effectively said as much, that if your team doesn't win the popular vote that she will find a way to manipulate the results. I know that undercuts the point of this entire affair, to see if you're actually popular or not. But that's not important anyway. From a practical point of view, and you've just said as much yourself: you're trapped in an echo chamber. I think everyone looks upon your club generally positively at this point. Maybe they think Alan is a traitor, but everyone thinks that at least you and Juliet are good people who are smart and capable. You have name recognition—can you say that you actually remember who your other class officers are? I bet you can't, and I also bet that barely anyone knows you're class secretary. So at the end of the day, people who don't know anything about your philosophy, just that you are generally trusted, will be liable to support you over some other no-name person. What are you going to do if you win? Have you thought that through yet?"

"When we look at the big picture, I want to transplant as many club policies to the school at large. Some are undoubtedly going to be impractical. But I've done some informal surveys of your colleagues and I think that some would be open to new ideas. Not new ideas, actually, but just some of those old-fashioned values that we discarded for no good reason. I think the Pledge of Allegiance is unnecessary puffery, but it gives us unity at club meetings, a predictable ritual during times when we can't always rely on predictability elsewhere. Things like that, simple things that are quite doable. Far less extreme than the drug bust."

"I don't know what to make of you at times, Frank. On one hand you clearly shouldn't be trusted with any position of executive authority, yet despite that you've done quite a good job. You remind me of Mr. T, and I guess you are his protégé in a way. I can't wait to see what things you accomplish." Ms. Liu's phone rang, and Frank left the room with a new urgency: if Ms. Liu, one of the sanest teachers on campus, supported him, he clearly could not be in the wrong at all.

As much as Regina's parents tolerated the occasional bout of childhood mischief, going to an illicit party at the beach was too much for them. They did not care that the drugs were fake, and in fact, this made them even more incensed; if it were just marijuana, at least they knew what was in it. Regina naturally defended Tom: Tom was not a bad influence who took too many risks, Tom was a caring person who was attentive to her desires and always knew how to make her feel happy. And thus she and her parents were at an impasse: they were willing to drop any punishment for the party, considering it a valuable life lesson, but they insisted Regina have a serious, heart-to-heart talk with Tom to clear up any major misconceptions regarding what was acceptable in polite society.

"You lied to me, Tom, you always have!" Regina began.

"What's gotten into you today? Didn't drink your coffee?"

"Shut up about coffee! All this time I've believed your generosity to be charity, done out of affection. But that's clearly not the case, is it? You buy me things because they make you happy, not because they make me happy too. It's like you're gaslighting me."

"That's not what gaslighting means, Regina. Don't get into hysterics."

"I'll tell you what gaslighting means then. Gaslighting means convincing me that dancing around on the beach is fun. You convinced me we were having a good time, but you may as well have taken me to a strip club! Don't you dare try to convince me that all of this is in my best interest."

"You're happy. It shouldn't matter why you're happy. Thinking you're happy is the same as being happy. People try to convince me all the time that I'm not perpetually living in my father's shadow, and I believe that. It's better than facing the facts. So I think the point is, we can all live in our fantasies occasionally, because the real world is a scary place. One of our classmates died, Regina. Someone I respected, not some no-name klutz. Alan's father is dead. That still pains me. We tell the people we love: do not go gentle into that good night. Old age should burn and rave at close of day; rage, rage, against the dying of the light. Yes, I have that memorized. I'm not some brute or 'ape,' as I heard you call me once."

"An ape who can recite poetry is still an ape."

"You're missing my point, Regina. We all need to lie to ourselves and lie to each other, otherwise society can't possibly function the way it does. We're all stressed these days. Get some sleep. I know I need it." Tom abruptly hung up the call, and Regina stared at her phone's home screen and cried. How could he be so crude and yet so lovable simultaneously? Tom could be wrong, but he at least thought he was right. Ernest died the other day. Regina still thought that sad. Tom's still alive today, Regina thought. That made her happy. "I'm still alive today," she told herself, "I'm still alive!" That made her even happier. This bout of emotion tired her, and she decided she would go to bed immediately after dinner.

Even if Ernest hadn't died, Ted would still have left Heller. He had acquired his GED, studying harder than he ever had before, just so he didn't need to deal with more high school drama than needed. Ted was told once that all the world was a stage, but there came a point when he wanted to stop acting and simply get things over with. For Ted, that threshold was somewhere after breaking up with Beth, somewhere after getting detention for buying fake drugs, and somewhere after Ernest's death. Ted did not tell many besides his teachers about his impending departure. Why did they need to know in advance? Maybe even a few days after he left, they wouldn't realize anything had changed; he would simply be gone. Tom deserved a special adieu, however:

"I'll miss the good times we had together. You made high school just a bit more tolerable for me, and what else could I really ask for? Wish Regina well. Keep in touch," Ted said with a pat on the back, and that was the end of that. Behrooz happened to walk by during this conversation, held in the student parking lot on that fine border between school and reality, and was immensely sad to see yet another vaunted figure of Heller leave. Truly too soon.

"I know we haven't always been civil with each other, but maybe I'll see you around sometime, Ted. Once a Tiger, always a Tiger." Behrooz looked out at the parking lot to see if he could spot Ted's car, but realized that he didn't know what it looked like; unlike Ted, Behrooz never loitered in the parking lot when he was supposed to be elsewhere.

"Cheers, Behrooz. Good luck with your student council bid. You deserve it, unlike those other jerks." Ted shook his head in consternation, but Behrooz rushed to defend them:

"We disagree on some things, but I respect them as people. I think President Underwood is a psychopath even though he's a Democrat; likewise, I admire their dedication to improving the school even if I disagree with some of their methods. They're reasonable people who are open to debate, and that's what really matters at the end of the day. I'll take them over zealots."

"That's why you're staying and I'm not," Ted laughed. "Besides, I have one more day. You won't see me after the weekend."

On his last day, which to everyone else seemed like any other, Ted didn't make a show of his departure. He told some of his friends and teachers, more out of necessity and a sense of obligation than a true desire, and after class on Friday, he stepped outside, took a deep breath; walked down the steps through a crowd of students scrambling to get to class on time; looked at the bushes and trees garnishing the concrete; surveyed the parking lot with its beat-up vans and brand-new Teslas; the steep, verdant slope that guarded the school from the houses up above behind the fence; the elementary school far more clearly visible across the street and up a few stories that the parents reached by driving along a serpentine path; the few parents already queued in the parking lot on their phones or blankly staring ahead; and extended one final middle finger to the sun up above before walking to his car. Before he stepped in, he spat on the ground and watched the bubbles fade into a dark dot. He drove off in the same direction he always did, and then he was gone.

Chapter 28

Behrooz frantically adjusted his tie backstage while Alan peered out at the building crowd.

"Looks like a lot of people," Alan observed, looking for friendly faces.

"Well, of course, the elections are mandatory." When two weeks ago, he had turned in his paperwork to officially launch his bid for class council, and when immediately afterward Alan shook his hand vigorously and offered "their" support, Behrooz hadn't quite expected the full display of posters and advertisements that culminated in one beautiful sham of an election. He knew that the four of them were the only ones running for office that anyone had ever heard of (a straggler persisted for the presidential position, who clearly had misjudged her odds), but he did not quite expect a political rally.

"Is everyone ready to take their positions? Don't forget your cue for the musical number during my concluding remarks—remember, it's 'I have one last thing to say.' Your own speeches had better be good too. We're going to need to do this twice more for the other classes, but I want to start off strong," Frank explained, tapping his microphone just to ensure it was there. "Anyway, it's time."

Frank emerged from the curtains to a roaring thrum of noise that astonished even him. He signaled for silence, and began reading, maintaining eye contact with the audience despite not having memorized his speech:

"Community. Identity. Stability. Three things all of us hold dear. Three things all of you ought to hold dear. In the interests of time, we all will keep our remarks brief, since we all know that this is a mere formality with an inevitable outcome—sorry, Kayla, but your chance at stardom is over. Over the last few years, I have built a thriving community here at Heller based upon nothing more than a few philosophical ideas I hold dear. Simple things, good old-fashioned values, many of which are familiar to all of you. I want to make one thing abundantly clear. I am the author. You are the audience. I outrank you—at least on merits of good person philosophy, which I think a good portion of us would consider the only philosophy of any merit. Through this sense of community, we create identity. A cohesive identity, but one with many complexities. We are all Tigers burning bright in the forest of the night. We are all familiar with the eye of the Tiger and the name of the fight. We are all crouching Tigers and hidden dragons. We are all so many things, each and every one of us, but above all, we are Tigers. By electing us, you are reaffirming your identity as Tigers, and your resistance is futile. Stability. The world is a scary place—in the last year, we have seen many changes. We have lost one of the great sages of our school. Some of us were caught in a drug sting which I officially cannot comment on further. College applications loom on the horizon, and will occupy much of our summers. So given all that, all I can promise you is stability. Reliability. Faces you can trust. Vote for me, and all will be well. Next up, Juliet Wong."

Juliet took the podium and cleared her throat a few times off-mic before beginning:

"Wow, so many people! Our future president really covered most of what I would have said, so I'll talk about myself a little. At the beginning of my time at Heller, people knew me as a cheerleader, little more. Maybe they recognized my face, maybe they didn't. It's all irrelevant now. But now, you all know me as a philosopher-in-training. I believe I have changed over the last three years, mainly thanks to Frank and his leadership. For the better, believe it or not. I cannot promise the same epiphany to all of you, but I can promise that if you listen to what this man has to say, whom I consider a friend of mine, a mentor, an inspiration, and so much more, all of you will become better people. And through that, we make the school a better place. I remember at the very first club meeting, he said 'where we go one, we go all.' I think that holds especially true today. Vote for us, and we will all improve." Juliet concluded on the verge of tears, not noticing Tom's chuckle at her concluding note—out of all the phrases Juliet could have remembered, she remembered the fascist motto Frank had co-opted. How fitting for a brainwashed maniac, he thought. Alan took the stage next and stood on his tip-toes to speak into the microphone before Frank ran backstage to grab a stepstool.

"Because Frank and Juliet have presented such optimistic messages about the future of our school, I think it fitting to deliver some brief reminders about what should happen if we fail. And by 'we' failing, I actually mean 'you' failing, because the burden does not rest on us for not delivering our messages passionately enough but on you guys for not understanding them. If any of you have watched the original *Star Wars* trilogy, you'll remember that common expression 'there's always a bigger fish.' We are sharks and you are minnows. You can swim forever, upstream even, but we will always catch up to you. Do you want to know what happened to those foolhardy minnows who thought themselves immortal? They got detention for daring to ruin the school's name. When I phrase it like that, the course of action should be pretty obvious, isn't it? Any rabble-rousing will not be tolerated. Join us or risk being forgotten. That's an interesting idea, isn't it? I don't even know most of your names! Maybe I'll learn them. Maybe I won't. Maybe I'll instead assign clever nicknames to all of you—let me try that now." Alan left the podium and walked to the front of the stage, towering over the front row: "Zingy,

Splotch, Fish-face, Dork, Bozo," he called out one-by-one, and the smart people in the audience laughed. "You see? It's not that hard for you to be reduced to mere nicknames, or maybe nothing at all. There is a way out though: join us, support us, work hard to be noticed through your merit. Make your high school experience one worth remembering. Last but probably least, Behrooz Ghorbani, everyone!"

Behrooz wanted to curl up in a ball and die of embarrassment. The speeches were nothing if not mortifying, laced with cruel subtexts even he picked up on. It was too late now. This is what he signed up for, and at this point, he really didn't have much of a choice, did he?

"I'm an outsider on this stage. I've always been an outsider, standing on the sidelines DJing or manning coat check while everyone else had their fun. And when you're an outsider, you pick up on some things. I'm the only person up here who isn't a club officer; I don't even attend their meetings. But simply by being in the proximity of these fine people, I've learned a few things. One: we may disagree on a few tiny details, but we both have similar goals. All of us here want to see Heller be made the best school in the nation. All of us here want to see each and every one of you just as happy with the results as we are. Two: these guys are genuinely good people. I know that phrase gets thrown around a lot without much meaning, but everything I have known them to do has been done with good intentions in mind. That's a hard ask, these days. When we all experience betrayal and backstabbing, it's a comfort to know that there are some people on whom we can truly depend. They're certainly the sort of people I'd like to have in charge. I don't know where next school year is headed — I'm trusting they have a plan, because I certainly don't. But I can promise that it's going to lead somewhere better than where we began. That's all I have to say, but Frank," Behrooz said with his best acting skills, "do you have any concluding remarks?" Frank confidently strutted back to the podium as the curtain drew back, revealing the three others standing behind him.

"I certainly do. I have one last thing to say, but I forget exactly what. Oh wait," he said with a grin as the music began, "Don't! Stop! Me! Now!" The club members in the audience had by then snuck out of their seats and assembled in the wings to wait for their entrances, and the lip-sync proceeded far better than would be expected from amateurs. Beth and Juliet had organized the choreography, which after months of marching drills was a breeze to learn. Those in the audience who didn't expect the plot twist, including Kayla, who had by then resigned herself to anonymity, watched with jaws hanging loose. Mr. T, who was filming the entire performance, flashed them a thumbs up. The song finished with bursts of confetti, and the entire audience roared in approval with the largest standing ovation Mr. Cathcart had ever seen.

"This wasn't how I expected them to secure the vote," Ms. Foster joked to Ms. Norris, who despite generally disapproving of pageantry decided to make a special exception for their performance.

"They've convinced me! But then again, I think this loses some of its luster given the lack of alternatives. If I were cynical, I'd go as far as to say that this is a veiled threat, 'don't stop us or else,' you know."

"You're such a funny one, Mary." By the time Frank and Juliet arrived to their TA period, Mrs. Huang had made up her mind based on that morning's assembly, and more importantly, prom that night. Frank had already confirmed that he had secured free tickets for all his VIP club members, which by definition included Juliet. And the previous day, when asked which special someones they were planning on going with, the answers proved inconclusive. Mrs. Huang would never get a moment like this again, she thought. This was the day.

"Great performance, both of you! I'm so proud!" she exclaimed, running over to give both of them hugs.

"It was nothing, really, just a bit of showmanship to keep them happy. Any credit should go to Juliet," Frank said.

"You're too modest, as always. This was your idea."

"So, my two favorite students," Ms. Huang interjected even more assertively than normal, "What are your plans for tonight?"

"I'm working. I'll be there. In the shadows. This is business for me," Frank answered.

"You're so studious even when you should be partying it up. I'm going for pleasure."

"Glad to see we're in agreement. Frank, do you have a girlfriend?" Mrs. Huang asked with a glimmer in her eye. Frank recoiled in horror and almost tripped on a desk.

"I am a bachelor, in fact. It's liberating. So, no."

"Juliet, do you have a boyfriend?"

"Well, now that you mention it, I don't," she said, looking at Frank with a smile that Frank perceived as uniquely threatening.

"So...tonight seems like just as good of a night as any, don't you think?" Frank looked at Mrs. Huang like she had just committed a crime, and Juliet could not decide whether she was supposed to speak first.

"Frank's my dearest friend, and—"

"Yes, we are dear friends. Anything else borders on impropriety, and well, if the president and vice president were dating, what example does that set for the rest of them?" Juliet did not seem hurt by this, and so Frank let his breathing steady.

"It was only a suggestion." Mrs. Huang took this as a partial victory: "dear friends" sounded like an euphemism to her, and if that's what they wanted to call themselves, she could still say that she had created a lasting friendship, even if it didn't have quite the same ring to it as "future prom king and queen." They continued the rest of the period working as usual, Frank and Juliet seemingly just as friendly as before, and the political incumbents walked together to the parking lot slowly, admiring the spring weather and the flowers in bloom. A few people stopped to congratulate them, who they largely ignored.

"Frank, you have no idea how much everything you've done for me means to me. In my speech today, I only mentioned this briefly, but I have so much more to say on the topic: I'm used to people treating me like an idiot just because of my pretty face or my personality or even because I'm a cheerleader. They automatically think less of me, like I'm incapable of having a serious conversation. It gets annoying after a while, you know? I have straight As. I probably have the same GPA you have. But nobody really treats me like a person of my own merits and not as an object to be caressed, not even my friends, besides you. You don't speak over me during meetings. You don't send me naughty messages by text. You don't try to test my boundaries and see how much you can get away with while nobody's watching. I can't tell you how rare that is, and how it makes everyone you know appreciate you that much more. If that's what being a good person is, I wish more people could be like you." Frank looked at Juliet with a newfound understanding. Whether he had known it or not, what he was doing was right. Even if he handled Juliet politically at times, a safeguard he believed he was increasingly able to dispense with, he had not done so out of malice; indeed, if he had truly thought her an idiot, he wouldn't have needed any precautions at all. Certainly, once, he had thought her a mere annoyance; but over time, she was slowly progressing beyond that to on the verge of tolerable. There was truly too much of a good thing, and that was Juliet thanks to the TA period, but Frank also knew just how much of a luxury that overabundance was. People would kill for the same.

"I believe I only act as everyone should, not with anything more."

"So while we're on such a good note, I have some quick little questions about everything. The drug bust was your idea, right?"

"Well, Beth gave me the idea and I turned it into something workable."

"Aha! It must have been you and not her—I saw her loading boxes into her trunk one day, and I thought her a drug smuggler. I'm glad to know that it was all for a good cause. But, you know, Regina got detention because of Alan."

"Well, Tom did too. And the school is a better, safer place because of his sacrifice."

"Do you really think so?" On any other day, Frank would be tempted to lie, but he knew better than that:

"Yes, I do. I wouldn't have spent the last two years fighting to make the school a better place, even if through unconventional methods, if I did not believe my actions had an impact." Juliet appeared to consider his words carefully, and Frank's left hand twitched with nervous energy.

"If you say so, Frank, I trust you." Frank believed what he was saying, but he was still impressed that Juliet did too. As much as he had hoped that she subscribed to the club's ideology not simply because of the brainwashing, perhaps Tom had been right. Juliet was a good person, even one whose moral compass was slowly slipping from the conventional, but she was not a "good person" in the sense that Alan was. It was a fortunate coincidence that despite their elitism, good people had many nice qualities too.

"Oh, one more thing, Frank, before you think you can get off so easily: why don't we do more charity events? It seems weird that a club dedicated to being good focuses its efforts so narrowly. What about a canned food drive to end the year?"

"Juliet, what a charming notion! Eminently practical and yet appropriate as always," Frank exclaimed gleefully. He stepped back with a dancer's grace, and Juliet suddenly reached out to take his hand in a delightful bit of improv; they did a brief waltz, avoiding the concrete barriers, until they realized that others might see.

"Well, anyway, I guess I'll see you at prom," Frank said with a chuckle, not quite sure what strange mood had swept the both of them that moment.

"Are you still going as a bachelor?"

"Well, I suppose you could phrase it that way, but you know I'm working. I'm just doing what needs to be done. I'm not much of a dancer anyway."

"Are you sure about that?" Juliet smiled, her expression and voice just as warm as usual, and she waved good-bye and went to her car. As much as she wanted to be disappointed in Frank for his unorthodox methods and gutsy vision, he made some good points. It wasn't just because of the club—Juliet had always admired those with initiative. Fortune favors the bold, after all, and besides, it felt good to be ahead of the game. Her parents had done the same, and had nothing but success and the occasional shiny bauble or trinket to show for it; that, and a loving childhood for her too that never seemed tense. In the span of two years, she had reached a new level of self-confidence and general competence, and a few bad people getting what they deserved maybe wasn't something a good person concerned themselves with.

Beth found John and Alan eagerly deliberating about something most likely of little importance in the central courtyard, and so she inserted herself in the conversation when she saw an opportunity:

"Who's ready for prom?"

"Ask for me tomorrow, and you shall find me a grave man," Alan moaned. "I need to wear a tuxedo because I'm apparently a waiter now—we have club members running the administration of the event, and while Frank's the one in charge I'm supposed to be his loyal second-in-command. I hate dances. I hate them, I hate them, I hate them."

"It's just a few hours, it can't really be a big deal, can it? Anyway, John: will I see you tonight?"

"I never make plans that far ahead." John was another lucky recipient of a free ticket, which was fortunate, as otherwise he had absolutely no intentions on going. He had no date, so what was the point? Beth encouraged him to think otherwise:

"All of your friends will be there. Tom, Regina, Juliet, Frank, myself. Behrooz will be DJing the entire time, so you can take some photos with me and we'll call it tradition, how about that?" This did not seem like a great compromise to John, but it was the best he thought he was going to get, so he nodded his approval.

They certainly could have hired people to man the coat check, feed the students, and check IDs; teachers would sometimes handle those tasks, but those who did show up were either telling students to stop making out on the dance floor or giggling in the corner in their own miniature dance party. So, in essence, the students did the bulk of the work and the teachers got to relax and drink sparkling apple cider. Frank felt pride in his work, even when it was his turn to shine shoes, and he hoped that his peers enjoyed the opportunity to boss around their classmates like he did when he ushered. Those sorts of events were rare, and he would hang a copy of the group picture of all the staff in their matching tuxedos in his room; due to a miscommunication with the Office Depot staff, forty other copies were delivered to the principal's office, who kept a personal copy to incongruously display among senior portraits and slowly gave the others out to teachers who expressed even mild interest. The theme was "A Night In Athens," and the overzealous students in leadership had spared no expense in ordering olive wreaths, faux marble pillars, white tablecloths, and food from the nearest Greek restaurant.

Beth found John wandering alone somewhere and insisted he go with her to the photo booth, where she smiled and John tried his hardest to not frown. As much as Beth was acting like a gracious host, insisting John meet all her friends and pose appropriately, this experience wasn't his. This wasn't what he was promised at the start of freshman year by an immature Regina: universal adoration and an arm that was exclusively his. Regina and Tom were inseparable, as usual, and walked decisively to greet everyone they knew. Perhaps this wasn't so bad after all; John had what many others did not, a friend who had apologized for her earlier outbursts, and who had never broken up with him. It had slipped John's mind that Regina and Tom's relationship was marked by stability, not outbursts, broken noses, and stormy affairs. Suddenly John wasn't thinking of Tom and Regina anymore, but of this clean, hard, limited person, who dealt in universal skepticism, and who leaned back jauntily just within the circle of his arm. Beth thought the same of him, even as she cast longing glances across the packed gallery to Behrooz, who was so absorbed in his craft he barely waved hello to her.

"It's important to treasure these memories while we can, John. We only get two shots at this. Next time, we'll undoubtedly have a professional DJ and Behrooz can take his rightful place by my side. But until then, I suppose this isn't a bad way to spend the evening, is it? Enjoy this—you can't repeat the past."

"Can't repeat the past?" John cried incredulously. "Why of course you can!"

"Very funny, John." But Beth's words reached John from a distance, as he was in his own dance hall now, somewhere quiet in a parallel universe. He wore a tuxedo with a red boutonnière, Beth wore a midnight-black dress. Some waltz was playing, a good one, maybe Shostakovich's second. One with a good rhythm he could appreciate—he had discovered that waltz one night while writing his *The Great Gatsby* essay, and it so enchanted him that he played it on repeat for hours until he finished the best essay he had ever written. It was just them there in John's dreamy landscape, one two three one two three one two three endlessly until John could no longer stand Beth's perfume and they had told each other everything they had ever wanted to say. The clock here ticked at a slower rate, and it was nothing John could hear over the one two three one two three one two three into infinity.

By the time John had come back to reality, he was not dancing in the reflected moonlight with his Daisy but really dancing the sirtaki with a large group of people, some of whom he had never seen before. Tom and Regina watched from a distance, and Juliet had finally convinced Frank to briefly join her on the dance floor, if only to serve as an example to the rest of them, and they led the crowd (despite Frank's professed disinterest, he had indeed practiced this with the other club members beforehand). This had its own good rhythm to it, and it took John's mind on a Mediterranean sojourn to azure seas and a lemony sun, where someone played the bouzouki in the background while he and Beth drank wine. John had never had wine before, but it seemed like the sort of indulgent thing people did when they were happy. They would then go swimming, and for once the water would be warm. This was even better than the waltz, maybe!

Frank had returned to his original duties after the sirtaki, thinking that needless nod to the prom theme more than enough school spirit for a night. Juliet still followed him, and he entertained their conversation and their one trip to the photo booth, but did not fixate upon them with any more attention than any other day; she was easy enough to keep at a distance with the promise that he'd still be at school on Monday, and then they could eagerly plan their next year. Just not now, he was busy, and unless she wanted to help him with his duties it would have to wait; OK, she did, but the conversation could still wait for another day. Tom had watched him all night, formulating a scheme that would be guaranteed to fix all his problems. Frank didn't like him much—that was as clear as day. Tom was a remarkably poor member of the inner circle, and he was well aware that he wasn't even in the innermost layer. But Tom did have one thing on Frank: despite Frank's superior looks, better charm, general intelligence, surprising physique, bilingualism, and so much more, Frank did not have a lake house.

"The lake? What do you even do there?" Frank asked while restocking the snack trays, laying out a tiled pattern of cheese and crackers next to the baba ganoush.

"We talk, play games, some of us even read," Tom trailed off with a minor hint of disdain, as if they were wasting what otherwise would be a fun experience. "You could even swim."

"PE was enough swimming for me."

"I'm sure you're not missing out, the water is cold."

"The cold never bothered me anyway," Frank responded, and Tom chuckled. "But I'll have to think about it. Who else is coming? I assume John and Regina at the very least?"

"Well, I'm sure you've heard plenty of gossip, but Beth and Juliet are also coming too. You'll balance out the genders."

"When you phrase it that way, that's an offer I can't refuse."

"It's settled then!" Tom proclaimed, reaching out to shake Frank's hand.

"And you aren't mad about the celery juice thing? You made a noble sacrifice."

"No, not at all, the past is the past," Tom assured him, and he walked away to find Regina before he was asked any more tough questions. Bringing a sixth person was a violation of tradition, but it wasn't as if he didn't have the room. Frank seemed like he would be a good houseguest, the type who would do their chores for them. Less work for him, Frank would think he was offered a peace offering, and he would gain more time to spend with Regina.

They danced long into the night, or really until ten, and all of the juniors left with little ceremony. This wasn't their time. Despite the fun they had, their main purpose in attending was to serve as a backdrop for the seniors. The seniors embraced, confessing secret love; some almost broke out in a fistfight in front of the building before Mr. T reminded them that he could take on all of them at once without a scratch himself; all of them swept themselves away in glitz and glamor and debauchery until they convinced themselves their high school experience was complete. There was still a month left, but to them, it was pure afterthought. Tests meant nothing. Final goodbyes meant barely more. Graduation was a ceremony to be dispatched swiftly, and few juniors attended. Frank had attended out of some lingering obligation to Pranav, and he wished him good luck in his future endeavors as Pranav did to him. But beyond those few exceptions, the juniors walked through that last month eagerly awaiting their turn at being on top. John passed by Heller once the day after graduation, when enough teachers remained on campus to keep the parking lots full even though the students were already on break. It looked feeble. Small. Completely unworthy of note, and John resolved to forget completely that he was still contractually obligated to attend for another year. He had vacation to look forward to, and even greater things than that. Tomorrow would be a new day.

Chapter 29

Frank lived closest to Tom and thus was the first one picked up. He had made Tom promise to keep his coming a secret from the others, and Tom was all too happy to do so. Mr. Langley made the bold move of stepping out of the car to greet Frank, as Tom had told him he was an honored guest:

"Our future president! Tom's told me so much about you—please, call me Steve."

"Whatever he's told you is undoubtedly more exciting than the truth," Frank reassured him. Frank had thought wearing a suit would be too impractical, even if it made a statement, so he wore jeans and a Heller-branded sweater. "Should I put my suitcase in the trailer?" Mr. Langley was driving farther north after he dropped off the kids to go hiking with some of his coworkers, and thus realized the inevitable necessity of more storage space.

"What do you think you're going to be studying in college? You strike me as a future lawyer."

"Finance, maybe, just something to pay the bills, you know." Frank considered taking the middle seat in the back of the van for the most foot room, but as he was about to do so, Tom reminded him (as if he should have known) that John always sat there, and so Frank shifted to the right. Mr. Langley was surprisingly enthusiastic about chatting up his new arrival, knowing from the past two trips that he wouldn't get any other chance:

"You must be a busy guy. What are you most looking forward to at the lake? Tom told me you weren't much of a swimmer, but don't worry, neither am I. That's more of a teenager thing to do."

"I've had a busy year, and sometimes it's nice to settle down and read a little," Frank said while waving his copy of *Lolita*.

"*Lolita*, that's a very mature book, I'm impressed," Mr. Langley marveled. Mr. Langley didn't read much in his spare time, a trait he instilled in Tom, but that didn't make him illiterate by any means.

"One must always have something sensational to read in the car. Is this John's house? I imagined it to be a bit bigger."

"Yep, it's John's," Tom commented. John climbed into the van as he normally did and was about to sit in his usual spot when he realized the seat next to him was occupied; this wasn't what was supposed to happen. "What are you doing here?"

"I'm on vacation like the rest of you. I come in peace." John immediately needed some fresh air to clear his head, and decided that he would very much like to sit by a window, and so he went to sit behind Mr. Langley. Juliet was still next on the list; as soon as she entered the van and saw John directly across from her, she knew that there was something terribly wrong, and the thrill of knowing exactly what resolved quickly when she sat down in John's normal spot and saw Frank to her right, reading some sort of book, and seemingly unaware she was next to him. Why did nobody tell her this was going to happen? The fault clearly lay with her for not psychically knowing; her entire vision for that week's entertainments had to be scrapped. This was the good sort of surprise though: she would finally have someone to talk to who understood her point of view and did not treat her as secondary. After her embarrassment and her unreasoning joy she was consumed with wonder at his presence, and this wonder finally manifested itself in a tap on his shoulder.

"Surprise!" she said, as if he were not the one who had surprised her. Frank looked up and was just as astonished as she before he remembered that this was supposed to happen. This was not an all-expenses-paid vacation but a social gathering with his classmates, just like any other.

"What a nice surprise it is indeed to see you here, Juliet. I would have never expected it," he responded with a tinge of sarcasm.

"I'm so glad I finally convinced you to come. This is going to be so fun! What book are you reading? I'm delighted to see your literacy isn't all an act."

"I'm reading *Lolita* by Nabokov. It's interesting so far, not too dense."

"Cute name. What's the book about?" Juliet's persistence took Frank by surprise, and he immediately regretted his lack of foresight.

"Well, it's a romance in a way. There's this man who loves a girl, and well, I don't want to spoil anything, so it's best we leave it at that."

"I always knew you were a romantic at heart," she teased, and by the time Frank had steered the conversation toward something school-appropriate, Regina and Beth had taken their positions. After an initial frenzy of conversation, it became quite clear that all the good conversational topics had already been exhausted and did not need to be rehashed in Frank's presence—Frank in fact had seen deer before, and he explained he had no need to fawn over them like everyone else did—and so they remained quiet until they arrived. Tom watched Frank eagerly as he disembarked and viewed the house, hoping he would be impressed; Frank instead remarked simply, "It looks nice." Frank was more impressed by the groceries that awaited them in an unlabeled brown paper bag on the porch, and as soon as they came inside, he looked through the bag hoping the Monroes intended the bottle of Zinfandel for cooking.

"Welcome to my humble abode!" Tom announced with fanfare, and he led Frank downstairs to the study, where Frank immediately went to the bookshelf as if by instinct to find his copy of *Don Quixote*; through the family room; back up two flights of stairs; and to the master bedroom, which Tom all but insisted Frank take.

"Where will Juliet sleep then? Unless someone wants to sleep in the attic, well, I don't mind sleeping on the couch. It will be no inconvenience."

"No, no, you're an honored guest, Frank. Juliet has a sleeping bag and can sleep in the living room. By the piano. It's not as cold as downstairs."

"If he's the honored guest, surely he can have the honor of choosing where he wishes to sleep," Regina suggested, secretly hoping that she would be next in line for the master bedroom.

"He isn't that honored," Tom laughed, and Frank decided there was no need to make waves, and so he brought up his suitcase and started filling up the armoire. He pulled out a small pair of black socks that were left inside and clearly weren't his or Tom's; probably Juliet's. He tossed them out his door and into the hallway, hoping that someone would find them eventually. Tom and Regina had returned to their usual rooms by then, John was taking too long in the downstairs restroom as usual, and Beth and Juliet were left with grocery duty.

"Can you believe this is our last summer here? My, how time flies!" Beth observed.

"Time does fly, and thankfully the weather's nicer this year. It's like the whole squad is here: Tom's with Regina, you and John can be best buddies as usual, and I guess that leaves Frank and myself."

"What do you mean, Frank and yourself? Do you mean what I think you mean?"

"Well, knowing how much he dislikes this sort of thing, I can only presume he has a special reason for coming here."

"If I had to guess, it's because he's president now and wants to cozy up to other people with fat wallets."

"You're too cynical, Beth, of course he's here because of me. Why else would he keep it a surprise?"

"Well, if he had told you, I assume you'd have shown up with a box of chocolates and a bouquet of roses to mark the auspicious occasion. I know you well, and something tells me you finally want your turn at romance. If anyone can turn Frank's stony heart to a living, beating thing, it's you, and I promise I'll try my hardest to help you out."

"You sound like Mrs. Huang!" Juliet exclaimed. "I never thought you'd be so brazen."

"Desperate times call for desperate measures."

As much as Frank really wouldn't have minded quiet reading time for the majority of his break, of course in conjunction with creating a detailed outline for the following year, he was fully aware he ought to be a good citizen too. At Regina's suggestion, Frank examined the game cabinet, and he turned around to see Tom standing behind him with a gracious smile.

"What do you say, are you up for a little challenge? Chess, checkers, Scrabble?"

"Scrabble seems fine," Frank said.

"Be warned, I'm a good player. I beat my dad every time and he hates it."

"I play a little too, but we'll see who wins, shall we?" They moved downstairs to the small table in the kitchen and set up the board; Tom spun it around a few times for good luck, and generously let Frank go first. John sat in the corner on a barstool with the dictionary in hand to act as an unbiased observer.

"Hmm... I'll play 'qanat.' 48," Frank announced after only a few seconds and with the appearance of heavy deliberation.

"What the hell is a 'qanat'? You need to play real words."

"It's an underground channel for carrying water, John can verify." John adjusted his glasses and looked up: "It's indeed valid."

"I don't believe you," Tom insisted, and he walked over to John to scrutinize the dictionary. He shook his head a few times and resignedly walked back to his seat. "Well, if we're going to play that way, I guess I need to put on my thinking cap. I'll play 'tongue.' 7."

"8, you forgot the double letter tile. Hmm..." Frank continued, "I'll play 'quixotic,' as seeing the book earlier reminded me. 92." Tom immediately looked at John with disapproval, but he verified the word again. "Do you have this dictionary memorized or something?"

"I played a lot of Scrabble when I was a TA last year. Keeps the brain going. Your turn." At this point, the others in the house heard Tom's expressions of exasperation and came to watch, and Tom felt all the more pressure to play the best he ever had in his life.

"You can play clever words, I can play clever words too. 'Nob.' 11," Tom said as he triumphantly lay out his word in the middle of Frank's 'qanat.' Frank appeared nonplussed, and the others watched him rearrange the tiles on his rack with bated breath.

"'Zax.' 55."

"Nice word, Frank!" Juliet exclaimed, and she leaned over to .ine up the tiles on the board.

"What the f— is a 'zax' or an 'oxo'? You're just bulls—ting me," Tom declared, too irritated to censor himself or consider the shocked expressions of those around him. Frank responded coolly:

"A 'zax' is a tool for cutting roof slates. Everyone knows that, Tom," and Juliet and Beth nodded their heads in approval. Even Regina was forced to admit that the winner seemed obvious.

"I give up," Tom shouted, and he dramatically swept off all the tiles onto the hard floor before storming upstairs. Regina immediately ran off to reassure Tom that he wasn't an idiot just because he didn't know his qadis from his qaids, and the others silently picked up the pieces. "Anyone up for another game?" Frank asked them. "You all can be on your own team. It will be fair."

The game still wasn't fair—Frank won by a wide margin without any seeming exertion—but they all had fun, and in the process worked up an appetite for dinner. Meanwhile, Tom sat on his childhood bed with his head in his arms while Regina guarded his side.

"It's not fair! He's been here for 30 minutes and he's already ruined this vacation. He always wants to hog the spotlight; sure, he can do that at school, but he isn't supposed to do that in my house. This is my house, my rules, and nobody's allowed to make me look like an idiot. You can hear them laughing down there, having fun even while he's undoubtedly crushing them." Tom saw something awful in the very simplicity he failed to understand. Tom had already envisioned a full vacation with Frank, and really the others too, comfortably out of sight, out of mind. Not this, whatever it was.

"Whose turn is it for dinner?" John asked everyone assembled after they had cleaned up the Scrabble game. "If we follow Mrs. Monroe's plan, we're preparing, uh, chop suey? How kind of her to consider her audience."

"Nonsense," Frank declared. "I checked on Google Maps, there's a 99 Ranch and Whole Foods just a half hour's walk away. If we're cooking, we're doing this right. Who wants to join me?" Everyone grabbed an empty grocery bag and walked out the front door without any deliberation, and the sound of the closed door and eerie silence afterward was enough to draw Tom and Regina back downstairs. "Good riddance," Tom declared. "Now we have the house entirely to ourselves."

Before they could get too comfortable, they heard the front door unlock, and without even saying hello they went to the kitchen to start chopping vegetables, boiling water, and creating a maelstrom of activity, marshaled largely by John, who saw this as his chance to prove his worth. Regina was about to stand up to help them, but Tom cautioned her: "This isn't the time. It sounds like they have everything under control." About an hour later, Regina pulled herself up from the gray couch where she had been reclining on Tom's lap to help set the table, and nearly gasped when she saw the prismatic array of eggplant, bitter melon, and other garnishes to the pièce de résistance, a whole steamed carp.

"It smells like home!" Regina declared. "Where did all of you learn to cook like this?"

"The things you can learn online," Frank joked. "I took the chop suey recipe as a personal insult, and this seemed like the best way to make up for that slight." Even Tom was forced to see what joys awaited him on the dinner table, and he was about to reach out and touch the fish until Regina held him back. "Why would this be a personal insult? You aren't Chinese," Tom asked.

"That reminds me: we can all gossip about Tom without him understanding us!" Frank laughed, and that infectious cheer carried them through the meal, where John tried his hardest to remind Tom how to use chopsticks while using them badly himself, the girls nearly force-fed Tom and John the "medicinal and very healthy" bitter melon, and the fish was picked to the bone. As they concluded their meal and sunset was beginning to fall, the oven beeped, and John returned a few minutes later with piping-hot egg tarts.

"You're spoiling us," Regina declared. Juliet blew on hers and immediately took a bite. "Tastes like home," she announced, and Frank smiled. Tom had gone silent long ago, disappointed at the table conversation that didn't seem to include him. He still was decent enough to wash the dishes, even when Frank generously offered to take over.

"Isn't the guest supposed to help clean up?" he asked, and Tom drew out a sigh: "You've done plenty, Frank. Go sit down." There was something menacing in that, enough that Frank for once did what he was told and sat down with the others.

"I guess we can call that a success," John commented. "Everything besides the bitter melon. Disgusting."

"We should start a catering company, wouldn't that be fun? I think I'm going to burst if we have any more meals like that," Juliet added.

"No, of course not, you're skinny," Beth assured her, casting Frank a glance to make sure he heard the compliment.

"I think most of all, I'm disappointed in the Monroes. To think we abused their generosity for so long! I'll not stand for it," John continued, and before he could vent any further Frank interrupted:

"We can't possibly let one meal stand in the way of what you said has been three years of a legacy. We will eat well, I promise that personally. You can't let this leave a bad taste in your mouth, John."

"I suppose I can't, but it's just so bothersome. It feels unstable. Anyway, I don't know. I'm tired, I don't know about you guys. I'm going to head off to bed." As usual, John spent a few minutes staring out at the lake from downstairs. It felt completely transformed without the fog: he could see the faint outlines of lit windows out across the water, and using the binoculars that he had finally remembered to bring, he could look even closer. John stood just outside the door so the glass doors couldn't block him and listened, but most importantly, watched: the silhouette of a young kid playing piano behind a curtain could have been taken straight out of a movie. What interesting lives everyone else must live, John thought, so interesting that their paths never intersected. The wind grew too bothersome eventually, and John went to brush his teeth and turn in for the night.

Frank enjoyed all the comforts of his new position: his armoire now most definitely clean of Juliet's essence, space for morning stretches, a bathroom with a cold shower and no ambiguity as to which toothbrush was his, relative seclusion that let him sleep at a reasonable time, and a view of the lake that made him wish he had come here earlier. Frank woke up early as usual, took a morning shower, and got dressed quickly enough that when he came out, he was definitely the only one awake, unless Beth was somewhere on her phone browsing Instagram. Treading lightly as to not wake up Juliet, he opened the fridge and surveyed the cornucopia of eggs, butter, milk, fruits, ranging all the way to the now-classic duck breasts, salmon, and even some liver pâté. Normally he'd fetch the newspaper and make himself a bowl of cereal, but that brioche looked so good, and he searched the wall of cookbooks for something that would have French toast and got to work. Frank did not consider himself a natural-born cook, but he certainly could follow a recipe; was it really any different than a lab in biotech? As he started cracking eggs into a metal bowl, cracking one of them one-handed just to see if it was as easy as it looked on *Chopped*, he wondered if French toast alone was too pedestrian; too many carbs, and with the fridge well-stocked, anything but decadence would be disappointing. So he opened the fridge again, took some berries, the mascarpone, bacon (a crowd-pleaser, even if he wasn't a fan), and maple syrup, got out another pan, and got to work, the sizzling music to his ears. The smell of hot breakfast drifted through the kitchen and down the stairs, and roused John, Beth, and Juliet just as the meal was nearing completion. Juliet initially thought that the kitchen was on fire, a notion thankfully dispelled when she peered into the kitchen and saw Frank clearly hard at work. Not wishing to intrude too annoyingly, she took the long way around to enter the kitchen, sitting at the table and waiting for Frank to turn around, which he did fairly quickly.

"Good morning! Breakfast is served!" Juliet tucked into her food voraciously, stopping only to ask for a glass of milk which Frank immediately provided and to encourage him to sit down with her, which he did, and Frank ate even more voraciously than she. By the time John and Beth had greeted each other appropriately and decided to investigate the source of the delicious smell and hubbub above, Juliet had already finished and was attempting the crossword with the same vigor.

"You're up early," Beth commented, and John took a break from chewing—he had never had maple syrup before, but it seemed like heaven in a bottle—to interject: "We're always up this early. Remember last year?"

"It was cloudy then, we had nothing else to do. And besides, we meditated, which doesn't really count," Juliet added.

"I thought you loved meditation and yoga and all that sort of New Age-y stuff," Frank said. "Why shouldn't it count?"

"It's more passive. And I'll have you know that there's nothing New Age about it. People have practiced meditation for millennia, and there are countless health benefits. Even you aren't too busy."

"Look, I'm not going to be the person who denies the value of a morning stretch, but I've never been a fan of meditation. It brings back too many bad memories of middle school. I'm sure Jason's told some of you about this at some point, but on our field trip in eighth grade we meditated at a Buddhist monastery where monks whacked us with sticks when we shifted out of seiza. It was very traumatic."

"It sounds beautiful," John said, "I mean the scenery and not the whacking. It's still early, so what do you say?"

"The early morning is my favorite time of day, but in the summer when it gets too light the entire mystical aspect is lost. There's that certain *je ne sais quoi* about it. Although, with everything so quiet around here, maybe not. Shall we have a vote?"

"Don't beat around the bush, we're going outside," John insisted. Frank portioned out two more servings of French toast for the late arrivals when they chose to come down, and as usual the others went outside to the backyard, and they took their positions in the garden. John directed everyone through breathing exercises until it became clear everyone already knew how to meditate. Tom peered outside from the living room warily and licked mascarpone off his lips. "So they got to him too," he muttered to himself.

Later in the day, the six had split into two pairs of three, as by then seemed established custom. John and Beth had migrated downstairs, as the clearer skies made the lighting less ominous and John objected to the window upstairs being cracked ajar. Tom and Regina were somewhere, probably on the top floor, and Frank sat in John's typical spot, with Juliet across from him.

"Do you play the piano, Frank?"

"Not as much as Regina, and I most certainly wouldn't phrase it as a habitual action, but I do play. Do you?"

"I never learned, too artistic for me."

"But I thought you were an artist?"

"I'm a disappointment in many ways, I know. Can you teach me how to play? I promise I'm a quick study." Frank groaned, set aside his book, and walked over to the piano, gesturing for Juliet to follow.

"There's a simple duet, I'm sure you've heard it, 'Heart and Soul.' You know, doo doo doo, do doo do doo do doo, and so on. Watch me," and Frank demonstrated the right hand. "Put your hand over mine. See? It's a simple rhythm. You can add all the embellishments you want—many classic pieces have themes and variations, but you're a quick study, you'll figure it out." After a few minutes of practice, they began playing, switching parts when it seemed like Juliet understood everything.

Tom found the sound of people having fun without him repulsive, and he peered from the stairs to see them jamming together with laughter that seemed too genuine and too carefree. That piano bench was meant for one person, namely Regina, and not two. John silently crept up the stairs from the family room, not wishing to disturb Beth nor the picturesque scene unfolding without him; he wanted to do the same with Beth, maybe when the others were gone, with Frank's full range of musical improvisation and Juliet's joy—far more romantically, of course.

"I don't know what I'm doing wrong, John. Not even 24 hours and he acts like he owns the place. It's absolutely ludicrous."

"You are a king by your own fireside, as much as any monarch in his throne. No matter what they do, before Frank came this was your house, and after he leaves this will still be your house. It's nothing to worry about during vacation, no less."

"There's more to it than that. It's that male-female aspect too. If I had known I were inviting boyfriend and girlfriend, I'd have left one of them at home."

"But they aren't dating," John insisted. "She's just friends with him."

"That still doesn't make me feel any less threatened. That's worse, even; now Frank's just rubbing it in my face that he can have a healthy relationship. I find the moment that a woman makes friends with me, she becomes jealous, exacting, suspicious, and a damned nuisance. I don't see why it shouldn't be the same for him."

"Well, Frank is a good person, and clearly his policy is paying off."

"Pah, don't believe any of that propaganda they tell you. Just because Lady Macbeth is always whispering sweet nothings into his ear doesn't make him any less misguided. I'd go as far as to call it sorcery. Let me paint you a picture with a classical allusion, to take a page out of Frank's book: the policemen are running around trying to track down the famed temptress Carmencita. She comes out on stage, sings the habanera—all the soldiers stare at her, she rejects all of them, except Don José, who's sitting there minding his own business undoubtedly thinking of something stupid. She hands him her flower, and at once he is enthralled. But does Carmen care about him at all? Quite frankly, she doesn't give a damn. She plays with him a bit, leads him astray, and then when Escamillo walks in and sings his song about how heroic he is, Carmen immediately falls for him! Don José is left despondent, and I don't want to spoil the entire thing from there, but that nasty Carmen! I hate women with loose morals like that."

"Is Don José supposed to be me or Frank? Because what you cescribed sounds a lot closer to what I've gone through. With the whole Jezebel thing. And I never took you for the opera sort of guy—I'm impressed."

"Regina made me go with her, but that's beside the point. Perhaps this is something all high school boys must go through, the deification, defenestration, and domestication of the opposite sex."

"Not the gay ones, Tom, don't forget to be inclusive."

"You're right. Adrian and I still are good friends, but I haven't asked him much about his adventures on the dating front. But let's just discard convenient exceptions like him and Frank. We should concern ourselves exclusively with our own kind." Frank and Juliet finished their duet, and Tom and John politely applauded so as to not seem too sinister. "Bravo! You have a natural talent," John shouted, not entirely insincerely.

"Any song requests? I'll try my best to humor you," Frank promised. Juliet stood still by his side, curious to see if he could replicate his virtuosic Scrabble performance. Tom quickly Googled "hard piano pieces," and suggested "La Campanella" by Liszt; Frank groaned and gave Tom a knowing sneer, then began. This was enough to attract Regina and Beth, who joined Juliet in watching from behind. Tom kicked himself—somehow in the process of hazing Frank, he had only made him look more skilled. Frank kept up brief snippets of conversation with Tcm, asking him repeatedly if the piece was being played to satisfaction or if he ever had played it before, but Tom ignored his questions.

"Is this a hard piece?" John whispered to Tom, who refreshed his search engine a few more times to make sure he had not made a mistake.

"Google lies! Everything lies these days! No wonder civilization's going to pieces. Let me tell you something: you can't trust anything besides your own brain. There's nothing like the brain, and we only get one of them. Clearly I haven't been using mine wisely."

"You play just like Mr. T, I'm surprised you had this piece memorized," Regina commented after Frank had finished and exhaled a sigh of relief.

"I'm a professional, and even I wouldn't go with this as my first choice. Maybe a Chopin etude or something instead."

"If you wish to play Chopin for us, go ahead; I think my hands will fall off if I play any more." Frank stood up and went to the couch, where he slumped in an unprecedented display of exhaustion. "I need some water."

Frank's largess continued the following morning with eggs Benedict on homemade English muffins. Juliet knew by now to wake up early if she wanted Frank's undivided attention, and still in her nightgown she sat down and dug into her meal. John and Beth also knew by now not to be late, and while they chatted and imagined themselves the only people in the house, Tom and Regina ambled down the stairs at the same time, both still in their pajamas. Beth looked at the others and rolled her eyes before trying as hard as possible to say "Good morning" happily. John didn't immediately understand Beth's exasperation, but after a few seconds of Tom dramatically sniffing the air he thought he figured out why he and Regina were holding hands. They couldn't be—but did they? He struggled to remember if Tom and Regina were even more attached to each other than usual. She never came down for group reading time anymore, and not even a hot breakfast could entice her to adjust her sleeping habits; this wouldn't have stood out as much if not for everyone else in the house having acclimatized themselves to waking up early. The forbidden word, s-e-x, didn't immediately occur to John as an explanation, but Beth discreetly mouthed it to him and he suddenly could think of no explanation less natural. Frank, really, didn't mind: the food was still fresh and the hollandaise hadn't congealed. He went back to the kitchen and brought two more plates, still smiling and trying not to think about what the other people in the house got up to when they were alone.

"Wow, you guys are up early," Tom exclaimed, immediately seeing Frank and thinking him the culprit.

"We were up this early yesterday too, Tom, you just didn't notice," John responded. "Eat up, this isn't going to eat itself. Can you believe that Frank's never made this before? It's divine."

"Oh, I'm sure," Tom grimaced, and he and Regina took their plates to the dining room table, separated comfortably by a wall from the rest of them. After breakfast, John decided to conduct some intrepid investigative journalism and check out their bedrooms. Regina's bed was fastidiously made, but not without imperfections; one corner of the blanket hung loose, and the pillow on one side wasn't quite as fluffed as it ought to be. He was tempted to go and fix it, mistakes like that bothering him, but that wasn't the evidence he was there for, and so he walked directly across the hall to Tom's room. The blanket and sheet appeared ripped from the mattress, and the light was dim. Scattered piles of socks and shirts were strewn about the room as if Tom had in a fit of madness decided to build miniature altars to some eldritch god. John believed people's rooms reflected their state of mind, and if Tom's room was any indication, he was clearly demented. He searched quietly, trying as hard as possible to leave everything just as before, for any evidence of Tom's impropriety, but John did not know what besides woman's underwear, a sweaty bra, or a lock of Regina's hair could possibly be the proof in the pudding.

Tom came back to his room a few hours later to change into swim trunks and saw that someone moved his blanket. John, it must be John. That silly John who thought he understood the world. Such a prude, really. That anyone should care in this heat whose flushed lips he kissed, whose head made damp the pajama pocket over his heart! Tom wasn't crazy—they didn't go beyond snuggling—but the lack of trust clearly apparent in all of his friends was too much to bear. He pulled out more clothes from his suitcase, throwing some on his chair, some on his bed, and when his aim failed the floor, looking for some sort of proof of his good character. He wanted something like photographic evidence he could strut downstairs with and yell, "I am innocent!". Even now, the longer he took to get changed, the more time that gossipy Beth and John would turn everyone, even Regina, against him.

Everyone, even Frank, assembled at the lake; as promised, Frank did not swim, and so he set up a chair and continued to read. Occasionally he would take out his laptop and type furiously, and other times he would just stare at those frolicking in the water with a wistful expression. Juliet's initial excitement at being able to swim in this mythical lake, which Regina had once jokingly promised siphoned from the Fountain of Youth, dissipated when she jumped in and found the water frigid. This wasn't Hawaii. Frank laughed when he saw Juliet's awkward strokes, shouting "I warned you!" This did not stop them from playing until the chill became too much for everyone but Tom and John, who each seemed determined to win an endurance contest. Juliet went to get her own chair and sat down next to Frank after cleaning up.

"What are you working on? Your master plan for the school?"

"How could you guess? It's just a bit of work, no big deal. The weather's nice, enjoy it while you can; don't feel obligated to wait with me."

"You have months, Frank. I don't understand why you need to make everything so professional. Come on, put away that laptop; the weather's nice, enjoy it while you can." Juliet leaned over to close Frank's laptop, and she walked back to the house to put it inside before he could voice any objections. From the moment Frank got into Mr. Langley's car, he had felt a constant desire to be productive; he was under constant scrutiny, and any mistake could undermine everything he had constructed up until that day. Frank was a good actor, but he wasn't that good, and he thought slips like his piano performance earlier were pushing him toward a precipice. Juliet came back with her own book, and they waited until Tom finally conceded and dragged his soggy frame inside.

"John, what are your thoughts on love?" Beth asked him when they were alone at last.

"Love is a fabrication of the mind. Love is inherently unjust. I hate talking about it."

"Sounds like someone's been rubbed the wrong way by Tom and Regina."

"It's not them, it's everything. Why can't we live in a society where people mind their own business?"

"Geez, I'm sorry I asked! But I was just thinking, Behrooz and I have gone through so many ups and downs, and in the meantime everyone else seems to have everything figured out."

"The course of true love never did run smooth. But you're right, Tom and Regina most certainly have all their ducks in a row, and it's only credit to Frank's willpower that Juliet's seductive charms haven't gotten to him yet." This elicited a rare laugh from Beth.

"Seductive charms? The only person that would ever say something like that is someone who fancies her, John."

"This wasn't my idea, Tom was saying that earlier. While they were playing piano."

"So Tom's the jealous one now, isn't he? He's compensating for something, I'm sure, but I haven't gotten a good enough look at his swim trunks to find out. I m only comfortable saying this because he's not in earshot, and maybe it's just me being paranoid, but Tom is mean to Regina sometimes."

"He's assertive. Masculine. I can't say, I feel like I'm unsexed compared to him. So weak."

"Don't say that about yourself, John. I've been known for my predictions recently, so I'm going to make another one: this entire situation is a powder keg waiting to burst. Tom's going to make a fool of himself at some point again in a misguided attempt to make things right, and then we're only going to laugh at him more. This will be the worst vacation of his life! But he deserves it for being a spoiled brat."

"That's big of you to say when we're all here thanks to his generosity."

"Caveat emptor." Beth did turn out to be right, as always. The following night, Frank had decided that because nothing succeeds like excess, beef Wellington would be on the menu. Compared to all else he had done, this was no Herculean challenge, and only John was conscripted to help him; Frank respected John's prioritization of food quality above all else. The others sat downstairs and watched *The Office* reruns, trying their hardest not to salivate too much at the smells from above. Tom could not bear this any longer, and he had the perfect argument planned that would expose Frank for who he was, a lying and cheating conman. Tom lumbered upstairs and barked Frank's name, and when this did not receive an immediate response he walked closer, just a few feet away from him and John.

"Why are you trying to steal Regina from me?" Tom asked in a near growl. Frank refused to make eye contact, continuing to swirl butter in a saucepan.

"That's preposterous. How could you possibly come to that conclusion?"

"Don't you dare lie to me. You've been abusing my generosity this entire time, eating my food, talking to my girl, playing my piano, sitting in my chairs, beating me at my games, and nobody else is brave enough to call you out on it. But I am. Is that what your agenda's been the entire time, this past few years? John failed first, so you thought you could do better than him. Is that right?"

"This savors of anticlimax, Tom. I'm not going to say anything more that will be spun into your conspiracy theory, but clearly you took me too literally when I said that paranoia is a sign of intelligence. I have no designs on Regina, nor any of you for that matter. I'm just trying my hardest to enjoy my vacation like the rest of you, and if cooking dinner is too much, then I can easily only prepare dinner for five. Would you like that, Tom?" Tom sniffed the air again and decided that this fight was not one worth sacrificing dinner for; he did not believe in principles enough to stick by his word. He returned downstairs silently, and John could only remark, "That was strange."

"He's a strange guy, John. There's no doubt about it."

"But he has a point, you know. Don't you think you're trying a bit too hard? Whatever Platonic ideal of yourself you've made, it's... I don't know, but I can see why Tom would be bothered."

"This wasn't my idea to come here originally, John. Tom came to me during prom and offered; I thought it noble of him how he wanted to put the past behind him and focus on the future. Clearly I was wrong. But I think of this as a life lesson for him. Holding grudges does nobody any good. Besides, if this is a democracy, I think Beth, Regina, and Juliet all certainly aren't complaining. Even if Regina is loyal to Tom without a fault, she has a good head on her shoulders." John did not know how to express his argument further, so he went mute and focused on finishing the meal. Nobody dared bring up Tom's outburst at the dinner table, but they still complimented Frank and John on another meal well done; Tom barely touched his food, slicing it into tiny pieces but refusing to eat any until it became clear nobody else would keel over from poison. He didn't trust Frank; he was too clever to poison everyone's food, he would just touch his, and then he and Regina would embrace over his stone-cold body. They'd paddle out at night when the moon was bright and not a sound could be heard elsewhere and dump his body into the lake to sleep with the fishes, and they'd return to raucous celebration. That sneaky bastard.

The sky was preparing to turn dark the next day, and everyone was feeling sufficiently sanitized from their swimming, when Juliet found Frank and suggested he go with her to the dock and admire the view; the closest he had actually gotten to the lake itself previously was shaking his head at John's wet towel that had been draped over a chair. Frank looked around the room to see if anyone else was still in earshot, but they had all disappeared somewhere else, so he hesitantly said yes and followed her outside. They walked through the backyard and down the path, Juliet for once leading the way. Frank gently closed the gate behind him, and they sat with their feet off the edge of the dock dangling safely above the water, sitting a few inches apart.

"Isn't this nice?" Juliet ventured, and Frank agreed without hesitation. There was something oddly mesmerizing about still water, shimmering in the sunlight, and framed by the trees and the shadows of other houses. It was oddly Zen, and the water was still enough for them to see their reflections as clear as glass. Even the kayakers faintly in the distance were as much a part of the natural environment as a flock of migrating waterfowl. Frank was content to sit there and imagine quiet orchestral music, a string quartet perhaps, while relishing the comfort of the breeze; Juliet, after enjoying a few minutes of the same, turned to him.

"You know, I never would have thought that we'd become such good friends. I still remember that day in Ms. Bracknell's room when you tutored me, and then I knew you were a good person. So good that you devoted so much time to teaching others how to be good."

"It's nothing. Any other person in my position would do the same."

"You are the kindest and smartest person I have ever met. Nobody could possibly have done the same."

"I wish I could agree. But what I can say is that you're also one of the kindest people that I've ever met."

"That means a lot coming from you, Frank." They sat for a few more quiet minutes, thankful that the mosquitos weren't out that evening.

"I would love to live in a place like this someday. Like all those retirees across the water. It may just be me, but I think we're the youngest people here."

"You know, I would love to as well," Juliet responded with her charac-teristic smile. Frank walked back to the shore and picked up a few small pebbles. He threw one with some intensity at the surface of the lake, hoping it would bounce and arc; instead, it simply broke the surface tension of the lake and disappeared, leaving concentric circles that quickly faded. Juliet tried, with no more success, and they alternated, none of them accomplishing anything but creating an ephemeral patchwork. This amusement took only a few minutes to resolve itself before they ran out of pebbles and established that neither of them knew how to make the pebbles skip and dance. Frank was starting to get a bit antsy at this point, as he'd much rather be sitting on a couch; seeing no particular obligation to stay longer, he stood up and began walking back, Juliet rapidly following behind. Frank felt like he was doing something sneaky when he opened the sliding door and climbed the stairs. John and Beth were in their usual positions reading their books, and paid them little notice. At least they probably weren't making out, Beth thought, unlike the last time Tom and Regina proclaimed they were going for "a little walk."

"Hey, uh, Frank, I think I left my swim goggles outside by the lake, could you do me the great favor of checking if they're out there?" Beth asked, hoping Frank would take the hint. Frank immediately darted off downstairs, and Beth turned to Juliet with a smile. "Tell me everything."

"He's like a brick wall. I can't get through to him. I don't know how I can make my hints any less subtle besides acting like Regina, and that's not a good look for anyone. It's not classy."

"So your issue is that Frank is too much like a gentleman?"

"Yes, exactly! He spends too much time reading and working and not enough time relaxing."

"I know for a fact that as nice as Frank may be, he certainly does not consider himself a gentleman. Good things take time, don't force them. Otherwise you'll be like me and Louis, or me and Ted, or..."

"You and Behrooz?" Juliet asked, a bit too eager to fill in the blank.

"You're right, you know. This time I think we're enjoying each other in moderation, and that makes us treasure our experiences just a bit more.

This isn't a symbiotic relationship; we don't burst into tears when we can't see each other for a few weeks. In fact, and this theory may be just a bit too outlandish for you to believe, but have you considered that maybe Frank is perfectly happy the way things are now? He has feelings, you know."

"He has feelings, but I have feelings too. I'll keep trying," Juliet finished when Frank came back upstairs and reported that he could find no swim goggles, and it was kind of funny because he couldn't remember Beth actually wearing any that day, now that he thought about it.

"You tried your best, Frank. Sit down with us, relax a little," Beth urged him, and Juliet patted the couch next to her; Frank sat down next to her obediently. John finally looked up from his book to see the reshuffling, and thought it prudent perhaps to go join Beth as well. What was the point of sitting in the armchair, from which he could observe all, if he did no observing? Inaction was lazy, but perhaps it was the intellectual thing to do; Frank had said once that a philosopher was characterized by the abundance of time they possessed: a philosopher could always find time to think before they acted, they were never consumed in a fiery tempest of energy that drove them to lash out at others or turn every dinner into something out of Martha Stewart. All of them thought they had no time, that's what the issue was! Their lake trip only lasted a week total, but what did that leave them, a hundred waking hours if not a bit more? How could there not be enough time in all that to take a breath? There was something gravely wrong with the world, or maybe just with them, and Regina had private thoughts about that that evening when they spoke in her room:

"This is stupid, all of it. I thought the lake was meant to be a refuge from teenage drama; we came here because we thought ourselves better than that. Instead, look what we get: Tom hates Frank for no apparent reason, Frank is working himself to the bone maintaining his perfect persona, Juliet is hopelessly infatuated with him and he doesn't even know it—and Beth's goading her on all this time! When have we had one meal with the six of us not finding some clever way to snap at each other's throats? It's shameful, and I'm disappointed in everyone, besides maybe you, for contributing to it. I'm going to wake up one day to see Frank's corpse floating on the water." John sat on Regina's bed next to her, staring at the wall hoping for some insight to reveal itself.

"Everything was perfect last year. Maybe the secret is cloudy weather. Too much sunlight hurts the eyes."

"Do you know what I like about you, John? Your honesty. I can always count on you to tell the truth. Even when it hurts."

"Life hurts," John plaintively declared, and he collapsed into tears. Regina wasn't sure how to soothe him—he took up too much space in her room—so she brought him a tissue box and went back downstairs.

For their last meal, Frank thought it finally time to touch those duck breasts, and for lack of any original ideas he settled for a classic duck à l'Orange. Everyone had promised themselves beforehand to shelve their concerns and lingering insecurities, and at the end of the meal, John proposed a toast:

"To family!" John declared, and everyone raised their sparkling cider in celebration. He looked at all his friends, who were comfortably chatting—even Frank and Tom had appeared to have worked out their differences—and he wondered how much of it was due to him. There was a peculiar chain of cause-and-effect which John had started to formulate over the past few days. If Regina hadn't been so nice to him, it was unlikely Tom would have recalled who he was, and at the lake that was undoubtedly when Tom and Regina first met. If John had not told Behrooz such nice things about Beth, which he still earnestly believed, they would not be together. And as for Frank, Frank had enabled John's current state of mind with his tactical book loaning. But at the end of the day, ultimately John was the protagonist of his own story; he was the one with emotional depth, with wisdom acquired through experience, a wandering eye, and so much more that even he could not quantify. He was the linchpin of their ragtag band, and nothing could change that. He thought back to the previous year, once more; was the food really that much worse? If one thing was for certain, he felt happier then. John slept the best he had ever slept that trip, and was surprised to walk upstairs and hear no sizzling pans, just Frank and Juliet reading the newspaper and eating cereal. A boring end to a boring trip.

Mr. Langley was the star of the trip back home because everyone wanted to hear about his hiking; he described in grandiose terms the mountain peaks, the arduous trail, and the male bonding, and went as far as to suggest that next summer, if it ever came, instead of lounging in luxury they should do the same.

"Why should we do work during vacation?" Frank asked rhetorically, and they all laughed.

"Says the wannabe Gordon Ramsay," Tom responded sharply. After everyone else had been dropped off, Frank took the last few minutes to address Tom earnestly:

"Look, I'm not sure what exactly sparked this cold war between us, but I hope it's all over. I understand that you felt attacked in some way, but if there's anything I could do better for next time, please, just tell me."

"It's exactly that perfectionism that's bothersome. But it clearly makes you happy, and everyone else absolutely loved you, even Regina, so why should I complain? My duty as host is to make sure all my guests are happy. It's as simple as that."

"When I start my catering company, you'll be first on my client list," Frank laughed. "Well, there's my house. I'd better head out. Catch you on the flip side." Frank, still somewhat wary of Tom, quickly grabbed his bags and went inside before he could do something stupid. It wasn't as if he was ever in any danger, but he couldn't shake the image of Tom standing in front of the knife block and potentially being able to grab one and lunge at him before he could react. 'Tis but a scratch, he would say, if he couldn't indeed duck and kick Tom's leg out. Maybe he would have won, but that wouldn't have been a fight worth winning—he probably would: Tom did not seem as nimble as he could be. And the police, everything else too, would make an awfully embarrassing mess. As soon as he left, Tom switched from NPR to a hip-hop station and spent the rest of the way home singing out of tune.

Chapter 30

When not struggling to start his college applications or playing video games, John occasionally found the time to go socialize with his friends. The classic core of Beth, Regina, and Juliet proved most forthcoming, mainly because they saved him the trouble of taking initiative, and their idea of a good time was eating food with little else needed. John walked up to the rose garden and saw Beth sitting on the bench texting the others; she looked up at him and beckoned him to sit down instead of awkwardly hovering around her.

"What are the odds that Juliet will have guilted Frank into showing up?" Beth asked after the usual pleasantries and upon realizing that both of them were a bit early.

"I don't think Tom is coming, and although Frank does live fairly close by, I know he's busy prepping for the club. I'm sure he has better things to do."

"I think it's more likely he wanted to avoid a repeat of last year. Regina and Juliet were, shall I say, sociable."

"If Frank didn't at least tolerate her presence, I doubt she'd be vice president of the club."

"He may tolerate her, but if I know her, I think she more than tolerates him."

"Maybe he just likes the attention. I know I would," John remarked, now thinking back on all the "attention" he had received over the years. There was something about the park in the summer, maybe, that drew out those feelings—the heat and fragrance, perhaps. And it was this that John and Beth savored for a few minutes before Regina and Juliet arrived, and without wasting any time they left.

"Why don't you bring Tom with you, anyway?" John asked Regina while they stood in line at Dirt & Grass.

"That's a great question. Hmm, why don't I bring him? Beth, why don't you bring Behrooz?"

"Some things are best enjoyed privately. That's less about socialization and more about obligation—the good kind of obligation. But nowhere in my visualization of the perfect date with Behrooz is a whole supporting cast. We can't leave you out of this, Juliet—why don't you bring Frank?"

"Well, Frank isn't hers to bring," John muttered, but Juliet interrupted as if she had an epiphany:

"It slipped my mind completely, but you're a genius! You're all genius-es! I never quite thought about it like that before; I know he's not to be disturbed this summer, but, just but, when the time comes he will be brought whether he likes it or not. Anyway... ice cream. You should try the smoked salmon, John."

"Ugh, smoked salmon! Who would order that?"

"Frank," Regina groaned. They took their ice cream back to the park, and John still could not believe his good fortune. He was an outsider, a casual watcher in the darkening streets who did not really know anything about his dining companions besides what they presented outwardly to him. He enjoyed his infrequent social outings with the girls because they made him feel interesting. What he said held great importance to them, choosing ice cream flavors or deciding where to sit down. He used to clearly bristle whenever social media was brought up, but now he didn't turn frigid when they inevitably Snapchatted and Instagrammed their adventures. He really did stick out, though, three people with sunglasses and stylish outfits, and then John in jeans and a T-shirt awkwardly crammed in-frame. They outnumbered him, that was as clear as day; and if they wished to dictate how it was John felt at any moment, he couldn't stop them. He was more than a token, but John did not know what to think of himself nor anyone else. At least the ice cream was good.

But why was he there? His visits to the lake had exigence; they were separated by distance and time from the mortal world. Time looped back on itself there, which is why sophomore year felt as close as yesterday and that year's trip had been filed before then, before John learned to be his own protagonist. So why was he with them in the park? John looked up at an unfamiliar sky through frightening leaves and shivered as he found what a grotesque thing a rose is and how raw the sunlight was upon the scarcely created grass. Raw, that was the word: there was no filter, no peer pressure, nothing to stop Juliet stealing a spoonful of his ice cream when he wasn't looking or her mischievous smile with milk-stained lips when she was caught *in flagrante delicto*. There was too much heat, and they had to eat their ice cream quickly before it melted. In the heat, everything melted together in John's mind, as if they were made of wax. Everything was made of wax, the textured leaves, the wiry men playing tennis, Mr. T in the far distance playing alone with his dog. John was tempted to go say hello to him, but he was so far away, and the others were so near.

"What's wrong, John? You seem more wistful than usual. Brain freeze?" Beth asked, seeing his eyes glaze over even as he talked.

"Nothing at all. Nothing at all. This is perfect, as always."

"Everything's always perfect or terrible with you, John. There's never any halfway," she joked, and they finished their ice cream and said their farewells. John had parked a few blocks away, and he sauntered slowly, stopping to smell the flowers and pet a dog who wanted desperately to be his friend. Everything about this was wrong. John was happy to be back inside his car because the air smelled clean; there was no trace of sugar that could condense in his brain. As had become usual when the world seemed too much to handle, John took a nap when he returned home.

The new leaders of the school assembled a few weeks before to meet with Ms. Foster, where she was supposed to in the span of a few hours brainwash them; it seemed an impossible task, and as soon as they sat down, Frank made it clear he had no intent of letting that happen:

"So, I've been reading the student handbook and some of the district policies—all of that boring legal boilerplate—and I think I've figured out everything we need to know. Are there any other documents I'm missing?"

Ms. Foster smiled and sucked in air: "Well, it's like you've done my job for me. I really appreciate that. That's the leadership I'm talking about. Yes, uh... have you met with HR yet?"

"Of course; I had a conference call with them and Mr. Kurtz earlier. Such lovely people."

"If you say so. Anyway, you know the drill: I'll give you tasks occasionally, you make other people do them for you, it's a simple system. Very hard to mess up."

"I think we'll be capable of making our own tasks, Ms. Foster. Recall the ¾ rule?"

"What's the ¾ rule?" Behrooz asked, mildly concerned that Frank hadn't seen the need to inform him about this, but everyone else clearly already knew.

"Oh, the ¾ rule is a beautiful thing," Ms. Foster explained. "Technically speaking, unless it's a matter of school safety, as long as ¾ of you agree on a rule and can champion its implementation, and nobody above us cares enough to interfere, you can do pretty much anything you want. You have no idea how many legal rights we have. If you want everyone to show up to school in Speedos, you type up your proposal, sign it, and voila!" Ms. Foster thought the idea of a student-run dictatorship horrendous. However, she considered her job to be facilitating student leadership, not enforcing her own vision of what ought to be, and so she shelved her personal concerns; besides, if any students were capable of taking on this challenge, they were.

Behrooz found it more surprising that Ms. Foster was willing to use the ¾ rule to delegate any authority to Frank that he wished than that he suggested rule by fiat as a more efficient way of doing things. Perhaps it wasn't a coincidence that so many leadership students were involved with the club. Behrooz weakly raised an objection, claiming that as an elected body, they had some obligation to represent the students.

"If they didn't want us, they wouldn't have voted for us. Democracy is the will of the majority, right?" Frank responded, and the leadership director nodded and added, "I am sure that we can all work out any differences we have, Frank, don't worry. I have heard such great things about you, especially with that celery juice project, and I could think of nobody who embodies our school values better. I have no doubts that you can take on as much responsibility as you desire, within the purview of leadership."

"And what exactly does this include, Ms. Foster?" Behrooz asked to clarify, a pit forming in his stomach.

"You can't change the curriculum, you'd have to make money appear with a magic wand to change the school lunches, and we have a love-hate relationship with the arts department. But don't worry, I'm here to help you out."

"Ms. Foster, I believe this is the beginning of a beautiful friendship." Frank announced, dramatically reaching out to shake hands; Alan followed, Juliet afterward, and Behrooz put on his best smile and did the same.

"It sounds like we may need to tap into that little nest egg we've been accumulating," Alan remarked.

"Oh, you have a nest egg already!" Ms. Foster cooed. "This should make things so much easier! We could use new printers for the staff room."

"Get me a list, Ms. Foster, of anything the school needs and we'll try our best to take care of it. Our philanthropy may not directly extend to our peers, but to our teachers, most certainly! It's trickle-down economics, everyone knows that," Frank added. Behrooz looked like he would burst into tears if he stayed any longer, and so the students left to assemble outside. Behrooz naturally did not wish to spend any more time than he had to with his new president, and Alan's desire to be a sycophant was outweighed by his desire to go home and play Call of Duty, which left Frank and Juliet alone once again.

"So... want to get lunch? I'll drive," Juliet asked coyly, trying to remember what exact intonation she used to invite John to group outings.

"I don't trust cars. They're hunks of metal with an agenda. And what may I ask is the purpose of this lunch?"

"Well, obviously it's not just so we can get to know each other better and enjoy shared company, but so we can discuss our shared vision for the school. Let's call this a working lunch; those are what professionals do, right, and we're professionals? You mentioned that nest egg of yours, so there's no harm in a little indulgence. Bill this as a business expense."

"Indeed we are professionals," Frank agreed. As if guided by an inner GPS, they walked as quickly as Frank could in his suit and dress shoes, so still a brisk pace, downtown to a restaurant Juliet insisted upon. The hostess chose not to comment on their oddly formal outfits, and instead asked Frank where "he and the lady" would like to sit. Juliet pointed out a secluded booth in the corner.

"If you could pick one word to describe Heller, what would it be?" Frank asked Juliet.

"Community. It's obvious. We have communities everywhere, your club, my cheer team, the drama kids. Without community, where would we be?"

"Are you still doing cheer? I thought you said last year you'd stop. Too much sin."

"My college counselor said I need extracurriculars. You would be great on the team. You have the right body type. It's fun."

"I'm busy enough as is, and if I say so myself, I've never trusted cheerleaders. It's a weird prejudice, I know—not you, don't worry."

While Frank and Juliet talked, Ted entered the restaurant to get his own lunch, and when he saw the only person wearing a suit, it was obvious he had to pay his respects.

"Hey hey hey, my two favorite people!" Ted laughed, towering over the two of them. Juliet decided then that she could really use a bathroom break, which left Frank and Ted to catch up.

"First off, what do I call you now? Sir? Dictator? Grand poobah?"

"President will be fine, Ted."

"So you won?"

"We had a meeting with Ms. Foster earlier, and now we're just enjoying a lunch to discuss what to do now. There are so many possibilities and there's such little time. Time is a rare commodity these days."

"And so you're dating Juliet now? Nice!" This prompted immediate denial from Frank:

"Oh, no, no, not at all. She's vice president, I'm president. How else are we supposed to do things? This was her idea, actually. These things are always her idea."

"And you don't think there's anything that could potentially be misconstrued here? The very essence of romance is uncertainty, you know, and what I'm sure myself and everyone else would think is that there's a little, you know, spark."

"At least from my perspective, I'm just enjoying a nice lunch while trying to plot school domination. I really don't see what's so weird about that. Besides, we need to spend our profits somehow—Alan's been into cryptocurrency recently, and he's increased our profits probably more than fifty-fold, and he projects more growth through the year. That kid's a genius," Frank explained in between bites of his Caesar salad.

"The way to a woman's heart is through her stomach, after all. Wining and dining always works. And this was her idea, you said?" As much as Ted should have been impressed by Frank nonchalantly revealing that the club now possessed over a hundred thousand dollars in assets through some stroke of sheer luck, he was more interested to know just how that money was being spent. Frank was just like Tom now, even if he didn't want to admit it.

"It was. I was going to head back home, but she wanted to celebrate, so here we are."

"Why didn't you bring Alan and Behrooz then if this was a celebration?"

"They didn't respond to my text messages when I tried to change their minds, and I was hungry. I didn't feel like waiting." Ted sat down in the booth across from Frank, staring him down slightly with a thin smile; they were buddies, Ted thought, why did he have to be so coy?

"Regardless of your exact status with her, she's a catch, either as a partner in crime or a girlfriend. I'm surprised more people haven't been flirting with you."

"She's not flirting, she's just being nice. A good person."

"We both know that doesn't mean what you think it means, Frank. But anyway, what can I say? You've won. In every sense of the word. I'd love to pick your brain a bit more, but Juliet will be back at any moment and I have my own lunch to eat, so enjoy your date."

"It's not a date, it's a working lunch."

"Whatever you say," Ted said as he slid out of the booth and wandered off. Juliet came back a few moments later and sat down across from Frank again, and he finished his lunch without thinking much about exactly why he was there or if he'd want this as a part of his routine.

"I've never liked Ted. The school's better with him gone," Juliet declared. "What did he even want to talk about anyway?"

"Everyone contributes in their own special way to the school. I try not to let my own personal dislike of romance applied irresponsibly get in the way of a cordial conversation. That's what he was curious to know, actually; he presented this astonishing hypothesis that to him, this looked like a date. Absolutely unprofessional and ridiculous, right? That silly Ted, he never knows what he's talking about."

"Oh, we are undoubtedly extremely professional here, not a trace of anything uncouth," Juliet laughed as she tapped Frank's arm. "I wouldn't trust anything that man says. A broken clock is never right—isn't that the saying?"

"Close enough," Frank said while looking at his arm to see what necessitated any tapping.

"You know, I've enjoyed this little lunch of ours so much that I think we ought to do this at least weekly, right? After all, there's so much work to do; have you ever been to my house? You're such a good cook, I think it would be an excellent teambuilding exercise. I'm sure you knew this already, but girls love it when guys know how to cook."

"I love this new inside joke—yes, what a funny joke. But," Frank admitted, "I don't think the occasional repetition of this could hurt at all, we could bring Alan and Behrooz too, really make a difference."

"No, they can do their own thing. We're the most important people, you said so yourself. Anyway, just know that if you say no, you'll be disappointing me." Juliet did her best attempt at pouting until Frank gave up and agreed. Juliet saw Frank off at his door, either fortunately or unfortunately having a commitment later that afternoon. Frank could not get inside soon enough; he understood this situation from the sexual harassment training Mrs. Huang made him complete to be a "hostile work environment." Well, it wasn't hostile, quite endearing in a way, but what irritated Frank most was the uncertainty. He had spent three years staking everything on certainty: he wished for something to unfold in a certain way and it happened. But now, he was faced with a dilemma:

Juliet had always been this friendly, there was no doubt about it, and he did not know if her recent attempts at pushing the envelope came from her own impatience or were simply statistical inevitabilities. Accepting that Juliet was nothing but a sycophant was the only sustainable option; anything else undermined his entire worldview. Frank believed that he was truly changing people, turning them worse and yet better; he had hoped that people would have grown to see past the literal and accept a well-rounded, even-keeled perspective. If Juliet had indeed been flirting from him since the beginning, using whatever techniques of flattery she could to become his irreplaceable best buddy, he was nothing but a misguided ideologue and a failure, and Frank would not let himself be a failure.

Cognitive dissonance would be best, then, and so Frank was tasked with his hardest task of all: brainwashing himself. Juliet was a friend, a loyal lieutenant who simply was a bit, he supposed, touchy. All friends insisted on taking their friends to the lakeshore to confess their secrets; all friends talked for hours on whatever they pleased; all friends wished to meet for one-on-one meals in all sorts of locations for the sake of teamwork; all friends texted constantly, and sometimes ever did video calls, just to say hello; all friends saw nothing unusual in hugs or sitting directly touching; dear Lord, what a fool this mortal was!

Juliet, after waiting a few seconds to see if Frank would suddenly open the door and invite her in, texted Beth one word to sum up the situation: "Victory."

Chapter 31

Mr. Cathcart arrived exactly when he always did on the first day of school, fifteen minutes past when he was supposed to. The massive iron-barred gate that isolated the theater's distinct outdoor space from the common ground surrounding it was unlocked, which Mr. Cathcart took as a bad omen for what was to come. He swirled his coffee cup a little and was relieved to discover he had plenty left. When he entered the back room of the theater, he was greeted by a tiny and officious leadership student who demanded to know who "Mr. Cathcart" was—it sounded like a pseudonym—and why he dared intrude until he realized he was talking to someone who was supposed to be there; instead of apologizing, the student shouted something behind him, and Ms. Wolfe came out.

"Hey, this is my theater! What are you doing here so early?" Mr. Cathcart said jovially, trying to disguise his irritation with humor.

"The theater is school property—you just work in the back and do your little theater things whenever we need them, and if we decide you ought to work outside on the damp asphalt, you'd better bring a blanket. You're late, but no matter. We already have everything under control."

"Already have what under control? Your little leadership kid in the suit was about to drag me out of my own theater until I told him who I was."

"Growing pains, Mr. Cathcart. Everyone gets them. We need a few more teachers to supervise the assembly—you'll do. Come with me," Ms. Wolfe insisted, and they walked at a brisk pace to the lobby, where a few teachers milled about and clutched paperwork, consulting with the leadership representatives present.

"Since when did we have this much paperwork?" Mr. Cathcart asked in astonishment.

"We have a new way of doing things. More efficient. We decided, in consultation with our new student council, that this school lacks discipline. Many of the current students are beyond hope; everyone but a few idealists believes that. But the new kids... yes, I think we can get something done there." Mr. Cathcart refrained from commenting further, wisely assessing that now would be a poor time for dissent, but Ms. Wolfe kept talking verbosely to anyone else who would listen.

Mr. T led a few other teachers in supervising the assembly, which as club members were generously volunteering their time, really meant scowling appropriately at the right times to get any freshmen with attitude in line. As they queued outside in the cold to enter the theater, they were checked for appropriate paperwork; those who had lost their papers or simply creased them too badly were sent to a separate line, where their infractions were marked. Improper posture was corrected appropriately, or as appropriately as they could without using a meter stick to slap hunched spines. Ms. Norris, despite generally trying her hardest to avoid freshmen, came out too under the belief that it was never too soon to teach students something new. It was a remarkable transformation indeed to see shrill, shrimpy youngsters learn in an instant the value of following orders! Most teachers who taught freshmen were split on whether their boundless energy and occasional snark were things to be encouraged, and as much as these traits had their time and place, this wasn't it.

Frank sat in the back of the theater, even more out of sight than his usual seat as usher; Juliet had earlier expressed a strong desire to be the new freshmen's first impression of Heller on stage, saying that he was a bit "severe." An observant freshman who appeared not to know anyone else came to sit next to him and immediately noticed something wrong:

"What's up with your suit and tie? There's no dress code here, you can relax a little."

"I'm not a freshman, don't worry. I'm Frank, your school president. Nice to meet you," Frank said, extending his hand.

"Why are you back here instead of on stage?"

"Juliet thought she could do a better job, so I thought I'd humor her a little. Leadership is about delegation, and to be honest, it's been far more satisfying admiring my work from afar. You lose that perspective when you're in the thick of things."

"Well, since you're president, why don't you help me out: your class-mates out there were being bullies. One of them had a megaphone. Can't they just chill a little?"

"You seem like a smart kid. Come to the How To Be A Good Person Club today; that's where all the real cognoscenti meet. You can either be shepherded around all year or work to be the one cracking the whip yourself—how does that sound?" The freshman meekly nodded. "Anyway, we'd best be quiet now. A pleasure to make your acquaintance."

By the time the freshmen had come up from the theater, some wearing red stickers to indicate their disobedience or blue stickers to signal good conduct, Alan and his squadron had scrubbed the hallways to a shiny luster and carpeted the walls with motivational posters, one of which explained the new caste system. Frank had enjoyed reading *Brave New World* greatly, and Ms. Foster had verified that as long as no students were denied food and rankings had no direct bearing on academic performance, color-coding the student body was merely immoral, not illegal. The TVs that typically displayed boring motivational quotes in the hallways now displayed exciting pearls of wisdom, many taken from *How To Be A Good Person*, and showed brief motivational skits:

"I'm so glad to be an Alpha," Juliet announced as cheerfully as she could. "I get to sit on the lawn and I have priority seating for assemblies. I'm glad I'm not a Delta, or even worse, an Epsilon. They aren't allowed to sit at all during breaks, and they need to perform community service. They also attend reeducation sessions after school. I'm a good kid. I don't talk with Deltas or Epsilons. Everyone works for every one else. We can't do without any one. Even Epsilons are useful. We couldn't do without Epsilons."

"I'm only a Beta," Behrooz declared. "I have some of the same privileges as Juliet, but not all. I'm not invited to Friday breakfasts or Monday movie nights. But I can still sit in most places, and I am deserving of respect due to my seniority. If I work hard enough, I can become an Alpha."

"I'm an average Gamma," Alan continued. "I do what Alphas and Betas tell me, and I tell Deltas and Epsilons what to do. I can check my social credit score on the free TigerTalk app, where I can also see my grades and caste-level announcements. Regardless of my ranking, I'm proud to be a Tiger."

"I'm a lowly Epsilon," Frank slurred. "I'm of below-average intellect and hold defiant tendencies. I am physically weak and generally deficient, not because of my genetics, but because of my lack of willpower. It is the burden of those above me to take care of me, and only through impossible effort may I advance in the ranks. There is no hope for me."

"We all are proud to be Tigers," the four of them announced in unison.

Jason needed little encouragement to dislike Alan, and Alan's new attitude was impetus enough. Alan wasn't quite clear on what conventional formal dress entailed, and wore a fedora along with his slick, black suit; his hair appeared gelled. And when he saw Jason in the hallway, he walked straight toward him, ignoring the others who tried in vain to weave around him smoothly, grasping his hand with his own simultaneously icy and oily hand to say hello and welcome him to a new era. Jason didn't think it was sweat, as his own hand now smelled of cheap cologne that in another reincarnation probably could serve as paint thinner. And off Alan went, not even pretending to have any interest in conversation, only making sure that he was seen and that it was known who was boss—in case any of the freshmen didn't recognize him from the assembly, his face on posters with such tasteful slogans as "Avoid bright colors" and "Don't be a simpleton" would endure his memory was forever seared in everyone's mind. Nobody dared tell him he was tasteless, as the consequences were unknown. The smell on his hand bothered Jason, so he went to follow Alan to make him apologize, snaking through a crowd of students who parted like the Red Sea to respect Jason's Alpha status. But by the time Jason made it outside, he couldn't see him anywhere; he went to pick up his complimentary hot chocolate and watch the nearest TV screen, which flashed frenetically between visuals.

Jason was willing to admit his involvement with the present situation; he had helped code TigerTalk partially because Frank paid him $1000 in cash and partially because they were friends. Frank had promised Jason a cushy position in the administration as befitting his unwavering support in the cabal, but neither of them knew exactly what would be suitable until Jason suggested "chief propaganda officer." Frank thought this such a crucial position that he couldn't believe he didn't think of it earlier, and Jason was happy to be in a position that seemed suitably Stalinist. Unfortunately, this meant he couldn't always ignore Alan:

"Hey Jason, what's up!" Alan had shouted at him during a robotics meeting a week before school officially began. Jason groaned; this was supposed to be neutral ground. He was the new leader after Pranav left, and he was thus entirely within his authority to make such declarations.

"So, I was thinking," Alan continued before Jason could acknowl-edge his greeting, "isn't this so exciting? We're finally in control of the school—or we are, you're just a consultant—what better validation of our philosophy could you ask for?"

"I'm just as valued in this as you are, Alan, if not more so," Jason insisted. "We knew about the 'juice' sting sophomore year, long before you ever did. You just follow orders, Alan, you don't take initiative with anything. Keep yourself busy with your paperwork and leave us to do the real thinking."

"There's nothing wrong with following orders, Jason. We're all human, and humans need something to sink their teeth into or their minds wander. And when minds wander, all sorts of bad stuff happens. It sounds like your mind has been doing a bit of wandering itself, so buck up, Jason. Change is hard for all of us."

Jason pretended to consider Alan's words carefully: "Oh, well that's a different matter then. For a moment there I thought you lost your marbles." Alan was such a brat. Frank had told Jason that privately, and so it was really true and not just another layer of deception with no end in sight. It wasn't that Alan's vision was inherently distasteful; he was a good ideologue and believed as told. He was merely inelegant, and much of that was because he had chosen to be visible. Visibility had its place—Juliet and Behrooz were visible, and nobody thought them crude or heartless—but it was better to speak softly and carry a big stick. Everyone knew about the KGB, and yet they operated silently; why couldn't Alan do the same?

Frank and Alan met a few days later at school, silently staring with eager eyes at the school that was entirely theirs. Alan still felt hurt after Jason had doubted his leadership ability, and now saw an opportunity to curry favor:

"Can we get rid of Jason already? He's so annoying. I think we should make him a Beta, show him who's really boss." Frank burst out in laughter.

"That's nonsense, Alan. Jason is an invaluable member of our team, and even if you can't see the tangible benefits of his actions, I certainly can.

Let's focus on the future, because the future is only what we make today. What do you think about patriotism?"

Alan sat up like a shot. "That's it," he cried excitedly. "There was something missing—and now I know what it is." He banged his fist down into his palm. "No patriotism," he declared. Frank rolled his eyes.

"I appreciate your enthusiasm, and even before I told you what I had in mind too. How about the national anthem? Every day during first period—take out the ten minutes per week we waste on leadership announcements and spread it out a little. Everyone knows it, and the best thing is, anyone who's against it is against America."

"I never knew it was that simple!"

"It really is. I'll draft the letter and print it, we can all sign, and I know Mr. Kurtz will be glad to see this happen. We don't need to announce this to the students in advance, right? It will be a surprise."

John encountered a surprise of his own during his first period, tutoring with Ms. Liu. She had come to him at the end of the previous school year, believing he would be suitably altruistic while not simultaneously being busy, with the tempting offer of having a tangible impact.

"These aren't the AP kids, you know. They need more support, and it's our duty to provide that. You can do anything you want to do with them, John—if you want to teach them how to be good people, the power's all yours."

"I wouldn't want to infringe on Frank's authority, Ms. Liu."

"Well, that's not the point anyway. I trust you to be patient with them and show a little sympathy. That's what a good person does, right?"

John was the first to arrive to class, which surprised him; he did not think he was that punctual, but clearly the freshmen had not yet learned respect. That would change, John hoped. Ms. Liu was once again pleased to see him, and urged him to sit down in the back; none of the freshmen would be so precocious as to require academic support before their first real classes.

"The other tutor's getting her schedule sorted out in the office, but she'll be here in a few seconds—I see her walking now," Ms. Liu told him while John stared at the ceiling lights. John's gaze shifted to the door just as Regina pushed her way in. John's face contorted into a brief scowl, which Ms. Liu but not Regina noticed, and Regina went to sit a safe distance from him eagerly.

"Do you two, um, know each other?" Ms. Liu asked with a tinge of worry.

"Oh yeah, of course we do! John and I are the best of friends," Regina declared, and before John could voice his objections Ms. Liu laughed with glee: "I'd expect nothing less. Things are going to be a bit different this year, as I'm sure you know, so we have an especially important responsibility this year. Not that our work is never important—it's always important—but it's just that there's a lot to take in. My chart here tells me you're an Alpha, John, and Regina's a Beta. These students are likely to be Gammas, Deltas, or even Epsilons. You've all read *Brave New World* right, you know how this goes?"

"Yeah, it's really ingenious," John admitted. "I've always felt like high school has all these unstated social hierarchies; even I struggle to understand exactly where I stand. How nice of leadership to take away that cognitive burden and do the thinking for us."

"Not quite, John. I think I may be judging this too early, but while we still have a few moments, I think this is kind of clever, actually, demonstrating how absurd and harmful those distinctions are. Well, Frank didn't actually have to do this—this was an idea he maybe could have left on the drawing board or as a club exercise—but if after a few weeks, people are sick of this and demand to treat everyone equally, maybe that's progress? I take what I can get."

John was privately seething. What sort of role model was Regina for impressionable young minds? For one, she was a Beta, but her flaws extended beyond that. No good person would dance on the beach with classmates or kiss her boyfriend at school; both those reflected an inability to separate business and pleasure, and the last thing he would want in his classes is to see more people flirt. Her attitudes in general skewed liberal; Regina believed in personal choices as long as they did not affect others, but for some reason she was completely apathetic about John's emotional anguish at his classmates fornicating or drinking beer or smoking marijuana. What a hypocrite! One thing was becoming extremely clear, and that was that any flaws in the class were due to her and her alone.

After all the students arrived, Ms. Liu engaged them in mild small talk about seating arrangements and stationery until the PA system turned on with a chirp.

"Hello Tigers!" Ms. Wolfe's voice radiated, still simultaneously energetic and flat like always. "In order to ensure compliance with, I want to make sure I'm reading this correctly, the 'Committee for Rejuvenating American Principles,' we are going to start every day henceforth on the right foot and recite the Pledge of Allegiance, then sing our national anthem! Please turn and face the flag; you will be expected to memorize the words by next week. Teachers, please assign merits and demerits appropriately." Ms. Liu's students turned to each other with puzzled faces, but were too shell-shocked to raise any fuss.

"I pledge allegiance..." everyone continued, all the way through a desultory crescendo at "the home of the brave." Ms. Liu tried her hardest to set an example for her students and sang the loudest out of all of them; Regina had considered joining the choir once, and articulated every consonant even when John seemed to be content with verbal mush. John thought he was an excellent singer; nobody ever asked him, but if they ever did he'd be sure to indicate as such. He strove in vain to emulate his idols, mumbling Marlon Brando and crooning Frank Sinatra, and while he imitated their styles he did not imitate their musicality.

"Ms. Liu?" The same freshman who had met Frank earlier raised his hand tremulously.

"Yes, uh... Harry!"

"Will we have to do this every day? At the assembly this morning I met a kid who said he was the president, and he seemed pretty happy about all of this. But I don't know, we've never had to do anything like this before. Wouldn't our time be better spent on learning values like dignity besides empty, symbolic gestures?" Ms. Liu chortled—she told every student besides the really bad ones that they were her favorite, but with Harry she was starting to mean it:

"Good point, Harry! I don't think it's an entirely symbolic gesture, not any more so than anything else. There's a certain value in tradition that we just need to accept for its own sake, and I think all of you have your own traditions that you or your parents do without any greater purpose. Do Christmas trees alone teach us charity? And I think just to bring us all into the year and get to know each other a bit better, that would be a great discussion topic. So let's move our desks in a circle..."

John already felt his attention wander, even as he and Regina moved their desks to join the rest. He was promised heartfelt moments of mutual understanding—not that he'd know what they would look like—but this wasn't at all what he had hoped for. John did not know what he was hoping for, really; he did not even know why he was tutoring. He had taken Ms. Liu's off-hand suggestion as an order, and for that reason he was with faces he did not recognize, faces which looked very different from his. John was in disbelief when one kid described how every November, they would build an altar with a name he knew he would immediately forget to celebrate those lost, or how kids felt guilt because their grandparents lived in another country and spoke a different language. John wanted happy stories, not ones tinged with the bittersweet; he wanted algebra worksheets from which he could discern no morality, not buzzwords like empathy and socioemotional learning. Ms. Liu thanked both of them effusively as they left; he did not think the thanks were deserved, as what had they done?

John hated to admit that a freshman, a mere Beta, could be right about something, but what Harry had said about the anthem gnawed on John's mind enough that John went to talk to Alan after school. Alan stood above the student parking lot waving at all the students leaving, none of whom he knew and none of whom cared to return the gesture. He did the same to John too before remembering that despite his dopey expression, John was not a freshman.

"Hey John, what's up? It's a new day—be your own sunshine."

"I saw that poster already. I don't have much time to chat, but I just wanted to get your thoughts on a little something that came up in class earlier. A freshman made a good point earlier—"

"And what's the freshman's rank?"

"Beta, but that's really not relevant. So he, Harry, was wondering that if we play the anthem every day, then won't it lose some of its meaning? It's a symbolic gesture, anyway, a trinket of our patriotism like all the flags in the classrooms I didn't even notice were there until today."

"John, John, John... do you think our brave soldiers view the national anthem as a symbolic gesture? When President Underwood wept last year at the 9/11 memorial as they sang the national anthem, do you think that was just a puny symbolic gesture? In fact, it's nothing of the sort. Our nation's fate rests on moral virtue, and nothing is more moral than the national anthem."

"So tell me Alan, what's one moral that comes from the national anthem? If someone isn't roused to tears through Pavlovian conditioning, what's their next move?"

"Well, uh, the answer is obvious, yes, umm..." Alan stalled confidently, "Loyalty. There's nothing more important than loyalty."

"Loyalty to whom? The school? The nation?"

"Well, those two things are really synonymous when you think about it. We attend a public school, ultimately run by the state, and then run by the nation if you go up the food chain far enough. So you can't have one without another, just like you can't have peanut butter without jelly."

"So why should we be loyal to our school? We show up, get an education, meet friends, then leave. Isn't that all there is to it? Do sinners look covetously at the other team during football games? I want to understand your point of view here."

"Like I said earlier, that's what our nation is built on. Our army serves the United States and is not a mercenary force—let's ignore Blackwater for the sake of argument—there's no other way you can have it. Likewise, we serve the school and think little else. What's good for the school is good for you. With our flesh and blood we build our new Great Wall."

"Huh?" John raised an eyebrow.

"It's a Chinese proverb Frank told me. But he says that we'll be just as formidable as an army if we work together with one concerted spirit."

"The Great Wall was sieged by Mongols, remember."

"You're missing the point here! So I think we both agree that without patriotism, our society cannot function. So what's more patriotic than the national anthem? You tell me." Alan looked even more smug as usual, and he still waved at scared students as they walked down the steps to freedom.

"So just to recap, we play the national anthem now because it embodies moral virtue, and moral virtue is important because it's patriotic, and there is nothing more patriotic than the national anthem? Am I getting that right?" Alan eagerly nodded: "Exactly, John. I hope now you understand the importance of our fight. We're the first ones bold enough to make these changes." Alan walked away with a smirk, and John left too. Maybe Alan wasn't good at explaining things. John didn't see why a song out of all things, one with no complex plot or theme, could hold such power; based on the lackadaisical delivery in class earlier, his peers thought the same. He didn't object to the anthem being played at club meetings, as there they were fighting for order and dignity. He just didn't think that every student had volunteered for that duty.

Beth's communication with Behrooz followed a predictable daily routine: they'd talk before their first class, maybe a bit at lunch if Behrooz wasn't with his friends or if she wasn't with hers, definitely a bit in the evening, and they always said good night. She found that they had exhausted most of the novel topics that they had strong opinions on long ago—greatest hits never failed to disappoint, even if most of them were Behrooz explaining how well his DJ gigs were going. She rarely attended his parties not only for fear of a conflict of interest, but because she found them banal. Louis bothered her, Ted too when he occasionally showed up, and she had better things to do than drink beer and be flirted with. They weren't even best friends on Snapchat (as much as a good person ought to avoid social media, the practical interpretation which most in the club followed who were interesting enough to be popular on social media used was "avoid frivolous usage of social media—act with purpose").

For this reason their conversation had begun to wane, and sometimes she went days without even seeing his head in the hallway. Beth had been promised that with the new school year, they would see each other more at school events, but things like "Alpha Meet And Greet" didn't sound like they would offer much one-on-one quality time. She still was going to go that night—it was only proper—but she planned on not enjoying the experience at all. Beth hoped for more community at cheer practice with Juliet, but found instead resentment and petty rivalry: the cheer coach, whom the members of the team called "Coach Mama" for reasons unclear, proved a surprising supporter of the new system in place, and consequently declared Juliet the head of the cheer team because of her superior social credit score. Beth and Juliet were the only ones happy about this change; the others chafed under Juliet's peppy authority, knowing fully that she never attended their parties or did anything exciting. Some Deltas and Epsilons who were forced to run extra laps for no reason but their rank had the clever idea of filing an official complaint through the TigerTalk app, but discovered the feature was only available to Betas and above.

Frank, who had spent a few hours with Mr. Kurtz and Ms. Wolfe sorting through the first day's worth of feedback to discard all even vaguely critical, and Juliet were some of the last few students left on campus. Frank had made the calculated gamble of taking the route that wound past the football field to the street, hoping that the cheerleaders would have been long gone, but his legendary luck had failed him: Juliet was zipping up her bag when she saw Frank's frame in the distance, and she immediately hurried over to say hello. This wasn't their first encounter that day: all four of the student council officers were required to share a class period for leadership, which meant they all sat at a tiny round table and did their other homework, and Frank also had decided in yet another spurt of goodwill to serve as the TA for Mr. T. He was greatly excited about this initially—statistics was a strong subject for him, even at the college level, and Mr. T never failed to keep him occupied—and less excited when he discovered Juliet was a student in his period.

"Third time's the charm, right?" Frank laughed meekly, looking around to make sure that nobody saw them. As usual, Juliet launched into a passionately-delivered summary of her day, putting particular emphasis on how much everyone loved singing the national anthem and her newfound seniority on the cheer team. "I hope every day is as good as this one," she proclaimed, and added suddenly: "With all our new work, I think we ought to have another meal somewhere, it's been a few weeks; I heard there's a new Indian restaurant downtown. The weather's still warm, we can sit on the patio, and you know what you always say, fresh air builds a healthy body and healthy mind."

"I'll message Alan and Behrooz then. You're right, as always: each day is going to bring more and more work, and since we aren't spending all our time at school together, we can make up that time elsewhere. Emails, maybe, like normal people. Now that I think about it, Alan and Behrooz are handling the meet and greet tonight, so I think we'd have to wait for the weekend. Sorry." Juliet rolled her eyes, interpreting Frank's purposeful denial as mere obliviousness.

"Why do they have to be brought into everything? They're self-sufficient. We all are. I could invite Regina and Tom if you're not interested then. They're Betas, but you know, they're the next best thing." Frank bristled at his own logic being used against him, but he considered himself a good sport; it was only fair that she try to compensate for his history of half-truths and misdirection. He could spin this into propaganda somehow, he hoped. Good publicity, that was the term.

"I'll make the reservation. My treat," he resolutely declared, and Frank walked Juliet to her car before heading home himself.

Chapter 32

John realized halfway through Mrs. Huang's lecture that in the shuffle of seats that took place at the beginning of the period, a procedure that occurred whenever she suspected her students of excessive fraternization, he was sitting where Ernest used to sit. The vase of flowers constantly replenished last year had disappeared over the break, and with the custodial work that always happened over the weekends, what were the odds that he was sitting at that same desk which seated a dead man? Any special protection that the vase and Mrs. Huang's watchful eye afforded probably didn't last over weekends. This conundrum did not seem to occupy his group partners' minds, but why would it? They didn't know him. John's unique brand of melancholy clashed with Mrs. Huang's ever energetic temperament; he was one of the few students who had stuck with Chinese for all four years, most of his classmates being freshmen and sophomores, and so Mrs. Huang relied on people like him to be academic role models. Mrs. Huang had finally learned John's name, and after spending a few weeks trying to discern some identifying trait to create a nickname (Beth was the diligent one, and Juliet was "her little angel"), settled on "the philosopher"; this came from reputation alone, as Mrs. Huang avoided all philosophical talks unless they served to commend Frank: she had overheard Juliet call John that once and thus stuck with it.

But where was Ernest? Mrs. Huang thought it bad luck to keep any of Ernest's old papers, and once had presented all of them in a file folder to his parents with apologies. His name undoubtedly existed still in her gradebooks, not that John would ever be able to access them. It was like he had never existed at all, that he was a convenient fabrication to give John's inner monologue a devil's advocate and convince himself he wasn't crazy. John did not think Ernest had any distinguishing physical attributes; he looked, actually, very much like many of the other students, and while John's train of thought lingered there, he realized that he looked much more like an outcast. It did not help that he still talked with a curious accent that everyone with whom he talked placed as originating from a different part of China. John had hoped by now that he'd have blended in with the crowd, but a few weeks in and he was clearly still the foreigner—and not in a way which inspired pity from Mrs. Huang, one which made him sad he couldn't understand the students gossiping behind his back.

John knew that Frank had most likely gone through a similar experience, and asked him offhandedly before school one day:

"Am I one of them? I'd like to think we're beyond tribalism that isn't school-sanctioned."

"It's a reasonable question, Frank," John insisted. "You took the AP test last year. I see you chat with Mrs. Huang in the hallways. So I think it's reasonable to ask if beyond your comparative fluency, if you feel like they've accepted you as one of them."

"Culturally, besides eating a lot of Chinese food, my family isn't Chinese at all—why would we be? The closest we get to representing any particular ethnicity besides 'cosmopolitan San Franciscan' is having a British flag in a box somewhere. That gap isn't bridged simply because I speak with a good accent. You could ask the same question of Mr. T, who is far more fluent than I possibly would ever be in any reasonably common variety of Chinese—or any language—that you could think of: just because he's an omniglot doesn't miraculously place him in every single culture. He's no more Chinese than either of us."

"So how then would I go about absorbing more of that culture then, so I'm not missing out on aspects of class just because I lack that shared cultural heritage?"

"I don't know, John, go to Chinatown? Eat more Chinese food? Watch Stephen Chow films? This is a question best asked of Mrs. Huang, but I think the answer you'll find is that with greater fluency you'll find you get some of those answers."

"You're contradicting yourself, Frank. Language doesn't lead to culture, yet you understand culture better from language? You can't have it both ways." John was hoping for a magic bullet that did not boil down to studying more. Frank was smart, he knew a solution to everything. Surely there was a "good person" solution to this, like anything else.

"Do you know what filial piety is, John? It's a good vocab word; I'd think it would be in your textbook somewhere. Just because I know what that word is doesn't mean I automatically express a Confucian reverence toward my parents. That's a gross oversimplification, of course, but at least then, even if you don't share the same personal experiences with your classmates, you'll have a greater sense of empathy. Does that make sense?" John pulled out his phone to check his installed Chinese dictionary just in case the word looked familiar. It did not. John traced the characters in the air, hoping that like magic the air would glow around the glyphs.

"I'm not sure if I answered your original question that well," Frank continued. "When I was in Chinese class, nobody judged me for not having gone to Chinese school or not wearing slippers around the house. We eat mooncakes because they taste good, but we don't sweep my great-grandparents' graves, and that isn't seen as a sign of betrayal or inauthenticity. And I doubt they're judging you; why do you think they're gossiping about you and not just talking about their lives?"

"Well, clearly they didn't want me to understand."

"What if they assume that because you're in the same Chinese class, you're able to understand them?" John's eyes widened—he had never considered before that his personal exceptionalism did not automatically extend to others' perceptions. The bell rang, and John ran to class before he would be late. He related this conversation to Harry while they worked when Harry asked him for help with Spanish, a subject John was disappointed to discover he had not mastered via osmosis.

"It's cool that you're not taking Spanish. It makes you more unique," Harry remarked.

"Too unique, really. Do people look at you differently in your class because you aren't Hispanic?"

"It's an intro class, why would they? Chinese is too hard to learn, that's why I'm taking Spanish. I knew I couldn't handle it."

"That's a completely baseless assumption, Harry. You're a Beta—of course you could handle it!" Ms. Liu shot him a glare across the room; she was worried that the Deltas and Epsilons in the class would pick on Harry if they knew he was ranked above them. Ms. Liu believed enforcing inequality was not in her job responsibilities and treated all her students equally regardless of class; when her students struggled with food stability and familial obligations already, it would only be cruel to punish them more. The new caste system was a double-edged sword in that regard: with such a great emphasis placed on overcoming factors outside individuals' control, it was technically easier for those with surrounding socioeconomic factors to translate those into success at Heller, more so than the Lululemon-toting gossips who believed themselves entitled to special treatment. This created friction among those who sought to play the game, attending optional tutoring sessions and volunteering their time at approved off-site community service, and those who had started an Epsilon after the first assembly and resolved to never be anything else.

"I think it's more because I go to the club meetings than anything else. You know, I don't really like those people, the club people. It reminds me of Scientology."

"Scientology's a cult, though. It's completely different."

"You say that because you're a veteran member. I'm new, and everyone's a nice speaker, of course, but I wouldn't put my life on the line for them. They're asking a lot of freshmen to be so mature, you know; it's only been a few weeks. We're busy making our own friends and connections without the club doing it for us."

Regina watched John and Harry somewhat warily. Harry talked just like John, intellectually and without the vibrant charm that made Frank more clearly normal. Her biggest worry was that John would convince Harry to think exactly like him and be exactly like him; Harry would then be set up for years of psychological anguish that nobody truly deserved. Regina was extrapolating, of course—they had not gotten to the term in statistics yet, and thus she did not know why that was improper—but even in a new social hierarchy that prized such verbosity, it was still not something to be encouraged. Regina personally thought the other students a lot more relatable; they talked coarsely, but they talked of celebrities who had not died in the previous century, and that was enough for her. What Regina knew of mentorship told her that making a genuine emotional connection was the first step to progress; it did her no good to act with alien severity like everyone else normal thought John did. John had asked her once why she tried to become friends with "the Epsilons," as if they were not people at all—by the same logic, why would Regina want to build an emotional connection with Harry, who looked like he probably quoted Shakespeare daily?

"They're freshmen, though. They're younger than us, less wise. With a few exceptions, I'll admit," John argued.

"Age is just a number," Regina laughed; John looked at her conde-scendingly, clearly not detecting her sarcasm. "You were a freshman once. Don't act like you don't have any empathy, why else would you be tutoring?"

"It all boils down to, just like we've always been told, strength through discipline, strength through community, strength through action. Those are the traits we're trying to teach here, and you'll find that universal empathy isn't among them."

"You're such a downer," Regina groaned, and she walked away before John could apologize for his conduct and promise that it was just a slip of the tongue—he really was an optimistic person! John kicked himself again: he had forgotten to ask her about filial piety.

Alan was a man of mean understanding, little information, and un-certain temper. A division of labor began to arise out of circumstance as much as necessity when work began to accumulate. Frank primarily concerned himself with planning club meetings and dealing with ad-ministrative paperwork for other clubs that despite his grand plans, still needed to be done. He was willing to recycle old texts if they proved especially interesting, and the varied casts of the discussions ensured that the repetition bothered nobody; this eased his work somewhat, but he still pored over his old notes, annotating them with cryptic reminders and insights that even for him, were written in chicken-scratch. Juliet shadowed him, reviewing his tentative lesson plans, pretending she could read his handwriting with ease, and assisting with the bureaucratic drudgery that he did not need to leave for himself. These overlapping responsibilities ensured they mainly needed to talk with each other, after two years having developed some semblance of a rhythm.

Alan and Behrooz were tasked with implementation and more menial tasks that didn't require the help of upper management; Alan relished these opportunities to crack the whip, which, while metaphorical was increasingly supplemented with hand gestures. Behrooz tried his hardest to temper these flights of whimsy; he found Alan prone to fantastical ideas that at a moment's notice, he'd race off to investigate, only to return a few minutes later with seemingly no memory of his original attempt. While Behrooz tried his hardest to be fair to those under him, who were not particularly different in experience but simply had a different job title, Alan would pick on them individually, giving them nicknames and occasional tongue lashings. Once, one of the sophomores (whom Alan had nicknamed Bubba for some inexplicable reason) had grown tired of picking up beads Alan spilled on the floor, and privately vented to Behrooz; doing the right thing, he relayed his complaint to Ms. Foster, who promised to investigate further but clearly never did. At lunch, Alan would exhibit a convivial spirit that was rarely demonstrated elsewhere, jokingly referring to the other pair as "the bosses"; when all four ate together, this faded to what Behrooz believed to be blind obedience. It wasn't like he had anything to prove, so why did Alan insist on sucking up to Frank? Juliet seemed genuine, but Alan—the line was blurred there. It was not inconceivable, he supposed, that someone of such a mercurial temperament was entirely himself in all those different moments when he wore those different masks. Or that the truth lay somewhere buried inside, a mixture of all. Maybe this was why Frank and Juliet stopped eating with them.

During one of these lunches, once the others were comfortably out of earshot, Behrooz remarked to Alan: "What's gotten into you over the last few weeks? What did they ever do to you? They're just trying to do their jobs and follow your orders so they don't fail the class. It's hard enough as is with all the work we have to do, you don't need to make their lives living hell."

"War is hell!" Alan exclaimed, thinking that explained everything.

"War against whom?"

"Everyone. Everyone who isn't with us is against us, Behrooz, and if the bosses want us to fight the good fight, then I'll be damned if we don't! If we're generals, they're the commanders-in-chief."

"Everyone, you say. Everyone in this school is against us. Regina is. Tom is. Beth is. Ms. Foster is. All of them are against us?"

"I wouldn't slander some of those names, Behrooz. There are good people on both sides. But we have this hierarchy in place to keep the lower orders where they ought to stay, and maybe a few good ones will be filtered through and we can work from there. If we want to stay alive, it's what we have to do."

"Staying alive? Nobody's dying here."

"Open your eyes, Behrooz. It doesn't make a damned bit of difference who wins the war to someone who's dead," Alan fiercely declared, his voice grizzled. "Have you heard of Schrödinger's cat? You have a cat inside a box—it could be dead, it could be alive—"

"I know what Schrödinger's cat is, Alan. But what's that got to do with it?"

"The cat's dead, Behrooz. There's no ambiguity here. The cat's dead, and I'm no expert on cat CPR, but it's going to be a pain to resuscitate. We don't want to be dead either. The fear of death is a powerful thing, and that's the fear we want everyone else to hold, but we've earned the right to live comfortably without that. Because if that's not the case, what makes us any different from them? Am I making sense to you?" Behrooz prudently nodded and said that Alan was making perfect sense, so much sense that the conversation did not need to go on any longer.

While Alan occupied much of his conscious hours spinning elaborate hierarchies of secret surveillance networks and military stratagems out of thin air, Frank chose to dwell entirely in the practical, and there was no one more qualified to think practically than Ms. Foster. When Ms. Foster did not resign herself to the fact that her student council was self-sufficient, she'd walk by and offer suggestions offhandedly, ones which she only occasionally believed in.

"Have you considered expanding formal Fridays to be every day? I'm sure you have the money to cover any students who wouldn't be able to participate otherwise, and I think it would unify us as a student body, make us stand out a little. Heller's a remarkable school as is, but we're a public school with many other rivals in our district alone. I send my son to a Catholic school, and he wears a tie every day. I don't see why we can't do the same." On the spectrum ranging from "why don't we offer extra points to encourage students to see our music performances?" to "how about we monitor students' social media for signs of sedition?" of how much Ms. Foster earnestly believed in her suggestions, this sat somewhere solidly halfway in between the two.

"I'm not sure. The good students already are dressing nicely, and the Epsilons don't care. They already plot how to steal the free stuff the others get, and we don't want to reward that. They'll keep thinking in exactly the same ways as before, even if they look a bit nicer," Juliet advised. Beyond the color coding, formal dress also proved a quick way to distinguish the castes, as otherwise she sometimes had difficulties telling them apart.

"I disagree. I think that the way a person talks absolutely classifies them—our no swearing policy has proven that without a doubt. I don't see why we can't implement a bit of wishful thinking with a dress code. Who is it hurting, really?" Frank saw that Juliet still seemed torn, so he sighed and tried a little experiment: "I mean, haven't you said before that I look quite nice in my suit?"

Juliet's expression immediately turned sunny: "You do look nice in a suit! That's settled then. This is a great idea. I should have never doubted you."

"Well, it was Ms. Foster's suggestion..." Frank trailed off, but by then Ms. Foster had already left to dispense some more wisdom to other struggling students.

Jason found a less sympathetic ear in Mr. Ivanov, whom he was a TA for; Mr. Ivanov made frequent jokes about the new order of things, saying that if he had a ranking he would be an "Omega Minus" and that the work of exemplary students was "doubleplusgood." Mr. Ivanov's begrudging tolerance of Jason's authority began to fray when one day, Mr. Ivanov complained as he frequently did about his students' poor grades.

"Here, give me a name. Let's see if they're slacking off in other classes too," Jason perkily suggested.

"Uh, Eduardo Lopez." Jason pulled out his phone, typed something, and began reading:

"Eduardo Lopez, Delta Minus, GPA 2.8, email , password supersaiyan420—"

"Wait, wait, wait! You have his email password? Who told you that?"

"Nobody told me that, it's just data TigerTalk collects. I can see his social media accounts too, his address, phone number, contacts, anything that could conceivably be thought of as essential for security."

"That's just Orwellian! When are you ever going to check any of that info?"

"Of course I'm not going to memorize their Social Security numbers or anything, but it's always good to have this info just in case. We can even do GPS tracking; look here, and it appears that Eduardo is in Mr. Galantine's classroom."

"Who has access to this? Teachers? Other students?"

"The teachers have access to the info, of course, and the few students with admin accounts—mainly the student council and myself—can also look around."

"So if I wanted to look up Frank's birthday and Social Security number, I could just type his name into my computer and find him?"

"No, of course not, we aren't monsters: admin accounts like ours don't share that information. So no, you can't spy on your fellow teachers. Is that any comfort?"

"That's no comfort at all!" Mr. Ivanov exclaimed, tempted to grab Jason's phone from his hand to prevent any other breaches of privacy under his watch.

"I don't really see the big deal. There's nothing malicious behind the software's original implementation; justice is blind. But if there were someone I didn't like, for instance Louis, whom I still hold a grudge toward, with just a few clicks I own him. It takes very little under this system for students to know their place."

"You're a student, what gives you the right to be held to a lower standard? Even in Soviet Russia, you bet that all of Khrushchev's info was in a filing cabinet somewhere just in case a bit of kompromat was ever needed. Even then, everyone in charge lived on a razor's edge."

"The nice thing about history, Mr. Ivanov, is that we can reiterate on it to our heart's desire; while the same themes may hold true eternally, all of their succulent variations allow for some, I guess, flexibility." Mr. Ivanov had had enough, and after one more plead to be responsible, which fell on deaf ears, he returned to his desk. Jason was fortunate to be able to work in the backroom, where teachers kept their lab supplies, away from prying eyes like Mr. Ivanov's most of the time. He could take the network of back doors and end up all the way in the robotics room, which he had repurposed into his lair. Alan's words about war had found an eager audience in Jason, which to him justified many of his actions; Jason had received permission from a beleaguered Mr. Kurtz to monitor all the security cameras in the school, and when bored during class would idly switch between hallways, locker rooms, and the classrooms—there weren't originally security cameras in all the classrooms, but Frank was easily swayed, and who would deny such a small expenditure? As Frank walked by cameras, he would salute them, and they would blink their lights in response if Jason happened to be watching from the other side; he would prank Jason at times too and move the cameras around while he thought he was unobserved, which the two of them found amusingly dystopian. In his reports, Jason tactfully chose not to mention how he could see down shirts and watch girls shower and change; the former required some ingenuity and good luck on his part, but the latter was a reliable occurrence: any PE class, sports team, or even the cheerleaders were fair game. There was no way of telling if any camera's movements were the default random scan or a result of puppetry. Nothing so wonderful as war had ever happened to him before, and he was afraid it might never happen to him again.

The more Alan became sanguine, the more Behrooz became choleric, and this manifested itself in a growing frigidness with Beth. Behrooz sometimes scrolled through his old Instagram messages with Beth, some from before that great mistake and some afterward. It warmed his heart to feel the same warmth he did when they first started dating, when he asked her to homecoming, when they held hands looking at the moonless sky by his house. A winter night, hot chocolate in matching thermoses that Behrooz's mother had lovingly prepared for them, and not a hint of worry that the magic would ever fade. It was a clear transition: he read messages from years past, when he never knew that anything could and would go wrong, and he was happy. He caught up to the present, and his smile thinned. He no longer frantically checked his phone when he heard the little notification ping, typing and editing and rephrasing until he thought he was doing his feelings justice. Maybe this was fine though. He wasn't sad when he was sent funny memes or a casual invitation to grab a bite somewhere chic. He just didn't feel the same endorphin high that always left him racing, but at the same time, he could not bear absence either. Sometimes Beth would send a flurry of messages in rapid-fire conversation with the energy of a tennis match, and then for reasons unknown would go silent for a day. Other conversations proceeded languorously, so much so that they never could quite remember what they talked about. He tried to imagine occasionally what the world looked like on the other end, looking out from her phone screen: maybe she'd be splayed out on her gray bedding or tucked underneath her covers, or in her backyard overlooking the bed of vegetables her mother tended with her heart and soul. Maybe she was thinking the same—he really didn't know. But as long as she was happy, he was too.

Beth, in fact, was splayed on top of her gray bedding, deciding if it was quite time to change out of sweatpants into true bed clothing. He had guessed correctly. It was only 11:00. The night was young. Behrooz had been in her room only once, at least as far as she could recall. Probably just a few months ago, July? It was a hot, muggy day, and Beth s parents were late coming back from wherever they were. Beth and Behrooz had just come back from Jamba Juice, and Beth was still sipping on the dregs of her smoothie. It was too hot to linger outside on the porch and think of pleasantries, so Beth took Behrooz on the house tour. He had already seen most of the front floor, and so Beth took him upstairs through a hallway of dazzling monochrome; some doors up there were near-forbidden, even to her. And since he probably wouldn't need to see a bathroom that was very much like the one he had visited before, only larger, her bedroom was the last spot. He looked astonished when he stepped inside and found it quite ordinary. "What were you expecting, shelves of makeup and nail polish?" Beth asked, plopping down upon her bed and kicking off her shoes. Behrooz didn't respond, instead perceiving what surrounded him, including that little teddy bear that sat upon her bed still now. How wondrous it was to be allowed into someone's inner sanctum, a hall of mirrors that reflected every facet of their being! Alas, the only new insight revealed was that the teddy bear was named Cheddar.

Beth had naturally seen Behrooz's house many times before then, before and after his kitchen was remodeled and one of Beth's portraits was hung in the living room. Maybe he was sitting on the sofa looking at that portrait while he drank tea or watched TV with his family; that would be a nice image, wouldn't it? Perhaps she ought to paint a painting of him admiring his own portrait. She had a picture of that portrait of Behrooz saved on her phone, and as she admired its "life," as his mother had described it, she thought it amusing how he would be doing the same. An infinite chain. Behrooz's increasingly irascible temperament bothered Beth; the image of tranquility that had persisted over two years of DJing and schoolwork took only a few weeks to dissipate. He was too much of a gentleman to ever lash out at Beth, even when she offered her support, so he did not know any other way of expressing his emotion besides not expressing anything at all. There was nothing wrong with a little depression—she was no stranger to dismal moods herself—but Behrooz's spiral into discontent was too tragic, as it was so unlike him.

What she thought pained Behrooz most was having to lie. Behrooz abhorred lying in all its forms—that's what drove them apart in the first place, when Beth had denied ever having any feelings for Ted and ever making any promises of fidelity to Behrooz. So having to walk through the hallways every day as an Alpha and regard his former Gamma friends with apathy as they shied away from him, now that would be the worst torture of all! Behrooz had to tell Beth there was an insurmountable emotional distance between himself and everyone else; Behrooz had to lie and say that he and Alan were becoming fast friends, all while Behrooz held secret fantasies of running over Alan with his car if he ever saw him in the parking lot unguarded. Nobody would catch him, it would be the perfect crime: the ever-watchful security cameras were under his control too, and while it would be a challenge to keep them all turned away while the deed was done, the footage could also just disappear. Many things disappeared in those days—ethics, virtue, morality—adding one more to the list would really be a blessing where the pros outweighed the cons. He could never seriously consider murder, only its possibility, and that was almost equally frightening: there were at least three other students at the school, the teachers presumably being without any darkness in their hearts, who had the means to commit nameless crimes and get away scot-free!

One night, Behrooz had out of boredom spent a few minutes scrolling through Heller's security cameras, secretly hoping for there to be some illicit meeting he could disrupt and make himself a hero. The school appeared lifeless, no noises but fallen leaves blowing in the wind; he switched to one of the cameras in the gym and tried speaking through its loudspeaker, and he could hear his own voice reverberate through the room, bouncing off all the bleachers and becoming thunderous. "Let there be light!" he announced, and he turned the lights on with a dramatic flick. The gym was sterile without anyone else inside, the light a glaring white. This spectacle rapidly became uninteresting, so Behrooz turned the lights off and went to bed.

Chapter 33

It had taken Frank and other leadership students many hours to hash out a plan for implementing the school's new dress code, but even as they spoke, student volunteers were delivering outfits to everyone who did not already own something appropriate. Even Ms. Foster did not expect the level of student engagement they received, but as it turned out, free gifts warmed even the coldest of hearts. In a flash, the weekend passed with nothing but prelude to Monday. Frank left his house especially early, navigating the hilly sidewalks at an almost frenetic pace with a manic eye; if he even spotted one fellow classmate walking too, in a car, or anywhere, wearing formal dress, his victory was assured. Arriving at school without seeing much of anything, he positioned himself at the top of the main entrance and waited to greet everyone who arrived.

John privately mourned the loss of his sweatpants; his car wasn't heated, and now he felt cold as he drove. Traffic was heavier than usual that day on the freeway, and even though he had an unprecedented opportunity to admire the half-wooded neighborhood around him, he could only think of his sudden desire to be curled up under a blanket at home. John parked across the street from Heller, and as he waited for the traffic light along with everyone else, he could only marvel: people indeed were following orders! Even the Epsilons wore tight-fitting jackets, pantsuits, and garish ties, just like the rest of them. Some freshmen struggled to walk comfortably in their dress shoes, walking heel-to-toe like they had never walked before, but at least so far there were no protests. People looked nice, especially Beth, who John saw lingering by the entrance of the football field.

"How does it feel? Your tie's off, let me adjust it," she insisted; John had never tied a tie himself before, and had undue faith in his ability to follow YouTube tutorials.

"The tie? A bit tight."

"No, finally dressing formally. Everyone's equal now; it doesn't feel like the Alphas are simply rubbing it in anymore."

"You're an Alpha too, Beth."

"Well that doesn't mean I was rubbing it in before! This reminds me of what I imagine a Model UN conference to look like more than anything; what's the word... ah yes, professional." Beth was already regretting her decision to wear high heels.

"I would complain about my loss of individuality if I ever expressed that through my fashion originally. You know, it's always bothered me when people wore 'weird' clothes before. You know what I mean, strange designs and crop tops and clashing hues. This is a far more preferable aesthetic."

"You think crop tops are weird? Wow, you are sheltered. Wait up for me—it's a bit hard to climb stairs quickly in these; I don't know how Juliet does it."

One of John's fears when he heard about the new policy was that the teachers wouldn't play along too; to John, how a person dressed signaled authority, and if the teachers' outfits were ramshackle, then they lost their divine right to give instructions. Ms. Liu, at least, had chosen to set a good example for her students, not that she ever dressed too informally, anyway.

"I like the tie, John. Good color contrast—your shoe's untied too, by the way."

"Are you in favor of this policy, Ms. Liu?" She walked to the door where John was and tried to stare outside, where students were milling about in their by-now normal positions, some carrying briefcases instead of backpacks.

"My initial worry was that some students wouldn't have access to the same quality of clothes as everyone else, but as that problem was solved, I don't know what to think. I can say that compared to the celery juice or TigerTalk—Mr. Ivanov was telling me earlier how they can see all your data—this is a better idea on the surface. It looks like my students out there aren't complaining, and all of them are wearing their outfits, which given their compliance with other requests is absolutely extraordinary. It's funny really, when Frank talked to me last year with a fury in his eye and spoke of a complete overhaul of the school, I was expecting something a bit more fundamental, but all that's really changed is that we sing the national anthem now. Even the Alpha brunches were expanded to include free-lunch kids because they weren't able to eat breakfast otherwise. So yeah, why not, John. I'm in favor of this." Other students began coming in, all just as jovial as usual besides Regina, and Ms. Liu called a quick poll:

"Raise your hand if you like this new dress code—there's no shame in answering honestly." Everyone, besides Regina, raised their hand, and some looked at Regina disappointedly like she didn't know how good she had it.

"Regina, you didn't raise your hand; care to share your thoughts?" Regina cleared her throat and stood up:

"I have nothing against dressing like this. I think everyone looks quite nice. But it's forced on us, and that's the issue."

"Anyone want to respond to that?" Ms. Liu asked, and one of the Epsilons who typically had some behavioral issues stood up:

"We're already forced to do so many things, this isn't really all that bad, you know, in comparison. Ricky here looks especially dapper," he joked, and everyone laughed.

John felt an obligation to share his field research with Frank, who he found coming out of the administrative offices; Frank turned to him with a thin smile, knowing fully well by now to expect something unique.

"I must say, Frank, this dress code has actually been quite nice. How did you think of it?"

"It's not like we're trailblazers in any way. Ms. Foster said her son had a dress code at his Catholic school, and you know I'm somewhat of an atheist, but that doesn't mean I can't be religious when it's advantageous. I can't wait to see 1500-odd students at the rally on Friday all dressed alike. We'll have a moment for the history books."

"History, you say? But you said other schools do this all the time. That doesn't sound very historical to me, it's just how people dress. If they're forced into it, that says nothing about their principles."

"What principles, John? War criminals wear suits too." As much as Frank respected John, he was becoming increasingly frustrated with his naïveté; John had a peculiar way of sounding like he vehemently disagreed with him, even when he really just didn't know what he was talking about.

"When I think about formal dress—now what you think may be different, but this is what I think—it conveys a message. Discipline, severity. There's no sort of affable casualness that we typically get at school. Everyone means business, and that influences how they act; they close themselves off from others, I'd think. Right?"

"Well, have you seen people closed off any more than they were before?"

"I haven't, but maybe I haven't been looking hard enough," John admitted. "What's your plan for the rally? Just the usual fun and games?"

"In a manner of speaking, yes. I've been studying some historical tapes, not in a creepy way or anything, but I want to make sure I get that right intensity. I want to encapsulate the zeitgeist of the era all this new school business reminds me of."

"And what's that, Frank?"

"Hmm," Frank mused, "As they say in all the math textbooks, I'll leave this as an exercise to the reader. So, you."

"I don't know, maybe one of President Underwood's rallies?"

"Think APUSH. But it's really proving my point that you don't know, and that's exactly why this current system needs to continue. Schools have an obligation to teach their students what's right and wrong."

"You already do that though."

"Not well enough, John."

"Anyway, I just want to caution you against doing something too extreme. I don't like rallies already, and I doubt you can change that."

"When have I ever been known to do anything extreme?" Frank joked with a fist-bump, and he went off to find something else to do.

"I don't know," John mumbled, but it was too late.

Regina and Juliet were in the same group for statistics, and since Frank avoided interacting with Juliet as much as possible during the period, Regina was able to hold Juliet's undivided attention while they worked. Senioritis was a present force, and Regina thought that she had earned the right over four years to multitask a little, carrying on idle conversation with Juliet while they blitzed through worksheets.

"So, how are things going?" Regina asked, wishing to ease into her tougher questions.

"Things are going, and they're going quite well at that."

"How does it feel to be vice president? You're always so busy, we should get lunch sometime."

"It feels not that different at all—not as cool as being president, either."

"What does Frank do to make him cooler?" Regina's recent interactions with Frank had been defined by a quiet professionalism befitting his status as TA; while she saw him and Mr. T occasionally work on side projects, for the most part Frank insisted on serving his duties normally without any mention of the club or his political power. Frank, when normal, was not all that cool, Regina thought; he still had a certain wit about him, but it seemed to come from social obligation and not any genuine interest in who he was talking to, not unless they were one of his friends.

"He just is."

"I know you've been spending a lot of time together, can you tell me about that?" Juliet looked at Frank, making sure he was out of earshot—Mr. T was writing something on a miniature whiteboard for Frank in Chinese she couldn't recognize as he explained something to him too quietly to be overheard—and continued:

"I've been trying to get him to work less; I had always thought all this came naturally to him, but he seems to be somewhat of a workaholic. It's a struggle to get him to go out to lunch with me or relax; I've started playing Scrabble against him, even though he still beats me every time, to trick him into relaxing under the guise of 'practicing vocabulary recall.' At least I'm getting better at that."

"You're talking like you two are an old couple now."

"Well, I wish, but we're just two friends who spend an awful lot of time together."

"So that's why you never have time for any of us..." Regina chided.

"Don't take any personal offense at this, Regina, but I'm really busy. With the club, with president stuff, with cheer, with everything."

"You're not so busy that you don't drag Frank to dinner with you; mooching off his debit card, aren't we?"

"He pays in cash everywhere, which I find funny if not a bit weird, but your point still stands. I enjoy quality time and relax a little, he thinks he's still doing work even when he's hopefully increasing his serotonin levels or whatever; it's a win-win!"

"What do you mean by 'he thinks he's still doing work?' Are you lying to him?" It surprised Regina less that Juliet was practicing her own applications of good person theory than that Frank was falling for whatever she was doing.

"If he thought we were going simply for fun anywhere, there's no way he would ever cooperate. So I started calling them 'working lunches.' That did the trick. It's like boring dating, really, but I'm having my fun and he's maybe having his." Juliet finished with a smug smile, like she had just let Regina in on a big secret, and went back to work.

"One more thing, Juliet. What do you think about the dress code? I know that's been the hot topic these days."

"It's a great idea, like all of Frank's. Technically it was Ms. Foster's, but I choose to give credit to Frank. He deserves it."

"Do we need to talk, Juliet? Even freshman year when I was perhaps a bit too into John, I didn't credit him for being able to talk to birds, being able to levitate through sheer willpower, and inventing calculus."

"I said none of those things, Regina, but you do know Frank took calculus as a freshman, right? I can't believe that at all, but it happened. Who's to say that other impossible things can't be credited to him too?" Armed with a new mutual understanding, they went back to work.

Jason did not have his own office, as he was content commandeering a desk in the engineering lab that was safely away from any sawdust and sharp blades; as nobody else used the space while he was there, he considered it close enough to the real thing. Today, like any other day, he had a sheaf of complaints to work through, some from his own "secret police" (really just his robotics team, who had always sympathized with Frank's desire to explore the club and helped out when they could) and some from other students who considered themselves law-abiding. They ranged from mundane complaints about litter to the absurd: apparently some freshmen had taken down one of his posters, something about thinking impure thoughts, and burned it after hours. This account was corroborated by the whistleblower's photos of the poster's curled, charred edges having survived the grisly fate that befell the pile of ashes and embers next to it. If Jason were feeling particularly equitable, he would try to verify these reports before recommending punishment, but he also thought it important to build a habit of immediate reaction; otherwise, more people could start thinking their actions did not have consequences. Defacing school property was a crime, and altogether injurious to morale, so Jason forwarded the report to the school resource officer (the police officer on campus, except that too many parents became concerned with the former name, and thus the principal hoped this would quell their complaints) and carried on. There were always embarrassingly trivial reports too, ones that Jason was truly unable to investigate. He had no hope of verifying that someone used a real curse word instead of a school-sanctioned substitute; it probably did happen, but all he could do was mark them as having received a demerit. Jason thought his work was anything but honest—unlike Alan, he saw no need to conceal his new fondness for historical roleplay, and he wasn't trying to prove anything to the student council anyway. Frank knew he was no ideologue, but given how quickly he offered himself up as chief propaganda officer, that difficulty was easily brushed away. Jason did not plan on leaving for the rally early. He would rather blend in with the crowd and admire his planning from afar.

Alan toddled into Jason's space without an appointment, which demanded a brusque "What?" from Jason.

"Are you ready for the rally? It's going to be so fun, like the biggest rally we've ever had."

"Attendance is mandatory, right?"

"How else would we make it fun? Do you think people will ditch, Jason? Empty seats look bad on camera."

"People always ditch. Round up the usual suspects. We'll take care of them before they even know they want to leave." Mr. Ivanov had explained the concept of "thoughtcrime" to Jason earlier when trying to dissuade him of yet another dystopian vision, or how dissenting thoughts alone could be punishable without any deed to back them up. Jason did not have the technical knowhow to design brain implants or microchips, but he certainly could do the next best thing, checking known troublemakers' text messages through TigerTalk to see if any of them planned on quitting. Beyond punishing them, Jason would leave menacing messages on their phones' home screens telling them exactly what they did wrong. Jason considered styling himself "Big Brother," but instead chose to call himself "The Administration" in such vague terms that when the pitchfork-wielding mob descended upon the school, he could escape personal blame.

Alan looked upon Jason with impatience while he listlessly scrolled through his data looking for further signs of dissent. He had not bothered to play around with TigerTalk's cornucopia of features after discovering he could not spy on Juliet. All this technical stuff bored him. It, and everything else Jason insisted on handling judiciously and cleverly, ran counter to his short attention span and the very fiber of his morality. He was never quite still; there was always a tapping foot somewhere or the impatient opening and closing of a hand.

"Are you done yet?" Alan asked a few times, once every minute or so, until Jason put out his hand and shouted "Enough!".

"I emailed you the list, Alan. I hope you're happy now."

"See, Jason? That wasn't so bad at all. Work on that attitude in the future; you know what Frank always says, turn that smile upside down!" Alan went off in a hurry so he could be early to his rally—yes, clearly his very own rally, just to honor him!—and Jason reluctantly followed.

As promised, the gymnasium was indeed full; the people who claimed they were sensitive to noise were given expensive noise-cancelling headphones and told they could stand by the door. Alan saw the audience of suits and ties actually smiling and cheering and resisted the urge to cry. He always tried to fit in before, not quite knowing where to sit or what was going on, and he saw the club as an opportunity to finally be ahead of the game; it reinforced a notion he'd always had that he was better than "those" people, even if simply because they didn't give him the time of day ordinarily. A good person practiced stealth: they blended in, sticking to those they could trust in what was otherwise a vast ocean. But what was this vast ocean was one of friendly faces? Frank had mentioned before the idea of the "third wave," which was what they were doing now: each wave climbed in intensity, their sophomore year being forceful if constrained, and slowly over time spilling out and sweeping over the school. Awe-inspiring, if he said so himself, and the fact that he was partially responsible for the pageantry made it that much better.

When Frank made his triumphant entrance from a supply closet, some of his buddies in the audience started chanting his name, and to their astonishment, it spread.

"Holy Bosnia-Herzegovina, they're chanting my name!" he muttered to himself as he walked toward the podium, practicing the classic point-and-wave to keep the masses happy. When he got to the podium, he did his classic conductor's gesture, and the crowd turned silent. As usual, he had a speech prepared: "Tigers! Take a look around you. Everyone looks the same at first, right? Look more closely. Every outfit is unique in its own way, even simply because of the person who's wearing it. That is what our school has become: everyone united around one ideology, but still with that personal touch to make it just a bit more human. We have succeeded at what we originally set out to do: we have proven that as a school, we can change for the better. But who are we to stop here? Leadership has many festivities planned, and as you can see our cheer team is getting ready to perform; just because things are run a bit differently now doesn't mean we're going to ruin the rallies. Alan has a bit to say, and then we'll be back to your usual, familiar schedule."

Alan took the stage next, and just as he was starting to summarize the minutiae of the new dress code and all the other policies that people weren't doing quite right, his eyes wandered over to the Beta section, where Tom and Regina proudly sat in one of the front rows in tank tops; they glared at Alan, daring him to do something.

"As an example of the disobedience we are trying to crush out, I'd like everyone to take a look over here, where I'm pointing." Hundreds of eyes turned toward Tom and Regina, who were still maintaining their stoic expressions. The same rabble-rousers from before started booing and jeering. "Do we want these cockroaches to breed and multiply and infect the entire school with their sexual deviancy?" Alan shouted, and the crowd responded with an equally loud "No!". Frank was confused—calling them sexually deviant seemed like a stretch—but as this was such a poignant moment otherwise, he joined in.

"After all we have done to make this school a better place, do we want some stinky little toddlers throwing a temper tantrum? Tom Langley and Regina Wang, please stand up and come here. I want all the school to see the little snot-rags that think they're too good for us."

"Shut up, Alan!" Tom yelled, any signs of former friendship completely gone.

"Seize them and bring them to the principal's office!" Alan barked at some of his burly comrades, who were repaying Frank for his previous academic mentorship and really found all of this a hoot. They marched over to where Tom and Regina were still stoically standing, unashamed of their misconduct, and forcefully grabbed them both and effectively dragged them through the gym.

"They're lying to you!" Regina shouted, and Tom followed up with a simple "F— you Alan!". Once they had left, Alan asked: "Could we get a round of applause for our noble student volunteers? Without them, we would not be able to root out those harlots and their sympathizers. I am sure we will have nothing else to worry about now, right? After all, we are good people," and the crowd started cheering. Alan resumed from there, hoping that no other outbursts would occur. In the corners of the gymnasium, the teachers looked at each other aghast.

"I told you this would happen," Mr. Ivanov told Ms. Liu, who appeared conflicted but not quite to the point of anger.

"Of course it would happen. We all knew that. But I didn't see you remove Tom and Regina as they entered."

"If they knew it was going to happen, why didn't Jason use his spyware and cut the problem off at its root? That's not very Stalinist." Ms. Liu rolled her eyes—Mr. Ivanov used "Stalinist" as a catch-all term to refer to anything he disliked, about Heller or society as a whole (he skewed a bit libertarian).

"The point of this, Igor, is to set an example for everyone else. I saw Frank's eyes wander as he went on stage; he sees everything. And I bet he could have simply pointed and they'd have been removed immediately. But he took advantage of Alan's zeal to make a bigger spectacle of the entire thing, and I bet now nobody will even think to disobey them." Ms. Liu would have complained if Alan were targeting the people sitting in the Epsilon wing, but Tom and Regina were still Betas. They'd be fine.

Ms. Liu lingered after the rally, in all its otherwise-ordinary normality, to congratulate Frank on a performance well-done. Frank was popping balloons one-by-one with a sharpened pencil, and did not seem to find Ms. Liu's joke about a balloon massacre particularly funny.

"This didn't turn out badly at all. I'll take it."

"So, Frank, Mr. Ivanov and I were trying to settle an argument: did you know about Tom and Regina's protest before it happened?"

Frank thought for a moment, spinning his pencil idly in his hand. "Of course I knew. But really, I was hoping that Alan wouldn't mention it. I still had that morbid curiosity, my classic poor judgment, but maybe the illusion of unity is better than the truth. I think he handled it well though, better than I would have in the moment."

Ms. Liu grimaced. "He called them harlots. You'd have done worse than that?"

"Maybe I wouldn't have. There's something innately satisfying, and I know you probably won't admit it, in seeing two people who have had everything go absolutely right for their entire lives through nothing but family legacy face the brunt of systemic justice. Machines are inexorable things, they keep grinding their gears no matter what gets trapped inside. Now, you can call me a hypocrite for saying that with a straight face while simultaneously implementing a system from *Brave New World*, but maybe it's better that people discriminate against each other based on artificial constraints now rather than their race or sexuality."

"Maybe it is. Enjoy your balloon slaughter. Keep up the good fight," Ms. Liu remarked, and she left to the faculty room—pizza was on the menu, a personal favorite. She checked TigerTalk out of curiosity, and Tom and Regina were already demoted to Epsilons. A slice of humble pie for them while she ate her pizza pie; was that justice? Close enough.

Chapter 34

The energy of Friday's rally had faded over the weekend, especially for the leadership students who had worked themselves to the bone making it happen. Ms. Foster's room was being used as interim storage for the rally decorations that nobody had the heart to throw out, and so Behrooz walked under a balloon arch, pushed his way through hanging paper streamers, and brushed confetti off his seat before he started working. He still had "Uptown Funk" stuck in his head, and just as he was about to reach the chorus, he heard the distinctive clip-clop of high heels.

"Hey, Juliet," Behrooz waved when she walked in the classroom.

"Good morning Behrooz! What's up?" she chirped and sat across from him, immediately pulling out her laptop from her backpack.

"How did you enjoy the rally on Friday? Wasn't it a bit, you know, excessive?" Juliet thought for a moment, not wishing to speak unkindly of the people who were quite responsible for that excessiveness.

"I guess, yeah. But they're always like that. That's the point of the rallies, to have some of that spectacle. At least the cheer team still got to perform, and it was cool how the band got to as well."

"Oh, yeah, of course that was nice. But Tom and Regina were literally dragged screaming out of the gym while everyone was booing them. Tom seriously looked like he wanted to murder Alan."

"I can see where Alan's coming from. He worked so hard to get to this point—we all did—and it was so demoralizing to see people purposely being assholes just to spite them, you know? But I see your point: we should talk to Alan. They should apologize to each other so we don't have any bad blood."

"Well, I wouldn't say that I contributed much to this. You guys already had everything figured out, I'm just here for the ride."

"Don't say that, Behrooz. You're such a generous and warm person. We all look up to you to be levelheaded."

"Anyway, what can I do? If I vote differently from Frank and Alan, I'm in the minority, and any tie will be broken by Ms. Foster, and we all know she's on his side."

"What sides are you talking about, Behrooz? We're all in this together because we have the same goal: to make the school a better place."

"I guess you're right, but still... I don't know..." Behrooz shook his head and changed the topic. Before he and Juliet could grow too comfortable in discussing their impending English test, Alan walked in with a triumphant air, his face coated with streaks of face paint that had somehow intensified in hue over the weekend.

"*We are the champions...*" he sang off-key, sitting down with a thud and feigning surprise at seeing the others.

"Speak of the devil and he appears," Behrooz muttered to himself; Alan turned toward him, so he laughed as if he intended his remark as a joke. "So Alan, as you've decided to show up; what did you think of the rally? I must say, you really exhibited leadership! Some people in life are destined to be leaders, and some are destined to be followers, and nobody made that more clear than you."

"Where's Frank?" Alan grunted, not picking up on Behrooz's double entendre.

"He has a meeting with Ms. Wolfe. But we're all friends here, we can speak freely. Tell me what you honestly think," Behrooz continued sarcastically, not noticing the security camera behind him swivel to match his head movements.

"I think the rally was perfect. I've never seen such a beautiful, such a perfect, such an epic experience. The third wave has crested, and boy, it's a tsunami! I felt like I was running for president or something. I had so much fun—didn't you, Juliet?" Juliet was about to enthusiastically concur until Behrooz put his finger to his lips.

"Earlier Juliet and I were talking, you know, as friends always do, and we were thinking that what an upstanding gentleman like yourself ought to do is apologize to our mutual friend Tom. You know, you put him through a minor headache, back there, and well if I were him I'd be hopping mad. So what do you say, why don't we try to break the ice a little?" Behrooz needed no encouragement to dislike Tom—there was nothing a rich kid like him who didn't at least give back to the community a little deserved more than a kick in the nuts—but there had to be a line drawn somewhere between civility and revenge. Fifteen hundred scowling faces, screaming themselves hoarse, all directed their energy at now "nasty" Tom and "whorish" Regina. There was nothing civil about that, and Behrooz still thought highly enough of Frank to pin the blame on Alan.

"He's an Epsilon. He deserves no sympathy from us. We've won the battle, but we still have a war to fight."

"He wasn't an Epsilon until the rally—look at this from my perspective, Alan: if you were in his shoes, wouldn't you be a little mad too?"

"I see no need to engage in hypotheticals. If we were on Mars, or if everyone were buck-naked, or if instead of a three-legged race we simply hacked each other to death with swords, all of those would be very interesting situations to consider. But we're in the present now, and what happened happened. Que sera, sera."

"You're missing my point entirely; you can't just propose some sort of outlandish counter-example to everything I say and claim victory. Now if this stupid rally had never happened, Tom would still be a Beta, we wouldn't be fighting, and life would go on like normal. That's a hypothetical worth considering." Alan's social skills ran the gamut from obsequious to psychopathic, and in an instant he had calculated that some humor, some classic hyperbole, would diffuse the situation:

"You have no respect for excessive authority or obsolete traditions. You're dangerous and depraved, and you ought to be taken outside and shot!" Alan began laughing like a hyena, and Juliet chuckled slightly before turning to Behrooz and mouthing "He's joking," like that brought any comfort to him. In all of Behrooz's idle thoughts about Alan getting some sort of moral comeuppance, with Behrooz playing the lead role as the masked crusader, he had never thought that Alan would consider making the first move. It wasn't just the flippant nature of his death threat, no matter how facetious, but that Alan had trained himself to think "excessive" and "obsolete" marks of high praise. Somewhere in his mind, he had learned to associate the same rallies he alternately evaded in the library and screamed his lungs out at with everything and anything equally ostentatious. "Excessive" wasn't then a sign of poor judgment, it was proof that there was never too much of a good thing; "obsolete," similarly, was the manifestation of the good person ethos that said beyond the threshold of madness, somewhere far off in the distance, lay method.

Behrooz replayed that conversation in his mind, "you ought to be taken outside and shot... and shot... and shot..." reverberating with the echo of a bullet casing dropped on a linoleum floor, during lunch that day with Beth. They sat on the grassy green on a blanket that was an Alpha privilege; a string quintet played from a speaker nestled in a bush, and a freshman poured them lemonade from a pitcher, having somehow missed the memo that it was fall and not summer.

"I've been doing some soul-searching, Beth, and I was thinking that—"

"It's time?" Beth finished with no trace of sadness in her voice.

"For the last few months we've been in such infrequent contact that it's not like we're dating at all. I'm completely swamped with work, so it's not like I have time even though I wanted to, and those sparks of joy are completely gone. I'm sorry." Beth put down her glass of lemonade—nothing sweet seemed appropriate for the moment—and nodded sagely.

"I suppose this is now a working lunch," Beth smiled, and they stayed the rest of the period unburdened, talking freely of what a sad thing it was for love to die; that rebellious bird which nobody could tame needed to be euthanized.

Surprisingly for one of Beth's breakups, it was Regina who approached Beth first; Beth did not want to make a show of her separation, thinking it rather undignified, but Regina could smell her disappointment.

"I guess now I must say fifth time's the charm, right?" Regina teased, lightly elbowing Beth.

"Oh, stop it. You sound like Tom now. You know, he said something similar to me at the lake. I thought he was just being a jerk then, but maybe he was right," Beth said pensively. "Anyway, I need time to think. Those who don't study the past are doomed to repeat it."

"What are you now, a philosopher?"

"You know it's true." Regina pointed out John from the other end of the hallway, who was leaning against a wall reading a book she couldn't identify, but that appeared thick.

"Look, one of your kind!" Regina gestured, and was about to shout at John to come apply some of his wisdom to cure Beth's heartache that she could not possibly not be feeling, when Beth preempted the gesture by walking toward him. Regina followed from a safe distance, ready to coo with admiration if needed; by her math, it had only been an hour since lunch, and if Beth were to acquire a new boyfriend now, it would set a personal record.

"It's her," John groaned, not even bothering to point weakly at Regina.

"We're all friends here, John, you know that. Now's not the time."

"What do you want, Beth?" John asked far more cheerfully.

"Just advice, as always. The usual, you know."

"Cut to the chase—our time on this planet is finite." Regina silently clapped in the background; her job here was done, and she could sleep well knowing that John had met his match.

"All things are finite. Like my relationship with Behrooz." John's interest was immediately piqued—suddenly her sassy wit was, dare he say, attractive? He leaned in, his interest renewed. "Continue, if you wish. Tell me your diamonds." Ever since the beginning of sophomore year, when Beth was no longer his to idolize, John had let his only hate spring from his only love: Beth's dry humor was unpalatable, too pessimistic; Beth's wiry frame was clearly a sign of malnutrition. If John had not been all too happy to loathe himself and let his feelings swing like a metronome, perhaps he could have swooped in at the lake one of those years. But instead, he waited, and waited, and waited, and through some cosmic miracle it was time for history to repeat itself.

"There's nothing to tell, really. Have you memorized your poem for English yet? I haven't decided which one I'll do, but you've always been more into literature—what will you do, Shakespeare?"

"*If I profane with my unworthiest hand / This holy shrine, the gentle fine is this...*"

"So romantic, save it for class," Beth laughed, nudging John delicately in the ribs. She walked off, not thinking much of the conversation nor John's increased heart rate. All that John had ever dreamed of was walking away from him, footsteps in a steady rhythm that matched his heartbeat, and if he reached out to grab something, anything, he could imagine it was her and not empty air. Perhaps another waltz was in order, a delicate, springy, one two three rhythm; John could keep that up as he walked to class.

"I hate that son of a bitch," Tom growled. Regina gave a wan smile.

"Which son of a bitch?"

"All of them." Tom had spent all day being laughed at, talked over, and stared at with a disappointment he had only known from his father before. His first instinct was to throw enough money at his problem until it went away; Tom had earlier given Alan a nice watch, promising it would suit him well, but Alan looked at it, dismissed it with a sneer as an inferior model, and dropped it on the floor. And he, that little rascal, was about to step on it with his hard sole and grind the watch into the floor before Tom lunged down in the nick of time and saved it. What had gotten into Alan to make him turn so spunky, so confident? Tom was not used to thinking of Alan as anything but a kind, if chronically hopeless, sidekick. Intuition warned him that he was drawing close to some immense and inscrutable cosmic climax, and his broad, meaty, towering frame tingled from head to toe at the thought that Alan, whoever he would turn out to be, was destined to serve as his nemesis. There were grand stakes at play now, and Alan had messed with the wrong Thomas Langley III.

Tom's mind whirred like a motor in overdrive, but for all his tingling, Tom was a bit spineless. Knowing that was the mood Alan was in, Tom had wisely decided not to ask him if there was any chance that on account of his previous good behavior, he could be promoted from Epsilon to at least a Gamma. At least Gammas didn't need to pick up trash in bags that were hung from their backs; many played impromptu basketball with their milk cartons and orange peels, and really did not mind at all when their aim was poor and food scraps slid down Tom's neck. Tom would have gone to seek refuge in the club meeting, hoping for some sort of Christian charity, but while they accepted Epsilons, they did not accept his kind of Epsilon.

Tom then tried Frank, who by the end of Monday was still grappling with the issue of Tom as well. Tom's fall from grace was thematic, if anything, but it still wasn't as clean as it could be; Tom and Regina were still on campus—even he couldn't make them disappear. They clearly proved convenient scapegoats for everything wrong on campus and with the school, but the logical antecedent of that was with their disappearance, the school would somehow become infinitely better. And it didn't seem to be so. The school was great, of course, but somewhere out there was an irascible Tom. Tom had a mind, and Frank had noticed that people with minds tended to get pretty smart at times.

"Frank, you slimy, little, putrid bastard!" Tom yelled.

"Hello darkness my old friend, you've come to meet with me again," Frank began with a smirk, one which Tom used to think clever. "What's on the menu today, an apology? A misguided speech? Make it quick, please; there's a limit to my boundless wisdom that I share with Epsilons." Frank stared Tom directly in the eyes until he backed away.

"I can make it happen, Frank. I can pull the thread and unravel all of this. Juliet won't ever speak to you again, and quite frankly, nobody else but your cultists will want to even see you in the hallway," Tom snarled.

"It's not quite as simple as that, Tom. Nobody else really minds the costume change, and if they have principles that oppose what I'd call a slight reduction in freedoms, they keep quiet. That's the funny thing about principles, everyone claims to have them until not having them becomes advantageous. Is it really worth making a big fuss out of a dress code and the national anthem? They certainly don't think so."

"It doesn't matter what you're doing, it's still wrong. If they will not speak, I will. The truth is what matters here, and Juliet will agree with me. Unlike you, she has principles."

"My dear fellow, the truth isn't quite the sort of thing one tells to a nice, sweet, refined girl," Frank smiled. What would he tell her anyway? There was a moral event horizon somewhere already passed as soon as the celery juice scheme had been deemed a great success, and oh yeah, Tom got in trouble for that too, didn't he? As always, Tom would simply appear jealous.

"You're a terrible person, Frank, but I can't say I disagree. Juliet's brainwashed herself anyway, and if I had to guess, this wasn't a conscious effort on your part. God, maybe she's worse than you are!" Frank's expression briefly soured; was he mad?

"Well, nice conversation. Just remember to keep those displays to a minimum in the future, all right? Next time it won't just be detention and demotion."

"You despise me, don't you?" Tom called out with his last shred of ego.

"If I gave you any thought, I would." That one hurt. Tom stomped away, mumbling something under his breath that Frank could not overhear but assumed was incoherent. Tom had no greater fantasy than to be known, to be known by everyone, and occupy at least a good portion of their waking thoughts. He wanted people to think "gee, how is Tom doing today?" and "I sure wish I could be like Tom!", not whatever they thought now, which apparently wasn't much of anything! Ignominy was a terrible fate, but anonymity was worse. That was a good question, actually—which was worse: everyone in the school not knowing who Tom was beyond passing impressions, or everyone knowing Tom as the lowest of the low, the toddler who may as well have started screaming and pounding the walls of the gymnasium.

Mrs. Huang was happy to see Frank's silhouette behind the door, and ran to let him in. Heller only offered five levels of Chinese class, and as Frank had completed his last the previous year, he never had any occasion to swing by. She still saw Juliet in class, at least, who while vivacious felt in her perception incomplete without the other half of the dynamic duo.

"How nice to see you again! *Long time no see*!" Mrs. Huang smiled, urging him to sit down and scavenge some of the leftover mooncakes from class that day. "What's the special occasion? You didn't bring Juliet?"

"Don't worry, Mrs. Huang, I see plenty of her; one can have too much of a good thing, you know. I was here just to get a second opinion on our latest school controversy, seeing as I just had a tense conversation with one of the people involved."

"You have nothing to worry about, Frank. Now you know what it's like to be a teacher: we have to discipline people every day! I do really like your new system, it makes things a lot easier on my end. If you think dealing with two people is hard, imagine one hundred!"

"I can understand where Tom's coming from, and that's the issue. I've always had this unfortunate tendency of sympathizing with the underdog. Not to say either of them are underdogs, but you know, I can't help wonder if this system isn't helping them out as it should."

"Of course it is, Frank. There are hundreds of other people out there who are behaving exactly as they should. All my students are so well-be-haved now, and every other teacher has nothing but nice things to say too. I forget exactly how you wrote this, but I remember you wrote in *How To Be A Good Person* something like 'be careful of others before they betray you.' I don't know Tom, other than that he must be a very, very bad person, but I know that he would not even think to care about you if he were the one in charge," Mrs. Huang explained as if it were common sense. "Quit worrying and go change the world." Frank thanked her for the ever-practical advice and left her room, deciding if he wanted to mope around campus for a while or go home. Those days, Frank always had something to do on campus, enough that if he wanted, he could work the same hours as his teachers. One disadvantage of living within walking distance of school was exactly that: the journey was trivial, so easy as to be unimportant. Frank felt too tired to change the world, so instead he walked home, waving to Juliet through the chain-link when she waved first at him, patiently resisting the temptation to jaywalk, shivering slightly in the autumnal breeze.

Chapter 35

After his initial rage, denial, and bargaining with everyone he knew, Mr. Ivanov had settled into mute acceptance of the new status quo. It wasn't like him to be so bothered by what everyone else was doing; he was no stranger to the administration's harebrained schemes, and despite the new idea of student involvement, chances were that they'd have come up with something equally stupid in the future. When Mr. Ivanov saw Frank in the hallways, he thus didn't needle him too much; Frank was still a good kid, with a sense of humor Mr. Ivanov could appreciate, and despite Frank's refusal to ever censure Jason or Alan Mr. Ivanov was sure that Frank was on his side.

Jason, now, was another matter. Jason had grown emboldened over time, observing that nobody stopped him from spying on whomever he wanted whenever he wanted; it was like nobody cared at all. Jason had incurred some losses in his quest to see and hear everything: Mr. T had taped over his camera after seeing it follow Juliet around the classroom from too revealing of an angle. Frank assumed it was Alan, but some quick process of elimination proved that it couldn't be him or Behrooz. While both Mr. T and Frank assumed the most innocent of motives—it seemed entirely logical, in fact, that as Jason couldn't monitor Juliet's phone, this was the next best thing—when Mr. T casually brought up this observation to Mr. Ivanov, he was displeased:

"So you're saying Jason is a Peeping Tom? God, maybe I need to tape over my camera too!"

"I think you're overreacting, Igor," Mr. T assured him, "it's just some innocent espionage. I have nothing against it."

"But you taped up your camera, clearly you too are against this surveillance state they're building."

"Jason is free to spy on Juliet, Regina, Frank, or myself in any other place in the school. I personally would just like a little peace of mind. It's no big deal that I noticed, but what if someone else did? Then I'd look bad! Plausible deniability, you know. And if it turns out that I inspire copycats, well for the good of the school I'll take the tape off." Mr. Ivanov was not satisfied with Mr. T's train of logic, who after that conversation went to take the tape off in case he inspired Mr. Ivanov, and he accosted Jason when he came to class the next day as cheerful as ever. Jason's face betrayed nothing:

"Oh, Mr. T's classroom? Well, you know, I do routine security checks. Random chance. And if I just so happen to be following Juliet, Alan, or Behrooz around, from any angle I so choose, it's luck. That's all there is to it. They should be honored, actually, that they're so privileged to be examined so closely."

"And you don't see anything wrong with doing this during lecture, when you ought to be paying attention? Think of how disrespectful that is to your teachers. As a teacher, I take offense for all of them."

"I'm adept at multitasking. I serve a higher power, Mr. Ivanov, and He commands me to secure his legacy."

"Who, Frank?" Mr. Ivanov asked sarcastically, watching the security camera in his classroom from the corner of his eye.

"No, Joseph Stalin."

"Don't joke about Stalin like that. He massacred millions of people, and you think that legacy is something you want to implement here? My God, you're crazy! All of you are. Go sit down, Jason. And stop playing with the cameras when I can see you, it drives me crazy. Do you understand how scary it is to know that anything I say, anything I do, anywhere on this campus can be used against me? I'm going to have to start taking my calls in the restroom at this rate."

"We have cameras there, too," Jason added.

"Be quiet." Jason couldn't understand what all the fuss was about. Sure, spying on the club officers all day was going above and beyond whatever duties he promised Mr. Kurtz and Ms. Wolfe he'd handle, but then again, wasn't everything? And really, if Jason thought about it hard enough, their phones were spying on them anyway. Nobody walked around all day with their phone encased in aluminum foil. So what difference did it make? At least this threat was easily quantifiable; who wouldn't prefer kindly Jason to the NSA? That was why Jason left class that day entirely certain of his moral infallibility, and that was why Mr. Ivanov angled his desk so he was always facing the security camera; it was quite clever of Jason indeed to have the cameras randomly move, that way Mr. Ivanov never knew when he ought to start swearing loudly and flipping off his personal guardian. He couldn't always be watched; presumably he was not that interesting to Jason, who had spent enough time in his classroom to know that nothing interesting ever happened.

As if the universe had heard Mr. Ivanov's silent musings, at lunch one day Mr. Ivanov heard knocking on his door. Mr. Ivanov begrudgingly agreed to open his classroom during lunch for Tom and Regina, who at this point were starting to get tired of their newfound infamy, when Tom said he brought pizza. The three of them sat down at the desks and Tom passed out napkins and plates. The first meeting of the How To Be A Bad Person Club had begun.

"This is a complete violation of our freedoms. I don't care what Frank says, this is tyranny," Tom began with his mouth partially full.

"Jason during class today mentioned how Stalin's policies were an inspiration for whatever school project he's up to. Stalin killed my grandparents. Not cool," Mr. Ivanov added. "Thanks for bringing the pizza, by the way. One positive of this, I suppose, is that our weekly morning staff meetings have actual breakfast now. Frank and his people cooked us French toast last week."

"He cooked us French toast over the summer too! It's just a manipulation tactic."

"Whatever you want to call it, it tasted damn good. What disgusts me more about this entire thing, more than that students were given unfettered control over the school, is that all my colleagues signed off on it. Well, I wouldn't say that they're all in favor, but they just con't care. They think that just because it costs them nothing extra to wear a suit or say the pledge that it's of no consequence. First they came for the socialists, and I did not speak out—because I was not a socialist. Then they came for the trade unionists, and I did not speak out—because I was not a trade unionist. Then they came for the Jews, and I did not speak out—because I was not a Jew. Then they came for me—and there was no one left to speak for me."

"Niemoller, right? I remember Mr. Simon read us that," Regina offered. "It's a classic quote, and as much as I hate to admit it, history repeats itself."

"Mr. T would kill me if he heard this, and knowing the cameras, maybe he will, but Jason's been spying on everyone through the security cameras. He has access to your phones, too."

"We know," Tom admitted. Ever since he had become an Epsilon, someone had been rearranging the apps on his phone while he slept and changing the alarms by just a few minutes; Tom's first hypothesis was that he had suddenly began sleepwalking, but Mr. Ivanov's explanation made so much more sense.

"And does that bother you at all?" Mr. Ivanov asked, knowing fully the answer.

"Of course it does!" Regina interjected. "Some things, you know, are private business. There are some texts and pictures on my phone I hope Jason hasn't seen, girl business."

"It's not just him. I have access to everything through TigerTalk—not the security cameras, at least—but if I wanted to I could hack into your email right now. Just because I was feeling spiteful or something. Don't worry, I haven't touched any of those features."

"I think what bothers me most about all of this is that the balance of power is uneven. I talked with Frank the other day, and he made it abundantly clear I was just a number to him. It's not like they get performance bonuses for any of this, and they still have the rest of school to deal with. Classes, normal people things. If they were forced into it, I could understand some of this, but if they're doing it of their own volition it's just sadistic!" Tom continued.

"Let me ask you a question, Tom. Answer honestly. If you were in charge instead of, I don't know, Alan, would you be using your power in the same way? Would you be a force of good or evil, knowing that the power lay entirely in your hands?"

"How about you, Mr. Ivanov? It's a good question." Mr. Ivanov put his hand to his chin and wiped his face with a napkin.

"My high school self would have staunchly refused. These people would be my friends, whom I'd have known since my early youth. And I couldn't bear to see them reduced to statistics. I'm sure Jason has used this quote before, but: a single death is a tragedy, a million deaths is a statistic. It's not like anyone's dying here or anything like that, but they all start to blend together. I would know my friends not by name, but by their ID numbers. Now, as an adult with a great job, a loving wife, and a good salary, sure, why not? I don't think I would use my power in the same way as Jason; for one, I'd do what he suggested at the beginning of the year and use it to check for academic dishonesty, but it does make things very efficient. Before the celery juice incident and everyone shifted to just doing drugs off-campus, you'd get people smoking marijuana in the bathrooms at least once a week. Security cameras there would do a lot of good."

"But you see, Mr. Ivanov, that's the exact same argument Jason's using. Both of you think you're doing this for the right reasons. But all I see is tyranny, everywhere I look. I don't give a damn if Jason's busting people using marijuana, he's still looking at my phone for proof of secret Epsilon rebellion. They've all deluded themselves into thinking that they're doing the right thing, that they're good people. But there's nothing to keep them accountable."

"So do we want to keep up these meetings?" Regina asked, thinking next time they could eat sushi.

"I don't see the harm," Mr. Ivanov admitted, "when I'm free, of course. I think we're only scratching the surface of what's wrong with Heller, and together we will make it right." Tom and Regina cleaned up their mess and left, and Mr. Ivanov went back to his desk. Mr. Kurtz would have the solution, that was it! He would at least have a touch of sympathy and pretend like he cared. Mr. Ivanov began typing an email, but realized that Jason undoubtedly could be spying on that too; he took out a notepad from his drawer and began jotting down scattered thoughts. He wrote his reminder to himself in a heavy and decisive hand, amplifying it sharply with a series of coded punctuation marks and underlining the whole message twice. There were connections everywhere to be teased out and unraveled: this tangled web spanned from Jason to Frank, Ms. Foster, Mr. T, maybe Ms. Liu—she was a crafty one, and undoubtedly to anyone and everyone who could have some stake in this conflict. It was a war, one fought for the soul of high school education, and it was finally time for Mr. Ivanov to take up arms.

Mr. Ivanov would have thrown in the towel had he known that the superintendent was scheduled to come by the school that afternoon to meet with the "visionary" and "revolutionary" student council, as Mr. Kurtz had described them in an email. Mr. Mudd was a portly, squat man with a bushy mustache and the voice of a drill sergeant; all the teachers, and even Mr. Kurtz, spoke of him in whispers. They avoided saying his name, the rumor having been started a while ago that like Beetlejuice, if they said his name three times he would appear in a puff of smoke. Mr. Mudd did indeed often appear in puffs of smoke from fragrant Cuban cigars, although out of respect for the students he only indulged in his own office. Mr. Kurtz woke up one morning, a comfortable ninety minutes before he would have to think about work, to a voice message from Mr. Mudd:

"Patrick, I'm coming to check out your school today. What on earth is happening over there? Good things, I know, but I need to see this for myself. 3:30. Bring in the student council too. You aren't in trouble, don't worry."

The student council stood assembled in Mr. Kurtz's office, backs straight, waiting for the arrival of the mythical Mr. Mudd. Mr. Kurtz coached them on etiquette until it became clear they knew exactly how to hold themselves in polite company. At exactly 3:30, Mr. Mudd opened Mr. Kurtz's door and walked over to his chair and sat down, forcing Mr. Kurtz to stand next to the others. Mr. Mudd avoided the pleasantries and instead gingerly removed the photo of Frank and his staff from Mr. Kurtz's wall and examined it carefully.

"Who are these people? They look like waiters."

"Well, uh, I'm in that picture," Frank offered.

"So you must be the president then. You're the one we have to blame for all of this," Mr. Mudd laughed, and after Mr. Kurtz nudged them, everyone else started laughing too.

"I couldn't have done it without Mr.–Dr.?–Kurtz's leadership. Blame him for all the bad parts and praise me for everything good," Frank joked.

"I only go by 'Dr.' when trying to impress parents," Mr. Kurtz explained.

"But anyway, Patrick, why do you have this picture? Out of all the things to celebrate, this seems like a strange touch," Mr. Mudd continued. "The matching uniforms must have cost a fortune."

"I don't know why Frank had the photo taken originally, but I think it's a nice reminder that behind all the bright lights and celebration, there's hard work that goes into everything we do too. We can't just take the good parts and discard the bad. That's not how life works."

"So why did you have the photo taken, Frank? Do you agree with your principal?"

"You may not believe it from how I act, Mr. Mudd, but I try to stay out of the spotlight. I've settled into my role as deuteragonist, believe it or not. When I have such an excellent team of people surrounding me, I can occupy my time with delivering philosophy lectures, planning menus, and living normally. Delegating tasks I don't want to do to those below me, and trusting people like yourself above me to grease the wheels when needed. So I think that photo represents how I'm really happiest when I serve as a backdrop for everything else that happens. That's why I usher for the plays, too; I make things easier for everyone else, and thus I set the stage for each and every individual to live their life as they see fit."

"And is that how a good person acts? I've read your manifesto, and as illuminating as it was for reasons that I can tell by your facial expression, you don't want me to mention in front of everyone else, there seems to be a greater emphasis on realpolitik. That's what you've turned the school into, if I'm not mistaken. What do you think, Mr. Kurtz? It's unusual, dare I say unprecedented, that you're treating your student leaders as equals like this."

"Ms. Foster, if you know her—our student leadership director—had a good way of thinking about it. We can certainly control what goes on in the classrooms, but our goal is also for students to develop emotionally. And we can't control every facet of their being. You and I were teenagers a long, long time ago; we don't know how they think. We certainly couldn't plumb their psyches like Frank and his team do. It's efficient, if anything else. And we're still doing our jobs as teachers. I promise, the four of you, that any employer will be fascinated by this. I'm willing to write each of you a recommendation letter for college, and over the years I've built up a fair number of connections; Stanford's not that far away, and the dean and I play golf every Sunday. If you want an internship at Google, who cares about your resumé, masterminding this operation alone should qualify you!"

"I have an alternative offer," Mr. Mudd interrupted. "We could use folks like you working for the school district, or even as teachers. You won't become millionaires, at least not immediately, but as any of your teachers could tell you, we pay quite well for top talent. You can spend your days doing things exactly like this, mentoring students as they imprint on the school in new and exciting ways. Who knows what's next—you could come back in five years and we'd have a communist collective! But anyway, the school. That's what we're here to discuss."

Mr. Mudd found the conviction of Mr. Kurtz and his staff surprising; certainly it was nothing unusual to see the student council so attached to their Frankenstein's monster of a reform movement, but the principal spoke almost reverently of the progress made. The students let Mr. Kurtz speak for them as a whole, about how with a few notable exceptions, disciplinary infractions became infrequent, and even the students deemed troublesome that logically speaking, would not benefit from the good person movement at least did not seem harmed. Drug use had also declined dramatically, at least on campus; the superintendent was even more surprised to hear the catalyst for this change occurred last year. The drawbacks, at least according to everyone involved in fomenting these changes, were irrelevant.

"But does it bother you at all that your students are less free? They were promised a high school of astonishing new freedom and independence. A brave new world! Any freshman who came here not knowing how it used to be, unaware of the context of your little ideology besides what you force-fed them, would know that this wasn't right. It wasn't how things were meant to be."

"With all due respect, Mr. Mudd," Frank interjected, "most of the new rules enforced stringently now were in the student regulations before. They just weren't enforced. Certainly that doesn't excuse any particular rule, but they work. And I'm sure that in some distant past, before students had portable gaming devices in their pockets or I was born, those policies functioned flawlessly too. Consider me single-minded, but I'm not as much of a trailblazer as people think I am."

"Don't take what I say as criticism—I commend your chutzpah. And, although I hope this is clear to everyone in the room, high school students always complain. It's a fact of life. This is the time when they finally have enough of a functional consciousness to make intelligent decisions and have intelligent ideas, yet they're never able to do anything about it. I also wouldn't have expected people like you in this day and age to relive our former glory."

"Was it really that much better then?" Behrooz asked.

"I'd like to think that we are always making progress onward. Even if we revert back to old ideas, in a perfect world they'd have been refined in the interim. And I can say that as far as I can tell, you've done that. I would never have thought that propaganda posters would do the trick, but you learn something new every day. And TigerTalk, genius."

"If I may ask, Mr. Mudd," Behrooz continued, "what's your least favorite part of this new way of doing things?"

"If you're asking me just based on gut instinct, the caste system is a bit, I don't know, tactless? I know Mr. Kurtz waxed rhapsodically about it, but if I were in charge of creating these changes, I would come up with something a bit more subtle."

"Personally, that's one of my favorite parts!" Alan piped up, now no longer too shy to speak. "It's dramatic and most certainly excessive, but I cannot think of any other way in which we could enforce our new morality on over a thousand students in a way everyone can understand. Philosophy isn't approachable to the average person; only the most intelligent even come to the club, and so we needed to dumb it down a little for, you know, the others."

"You've convinced me then: under the logical premise that we want fifteen hundred people all to follow your new philosophy, it's not like you can fine them or send them to prison, so other incentives are needed. Fear is the most powerful incentive of all, I think. And you've been able to quantify that fear, into your point system, and it doesn't matter if you call them Epsilons or dunces or morons, the message comes through loud and clear. The more I stay here, the more I think I ought to have some conversations with other principals about expanding this system."

While those in the principal's office plotted the school's continual demise, Ted pulled up into the student parking lot, immediately noticing that someone had raked the fallen leaves out of the road. He checked his suit in his car's mirror before confidently strutting on campus. He was there as a tourist; he had heard such strange things about his former school that he knew he had to investigate, and it had already become clear he had entered a foreign land. His sister was a freshman, and as soon as she came back from her first day triumphantly announcing she was a Beta, Ted knew he had unfinished business. Ted admired the posters on the walls like he was visiting an art gallery. The floors were picked clean of litter, and the few students he saw in the hallways walked with hitherto unseen stiffness in their movements, like they were trying to speed-walk but hadn't quite figured out how. It was after school, what was the rush? He remembered that once freshman year, he had been sent on garbage duty for instigating a minor food fight; now, it seemed that garbage duty was everyone's duty, for how else did the school look so sterile? It was nice, of course, but it wasn't the school he remembered—the trash bins were even sorted correctly! Ted felt a twinge of guilt and paranoia as he walked around; what would happen if he were seen? Of course he knew what happened to Tom and Regina, and it wouldn't surprise him if repeated troublemakers were drawn and quartered in center court. He felt fortunate that the first familiar face he saw was Tom, who was lingering close enough to the administrative buildings to see the student council through the glass.

"Ted! What are you doing here?" Tom shouted at him. "It's dangerous here. Go back home."

"I had to see it to believe it, Tom. A little bird told me that you aren't taking this change as well as you could be—care to elaborate?" Tom didn't respond at first, instead pointing to the security cameras under the eaves of the buildings, far across the courtyard by the swimming pool.

"Why so sullen, Tom? You're typically bursting with energy." Tom frowned, and meekly gestured toward the office.

"So you don't much like civilization, Mr. Savage. I see how it is." This finally prompted Tom to speak:

"You can say that again for the people in the back. I feel like I can't even walk to my car without somebody breathing down my neck, telling me exactly what I'm doing wrong. All I did was one simple little act of defiance, and now it's like I'm public enemy number one. You'd think I tried to bomb the school or something."

"On the surface, I mean, everything looks great. Everyone's dressed nicely and the hallways are clean."

"The hallways are only clean because we Epsilons clean up the trash. If not for us, this entire place would be a garbage dump."

"I'm sure you aren't that important, Tom. How is everyone else doing? I saw Behrooz at a party a few weeks ago and he seemed to be happy, I don't know. I wouldn't go as far as to call him pleased, but he didn't seem depressed."

"Behrooz is a traitor and I hate everything he stands for," Tom declared resolutely.

"Isn't he Iranian or something? I thought they believed in theocracy and dictatorship," Ted asked.

"That's right, he's Iranian."

"That crazy bastard," Tom laughed, and he steadied himself: "Wait, aren't you Israeli, Ted?"

"That has nothing to do with it. So let me get this straight: all the Alphas are partying it up, and you need to clean up their trash?"

"Yep, that's it. The rich serving the poor. Look what society's come to."

"Never speak disrespectfully of society, Tom. Only people who can't get in do that."

"Who are you to speak of society, Ted? My dad's had the CTO of Apple over for dinner before. I can say with certainty I've beat multiple millionaires at Scrabble. What have you done?"

"I have a job. I take classes at the local community college. I may serve in the Navy or do some sort of ROTC program. I'm living life, Tom, and out in the real world people aren't Alphas or Epsilons, they don't wear suits everywhere; they get up, drink coffee, go to work, come home, and sleep. It's as simple as that. Don't let all this current confusion scare you."

"But Ted, you're working your way up from the lowest rung of the ladder. The fat cats in charge act like Frank and his band of thugs: they dress nicely, fraternize, eat fancy dinners, and tell the lower classes what to do. I know that life, Ted, and at this rate it won't be mine."

"Do you understand how childish you sound, Tom? You're a senior in high school, and you're talking as if your life's destiny has been dictated to you by someone else. We're about the same age; there's no difference between us besides that one of us is in the system and one of us is out of it. Maybe you're right and in the upper echelons of 'society,' people act like this. If that's really the case, who would want to live there?" With Ted's newfound lucidity, he began to feel a distinct pity for Tom; this wasn't his previous gut feeling that Tom was a bit too big for his britches, but Ted instead knew now that Tom was mortal, just as mortal as he was. And inside his pompous shell, there was a little kid who was never allowed to buy that lollipop in the candy store and never forgot it.

Tom took Ted's exhortation to heart too as they stood there, not daring to sit on the Beta benches or the Alpha grass. Morale was deteriorating and it was all Tom's fault. The school was in peril; he was jeopardizing his traditional rights of freedom and independence by daring to exercise them. How could he win a war where he was outplayed at every turn? He had nobody on his side but Mr. Ivanov, who he thought ultimately constrained by his official position to ever do anything daring, and Regina, who after her burst of energy in protesting alongside Tom had become feckless, passive, and complicit. Even Ted, one of his most loyal friends, thought him a loser.

"Being here depresses me. Let's go somewhere fun," Tom suggested. Ted had seen enough of Heller as well, and together they walked away, Tom pointing out all the places where change had been made, just as the student council finished their meeting. The majority vote ruled supreme yet again: the four of them had decided to be ecstatic about the superintendent's reception of their ideas. Immediately upon exiting the office, Juliet gave Frank a warm hug, and gave Alan and Behrooz clearly-lacking imitations. This occasion demanded celebration, they thought, and Juliet proposed they grab food downtown to celebrate. Alas, Alan needed to go to robotics, and Behrooz had a party to prepare for, and Frank was about to diplomatically propose they wait for another less cloudy day that didn't threaten rain. Juliet looked deflated again, but Frank looked at the sky—a bit of rain was no big deal, just a bit of water. So after the others had already left, and they were walking in the same direction, he changed his mind:

"You know, we have nothing to be afraid of. Just a little California dew. Want to get ramen?" And so they walked together, like they would have anyway, and Juliet was already rationalizing the walk back uphill as extra needed exercise.

Chapter 36

It took a special occasion for Mrs. Huang to take her family out for Sunday brunch, but the occasion demanded it. She had received an email last night from UCLA triumphantly announcing that Juliet had won a scholarship, and with it, admission; the logical thing to do would be to forward it to her immediately, but Mrs. Huang had a better idea. Mrs. Huang admired the chandelier and the lobster tanks, and was happy to be seated quickly by the old lady manning the front desk. She loved the frenetic energy and savory smells that permeated the room; for one, it made her hungry. She quickly conferred with her family before shouting some requests at the waiter who conveniently ambled by, and a few minutes later, an array of steamers and a bemused Juliet were delivered. Mrs. Huang insisted she sit down, and with little fanfare handed her an envelope and waited for her to open it.

"What is it?" Juliet asked.

"What are you waiting for? Open it." Juliet surgically opened the envelope and scanned the letter, her resting flat smile turning into jubilance. A few other tables noticed and began clapping.

"You're a future Bruin. Great school, great food. What's your major?"

"I know before I wanted to do psychiatry, but I chose political science. I think leadership has been good for me; I want more. Maybe you'll see me run for president in thirty years. Why did you come all the way here, Mrs. Huang, for this? You could have just sent me an email."

"Because then I wouldn't have seen your face!" Mrs. Huang excitedly laughed. "And I was hungry. I've been here before, but you must not have been there. I was very lucky today that you were here."

"This occasion calls for celebration," Juliet declared, and she took an empty seat at Mrs. Huang's table and hastily introduced herself to Mrs. Huang's husband with needless formality and her son, who was too young to understand the magnitude of the moment but happy to meet a new friend.

"I've told them such great things about you and Frank, this is no inconvenience at all. Where is he going?"

"He said he knows, but he won't tell me. Probably Harvard or something. He sure does love his secrets."

"People like you two will succeed anywhere. Don't even stress about it—but I guess your stress is over! You still have six months of high school left, enjoy it while you can. Let him enjoy it too."

"UCLA has been my dream school since I was a kid, but I never thought I'd actually be able to attend. Now I just want to leave here and move to the next stage of my life, you know. It seems pointless to stay and keep running out the clock; time is precious."

"Really, Juliet. I thought you loved high school. I thought you loved all of this. At UCLA you will be a nobody, at least at first; here, you are a superstar."

"Every star must fade. I feel like I've aged thirty years in the last few months. Everything that felt special about the new system, the new way of doing things, simply isn't special anymore; it feels like a job. And don't get me wrong—I really enjoy what I do—but it's like if you took a movie and added an extra hour before the credits. It's needless epilogue."

"Every senior feels that way, that's why they call it senioritis. If you think this is needless epilogue, welcome to the real world. I love my job too, but it requires people like you keeping it interesting, otherwise I only have my books and my church to add some energy into it. You can always find something to be happy about; that's a skill I learned long ago, and it's why I'm still at Heller. I bet you're such a smart kid that you can find more ideas for your student council to implement and make the school even better. That should keep you busy. But anyway, let s not talk so much of business here—eat up!"

With the homecoming dance approaching, Frank was faced with a dilemma: he could either maintain it as a bastion of normalcy in an otherwise-uncertain time, or overhaul the entire thing as proof that high school students didn't really care where they were as long as they were with their friends. The choice was obvious.

"Ms. Baldwin, how are you these days?" Frank knocked on her door a few times as warning and let himself in.

"Frank! I've heard such good things about you." Ms. Baldwin didn't have Frank as a student, but they had met in passing at multiple staff meetings, and at that point teachers would have to be living under a rock to not know who he was.

"So for homecoming this year, I was thinking about doing a *Pride and Prejudice* theme, and Mr. T informed me that you may have some experience on that front. Would you be able to help him lead a dance lesson for any students who want to be adequately prepared?"

"Why does it matter? People just shake their butts in the air all evening. You can't stop that."

"It would be a nice visual effect, and everyone is looking at us with high hopes. It makes us look like hypocrites now if we do something normal."

"Does tomorrow after school work?"

"Perfect, as always."

Ms. Baldwin and Mr. T addressed the assembled crowd of about fifty students, who had already separated themselves into pairs, with an artificial solemnity; they found their audience receptive, mainly because they were scared of losing points if they danced poorly.

"The difference between a lady and a flower girl is not how she behaves, but how she is treated," Ms. Baldwin explained. "Your dance partner needs to treat you with sense and sensibility; he leads, you follow, and when it's time to switch the transfer of power occurs gracefully. If your dance partner handles you roughly, well, we may as well be in the coal mines! Cue the music once more, Jason. Let's run through this again."

John originally intended on avoiding homecoming, as he did most other school dances; they were all the same, he was sure, and having experienced one he had undoubtedly experienced them all. As soon as Regina heard about the dance lesson, and confirmed with Frank that while he much preferred Tom didn't show up, she was perfectly safe, she begged John to go during their tutoring session:

"Come on, dancing is fun! Where else will you get to share your heart and soul?"

"I have no heart and soul to share."

"Don't be silly. John, this was meant for you! You'll finally get to become Darcy."

"Is this something I need a date for, you know, a dance partner?"

"Well, now that you mention it, why don't you go with Beth? She has some experience and those same peculiar sensibilities you have. Be a good sport." Regina would not have been so pushy had she not tried this with Beth before class, who said that as long as John truly wanted to, she had no objections.

"Beth? Why her?" John tried his best to ask innocently, while really imagining her sashaying down the wide marble steps in a midnight-black gown, delicately taking John's hand, and the beat—one two three one two three once again—that beat John could never escape, its melody found in birdsong and car wheels and anywhere the glory of life was to be seen. Regina could see beads of sweat forming on John's eyebrow.

"I don't know, maybe because I think she fancies you?" John turned toward Regina with wild eyes. "It's just a theory, a hypothesis as you smarties put it, I don't know. There's only one way to find out."

John stared down into Beth's eyes as they moved back and forth in the patterns that thanks to Ms. Baldwin's drilling, were becoming routine. She looked back warmly, but was there anything else in that implacable expression of hers? Any sane person, John thought, would consider dancing inherently romantic; even when they switched partners with other pairs in the room as they went through partner dances, they inevitably returned together at the end.

"Beth, want to go to homecoming with me?" John slipped out suddenly, trying to sound as casual and suave as anyone else would.

"Yeah, sure, why not?" Well, that was easy. Across the gym, Regina had made the mistake of choosing Alan as her dance partner, simultaneously feeling bad for his lonesomeness and seeing her actions as enabling upward mobility.

"Isn't this fun?" Alan nearly shouted as he stepped on Regina's foot once again, an example of an ongoing trend where Alan forgot left and right in the intensity of the movement. At least Alan could keep a beat; the music program had clearly done him some good, but Regina counted herself fortunate she had never entered those unhallowed crypts by the boys' locker room. Who knew what went on there that spawned such people like Alan.

"Yes, um, it certainly is."

"Where's Tom? Is there a reason, if you know what I mean, that you're here without him?"

"God no!" Regina exclaimed in disgust. "Originally neither of us were to be allowed in here, but Frank made a special exemption for my artistic experience. You're dancing with an Epsilon, you know—does that bother you?" Alan suddenly thought Regina's hand claw-like, her grace unnatural, and her face sinister. If Alan revealed that he had been duped, he would be the laughingstock of the entire school; instead, he shook his head and pretended this was part of a master plan.

The school could have afforded a classier venue for homecoming than the same gymnasium where the dance lesson took place, but by then it was established tradition for each dance to occupy an increasingly-ostentatious venue; the day of homecoming, the student council and an elite squadron of other leadership students stayed after school, scrubbing the room clean and carting in luxury decor. The spectacle gradually spilled out of the gymnasium, which would remain the dance floor, into the surrounding hallways, all so students would have places to dine and relax; by sunset, even the central courtyard was decorated and ready for visitors.

When Behrooz had confirmed that despite his DJ talents, he could not simultaneously play the violin and flute a few days prior, they had booked Heller students to act as the band; they showed up as a group with pizza stains on their face and expressions of terror.

"You spent hours rehearsing, right? This should be easy. You're all becoming Epsilons if I hear mistakes," Alan warned them. The Beta carrying the cello gulped and promised that under penalty of social death, they would make no mistakes. Slowly the guests began to enter from the student parking lot, walking through the covered path now flanked by displays of flowers and ribbon; Deltas dressed in tuxedos offered them snacks from platters.

"Not bad at all, not bad at all," John admitted to Frank, Beth standing safely at his side.

"I thought you hated these things, John. Did, um, Beth convince you otherwise?"

"I asked her, actually. I've spent four years waiting for good things to happen to me, so I thought, why doesn't silly old John be that good thing for someone else?"

"That's a great sentiment. Are you and Beth an item, or are you just here as friends?"

"We're just as much of an item as you and Juliet," Beth laughec. "I didn't see you two at the dance lesson, where were you?"

"For one, I would appreciate it if you didn't imply we were joined at the hip. I apologize for making the assumption about you and John—this is the 21st century, anyone can go do whatever they want with anyone else without any presumption of guilt. Secondly, we were busy." Frank knew he wouldn't be helping his case if he admitted that at Juliet's insistence, they had gone to Ms. Baldwin's room to practice the other day. They pushed all the desks to the edges of the room, and while Ms. Baldwin graded papers and occasionally offered feedback, Frank and Juliet danced until Juliet could not convincingly say the purpose of their activity was educational.

As the band launched into another waltz and new students filtered in (the PE teachers promised their students extra credit for participating appropriately, in what Frank believed was a gesture of goodwill but really was an experiment by Ms. Stevens to see how desperate her students were for po nts), Frank couldn't help but feel proud of himself. All of his favorite faces were there—even Tom and Regina, who Juliet had begged Frank to let n long enough that he finally assented, under the caveat that Tom spend an hour shining shoes—and it seemed like people were having a good time. He was no classical dance veteran like Mr. T or Ms. Baldwin, but they looked upon the display approvingly in their period costumes, and anything beat the ceaseless thrum of the human mob at most events. Sure, he knew a few people had ditched homecoming to go to a trendier party, where they'd probably be getting stoned right about now, but if they were here they'd undoubtedly have broken up the perfect tableau in front of him. There was certainly a bit of acting involved in the otherwise-picturesque image before him—Beth had to nearly drag John onto the dance floor, and Alan was elbowed in the face by a freshman and currently had an ice pack clutched to his forehead—but as long as people looked like they were having fun, did it matter? In an hour or two, undoubtedly after he'd be pulled onto the dance floor himself again a few times, they'd have to pack up the festivities and turn their space back into a basketball/volleyball/badminton court, but the magic could last until then.

"Can you believe this is our last homecoming?" Behrooz asked Alan, who was still nursing his minor wound. This was the first time in a while Behrooz was able to relax at a dance, and after observing the intricate spirals the dancers traced on the gym floor, wisely decided this was not his time. Alan stared emptily into space, gnawing on a crostini.

"It's my first. I don't see what the fuss is all about. I could be doing homework right now, but instead I'm sitting here watching other people have the time of their lives."

"Well, you know that's what we signed up for. In a normal universe, this is exactly the student council's responsibility. Welcome to the real world—we have obligations."

"When Frank recruited me for this position, he promised that all the hard work would be delegated to others. The natural order of things, that's how he put it. Why did he lie to me?" Coming from any other person, this would be the height of sarcasm, but Behrooz genuinely believed Alan felt betrayed.

"If you think this is hard work, sitting here and eating food, you don't know how good you have it. It's just a black eye, Alan. Get up. Act like an Alpha."

Frank had not wanted to tell Juliet that he got into Wharton because he considered it a fluke. A matter of circumstance, really, that was entirely out of his control; he had done all the right things: he had written a passionate essay about the power of satire as social commentary; aced all his classes and tests; and gotten the coveted, almost impossible to acquire golden ticket of a recommendation letter from Mr. T. Mr. T had connections everywhere and a near 100% success rate, the hard part was getting him to like you enough to write you a letter. A few days after he received the triumphant news, he got an email from a fellow future Wharton student, asking him if he'd care to meet the squad downtown for a casual meet-and-greet.

Somehow Frank was not surprised to see that the few other incoming Wharton students waiting at the Starbucks were not wearing suits and ties; instead, they wore starched polo shirts and shorts, even though it was a bit chilly out. They eyed him warily: while a few assumed he was merely weird, someone made the connection:

"Wait, do you go to Heller?"

"In fact, I do. Franklin Barnes at your service, but please, call me Frank." He offered his hand hesitantly, and Jack, who through his height and Patek Philippe was clearly the alpha, yanked it toward him in a far too aggressive response.

"I saw the rally video, the one where they dragged the kids through the gym. Hold on, wait—you must be the president then! I knew you looked familiar!"

"I suppose I am, but I'm off the clock now, there's really nothing to it." It was then that Frank knew that whether he liked it or not, his identity would be inextricably linked to his club. It did not exist without him, but he did not exist without it either.

"The things you can do at a public school, am I right? The name's Jack." After the initial pleasantries, conversation quickly turned to the miraculously egalitarian society in which they lived where someone from a public school like Frank could rub shoulders with the beneficiaries of trust funds.

"Your suit is nice, you must be rolling in that dough too. Why are you at Heller then? You don't deserve them."

"I always gagged on that silver spoon. I went to a small private school for middle school—Pemberley, if you heard of it. I found the atmosphere stifling. I wanted more. At Pemberley, with so few people, everyone was stuck in the limelight whether they wanted it or not. All your foibles were projected for everyone else to see; by the end of it, we all grew sick of each other. Is it really that preposterous I wanted to go somewhere where I could live my life exactly as I wanted with nobody leaning over my shoulder to tell me I'm not being a team player?"

"So you wanted to be a big fish in a small pond. I can respect that. Exploiting the lower classes—what did you call them again, Epsilons?—that's something I can respect. You're a good kid, you're one of us."

"I live comfortably, but without privilege. Sure, I have more money than I know what to do with, but that's shared with everyone. I consider myself the leader of a team and not a rogue agent. The difference between you and me, Jack, is that you consider yourself above others. I consider others above myself, and it's my ongoing duty to turn the tables."

"You may have started humbly, if we're to believe how you're telling your story, but that's not at all how you present yourself today. I'm not a student at Heller, I can't verify everything, but I sometimes watch your club meetings. The content is the same as always, but while before you just told everyone they were elite members of society, now it's all the more clear that they really are. If your goal was to truly even out society, to give to each as they deserved, you've failed. But that's fine, don't sweat it." Frank was an enigma to Jack: he was rich, but he didn't act like it, and was magnanimous without being narcissistic. Despite all evidence to the contrary, Jack chose to interpret Frank's attitude as a sign of weakness: Frank had merely gotten lucky in the short-term, but by the time they got to Philadelphia, so much for that.

"I'm still not sure why you're so fixated on what I've done—what have you been up to for the last four years then? As soon as we get on campus, I'm just your good old-fashioned Frank, an ordinary man. I'm not going to be some superhero whose voice can project into every classroom. You know how at the end of *The Wizard of Oz*, behind all the smoke and mirrors there's just a normal person in a world of fantastical, extraordinary people? That's me. Pay no attention to that man behind the curtain. Just let me take my classes, maybe get an internship through no personal merit, and maybe if I see the opportunity I'll become Frank the Ineffable again. Is that a deal?"

"Whether you like it or not, Frank, this is going to haunt you. That's a trade-off I'd take in a heartbeat, but if you think once you graduate, everything will be reset, don't think you'll get off so easily. This may not be a national award or an internship at Goldman Sachs, but the sheer audacity of the transformation you've effected at Heller puts you near the top. We already are calling you 'Supreme Leader,' and that's a compliment. I know you're used to public schools where everyone's a sycophant vying to get into lame schools like Berkeley or UCLA; you'll have more people like you here, people who are willing to be just as despicable as you without bothering to justify it under 'being a good person.' Anyway, this is such depressing talk. Any of you watch the Giants game last night?"

Frank left their meeting consumed with guilt. Frank believed what he had told them—he really was just an ordinary guy who made the most of unusual circumstances. He was no more mature than they, and in fact, maybe he was just immature; a mature person would have ignored the entire club thing, perhaps founded a stricter tutoring club, still made the same friends, and ended up in exactly the same place! If everyone at Wharton was like Jack, standoffish and aggressive, Frank didn't want to go. He'd much rather stay at Heller, or find the next best thing: kids just as smart, but pleasantly diluted. That was the issue with Pemberley, too, and part of why Frank had learned the value of Machiavellian manipulation. All societies relied on having an appropriate mix of leaders and followers: too many leaders and society fractured under the burden of their petty whims, too many followers and they would crumble under inaction and die a slow death. Everyone wanted Frank to be their "Supreme Leader" forever, but hadn't he earned a break?

Pranav, like Ted, had heard of the vast changes his beloved high school had undergone in his absence. Ordinarily, he would have better things to do—unlike Frank, he had chosen Berkeley over a private school, and a few weeks of euphoria had turned abruptly into an overwhelming deluge of work—but one day all his lectures were canceled, and so he took the train all the way back to San Francisco and took an Uber to Heller. Pranav had expected Mao-style murals of all the student council, and was relieved to see nothing but students dressed like clothing store mannequins walking in lockstep wearing colored armbands. "Home sweet home," Pranav muttered to himself. He found Frank standing on the bridge overlooking the swimming pool, not nearly as jovial as he expected.

"There's something about this place that brings people back," Frank said partially to himself and partially to Pranav. "What unfinished business do you have?"

"Why so grim? You've succeeded. I've kept myself apprised of recent developments—Jason gave me admin access to TigerTalk a few weeks ago. What reason do you have to be unhappy, a touch of guilt? Come on, that's not the Frank I know."

"Well, I got into Wharton. That was a downer, believe it or not. They're so entitled, paranoid, and narcissistic, just like unironic good people. And the sad thing is, I fit right in. The entire time, as I tried to defend myself, what we've done, I could feel my moral high ground slipping away as I spoke. There's nothing that makes me better than them besides that I thought I was doing the right thing. I still think I've done the right thing—even I can't deny my own results. I just didn't think there would be such a big price to it."

"Don't let some stuck-up Wharton brats tell you you're one of them now. When you set out here to make the club, you did so believing you'd be able to make some change, right? Leave the school better than you found it. Who says you can't do the same there? You're coming in with a good reputation and a natural knack for convincing others of stupid things. Take this from me, a college student: they aren't any less gullible than high schoolers. They may be wiser, but when has that stopped anyone?"

"Let's put aside those kids for a moment. Look at the people here, the ones walking across from us or already headed home. You know some of these people. Jason, your good friend, he's been embarking on a one-person campaign of vengeance against anyone and everyone. Those security cameras you see everywhere, he sees everything. I don't know how he does it. Watch me as I move my finger on my phone—do you see it moving? And you can look on my phone and see us standing. You could do this from your dorm room if you wanted. But beyond the entire surveillance thing, he's grown kind of scary. I merely thought him a bit too interested in history for his own good, I didn't realize he was a dictator reincarnate."

"Are you blaming him, Frank, for TigerTalk? That's the sort of thing that would get him court-martialed anywhere but Heller."

"I blame him, sure, but I blame myself too. It was an idea born of good intentions: the app we used before was awful, and we technically saved the school money by doing this in-house. But I should have thought of the little guys I thought we would protect, the people in the locker rooms that feel violated because Jason's seen their breasts."

"That's a bold claim."

"I don't know for sure—I don't know anything. But it's a slippery slope from where we stood at the beginning of the year to blackmail, and

we've been sliding down too many others to not consider it a possibility.
I can keep going, if you want. I have a lot to vent about."

Pranav did not know if he was supposed to console Frank or chastise
him. All his critiques of the people and system around him seemed
justified. Jason indeed was prone to outbursts, and it almost made sense
that he was specifically targeting those who wronged him previously. He
can't say that he knew John that well, but "saturnine" seemed an accurate
description, even if not the word he'd ordinarily use; as much as it was
crass to tell people in an authoritarian regime to cheer up, it was also a
bad sign when Beth out of all people was jovial. And at the center of this
tangled web, with strands reaching out toward names that by now were
unfamiliar to Pranav, was Frank. And by extension, himself too; if Pranav
had never been involved, Frank would certainly have managed to cobble
together a similar end result, but it would have had a different flavor and
less popular support. He really was responsible for this, wasn't he?

He chuckled at the brutality of the entire scheme, Tom and Regina being made laughingstocks in front of the entire school being a highlight,
but it certainly was not funny to them. And to most of the apathetic
audience, attitudes must have been mixed. It wasn't as if dissent was
encouraged before, certainly, but it was never punished—novel suggestions tended to rest in teacher's mailboxes and get lost in filing cabinets,
and that benign neglect was just what made high school high school. He
knew a few of his old classmates were secretly counting their blessings
after the school metamorphosed into tyranny, as things like the dress
code tested the limits of how much apathy was sufficient to numb the
high school experience. When Pranav ran into Mr. Ivanov earlier during
a passing period, he let out a resigned huff and said "It's an absolute
s—show. But I can't say that anymore, so I'll say it's a pile of steaming
hot cellulose. Yeah...". Pranav thought that was an inappropriate time to
admit his own complicity in the scheme. Not everything seemed bad,
even according to Mr. Ivanov, who admitted that test scores were up, the

school was cleaner, and more of his colleagues seemed to be enjoying themselves at work. But was this the school he'd have wanted to attend? If it weren't partially his idea, Pranav didn't think so, and perhaps Frank agreed. He asked to confirm: "So, if you were an incoming freshman this year, is this the high school experience you wish you had?"

Frank crossed his arms and stood still for a moment, then resignedly admitted, "As a leader, I could be sold on this. As a follower, I'd pass. But I really can't say. I would say that all through these three-and-a-half years, things have worked out for me one after another. No particular hardships that weren't of my own design. So I don't really want to dwell on some misfortune that could have happened. Don't forget what happened to the man who got everything he ever wanted: he lived happily ever after."

"Somehow, I have to agree: there's something oddly poetic about this ending. It's satisfying. But I thought you felt guilty about this entire thing? If you're going to be dogmatic, you should at least be consistent."

"When I say everything out loud, the more I'm convinced that this guilt is what everyone feels after making any sort of controversial decision. It's too easy to focus on the negatives when that's what everyone lingers on. But just a few days ago, we had homecoming; everyone survived that. Nobody rioted. That's the hard part of being a leader I think we were fortunate to have ignored while you were here: what's right or wrong isn't solely dependent on popular opinion. Besides, and I remember we discussed this when you interviewed me, I really have no choice by now. I can't stop now. I can't announce that everything was a joke, confess to everything, and politely let myself be led away in handcuffs. They'd kill me, for one. And too many people benefit from this scheme to let the power transfer peacefully back to the rightful owners."

"Are other schools going to adopt this scheme too? I know there have been a few gatherings at other schools, but I always assumed they were just weird kids."

"We're all crazy. But yes, the superintendent was quite amused to hear about everything going on here. Ask me that question again in a year or two. That's another reason—would you rather have students manning the security cameras, who can be held accountable enough through peer pressure and good old-fashioned violence, or adults simply following orders for a paycheck? I may not be able to claim the moral high ground compared to Jack from Wharton, but I think I can claim it compared to Mr. Kurtz. And that's what lets me sleep at night."

Pranav checked his watch. "Show me around a little. Do you have some secret lair under the swimming pool?"

"Mr. T should still be around. He's always up for a chat."

Chapter 37

Behrooz knew something was wrong when Tom didn't invite him to his birthday party. Tom paid well—this was a lot of money he was missing out on, and Behrooz certainly wasn't a recipient of the slush fund Alan still spent hours every night cultivating. He had sent a DM on Snapchat just to make sure; Tom opened it, but Behrooz received no response. Perhaps that was some sort of glitch in the software; he tried again through Instagram, with the same result. He even went as far as to send an email, still with nothing.

"Is Tom ghosting you too?" Alan asked knowingly. "He blocked me as well. What a loser."

"Don't call him a loser, I'm sure he's just working through some hard feelings. All of them are."

"All of them?"

"The longer this goes on, the more all my friends hate me. Maybe they weren't ever truly my friends. They say nasty things behind my back and get angry when I don't sympathize with them. Now I know how you feel."

"Hey! I have friends. They're just busy. Or forgetful. Who needs friends when you have a mission like this? It's enough to put some fire in your belly. Everyone needs to make sacrifices."

"You're in denial, Alan. We're all losers here. Frank and Juliet are robbing us blind and making out like bandits, while all we do is clean up their messes. It's not fair."

"I wouldn't go as far as to call it robbery: the fault lies with us for not being sufficiently disciplined studies at the club. No wonder why they don't trust us."

"Call me anti-intellectual, but I don't see why anyone would go to the club if they weren't jockeying to replace Frank once he graduates. But I suppose I can see some positives in this. Are you going on the charity walk tomorrow?" Behrooz rarely volunteered before he joined the student council, but he was starting to like the feeling. It felt good to use his position to help others in ways that did not require a manifesto to understand—it was certainly cliché, he thought, but he knew that one must be the change they wish to see in the world. If anything, when his parents asked him what he did in school that day, he could tell them something they'd be proud of.

Louis had asked him at a party once after Behrooz expressed his distaste for Alan's actions if he was part of the resistance, working to dismantle the club from within. At the very first meeting with Ms. Foster, that night Behrooz had assumed that would be his role. But as it became very clear that nobody else would be afflicted with any pangs of conscience, and that most in the school were happy to live their lives as they always had, fighting would be pointless. Ms. Foster had already told him not to be a sore loser the other day when he was the sole person to argue that maybe it was kind of mean to make Epsilons serve as custodial staff late at night. So at this point, once again, Behrooz had no choice. He did not think it was the right thing to idly stand by as the triumvirate did its thing. But it was also not the right thing to stonewall three people who, to varying degrees, had their own definition of the right thing. It was senior year anyway. Life would go on. He was supposed to relax, chill, and enjoy his time as ruler of the roost.

"What charity walk?" Alan was not told about this—was this proof that Behrooz didn't lie, that he was really being stabbed in the back? "We have plenty of money of our own, why don't we spend that instead?"

"Legal something something, or maybe that's another of Frank's lies. We're raising money for funding underprivileged elementary schools. They need glue and pencils and all the things we take for granted now; I'm sure they don't get French toast for brunch. We hope even the most cold-hearted of people can be persuaded to save the children."

"Nah, I'm not spending my Saturday doing that. Who else is going?"

"John and Beth. They've been surprisingly good friends, at least as far as I can tell, and you know how both of them are a bit strange. I guess this beats a candlelit dinner or something involving sun. We have clouds projected, clouds everywhere. What a great day for my morning constitutional, right?"

"John's cool. I respect him. Have fun."

The three of them assembled by Behrooz's house a few hours after the sun had crested the horizon, through the clouds shading everything in light gray.

"You have a nice house, Behrooz. Is that a Ferrari?" John asked with curiosity, leaning over to feel the car in case it proved to be a mirage.

"It's nothing much, and I certainly can't drive it. You have no idea how many hours of work my dad put into fixing that thing up. It was destined for the dump, and look at it now."

"My car feels inadequate now. Let's go—these pledges don't sign themselves." Behrooz lived in a neighborhood that made Heller's look like a dump. They walked up and down ridges and hills, grotesque gardens with topiaries and faux Tuscan facades, looming modern monstrosities with sharp angles and glass walls revealing fireplaces and curved plastic furniture. One house at a time, they navigated past garden gates past fountains to doors with smart doorbells and brass, leonine doorknobs; a few knocks, someone in slippers turned up at the door, complimented their outfits, and pledged a few hundred. John had never seen peacocks walking on lawns silvered with dew or butterflies flying in cages before outside of zoos, and only a lingering instinct of self-preservation enabled him to dodge nimbly when one of those aforementioned peacocks tried pecking at his leg.

There were normal houses too, without gaudy topiaries or sculptures or fountains, normal houses with yards John recognized as being like his own; the three of them were astonished to knock on one of these houses' doors and see Mr. T behind the threshold, his wife visible in the kitchen.

"This must be the charity drive Ms. Foster was mentioning earlier. Care to come in? Breakfast is almost ready and the scones won't eat themselves. It's cold out there, charity can wait."

"Thank you," John said with a thin smile, and they made their way to the dining room.

"Welcome to my Xanadu," Mr. T announced as he sat down and offered them coffee. "This is the first time I can think we've had such a coordinated fundraising effort. It's impressive what a bit of elbow grease can do."

"I think it's all smoke and mirrors, if I say so myself. I'm the only student council member here, but I can say with certainty we've been robbed and cheated. Each and everyone of us cannot think that just because we may be raising money for a good cause, that we do not all share in a moral burden. It's an absolute travesty," Behrooz explained.

"I don't remember you sounding this academic," Beth teased. "I think it's tempting to say 'how did we let this happen?', and I'm just speaking for myself here, but this has been pretty nice for me. I've been able to maintain my friendships without any great sacrifices, I've even started logging some volunteer hours with the Epsilons entirely of my own volition. I think it's humbling to do community service; it's one thing to tell others to do it, but it's one thing to lower yourself and serve others with pure benevolence."

"You've always been like this, Beth, for as long as I've known you. Your personality matches this far better than mine. I've been forced to change, to pretend to be someone I'm not—apathetic, shallow, calculating, emotionless. That really takes a toll on you, you know, when you wake up every morning dreading the punishments you'll have to inflict on others who don't deserve it at all. I'd rather be myself. Myself and nasty. Not somebody else, however jolly."

"How come every conversation needs to circle back to the club?" John asked. "We have lives, you know. I hope all of us have lives outside of school, private passions and hobbies, relationships not defined by who's appropriate given our social credit score. I think it's all very childish to keep running around in circles about something we're in no position to change. We're making a difference, none of the people involved are monsters, that's the end of it."

"That's not true at all," Behrooz insisted. "I care about my classmates. We're all in this together, and all that jazz. When Frank reminds us all privately to 'be careful' about which lower-class people we message, like they're going to infect us with some disease, I'm just supposed to shrug my shoulders and accept it?"

Mr. T looked up from his coffee mug and decided to join in: "You give him credit for too much cleverness. Everyone loves talking about Frank—it's hard not to. What Frank said in his speech, what Frank didn't say in his speech, yada yada yada. But I'd like to think of Frank as the product of an abusive system, an inevitable product. He's no monster. He's just a smart kid who leans a bit capitalist. He didn't have to be this charitable, but things are working out nicely."

"Exactly. You weren't there, Behrooz, but Beth and I were at the lake with him. He cooked every single meal. If I only knew him from that, I would think he's one of the nicest people I've ever met. So when I see what the school is like now, and his club meetings, and everything else, I only see charity. I see the person who had Pranav tutor me when I was struggling, who worked with me on math homework one time before school, who did all these other great things. How could anyone hate him? People have too much free time to think about others instead of themselves."

"I think this proves the importance of separating the deeds from the person. I'll spare you the origin story of *How To Be A Good Person*, or how I remember it, but he came to me one day asking for help in taking full advantage of his surprising new popularity. He expected everything to blow over in a few periods, but somehow the idea struck him that maybe, by some statistical fluke, he had struck gold. Now, his normal altruistic, kind, prankster self would not suffice. He needed to be a leader, charismatic in a loud way, boisterous and domineering and everything a good person is and Frank is not. So he invented just the sort of Franklin Barnes that a fourteen year old boy would be likely to invent, and to this conception he was faithful to the end," Mr. T mused. "Does that make sense? So if you're trying to look back at what's happened and tell everyone else what they need to know, it isn't enough to tell what a man did. You've got to tell them who he is."

"I think we've talked enough about Frank. So, Mr. T. Who are you then? What's led you to this point in your life?" Beth looked at Mr. T with expectant eyes, and the others followed.

Mr. T cleared his throat and took another sip of coffee. "I went to a small private university in Boston that some of you may have heard of—'pahk the cah in Hahvahd Yahd' and all that. That took me into finance and doing a bit of globetrotting. I ended up in Hong Kong, then Beijing, then Moscow, then Zurich, and so on, picking up a little of everything along the way, and eventually I ended up in New York. Things were going great; I met my lovely wife, I worked hard daily, but there was something missing at the end of the day. That human touch. I felt like I was the only sane man in a group of mobsters. So I came back to where I grew up, here in California, got my teaching credential, and I realized this is where I belonged. This is my second career—working for McKinsey paid the bills, it's not like I needed to do this to retire quite comfortably—but that's not all life is. You can't live every day just looking to pay the bills, because that's not life, that's drudgery."

"Do you believe power corrupts, Mr. T? When I imagine New York, I imagine people on Wall Street, looking just like we do but a bit older, all going through the motions and plotting how to stiff the common man. Were they always that heartless, or is it something you learned on the job?"

"You sound like a communist," John joked.

"Forgive me for bringing the discussion back to the school, but I think the comparison is quite close, and none of you were ever on Wall Street and I'd honestly prefer not to dwell too much on the past. I really don't think power corrupts. It just reveals what was inside all along; every man is as Heaven made him, and sometimes a great deal worse. Could you pass the butter? But anyway," Mr. T said as he lathered his scone with butter and blueberry jam, "the fact that you came to my doorstep canvassing for a charity event, run by this very same student council that implemented a dress code and finally put ad-blockers on the Chromebooks, should answer your question. We are trained to view the world through the lens of good and evil, but in between exist many shades of gray. I hope I've taught some people that lesson in English class."

"You said this was your second career. Do you plan on retiring? I can't imagine the things you've seen, you ought to write a novel," John remarked.

"Sometime, that will come to pass. I haven't thought about how I'm planning on leaving Heller. It certainly won't be a hastily written resignation letter and a middle finger walking out the door. Something simple, I think. 'Rosebud.' Yeah, that seems like a fitting end to all this. Have you seen that rosebush by the robotics room, the one that finally started blooming a few years ago? I planted that with my AP Environmental Science kids, one of the first years I was at Heller. In a way, we all leave our legacies. I wonder what mine will be."

Despite Frank's penchant for delegation and optimization, as fitting Ms. Foster's original warning, the drama department functioned largely the same as before, thus he served his usual duty as "head usher" along with a new cast of unfamiliar faces for Heller's first production of *The Producers*.

"If your goal over the last few years was just to make this happen, you've succeeded," Mr. Cathcart had joked a few months prior when rehearsals began. "I'd personally have gone to see the show in San Francisco instead of creating a cult of personality, but I suppose this works too. Do you want a role in the show?"

"I think I already have a role: quell any rioting in the theater. You should get one of the parents to storm out complaining about bad taste. Like the movie, you know. Or actually, I'm a poor singer, but I can lip-sync; Mel Brooks would be honored for me to use his voice—'Don't be stupid, be a smartie; come and join the Nazi party!' Hilarious, I know, right?"

"Sounds like a plan." Frank stood in his usual post, escorting people to their seats and directing any bemused inquiries to Mr. Cathcart. It felt good not to be his own boss, and less good to have to report to Mr. Liebkind, who couldn't stop gushing about how nice it was that Adrian was getting his place in the spotlight at last—this was apparently the perfect show for him, and as expected Mr. Liebkind didn't credit Frank one bit.

John and Beth had decided to see the show as a pair, if only to test out the idea of being a couple that wasn't just a couple of good friends. They had tried lunch that afternoon, with mixed results: the restaurant they wanted to go to was closed due to a burst water pipe, which forced them to go to the Japanese supermarket and walk downtown, sitting at the bench Beth recognized as where she always went with her friends. She immediately amended that statement—John was her friend, too.

"Do you remember how freshman year, we all sat together to watch the musical that was playing then? We planned that out on this very bench. No, it wasn't coincidence."

"What was the point of doing that? I never quite understood."

"Well, Regina was trying to work up the courage to ask you out, so she wanted to test the waters in a safer way. I'm surprised she never told you about that—you really thought you happened to get a free ticket that put you with us?"

"I don't believe in coincidences. Things happen for a reason, like that restaurant being closed; it brought us here, retracing the same steps you made. That had to have had a reason behind it. I remember asking Frank about my ticket, I thought there must have been some sort of mistake! All he said to me was 'today's your lucky day.' Luck, that's all there was to it, and that's what I thought all this time."

"I knew he was a romantic!" Beth shouted with glee. That experience brought them back to the show, where John was consumed in guffaws of laughter rather than pilgrimages to the Spanish countrysice. If John and Beth weren't staring at the stage slack-jawed at the girl dressed as a pretzel sashaying down the steps, they'd have noticed Frank standing in the back mouthing along to the lyrics before he disappeared to the side; they barely noticed when Frank showed up on stage, delivered his one line, and only a minute later returned to the back like nothing had ever happened. John and Beth walked out of the theater and back to their cars holding hands.

Over winter break, an email from one of the school counselors gave John the idea to write a letter to the editor of the local newspaper. Many other students had done it from other schools, writing passionately about the need for community service or career educatior or social justice or any of a myriad of things that did not interest John in the slightest. Nowhere in any of those asinine epistles did anyone represent him! That was a problem easily solved, with an obvious solution.

A few weeks prior, after Tom had read the local theater critic's positive review of *The Producers*, he realized that some negativity was needed. How could he write about the accurate casting choices or set design but not mention the dictatorship that had spawned the entire endeavor? Why was he writing about fake Nazis instead of the real ones around them? Tom sent a long, rambling email to one of the editors, including excerpts from official announcements, pictures, and even quotes from Heller's own newspaper with the singular goal of tarring and feathering his own beloved school. Surely the oil well of community outrage Tom was tapping into would burst, spreading foul ichor all over the land. Tom waited a few weeks with no response other than a perfunctory "Thank you." His father barged into his room one night commanding him to read the newspaper—they had dedicated four whole pages to Heller! They had interviewed the principal, teachers, Frank, and even the superintendent, all of whom had nothing but positive things to say about the system. Mr. Langley couldn't care about them in the slightest, but they had reached out to interview him; Mr. Langley didn't really know much of what was going on at the school besides that his son was punished for being a spoiled brat. Any other parent would demand an apology for the indignity, but to him this seemed like the sort of discipline that built character, so Mr. Langley too had said only nice things.

John had read that report because they had spent a club meeting discussing it, but he found it lacking in the sort of emotional, visceral reaction that to John made good reading. In those four pages, where did it say anything but that "Heller was destined for success" and "In this troubled age, might does indeed make right"? He spent a cold winter's morning wrapped up in a blanket and drinking hot peppermint-flavored coffee (a concession to the season), trying to anticipate all possible critiques to what one semester of tyranny had promised:

Dear Editors,

Not too long ago, I had the pleasure of reading your detailed report on my beloved school. Tears welled up in my eyes, and I felt a hitherto-unknown pride in my own school. I've walked its hallways for nearly four years at this point, and I never realized that everyone felt the same way as I did. To any member of the community reading this thinking "why isn't my child's school like Heller? This isn't fair," I offer you some words of warning.

If your child believes that their clothes define them, that memories are woven in their fabric, it is best for them to abandon that idea. I did not know how to tie a tie before I had to every day—your child should practice now. I barely knew the words to our own national anthem, and I only thought of it as something people sang at the Super Bowl. I hope your child is more of a patriot than I am, and if they are not, they may have some nasty words to say about school. If your child cusses like a sailor, peppering their speech incessantly with profanities, they will need to speak softly and choose their words with candor. We live in a world where words persuade; they hold magic, draw breath—they live! Most of all, that is what I must warn them: they will have a voice, and every action they make, any utterance no matter how profane, will grow to define them.

Before my school underwent its beautiful metamorphosis, my existence bordered on the tragic. I was always timid, I never took a chance. I was like a butterfly flitting about, never knowing if I were in a waking dream or cruel reality. Then, as I felt the swell of change deep in my heart, it began to dance. Frank (our leader), and Heller as a whole, filled up my empty life, they filled it to the brim. There will never, ever, be anything or anyone else like him.

Someday you may be called to vote on whether you want your school to be like Heller. Perhaps we are the black sheep of our community, as some naysayers claim. I think differently: I believe we are the vanguards of a brighter future, one which releases students to the world capable of thinking about others and capable of thinking about themselves. Students who do not shy away from discipline, and who meet the pressures of society with something equal coming from within! Students, who like myself, are able to spend hours in self-reflection, putting words together in long meaningless strings until eventually, they have meaning.

Sincerely,

John Zakarian

"Your last name is Zakarian? Like Geoffrey Zakarian?" Frank asked in disbelief, pointing to John's typed signature on the paper, which Frank had even circled as if to verify that it wasn't a trick of the eye.

"How do you know my uncle?"

"When we watched *Chopped* at the lake, you never thought to mention that the guy on TV was family? Cooking's in your blood, John, no wonder why you're so good at it! Do you think he could take over the catering for winter formal?"

"It's winter formal already? Ugh, it's only been three months. I suppose I'll have to ask Beth again and whatever. Such a hassle."

"It's obligation, John. Someday you'll look back on all of this and think 'Where did I go right?' You won't be thinking of the hassle of driving over to Beth's house, picking her up, taking pictures somewhere scenic before sunset, dancing the night away. You'll be thinking of the good parts, whatever those may be for you."

"I haven't even been to her house yet. Or, I haven't driven there myself; it's always been in the van with the others. I wonder what it's like."

"While you do that, I'm going to be booking the catering and doing exactly what I did those long, weary three months ago. Have fun."

Ms. Foster had vetoed Jason's theme suggestion of "A Night In Siberia" despite his promises of ice sculptures, caviar, vodka, and communism. A committee was hastily formed, consisting of everyone who happened to be in the room, and they settled upon the unoriginal, if consistently crowd-pleasing "A Night In Paris."

"Paris is romantic, I promise," Ms. Foster assured Jason. "I went on my honeymoon there. Far better than eating, I don't know, smoked trout on pumpernickel or whatever it was you suggested."

"Why did Jason even get a vote?" Alan protested. "He's not even in leadership."

"We live in a democracy, Alan; everyone gets a vote, everyone has a share," Ms. Foster reassured him. "I'll tell Frank about this later, but he's agreeable enough. He won't mind."

John sat down on a barstool watching the TV play recorded webcam footage from the Champs-Elysées, delicately prying mussels open with a fork and swallowing each in a few bites.

"The food's good, don't you agree? It's been so long since I've had good seafood," Beth asked him, leaning over to steal a French fry.

"I don't even know if I've had mussels before. I like the broth though, and what was the name of this again? Moules frites?"

"Yeah, that's right," Frank interrupted, giving an approving nod when he saw John was eating everything. "This is actually a Belgian dish, but it seemed close enough. Believe it or not, this is your uncle's recipe, straight from the Food Network website. He suggested the French fry recipe too when I sent him a message on Instagram; he knows what high school you're attending, and read your letter to the editor, but you didn't even mention anything at all before? That still boggles the mind. I guess while I'm here, I've been asking everyone this: where are you hoping you'll go to college?"

"I haven't really thought about it much," John admitted. "Wherever I'll go, I'll find something to be happy about."

"Really, anywhere you could go?"

"Well, if I could pick the perfect college: I would want to live on an island isolated from society. Society's too depressing, it dampens the mind. All of us would be philosophers, who spend all their time reading and debating."

"Sounds like the club," Beth laughed.

"Not quite. In this paradise, we wouldn't be continuously plotting how to overthrow the patriarchy or whoever else happened to be in charge. We'd be beyond such trivial things as that. Everyone would know their place, and we'd know happiness without anything else."

"*In Xanadu did Kubla Khan / A stately pleasure-dome decree: / Where Alph, the sacred river, ran / Through caverns measureless to man / Down to a sunless sea,*" Frank said spontaneously. "Legend has it that the words to that poem came up in a dream, describing a place so lovely that no mortal mind could imagine it with conscious thought; when he woke, he wrote and wrote until someone interrupted him, and in an instant, what else remained of the poem disappeared. We'll never know exactly what Coleridge imagined his Xanadu to look like."

"So how does that relate to this?"

"I think your island is just as mythical as this Xanadu. I don't mean to distract you or anything. Those mussels won't eat themselves. Oh, what about you, Beth?"

"Any college sounds good to me, Frank. I'll find my way."

Juliet found Frank about an hour later, after the webcam footage had already cycled through a few times, also eating a bowl of mussels.

"Who did you use for the catering? These look expensive," Juliet commented, doing as Beth did and stealing a French fry, although less covertly.

"The culinary arts teacher wanted her students to get some real-world experience, so we're using them instead. You can go look in the kitchen if you want; you'll see her in chef's whites teaching her students how to take orders and not drink the wine when she isn't looking. Have you eaten yet? I heard the scallops are good."

"Haven't you thought about how strange it is that a high school could end up this functional? You're right—these scallops are delicious! It's all thanks to you, and that leads me to another question. I overheard Ms. Liu the other day discussing with the other English teachers how she was going to add *How To Be A Good Person* to her class curriculum, and at first I was like, 'Wow, that's great!' But then I kept listening, and she said something about teaching students to identify satire and analyze it critically."

"Yeah, she cleared that with me, don't worry. I helped her with the lesson plan—I think it's great, actually, that we'll be educating the next generation of leaders."

"So you're missing my point here, *How To Be A Good Person* was a work of satire? We've been misled the entire time?"

"Well, I wouldn't say 'we' here. There's a value to using humor to blunt messages, that's what court jesters did all the time! *A Modest Proposal* carries a message, and we can recognize that Jonathan Swift wasn't telling us to eat babies. Look beyond the text of *How To Be A Good Person* and think instead about all the philosophy we've read; do you think we'd be able to get people to think critically about themselves and others, dare I say even be nice to them, without disguising the message a little? A spoonful of sugar makes the medicine go down. Let's use another example, the caste system: sure, at first, everyone was being a bit sarcastic and biting and haggling over exactly who was boss, but look at us now. People judge each other for the quality of their ideas now, not the color of their skin, and if someone of ill renown truly desires to become a better person, he is able to do that and is rewarded without judgment. I would like to think we are moving toward a functional society, slowly but surely. I couldn't exactly say everything outright without undermining the purpose of the entire thing. I'm sorry, Juliet, if I misled you into thinking I was ever ill-intentioned."

"I believe you, as always. Maybe this makes me the bad person here, but I don't mind being a little evil. Everything we're doing is quite palatable, with or without a guiding purpose. In fact, I think you're more fun when you're evil. I hope you have not been leading a double life, pretending to be wicked and being really good all the time. That would be hypocrisy." Juliet looked straight into Frank's eyes, showing all indications of being honest, and Frank did not know if he was supposed to lie again. Even he couldn't keep track of exactly whether he was supposed to be good or evil.

"Everything in life is relative, good and evil too. Our scheme here has transcended morality, anyway, and all I can say for sure is that if we were bad people, we wouldn't be rewarded with fine music and divine food. I think the universe is telling us that everything's all right just the way it is."

"To evil!" Juliet exclaimed, raising her glass. Frank clinked it and gulped down his ice water.

"To evil," he sighed, and went back to eating mussels.

Chapter 38

J ohn entered Ms. Liu's classroom like any normal day: he waved hello, tried to remember which desk he was supposed to sit at, sat down, waited for Ms. Liu to remind him that wasn't his desk, moved to the right desk, and stared into space. Today, something felt different:

"Ms. Liu, I've noticed that Harry's been absent for a few weeks now. Is everything allright? Is he ill?"

"Oh, no, nothing of the sort. His grades were so good last semester that he transferred out of the class—he didn't need your help anymore. You succeeded. Yay!"

"How often do people graduate out of this program? I hope frequently."

"Very few, if I'm being honest with you. This year we've had more than usual, but it's rare people don't need a guiding touch through all four years. That's why we're so lucky to have tutors like you and Regina who are able to make a difference. When you graduate, don't forget that you've made someone's future better."

"I always try to look out for the little guy," John admitted. "At the end of the day, when I'm wandering through the cosmos, I'll survive. If others can't say the same, well, that's my duty. That's what a good person does."

"Harry did mention that he attended the club meetings; do you think that was it, John? Maybe that's why..." Ms. Liu trailed off, staring at the club poster taped in the back of her room with a new sense of understanding.

"The other day when we had brunch with Mr. T, he quoted *Don Quixote*, something I really appreciated: 'every man is as Heaven made him, and sometimes a great deal worse.' But why can't the tables be turned there? We live in the 21st century, there's nothing stopping a wee bit of upward mobility, don't you think? Ultimately, I think teaching is about revealing that inner essence—the power that was within everyone all along." Regina had silently snuck in during John's monologue, and had taken her seat—unlike John, she always knew where to sit.

"I think that's the purpose of everything in high school, John; it's the definition of personal growth, and it doesn't matter where exactly that push comes from. There are some people who are easily impressionable, who soak up the world like a sponge and live all of eternity as a muddled mess of ideologies and virtues. If you want to talk of Heaven, maybe that's what all of us need here, a bit of Jesus to give us something to focus on," Regina offered; she was not religious herself, but had come to the realization over the previous few years that maybe it would be good for her. She considered herself adventurous enough, and whenever she felt like the club was a bit cultish, it seemed a tempting counterbalance.

"When I look up, I see people cashing in. I don't see heaven, or saints or angels. I see people cashing in on every decent impulse and human tragedy. I see sharks chasing minnows and cats chasing mice. I see all my classmates selling their souls to the highest bidder just to line their pockets. Heaven's a lie, if that's what we've been promised. It's not here, wherever it is."

"That's a cheerful sentiment," Regina laughed. "I choose to be more optimistic: I couldn't have done high school without my friends. I don't believe they're all out to screw me. Nobody's selling their soul here."

"In a world full of crooks and conmen, the one person you can trust is yourself. I'm not a crook. You aren't either. But we can't say the same for everyone, right? That's just how life works."

"I don't know what I would have done without my friends. You can always sit around and meditate on your own worries, but when that isn't enough, what can you do?"

"I'm only speaking for myself, of course, but I think over time, I learned to compartmentalize my anxieties. I think back to freshman and sophomore year, and I cringe—it's absolutely shameful how many mistakes I made! But then I think more rationally: I am the only person who remembers these experiences in the same way, if at all. Even if I cringe, I have an important duty here: to protect what would otherwise be forgotten."

"That sounds quite noble of you John, but did this really make you any happier?"

"It did, because I am being truthful and honest, and doing so makes me happy. Some memories make me sad, but that other happiness outweighs it. I remember when we saw *Man of La Mancha*, I don't want to say together, but I guess we kind of did—in a way, the impossible dream speaks true to all of us. We all have our own moral compass, and although we may not always agree, I think we all think we run where the brave do not go to reach that unreachable star."

"Friendships generally arise as a result of that shared moral compass though. We say opposites attract, but if you look hard enough, you can always find those common attitudes that are responsible for shared attraction. And I can say confidently that there are some people here who I believe have different values than I do, and because of that we never became friends."

"Would you say you and Tom are opposites attracting then? I'm no good judge of character, but I'm curious what you think you share."

"John, oh darling John, always asking the tough questions. As much as it pains me to say it, I find what I think are my worst qualities reflected in Tom, even though I didn't realize it first. But I still love him, and he loves me. He may be a bit of a narcissist, but we all are, and I've come to discover that with that self-assuredness comes outspokenness for what he thinks is right. That's his moral compass, and all of the school and so I'm told, about 5000 people on Reddit, saw that as clear as day. And I'm all the better person because of him."

"So he's no saint then."

"None of us are," Ms. Liu interceded, and she rang the bell to begin class.

During his leadership period, Frank delicately gave his portfolio of daily work to Alan and made the pilgrimage to the theater, saluting his peers he saw and trying not to slip on the damp concrete steps; the back gate was unlocked, as usual, and he knocked on Mr. Cathcart's door. Mr. Cathcart quickly exited out of his Minesweeper game before he noticed it was Frank and not Ms. Wolfe.

"How nice to see you again! What brings you into my lair?"

"I'm here to obtain your blessing," Frank said.

"For what?"

"I didn't think of this during the show and I'm kicking myself for it, but I'd like to buy a seat plaque. Or install it myself, whichever is fastest."

"Well, it's not like you need my permission; this isn't my theater, and if you decided you wanted to repaint the walls or something, it's not my call. But yeah, I can certainly arrange that. Did you have a message in mind? Is this in honor of yourself, or someone who's passed, or..."

"I was thinking something simpler. 'To The Ushers.' I don't know, maybe a bit too self-indulgent, but—"

"That's touching. For all the ways you've changed the school, you think of your most humble position first," Mr. Cathcart remarked while delicately rubbing his chin and re-opening his Minesweeper game.

"People have asked me before how I want to be remembered, especially as it's increasingly likely at this point next year will be like this one. I don't want to be remembered with a sculpture; I don't even want to be remembered by name. Ultimately, without everyone else here, I wouldn't have been able to become who I am, and I think that anyone with the same surrounding conditions would do the same."

"Without everyone enabling you here, you mean."

"No, not that. Even before I held my first meeting, simply by virtue of writing what's effectively an extended newspaper editorial I accumulated a throng of followers who would have shown up and stayed regardless of how I spoke. I would be a guru, and they would collect my words like falling lotus petals. Suppose I hadn't put my name on *How To Be A Good Person*, but instead given it to Jason to use as he saw fit; he would still have accumulated a following, different in its own way but still a following, and if he had made a club he'd be president by now too. There's nothing mystical about any of this besides human nature."

"While you're here, Frank, what should we do for next year's musical? People loved *The Producers*, but that's the sort of show that becomes only deeply ironic when you have this surrounding societal context. And since you seem like you're down-to-earth, give me your best shot."

Frank looked around at the old theatrical posters on Mr. Cathcart's wall for inspiration, all of which beckoned toward simpler times and eliminated a lot of his first choices. "Well, I don't know... given how much I know these shows have the power to influence young minds, I don't know what the first class to not know me should get as their first impression. How about *Joseph and the Amazing Technicolor Dreamcoat*? I remember I saw that once when I was but a wee young lad."

"Your wish is my command," Mr. Cathcart declared. Frank waved a quick farewell, and he took the long way out of the theater, walking through the house and its rows of identical, darkened seats. Frank found the seat closest to the door, where he often sat to stay out of view. It was separated from the others in its row by an empty space, where anyone with a wheelchair could position themselves as if they were sitting down anywhere else; nobody in their right mind would ever willingly choose to sit here if they paid for their own ticket, but perhaps, Frank thought, one of his brothers-in-arms would sit in that seat, notice the plaque, and smile.

In his zeal to distinguish himself from Behrooz, thinking that Frank and Juliet would otherwise not give him the attention he deserved, Alan had accidentally volunteered to be the head of the dance commission. Alan had initially told himself that his outsider's perspective would be valuable, but his attention span waned when he was asked to pick color schemes for winter formal besides "I don't know, what's the French flag again, American colors?"; now, a far more monumental task lay ahead of him: picking the prom theme. This was, by tradition, the sole responsibilities of seniors, and so Alan's committee looked at him sheepishly when he insisted they do the hard work for him. This proving impossible, he then created a ballot and gave one to every senior, voting mandatory under pain of demotion.

"Isn't this a waste of paper?" Frank had asked him after watching Alan struggle to carry reams of printer paper into Ms. Foster's room.

"Relax, trees are renewable resources. Besides, it's democracy. What were you thinking as a theme?"

"Seeing one of the posters in Mr. Cathcart's office reminded me: maybe five to ten years ago, they did a Gatsby-themed prom. Some may say you can't repeat the past, but why of course you can!"

"You're a genius!" Alan declared. "I hope the ballots agree with you."

"It doesn't need to be that literary, just that old-timey, gin and cigars without real gin and cigars, vibe. You'll see what I mean. Carry on, Alan, with your merciless campaign against our ecosystems."

When the ballots arrived, Alan insisted on counting them one-by-one, despite Ms. Foster's insistence that Alan was really making a fool of himself.

"You don't understand, Ms. Foster, this is our democracy at stake!" Alan explained, his fingers stained with ink. "If we can't get this right, there's no hope for us." Ms. Foster sighed and walked away. Alan spent about half an hour counting before he grew increasingly uncertain in his own abilities to do math; his tally marks had begun to take a life of their own, some sets of five turning into wavy scribbles. Alan looked around to make sure that Ms. Foster couldn't see his own weakness and dumped all the remaining ballots into a paper shredder, thus declaring premature victory for "A Night With Gatsby." Democracy was still undoubtedly important to Alan: he lived every day under the mistaken assumption that his actions were justified by popular support. But Alan knew what defeat meant, too, by that logic: if something, some undefinable force existing outside of the four dimensions, were to overturn Frank's demands, that would be the toppling of the first domino that took down everything Alan had ever dreamed of. He sent an email cryptically titled "You've won" with no further content to Frank, who read it, shrugged, and deleted it.

A brief spark of humanity wormed its way into John's mind one early winter morning, when the sun's first rays crept over the fence, through his window, and melted his heart. He and Beth had been Snapchatting for some time, John mainly attracted by the extensive arrays of emoji and the promise of immediate gratification when Beth happened to read his messages instantly.

"Hey friend, brunch today? Waterfront Pavilion?" he typed out, his hands still stiff.

"Yes, friend," Beth responded after a few minutes of tense anticipation. John would have screamed in delight, but he knew his parents would get mad if he woke them up. While his dad drank coffee at the dining room table and typed angrily on his laptop, John waved adieu and promised he'd be back "whenever."

Beth was already standing by the fountain, wrapped up in a scarf and mittens, when John aimlessly wandered past her; she said his name once with no response, and the second time made John stop in his tracks.

"I'm not used to seeing you dressed casually," John admitted, looking over Beth's face to make sure it was really her.

"When was the last time I saw you in sweatpants? It must have been August or September. I'm freezing. Let's go eat. Have you had dim sum before?"

"Huh?"

"You know, all those little buns and everything? Why else did you suggest this place?"

"Oh, yeah..." While Beth took the lead, John took a moment to throw a penny into the fountain, watching it settle among an even coating of other loose change, making the water shimmer.

"What did you wish for?" Beth asked.

"You'll find out."

"I've been on many dates with a lot of my classmates, and this has been my favorite," Beth said as she tucked into another shrimp dumpling.

"That sounds really weird coming from someone the same age that I am," John remarked, continuing after pointing out a pair of cute ducks outside, "It's impressive how despite our high school experiences having such different trajectories, ours both converged to this moment. Looking out over the water, drinking tea, being content."

"We still have a few months left, but you're right. I feel so wise right now. Let's see... What is past is prologue; what is future is epilogue."

"You sound wise, indeed—what do you mean?"

"For the last three years, our lives have been converging to this moment. We may have many more of these moments in the future, or something more exciting—maybe we'll discover this is all a hologram made by Alan and Jason in their robotics club—but whatever that is, it's hazy and undefinable. I'm not a math person, so I can't precisely estimate the probability of anything. There are so many possibilities out there, and I don't know which ones will lead to us drinking tea like this again. Any action I make now or in the future will lead to a slightly different timeline, or maybe not. I could throw this teapot out the window, and maybe that's the gesture that leads me on the road to prison, or maybe because of it I'd become a millionaire."

"When you phrase it that way, it certainly becomes overwhelming. I'd be even more crippled with anxiety than I would be otherwise had I known that every decision I made in the past at school would either lead me to this moment or away from it. What matters now is that we are here together enjoying a nice brunch, and that we are enjoying it the best we can, while we can. Here: you know I'm not much of a social media person, but let's take a selfie. Post it if you want, or don't," John said as he awkwardly pulled out his phone from his pocket and held it to the side of them, clearly not having thought through this plan fully. Beth playfully swatted his hand away and pulled out her own phone. "Smile!"

They walked briefly in the park nearby, where Beth explained she had once been with Behrooz—or maybe it was Ted, she couldn't remember—and pointed out a flock of other ducks, just like the ones John had seen out the window.

"Those ducks look different. Look at their plumage—it's like a rainbow!"

"They're called mandarin ducks, native to Asia. I never realized we had a feral population here. The male and female pairs you see are said to mate for life. Or that's what Mrs. Huang said once, if you remember. I don't believe in omens like that. You can sit here for hours if you want, but eventually they fly away. Where do the ducks go?"

"It's winter, so I think they're coming here from somewhere else. Maybe they really flew all the way over the Pacific, wouldn't that be lovely?"

"They're birds, Beth. Enjoy them while you can." John had been right, John was still right, John was always right. How could he have doubted himself? The reason he saw no angels up above on moonless nights was because they walked the Earth instead in mortal guise. All the temptations that John had experienced served a greater purpose, to ensure that he would be ready to be rewarded for his faithful devotion. Who knew that reward was sitting on a cold bench holding a gloved hand?

Another time-honored tradition at Heller which remained remarkably unchanged with the new political party in charge (after growing tired of constantly being called a cult leader, Frank had reinvented himself as a liberal, portraying those who still valued the old way of doing things as wantonly backward and conservative) was the teacher Open House night: teachers opened their classroom doors to inquisitive parents who stuck their noses in everything and demanded special treatment for their children. Mr. T considered the night glorified babysitting, and had conscripted student volunteers to answer the most obvious questions and let him deal with the interesting ones, which was typically an excuse to discuss Iranian politics or supply chain management with a few and let the bothersome ones grow bored and quit.

Juliet's grandmother lived with the rest of the family, and had made the minor mistake of expressing interest in learning what exactly it was Juliet went to school dressed up nicely for; Juliet's parents, seeing the opportunity to get a night alone, gladly obliged her request. Juliet walked slowly up from the parking lot and across the school as her grandmother used her cane to keep up as well as she could. They walked in silence, and not because of any particular animosity, but rather because Juliet could not speak Cantonese. Despite her parents owning a dim sum restaurant, they had decided at some point in Juliet's youth that Mandarin was the language of the future, the one that would open doors where none had existed before, and thus made that the language of the household.

"This is my grandmother!" Juliet announced to Frank and Beth, who had all assembled in Mr. T's classroom. "*Grandma, you go the sitting chair?*" Juliet's grandmother and Mr. T looked at Juliet skeptically, as she gestured the rough outline of a chair in case somehow her message wasn't clear.

"*Feel free to sit anywhere you like—here, let me help you. Do you want anything to eat or drink? You are an honored guest,*" Mr. T offered, taking Juliet's grandmother's enthusiastic smile as a sign his message was more than partially grammatical.

"*I appreciate the offer, but I don't need anything. You speak well, where did you learn?*"

"*I did business in Hong Kong after I graduated,*" Mr. T continued, ignoring that everyone but Frank was staring at him, "*and I kept studying after that. I'm a bit rusty, though, but I hope I don't offend you.*"

"*You flatter me. But don't worry, you speak like a native. I've never visited this school before, but I saw my granddaughter's face on a poster out-side—what's the meaning of that?*" Frank stifled a fit of laughter while Beth and Juliet continued to look at Mr. T with mouths agape.

"*How do I put this? Your granddaughter is the vice president of the school; she has shown remarkable leadership and personal growth, truly one of the best students I have ever had.*"

"*Oh, really? Could you show me around a little? My body may be weak, but my mind is sharp; I don't want to sit here all night.*" Without any further comment, Mr. T and Juliet's grandmother left the room slowly, and Beth and Juliet turned to Frank looking for an explanation.

"It's Mr. T, what can I say?"

"Is this normal?" Beth asked.

"It's Mr. T, so yes. We've learned to accept his surprises." Juliet shyly responded, clearly avoiding Beth's intent.

"No, silly: that your parents would leave your grandmother with you, seemingly not in accordance with her wishes, knowing perfectly well that you two struggle to communicate?"

"I love my grandmother, and she loves me. Just because I speak at the level of a dumb toddler doesn't mean that I don't care for her. My parents are busy and can be a bit distant, but they show their love in different ways. I can't judge as long as she's in good hands."

"So more importantly, what do we do with the parents?" Beth asked, noticing a few looked askance at them as they lingered near his desk.

"I'm used to people shepherding," Frank explained. "They'll go away eventually. So, uh, how's everyone doing on this fine evening?"

John wandered into Mr. T's classroom a few minutes late as usual, and was about to start addressing the empty desk when he realized that Mr. T wasn't there.

"You missed the fun; Mr. T took Juliet's grandmother for a walk, or I think—none of us could understand what they were saying," Beth explained, and when Frank appeared he was about to start laughing again, she corrected herself: "well, neither of us could, maybe that joker over there."

"Yeah, Frank, explain yourself," Juliet said sternly.

"I have absolutely no idea—I'm just as clueless as any of you, and I wouldn't know anything about your grandmother being an honored guest or you displaying 'remarkable leadership and personal growth.' I'm just as clueless as I always am."

"Oh, OK then," John remarked. "We'll just have to wait for him to come back."

Mr. T did not take terribly long to return, simultaneously opening the door and making some sort of joke that put Juliet's grandmother into peals of laughter. Beth, Juliet, and John now stood staring at him, while Frank coincidentally decided that something in the opposite corner of the classroom seemed very exciting; Juliet's grandmother leaned and whispered something in his ear with a smile as he walked past.

"You need to talk with your grandmother more. Frank's Cantonese is far better than yours, he can help you practice. It would make her so happy if you improved," Mr. T chided, still with a smile that made his advice more loving than critical.

"Hold on, what?"

"I've been teaching him during his TA period. Surely you've overheard us at some point. Hong Kong is a great place to do business these days. Sure, they speak English, but you never know." Frank blushed, and worked up the courage to walk closer again.

"This is embarrassing. My parents are going to find out and think I'm stupid."

"Let's not mention it again," Frank proposed.

"Anyway, I'm no good judge of character, but she seemed to enjoy my little tour of the school. I made sure to tell her only nice things about what you've been up to." Mr. T looked around his classroom, which seemed completely undisrupted in his absence. "Glad to see you didn't set any fires while I was gone—hold on, another phone call. Lovely." He went back to his desk and took out his phone.

"I wonder what language it will be today. I'm guessing Navajo," John joked.

Chapter 39

Over time, most of everyone had abandoned Frank's side: Alan grew disappointed he was not always the center of attention, and thus wandered about the other leadership students until he found kindred souls who believed in wholesome values like loyalty and blind obedience; Behrooz had after one too many conflicts grown introverted, almost to the degree of reclusion; and even Ms. Foster, who had the patience of a saint, became convinced her advice was beyond them—she counted the days until they'd graduate and she'd be able to go back to running her own school. That left Juliet, who sat across from Frank like she always did, and tried her hardest to recall the good times they had had the previous year when it was just them.

"Do you remember, Frank, when Mrs. Huang suggested we go to prom together? Wasn't that funny of her?" Juliet smiled, looking around to make sure nobody was listening in.

"Yeah, it was quite funny. What about it?"

"Well, I was just thinking, you know, what do seniors usually do before prom, their last main social event of the year—what should we do as leaders, you know, to celebrate everything we've done? Do you get what I'm saying?"

"Enlighten me."

"How about we go together? Like as an actual couple, not just as coworkers." She reached out her hand, and Frank hesitantly shook it.

"Life's short. Shall we rent a limo? You know I can't drive."

"Fine," she huffed.

"Just the two of us will be a waste of money—how about we get John and Beth, and dare I say, Tom and Regina? Time heals all wounds, and I think it's time I give people credit where credit is due."

"Go with Frank? What are you, nuts?" Tom shouted at Regina, who was too scared to react. "He's going to murder me—he'll push me out of the limo and I'll roll down the hill and fall into the reservoir. You've got to be kidding me."

"As much as I hate to play this card, I'm a Gamma; I outrank you. If I say we're taking a limo, we're taking a limo, unless you'd rather walk instead. This is a special night, and if you ruin my last shot at the high school experience, Frank won't be the one murdering you." Regina had come to the realization one day while tutoring some particularly incorrigible children that in all senses of the world, she was better than them: she wanted to go to medical school, what did they want to do? Shoot hoops all day? This attitude served her well, and enabled her ascension to the respectable level of society, all while Tom staunchly refused to do anything noble and thus remained a lowly Epsilon.

"OK, fine, fine, fine! We'll go, just please, shut up."

"Tom!"

"Whatever—'please be quiet, my dear friend.'"

The six of them met at Heller and waited for the promised limo. Springtime was in the air—it wafted from every fragile bloom and radiated from every door. Juliet insisted on a group photo to commemorate the then-infrequent occasion when all six of them could be in the same place with the illusion of civility.

"Who's going to take the photo?" John asked. "Someone needs to hold the camera, right? We can't all fit in a selfie. Who wishes to be erased from the annals of history?"

"Don't be so dramatic, John. I will," Frank declared, and he directed them all to the entrance to the student parking lot, in front of the wooden "Heller High School" sign that had greeted all of them on their first day. John put his arm around Beth's shoulder, Tom and Regina embraced more tightly, and Juliet did not want to be excluded and stood next to John, flanking him. After taking a few photos, Frank watched the five of them silently, weighing his phone in his hand like it were a lump of gold. Photos contained power, John was certainly right about that—how else would people understand the recent past? The distant past was a lost cause altogether, just dusty tomes and steles one needed a PhD to read. But photos, those had some merit. Anyone with two eyes could see the lavender hue of the lilac trees behind them, the orange and black banner in the far-off distance, or the shaded emerald hall of bamboo. There was some texture there.

Frank would not be entirely erased from history: Juliet had come to his house for an early dinner after Frank could no longer deny her requests to see his house beyond the front porch. His parents, too, were curious to understand what exactly it was that forced Frank to keep his school and personal life separate—was Juliet some hideous, unkempt, socially stunted wretch? They were delighted to discover their first impressions of her were not inaccurate, and naturally, they insisted Frank take a photo with his "partner in crime" at his side. So at least one photo remained extant, that was for sure. But what would that photo, Frank in a tuxedo and crimson boutonnière politely grimacing as he held Juliet in a trailing, majestic midnight-black dress next to him, reveal about the past should some historian dig it up? The backdrop told little: it revealed Frank lived on a street, which was a fair assumption to begin with, and that it sloped upward slightly. The time was a few hours before sunset, which still did not explain much. If one were to examine the sides, as Frank did when deciding how to crop his one novel historical relic, they would see a wicker fence, a Gravenstein apple tree, and a rosebush. That still told little, except that when Frank had written the saga of Frederick and Gertrude for drama class, he had drawn upon his own life. Life imitated art, and art imitated life; before Frank could reflect more, the limo arrived, and exactly as Frank had timed, they were brought to prom early enough that Frank could greet the first guests and verify that everything had been assembled to satisfy his exacting standards.

"Eat, drink, and be merry!" Frank proclaimed to everyone he met, weaving between sophomores in tuxedos delicately carrying trays of canapes. The theme was still Gatsby, or a variant plucked out of time incorporating some modern sensibilities—more variety in music, for one, and the hors d'oeuvres were fairly cosmopolitan. They had spent a good chunk of their earnings to make this an appropriate sendoff to the first epoch of club domination, and Frank played his role as toastmaster extraordinaire with supreme aplomb. For a night, he hoped that everyone's dreams would come true.

John did not know whether he were in the past or present. Everything felt suffused with emotion, with every table having a story to tell. Beth wore white instead of black, but she still walked with elegance, and every time John watched her walk, he expected the band to start playing and everyone, everything else to disappear in a flash of light. Frank's loom of fate had spun out an universe of ineffable gaudiness, one which trapped John in its threads; John did not know whether he was supposed to talk with his friends or remain in awestruck silence.

"Willkommen, bienvenue, welcome!" Frank had greeted Tom before remembering that he was no new guest. "Not bad, right?"

"You've outdone yourself again," Tom sneered. "I thought you were heartless, but even if this party's built on the back of Epsilon labor, not bad at all. I'm not kidding here, have you considered a career in event planning?"

"If it pays the bills, sure. This is the stuff that dreams are made of, Tom. Look down," Frank said pointing from the balcony to the dance floor framed in shiny marble. "I can guarantee that someone down there is having the best time of their life because of me. Good old humble Franklin Barnes. John and Beth, those star-crossed lovers, are finally together. Alan and Jason are having fun in their own way, bossing around all your compatriots to keep this well-oiled machine running. Regina's somewhere down there waiting for you, go. I'll watch."

"Where's Juliet? I thought you were here together."

"Probably looking for me," Frank laughed. "If you see her, tell her to look up."

Frank had instructed the band to cycle through a good mix of historically accurate music, with exceptions for classics like the Cha Cha Slide that even he could not deny. One of these songs was Shostakovich's Second Waltz, which through some cosmic coincidence Frank thought would be the sort of song Gatsby would listen to on repeat, alone in his office, crying into a handkerchief. With the first downbeat, John's promised epiphany came: the room became empty, silent, and then pitch-black except for the bright, full moon, which shined through a window overhead and acted as a spotlight on just himself and Beth. Each step was precise, exactly as John had been taught long ago: one two three one two three until in yet another flash, the illusion was dispelled and he was back with everyone else. John could have danced all night, he thought, through day and night and as the Earth grew weary in its pendulous orbit around the Sun, and even as the Sun grew red and burst in a wave of hellfire.

By this point, Frank had made it downstairs, and snuck over to where the band was to watch from the periphery, where Mr. T also stood "supervising" the least he could. The piano player muttered something in Mr. T's ear and left, and Mr. T shrugged and took his place.

"He needed a smoke break," Mr. T explained. "So, any song requests? This is your chance to complete the cycle, to leave an indelible mark on everyone here. Suggest something soulful."

Frank grinned thinly and remembered the pure ecstasy he had witnessed on John's face as he and Beth danced. There was some ultimate climax in the crescendo of the last four years, the ribbon on top that would tie everything together. Frank held the keys to the universe, and with a stroke of a pen he could rewrite history. "For John," he thought to himself. "For all the dreamers."

"Play it, Max. Play 'As Time Goes By.'"

"D-sharp major, just like the movie," Mr. T told the singer, who nodded knowingly. Frank listened and felt his apotheosis complete. Even from across the room, he could see John's dull expression suddenly brighten as memories flooded into his head from all directions. Past, present, and future crystallized, unified; it was a miracle John did not collapse from the sensory overload, but instead remained upright and resolute.

"This is the song from that movie we watched," Beth whispered, not wanting to speak too suddenly and shatter the enchantment of the music.

"I know, I've always known." John remembered vividly then that when at the lake, in their mist-shrouded house where storms raged and battered, Beth had worn blue. Watery blue, a deep aquamarine, that shone from the sea and down from the sky when she swam, whenever it was that the sun had come out to play—not that year, it couldn't have been, it was dark then. Must have been the year afterward. Blue skies, nothing but blue skies then; John had never seen the sun shining so bright as it did then, and he thought he would never see it again. Now that he thought about it, the sky was blue on the day of winter formal, that day that passed by a blur with nothing but bread, butter, and Beth. He'd always have Paris, that was a fact on which he could rely. Bread was good, John thought; he liked food. One time Beth had rung his doorbell one early Saturday afternoon, a cloudy day like any other; John had heard the noise and casually sauntered from his room to the door, expecting his new gaming mouse, and nearly dropped his coffee mug in astonishment when Beth stood on his porch instead. A few minutes later, John was in her minivan, where he thought he could see his reflection in the polished backs of the car seats. They drove somewhere to eat, he couldn't even remember where at that point, but it was just the two of them. Like it always was. John's mind kept jumping between times—only the good ones, of course, as there was no room for the bad in a moment like this. Moments which evoked no pathos could simply be discarded; nobody would miss them. With the final chords, John's breath slowed, his heart dropped, and their steps ground to a halt.

"My dear protégé, you seem to be displaying signs of triviality," Mr. T remarked after the song finished and the piano player returned to his post.

"On the contrary, Mr. T, I've now realized for the first time in my life the vital importance of being Frank." Instead of laughing, they watched the dance floor silently, following John as he roused himself and went to the snack bar to sit down and sob.

"I miss him. I really do," Frank admitted, shedding a solitary tear that worked its way down his cheek and landed on his boutonnière. "I hope if he's watching, he'll forgive me for my sins. He probably wouldn't—he's never been that nice—but I think he would understand."

"I don't know to whom this entire party is a tribute, but whoever they are, I am sure they are pleased. And that they forgive you for all your sins. You have a date, don't you? Daisy calls." As if by magic, Juliet walked up to them and forcefully grabbed Frank's hand, and they walked to the dance floor. Throughout the night, people came to pay their regards to them, thanking them alternately for the food, the music, and the "vibe," whatever that meant. It was no surprise, then, that Frank and Juliet were voted prom king and queen; Alan didn't even have to rig the votes. Frank wore his plastic crown a little, then when nobody else was looking threw it in the trash; he folded the sash down into a tiny square, which he tucked in his breast pocket as if it were a fashion accessory.

Juliet's sporting kiss on the cheek at the end of the night was a gesture Frank was quite surprised by, and also one he did not think was necessary to return. It was their first and also most likely their last, he assumed. They were just a couple of people living their lives, not a couple in the other sense of the word. That's the answer he gave other people when they asked if they were anything but partners in crime. As much as he loathed the term, perhaps they were BFFs. They waved goodbye to each other couple as they left down the steps and to their parents' cars.

"I'm sorry," Tom mumbled with a pat on Frank's back. "You're a good kid."

"You don't need to apologize. I forgive. I always have," Frank responded, waving to Tom and Regina as they left; once they were out of sight, Frank took out his phone and logged into TigerTalk, and Tom and Regina became Alphas once more. The subtle April heat began to wane, even though it was only 10 PM, and Frank grew tired of well-rehearsed goodbyes just as he saw his parents arrive; being the gentleman he was, he helped Juliet into the car, and together they drove back to familiar ground. Ordinarily Frank would have wanted to help clean up the mess, but Alan had insisted halfway through the night that he finally be put in charge of something, all with such a furious intensity bordering on tears that Frank stepped back and kindly bequeathed the responsibility.

Alan sat on a box of chinaware and stared at the grand hall, which without any decorations seemed pedestrian; even the statues had to go, which were lugged onto carts and dragged to trucks. Where was his happy ending? Why had his heart not burst out of his chest in a bloody ba-boom? He had been cheated out of something everyone else in the room had earned; even Jason, who also had no date, had found his epiphany in the choreographed movements of his waitstaff. He had lost the war.

The euphoria of prom rapidly reverted to more practical concerns the next school day, where those who had spent the entire weekend riding the sugar high of that magical Friday night rediscovered mortal concerns like tests and essays. For Frank, prom proved a reminder that for all his visionary spirit, if their well-oiled machine were to persist once its progenitors left, the coming election proved to be of utmost importance:

"Wheels must turn steadily, but cannot turn untended. There must be men to tend them, men as steady as the wheels upon their axles, sane men, obedient men, stable in contentment," Frank explained to Jason. "I need a list of the top-ranked students at the school. The most alpha of the Alphas. Most importantly, we need people who understand exactly what the complicated, twisted legacy they're inheriting is. We need stability—community, identity, and stability are pillars of our society, are they not? We need followers who understand, or can be made to understand, that *How To Be A Good Person* is satire, but that that has no bearing on society today. Get someone sensible like Behrooz to give his opinions on them. Sense, that's what we need."

"I have four loyal members of the robotics team who would be perfect for the job. Pranav chose them himself, long ago; I'd like to think he knew somewhere in the back of his mind that they would be destined for greatness."

Behrooz stared at his four new lieutenants, trying to read in their faces exactly who they were—with Frank and Juliet, he had at least known them as people with heads on their shoulders and brains sloshing somewhere around in their cranial cavities. But these juniors, with names he had never seen before, promised nothing. They may as well have been anonymous.

"What's your goal for the school?" Behrooz asked nobody in particular.

"Sir! Our goal is to repeat this year's success tenfold!" The tallest of them, who Behrooz believed was going to be the new president, announced.

"And how exactly will you do that?"

"Sir! By focusing on our scriptures, and by crushing all dissenters like bugs!"

"Very well. You have my blessing," Behrooz sighed. All of them were perspicacious in their own ways, possessing perfect GPAs and a laundry list of extracurricular activities between them, but where was that passion? Where was that genuine desire to make the school a better place? What they possessed, and he did not, was an earnest belief in the righteousness of their actions; they had never complained one bit about the security cameras, the caste system, or the uniforms. They had been groomed over the years to accept nothing but that, and their casual disregard for anyone opposed to that goal made them perfect candidates to take up the torch. There was little need for pageantry with the elections that year: there was only one set of candidates, the ones Behrooz had reluctantly approved, and so they used their speeches to hearken back to the year's successes and promise many more in the future. Their speeches were reserved, with no pounding of the lectern or hoarsely shouted appeals to unity, and the audience clapped timorously while troublemakers were quietly led outside. The seniors did not get to vote, and so it took some time for the news to spread that next year would be a repeat of this year; that elicited some laughter and wisecracking, but why did they care? It wasn't their problem anymore.

One day, Tom and Regina were driven by a strange sense of curiosity to check out a Monday club meeting, when new material was introduced and they consequently were less likely to be out of the loop, to see what had transpired in their absence. The desks were arranged in little pods of four, and Frank talked in a muted voice introducing *Euthyphro*; he pointed to a table to the side, where copies of the text were available, displayed next to a table with an array of fresh fruit and other snacks. The MPR was just as packed as usual, but unlike before, no inquisitive eyes peeked through the glass walls. It seemed peaceful enough, and so Tom and Regina grabbed packets and found empty seats.

Epilogue

M r. T signaled the orchestra, and at once they began the opening bars of "Pomp and Circumstance". All the students, arranged in alphabetical order, walked ten at a time down the aisle, their shoes sinking into the artificial turf. The somber procession turned to the right, tracing the edge of the track, up the few steps to the water fountain, then back to the left, before settling in the bleachers. The sun had not chosen to bless their ceremony, and the students shivered on the cold metal benches. Mr. Mudd walked down from the bleachers to the podium, cleared his throat, and began:

"First, I would like to once again offer my warm congratulations to Heller's 50th graduating class! Typically, as superintendent, I'm shuttled between schools to deliver long, boilerplate, impersonal speeches about bright futures and maturity and you know, the 'land of hope and glory' rhetoric that makes all of you fall asleep. You're fortunate today that I've had a bit more personal involvement with your class than others due to the, shall I say, political circumstances of this year. You've all heard plenty about those from your kids, I hope, and as much as there's an interesting story to be told there I'll save it for their memoirs.

As a former teacher myself, and someone who by virtue of my job description spends a lot of time talking to other teachers, one lesson we always talk about teaching is problem solving. Sounds simple, right? All of you solve problems every day, from the mundane—how do I decide what to eat for lunch today?—to the truly earth-shattering, problems completely beyond my comprehension. For us, who've been around the block a few times, problem solving comes by instinct. Unfortunately, that intellectual independence I'm really getting at doesn't come naturally to students. It's sad, I know: somewhere along the line, in your children's thirteen years before they've come to Heller, none but a precocious few were taught how to solve problems. All they were taught is a rigid set of rules, a flowchart—divide both sides of the equation by the coefficient, subtract the constant, solve—but not why that flowchart exists, or how some bright mathematician years ago came up with that procedure!

If there is one lesson I want your students to take away from their time at Heller, it's the importance of this skill. Many of the people on-stage have taken calculus. Fewer will use it. But that does not mean we should stop teaching calculus, even if the few going into engineering or economics would clamor not to be left behind. Part of why we teach it, and really encourage everyone who can to take it, is so they learn how to tackle new problems, unlike any they've seen before. How they can use sheer force of will to dominate what's on the page. How to cope when intuition, that unreliable compass, fails.

You may think this is a strange time to bring up problem-solving, but I promise there is a point here. What do people do in the course of solving problems? They innovate. They find ways out of whichever ruts they're stuck in at the present moment. That is what takes us to the future and brings us out of the nasty, ugly, backward past: being able to identify problems, and instead of moping, solve them. *The Great Gatsby* ends 'So we beat on, boats against the current, borne back ceaselessly into the past.'—great book, by the way, I'm sure your kids can tell you all about it. How I choose to interpret that quote is that it's saying something about human nature, how society is wont to rise and fall. And without doing something about it, that's exactly what we do: we go back into the past, cascading down waterfalls and damn near shipwrecking ourselves!

So in closing, I personally don't care if your students forget how to do physics, calculus, or whatever else—their teachers here may feel a bit sad, but that's not my concern. If they've learned a more efficient way of tackling the world, a more effective one, then your students did not waste their time. Thank you."

Mr. Mudd stepped to the side and gestured for Frank to descend, who gingerly stepped over his classmates' feet and nearly slipped down the steps. None the worse for wear, he came to the podium and pulled out a neatly stacked sheaf of index cards from his pocket.

"Dear friends, classmates, and Epsilons,

First, I would like to congratulate all who survived high school. From the endless days swimming laps in the pool to that palpitating, crushing fear right before taking a test, or whatever path you followed to survive, your hard work has paid off. You have earned this moment standing before your peers and your adoring family. Take a deep breath, smile, and center yourself. Think of your successes, when your team won the badminton championship or when the audience gave you and your castmates a standing ovation after a performance of *Sweeney Todd*, but do not forget your disappointments. Very few of us are standing here today without regrets. Tenacity has brought us success, and if we keep that value dear to our hearts, we will continue to succeed.

Now, onto the sad part. It is far too easy when living in the moment, no matter when that moment may be, to forget that this too shall pass. In a few months, when it is summer and all you can think to do is anticipate the next stage of your life, you will begin to forget many of the familiar faces and names that surround you today. Even if you talk with your dearest friends daily, the rest of us will fade into white noise. In a few years, as we make new friends and memories, these new experiences, vivid in the moment, will push out the old ones, and what we regard today with deep significance will be mere footnotes.

High school will be something recalled in friendly conversations that happen every now and then, when in the back of your mind you may wonder what happened to that person you used to talk to daily. Maybe you will send them a quick message just to say hello, but even if for a few hours they have reclaimed their position on a pedestal in your mind, they too will fade. Some of us in English class read the poem "Do not go gentle into that good night" by Dylan Thomas; I encourage all of us to "rage, rage against the dying of the light." We must all squeeze every last ounce of happiness out of those memories, and only when we are truly content move on; do not go gentle into that good night until you are ready to never return.

I do not want to dwell on negativity forever, no matter how tempting it may be for all of us at this troubled time to do so. All good things must come to an end, but who is to say that more good things may not follow that end? We may feel now that we have no choice but to sacrifice that comfort we intimately know for a future that seems cold, foreign, and scary, and it is natural to feel that way. Nobody wants to feel weakness when they once felt strength. Especially when we look at our own bright futures and cannot resist the temptation to look at someone else's bright future and call theirs brighter, we may look at the last four years as a failure. The great captain Jean-Luc Picard wrote, "It is possible to commit no mistakes and still lose. That is not weakness. That is life." Do not look out at the future, the brave new world that awaits us all, as something to be feared, driving us back into sweet memories of the past. Look at it as a blank canvas: the future is only what we make today. We must take this sacred responsibility seriously, as the alternative is that we spend our lives shrouded in misery; live every day as if it were part of our own brightest future. Some day, we will be there, and each day of us manifesting dreams into reality gets us a bit closer.

From the bottom of my heart, I wish you all the most sincere congratulations. I will miss you all, and once again, never forget how to be a good person.

Sincerely,

Franklin Barnes."

"Wasn't he the cult guy?" one parent whispered to another while they politely applauded.

"Must not have been. Sounds like a good kid though."

The ceremony proceeded from there to the long and tedious handing out of diplomas, where Mr. Mudd and Mr. Kurtz tried their hardest to give every single student a personal touch, overcompensating with some names by heavily rolling the "r"s in an attempt to be authentic. Nobody dared open their diploma just to make sure that there was indeed the promised slip of paper inside; everyone, even the Epsilons, wore the same black robes and carried the same black leather cases. The banalities continued, and a few young kids did what Mr. Mudd promised would happen and fell asleep, heads laying on their parents' laps. Mr. Cathcart delivered the concluding epilogue, reading some sort of Shakespeare passage that elicited polite nods from the audience, and with a final thunderous standing ovation the students descended into the warm arms of their parents.

"Some day, we shall meet again," John forced himself to say, a tear in the corner of his eye.

"How about Monday?" Beth retorted.

"Yeah, that works. And I thought I was building up to something dramatic," John laughed, and he went off to perambulate more, hoping to find more of his peers to deliver prophetic pearls of wisdom to. He found Alan standing at the periphery of the field, looking over the assembled students laughing for the last time and those making hasty exits.

"What's your plan now, Alan? You always have a plan."

"I've always wanted to found a startup. I think I have some ideas to make even more money from my crypto schemes—let's keep this between you and me, but I'm not sure if this is a Ponzi scheme or not, so don't gab about it. Loose lips sink ships."

"My lips are sealed. How about this summer?"

"I'm going to take my mom to Tahiti. We've earned a break."

"It's a magical place," John smiled.

Tom prowled the field not knowing who he was looking for; he had already said goodbye to Regina, even if temporary, and who else really mattered? Frank must have sensed his angst, he thought:

"From now on I'm thinking only of me," Tom said, casting his eyes across the field.

Frank replied indulgently with a superior smile: "But, Tom, suppose everyone felt that way."

"Then," said Tom, "I'd certainly be a damned fool to feel any other way, wouldn't I?"

"I thought you changed. You're strong, did one year of high school really defeat you? Where are you headed for college, anyway?"

"I'm continuing my family legacy," Tom said with a swell of pride, "to USC. Right across the city from Juliet, fortuitously enough. This means I can continue cheering for her inevitable demise, and yours by extension!"

"The University of Spoiled Children. Figures," Frank groaned.

"Oh, are you coming to the lake this year? One last week to remember all the good times? Come on, it will be fun."

"Yeah, sure. A bit of nostalgia never hurt anyone."

Thanks to Tom's reminder, Frank went to find Juliet. Frank's luck put him right by Juliet as her parents and grandmother were beginning to take photos, so naturally he had to be included in the spectacle.

"*He's a genius,*" Juliet's grandmother explained to Juliet's parents, and everyone but Juliet nodded knowingly. Juliet's family saw other parents they knew, and they left without saying goodbye, leaving Frank and Juliet alone.

"Good night, good night! Parting is such sweet sorrow, that I shall say good night till it be morrow," Juliet said with a smile before bursting into laughter. "I finally got to use that. But anyway, I hope this does not mean the end. I can't imagine how boring my life is going to be now.'

"I have no intentions of this being the end, even when we inevitably end up on opposite sides of the country. We live in the 21st century, there's nothing a bit of artifice can't fix. I've grown far too accustomed to our working lunches—why, I've grown accustomed to your face!—but I suppose we can't call them that now," Frank explained, a sudden horrific epiphany dawning on his face.

"They're dates. Or, at least, that's what I've been calling them since September, Romeo. But anyway, what's in a name?"

"Very clever. Very clever. And I thought I was the witty one."

"I've learned from the best. Are you free tomorrow for a brunch date at my place?"

"Not a date, but yes."

"Whatever you say..." She left to take more photos, and Frank shook his head and sighed. Ted had had the last laugh after all.

Behrooz looked both ways to make sure the coast was clear and then sauntered toward Beth, his hands in his pockets and his expression needlessly morose.

"So here we are..." Behrooz said.

"Yeah, here we are..." Beth responded coolly. "When you look back on your four years of high school, what do you think? Personally speaking, I can't wait to get out of here. Don't take any personal offense at this, but I miss wearing normal clothes to school."

"I've already privately disavowed all my association with the last year too many times to count this night. I'd rather be remembered as the nice DJ, not the collaborationist. Apathetic attitudes are a dime a dozen these days; it's hard to find someone with a good head on his shoulders. Don't be like Ted over there—how did he get in here? Anyway, I wish you all the best, with everyone. Here's looking at you, kid."

Ted still felt some strange tether linking him back to Heller, no matter how hard he tried to sever it. Perhaps it was the newspaper article that jogged his memory, but in any case, he had hopped the fence into the graduation ceremony and politely sat in the back through the entire thing. Somehow he had expected absurdity like the sort he had been conditioned to expect, but on the contrary, everything seemed normal. Nobody even mentioned the cult, like they all had a gentleman's agreement to convince the parents that their children were not brainwashed; the seed of heterodoxy had already had time to bloom in many, and even during the ceremony they plotted ways with their peers attending the same schools to keep up the good times, except this time with them in charge. The third wave had long passed, but waves promised to resonate into infinity and crash on the rocky shores for eternity.

"Jason, best buddy!" Ted smiled, patting Jason on the back before he could lash out in disgust. "Or should I say, comrade?"

"What are you doing here?"

"Saying goodbye to old friends, what else would I be doing? Look, I'm sorry for picking on you always. I've felt guilty about that for the longest time, especially seeing as you're nothing but a winner. Crouching tiger, hidden dragon, isn't that how the expression goes? Keep up the good fight."

"You too, Ted?"

Frank handled the letter Ms. Baldwin gave him with wariness—it had his writing on it, but why was it addressed to himself?

"Remember freshman year when you were supposed to write letters to your future selves? I held onto them for all the teachers. Read it when you get a chance; I don't know what you wrote, but I'm sure it must have been fascinating. If I'm remembering my chronology right, you must have written this just after you published *How To Be A Good Person* and the world was irreversibly changed. Keep in touch, Frank. Even though I didn't have you as a student, I'm glad to have known you."

Frank delicately unsealed the envelope and began scanning through—yada yada yada, please settle a bet: will Bitcoin ever get big?, yada yada yada, oh, this was interesting: "If you say something enough, you begin to believe it yourself. No matter what the future brings, never forget what you stand for, no matter who tries to make you forget. To thine own self be true." How sweet, Frank thought. No wonder he forgot about the letter; Frank had disappointed himself, clearly. Then again, weren't freshmen immature and incapable of holding deep thoughts? He had said that himself so many times, when he was but a sophomore and the freshmen did not look all that different, and still as a senior when only a few freshmen had names. But was that a fact, or was it an opinion that became a fact only through repetition? Too late now.

"John! Don't think you can leave without saying goodbye to me!" Regina shouted when it looked like John was growing antsy. "My high school experience wouldn't have been the same without you. I know you're always busy thinking deep thoughts, but relax a little. Enjoy the simpler things in life." John walked closer. "Oh, can I get a hug?"

"Fine," John grumbled.

A single story dulls our perception. It makes us not question what we see before us, the incontrovertible proof that what happened really did happen. For every John or Alan, somebody goes unnoticed too, someone who has their own meditative reflections to deliver in the dead of night or in a scathing letter. Adrian, the dashing star of the drama department, who used his charms and threats to rise from a nobody to the lead actor senior year—give the drama teacher kudos for his accurate casting: gay Hitler was, in fact, portrayed by a gay fascist! Madeline, who, while everyone else was busy carrying boxes of vegetable juice or leading the choir in rousing renditions of the Soviet anthem was studying all day and night to get into Harvard, and who upon stepping into her mother's car after graduation promptly purged all memories of the maelstrom around her. Louis, who was nearly kicked off the football team for trying LSD, and if not for his parents threatening to unleash a litigation campaign would have descended into ignominy. All of these stories are just as interesting, if not more so, than the ones described. They had all the same twists and turns, betrayals and reflections, yet simply were so unfortunate as to be forgotten. And there are many more out there, but no narrator could do justice to every single story! Thus, a decision has to be made, and our dramatis personae are the lucky few to win the lottery and have their memories dissected and put on display. Even for those who through their good fortune have had their time in the limelight, what were they thinking the entire time? How did they occupy the boring days, the days subject to the simple routine of class, club, class, then home again? That first question is most important: what did they think? It is not enough to tell what they did—the facts are as plain as day, and not outside the realm of extrapolation. But no story can tell completely what everyone thought at any moment; the stories told with Juliet, or Regina, or Beth, or Alan as protagonist will never be told, and even if one grasps warily at them, all those stories remain in the dark realm of fiction. And certainly, such a clashing perspective would make this palimpsest a more honest tale, and perhaps someday as Hawthorne delivered us "another view of Hester," we shall have "another view of Heller." Because of this very fact, do not delude yourself into thinking John and Frank the protagonists, no matter how this iteration of truth may lie to you—just because they hogged all the attention does not make their stories inherently more complex! Good fortune, a roll of the dice. That is all it is.

The remaining teachers outside who hadn't disappeared already, feeling the wind starting to bite and the warmth of day fading with the sunset, quickly folded up the chairs and left, leaving the field empty. A popped balloon drifted across like a tumbleweed, its foil catching the ochre rays of sunlight fading through the fence until it lifted off and flew over the fence into a garbage can. Up the steps, a janitor locked the door into the central courtyard, hoping no students were trapped inside. A few classrooms still had their lights on, but those slowly turned off as teachers left in black coats carrying their backpacks. A crow flew down from a tree and hopped between the tables, then left carrying a piece of salami somehow left from that morning—a fortuitous find indeed. Eventually, the school was once again quiet.